"In a world where moral absolutes have disappeared, THE QUEST FOR FORGIVENESS is a G-rated book dealing with R-rated material. As a teacher, my heart aches for what our children are being exposed to everyday, and the realities that they experience. Our society has eliminated consequences for our actions and empowered our children with a feeling of entitlement. This book deals with the consequences in very real, powerful ways. Brianna must face the problems created by her choices, and it's not an easy thing to do. The way the main character takes responsibility is an inspiration to adults and young people alike. I highly recommend this book for anyone who enjoys a complicated story line that has a destination and a purpose. This is that book."

— **MELBA LACKEY**, Educator

"Caution! You hold in your hands a powerful book. Handle it as you would a box of TNT. It has the potency to stir and move you to tears and transformation. It can be life-changing.

THE QUEST FOR FORGIVENESS is the latest in a dynamic series by J. L. Rothdiener. Every gripping page will intrigue you as you read of a world-famous singer and her startling conversion to Christ.

You will witness her at the Motion Picture Awards. You will fly with her to her island paradise and vacation on her private island.

As you read these pages you will sit in a courtroom and witness an innocent man convicted for a crime he did not commit.

Travel and excitement await you as you journey through this book. But be prepared. It will affect you deeply and perhaps change you significantly.

You will find this action-packed volume hard to put down once you have started to read it. You will want to share it with young and old.

— **BURTON C. MURDOCK**, Pastor (retired), Former Editor of Baptist Publications

"Forgiveness is at the very center and heart of this soul searching story of love, sacrifice, spirituality, religion, separation and hurt.

A well-conceived tale that takes you on an emotionally moving journey that shines like a brightly burning candle on a church altar. This is the kind of book that just might inspire and motivate readers to examine their own personal lives. Truly a story worth reading!"

— **W. H. MCDONALD JR.**, Founder of The American Authors Association, Author, Award Winning Poet, Documentary Film Maker, Advocate for Veteran's Rights, Minister, International Motivational Speaker, Vietnam Veteran and Former Radio Show Host

THE QUEST FOR FORGIVENESS

THE QUEST FOR FORGIVENESS

She was on a collision course with her past...

J. L. Rothdiener

NAVIGATOR BOOKS

THE QUEST FOR FORGIVENESS

Copyright © 2011 by J. L. Rothdiener

Cover graphics © 2011 by J. L. Rothdiener

Navigator Books

www.navigator-books.com

Biblical references taken from the HOLY BIBLE, New International Version®. Copyright 1973, 1978, 1984, and 2011 by Biblica, Inc.™ Used by permission of Zondervan. All rights reserved worldwide. www.zondervan.com

ISBN-13: 978-0-9834168-7-6

Cover design by Navigator Books

Printed in the United States of America

Dedicated to the children
of the world who do not know or
who have lost their mother and father.
May the Lord grant you peace and bring you
loving parents through adoption.

Acknowledgements

I wish to thank my wife, Joy, and her parents, Burton & Sylvia Murdock, for their encouragement and tremendous help on this project.

Also a special thanks to Taylor Dickenson, the Brianna Bays model who adorns the cover.

Cast of Characters

Brianna Bays/Janna Anderson/Mandy Dawn Anderson/Madiha —
A young Iraqi girl with black hair, blue eyes, and a heart-shaped birthmark above her right eye; adopted from Kuwait orphanage and taken to the United States; music prodigy; runs away and becomes the world's top entertainer

Mira Mirada Murat — deceased mother of Brianna Bays

Sonya Ellis — Brianna Bays' lawyer, mentor, friend, and manager

Aahil — best friend of Sonya's late husband, Jim

Ethan Anderson — Janna's adoptive father

Sara Summers — Maricopa County Judge

Carol Moore — Prosecuting Attorney

Susan Anderson/Johnson — former Miss Arizona; wife of Ethan Anderson

Robert Cain — Ethan Anderson's friend and attorney

Doctor Alicia Burrows — psychiatrist; witness for prosecution

Tim Johnson — Susan Anderson's father

Allen Anderson — Father of Ethan Anderson

Eric Anderson — Ethan Anderson's son

Lonnie Anderson — Ethan Anderson's twin son

Alana Anderson — Ethan Anderson's twin daughter

Detective Hastings — detective; witness for prosecution

Randy Burns — works for Petrichor Music

Conrad Thompson — Brianna's head bodyguard; close Christian friend

Simon — investigator for Boarder and Simms Law Firm

Harry Stillman — partner with Sonya Ellis at Boarder and Simms Law Firm

Barbara Evans — President, and CEO of Petrichor Music

Odel and Adel Murat — Brianna Bays' uncles

Miridia Murat — Brianna Bays' grandmother

Emir Murat — Brianna Bays' grandfather

ONE

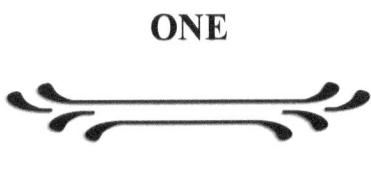

The Unexpected Visitor

Like cold water to a weary soul is
good news from a distant land.
Proverbs 25:25

The mood was electrifying, and the clamor of the crowd almost deafening as the singer began her final song. The high-intensity performance was fast paced from the beginning. She came to give her fans a show they would never forget, and once again she would not leave them disappointed.

The young star never was one to go slow on stage or off.

The stunning Brianna Bays danced around the stage in her five-inch stiletto heels. Dressed in a black, flowing dress, she looked somewhat angelic.

The entertainer's dark complexion was flawless. Yet it was her eyes, which enthralled her fans most. Her long coal-black hair enhanced her piercing blue eyes beneath her thick, black lashes—they were captivating, enchanting.

Her beauty mesmerized the crowd; it was nearly perfect, except for a unique birthmark in the shape of a heart above her right eye. Some might think it was a tattoo. She hid it with makeup; at times, she covered it with her hair. Only her closest friends knew it existed. Her blemish had never been captured on film.

Most of her life she was embarrassed about her distinguishing mark. Through the years she grew to accept it believing it was the only evidence to link her to her biological parents.

Brianna's sweet disposition and compassionate behavior made her a stark contrast to many in show business. Often she was on the scene after a disaster. She could be seen working in food lines in the aftermath of a hurricane, or bagging sand during a flood on the Mississippi.

She especially loved to entertain the troops. America's military made her proud, and she thanked the soldiers whenever she had the opportunity.

However, it was her musical talent that made her into one of the most well-known celebrities in the world. She possessed an incredible five-octave vocal range and was one of America's most recognized voices. She could sustain long notes without wavering in pitch.

Brianna was on the top of the charts among the greats. Her CDs sold millions; her concerts sold out within minutes.

The media reported her acting skills as phenomenal, multi-talented, especially for her age.

Success came to Brianna quickly, but as with many young stars it came with a price. At twenty-three, she looked slightly older and acted more mature than most females of that age. She was too busy to marry, but not too busy for a line of male friends... and that was what they were, friends, nothing more.

After almost ninety minutes, the concert was winding down.

Brianna always ended her show with her latest double-platinum hit, Coming Home Again. It was the sequel to Coming Home—a classic that made her an overnight sensation. The song began slowly and then intensified into an all-out bursting tempo, eventually winding back down. It was a perfect way to end a song, and a concert.

Cameras flashed all around the arena lighting it up like the noonday sun.

A laser-light show with pyrotechnics excited the fans as a curtain of sparks surrounded the young star, leaving her twenty-thousand fans standing in awe, wanting more.

It was the final concert of what she called her "Redemption Tour." The name seemed fitting after her Christian conversion seven months prior.

One hundred and twenty-seven concerts in ninety-two cities from Ottawa, Canada, to Mexico City, Mexico. In all, Brianna entertained almost five million fans.

The entertainer sang many of her tunes from her latest mega CD—all of them dealing with relationships and forgiveness. To date, the CD was at the top of the charts for twenty weeks.

She slightly bowed down to the screaming crowd, giving the worship sign with two hands together as if she was praying. One last wave, her right hand upward with her index finger extended, symbolized her newfound Christian faith.

She exited the stage surrounded by a dozen bodyguards and makeup artists who were cleaning the perspiration from her face and back.

Fans rushed to catch a close-up picture, touch her, or get an autograph. She stopped long enough to smile at them and shake a few hands.

The protective bodyguards always hovered nearby.

One spellbound girl, probably ten or eleven, stood close to the railing attempting to catch a glimpse of her favorite star. She gazed with unbelief as her idol neared her. Brianna stopped long enough to bend over the railing and give the young girl a hug. The girl's mother watched proudly. Brianna winked at the mom and then sprinted to her dressing room.

One of the guards readily opened the door. The drained entertainer hurried in with a towel wrapped around her neck. A number of her staff followed.

The singer noticed a woman sitting on the sofa. Next to her were a small briefcase and a box. The unexpected visitor stood, excitedly greeting Brianna with a heartfelt hug.

"Sonya!" Brianna's smile showed her delight. The star stepped back, holding the visitor's hands. "You look great!"

"You look exhausted!" The woman uttered a short laugh.

The visitor was Brianna's personal lawyer and manager, but more importantly, her dearest Christian friend.

Those close to her tried to read the expression on Brianna's face. They knew who the visitor was, but wondered why she had been gone for nearly seven months. Some believed the two had a falling out, a parting of the ways.

Brianna turned to the others in the room, her voice demonstrating urgency. "Everyone out, please! Close the door, and don't let me be disturbed."

No questions were asked—their job was to protect and obey their boss, after all, she paid their wages. They hurriedly emptied the room.

The singer walked over to a small refrigerator and grabbed a couple bottles of water. Handing one to the visitor, Brianna walked over and sat down in front of her mirror. Sighing, she glanced at her image; the sweat on her face and messy hair were noticeable. Obviously, she had been working hard; she looked like she had just stepped out of a gym after an intense workout. Actually, the ninety-minute concert and dance routine, along with the stage temperature, which at times reached over a hundred degrees, was more than a typical gym workout. She took a long swig of water, grabbed the towel from around her neck, and dried her sticky face.

The unexpected guest resumed her position on the sofa. Sonya Ellis was attractive, single, and tough. She would have to be to graduate tops in her law school; she was one of six women in a class of fifty-four. The men tended to ridicule her for being a woman. Even in a law school, sexual harassment was extensive. Some of her female classmates made it through school by giving favors to the male students and a couple professors. Not Sonya. She did it with hard work and a lot of prayer. She refused to give in to the pressure. Never compromising her morals, she stayed focused and driven. When she took her final bar exam—she was on the top of the list, graduating with honors. Sonya landed a job at one of the biggest law firms in California making a comfortable six-digit income.

The lawyer had been with the entertainer since the first day Brianna began her professional singing career. The day she discovered Brianna Bays singing in a small restaurant, her life changed. The young girl needed guidance; her life was in shambles. Sonya took Brianna under her wing and helped transform her into a superstar. The two beauties had been like sisters from the beginning—the air between them was easy.

"Sonya, what do you have?" Brianna leaned back, eagerly waiting for a response. She had a great deal of respect for her friend and confidant.

"Almost everything you wanted. I found out who your mother was, but unfortunately, not your father."

Brianna grinned and the lines on her face eased. "Who is she?"

Sonya stood up from the sofa and walked closer to her friend. "Not is, was. I'm sorry, Brianna, but your mother was killed during the war."

Brianna's demeanor changed as her hope was replaced by sorrow. "Which war?" Anxiously, she added, "Sonya who am I?"

The woman handed her a file with papers including a birth certificate. "It's a good thing you're rich. It cost a lot, but I managed to buy almost everything you hoped for." She drew in a deep breath. "Brianna, you were born in Baghdad, Iraq, February 13th, 1991. The death certificate states that your mother, Mira Murat, was killed when American bombs hit the hospital she was in."

Brianna glanced up from the paperwork she had been thumbing through, her lips trembling. "American bombs!" A sense of shock engulfed the superstar. She had been a major supporter of the American troops.

Sonya lowered her voice. "Actually, I have it from good sources that she was killed by her family, not from American bombs."

"What? Why would they do that?" Brianna reminded herself to exhale.

"Your mother was born to a rich Sunni family. Unknown to them, she met an American man while she was at school in France. Her family never met him, or even knew there was anyone special in her life."

"Why all the secrets?" Brianna's heart beat faster.

"There are a lot of unanswered questions, but it all boils down to their religious beliefs." Sonya shook her head sadly.

She knew how difficult it must be for Brianna to absorb the information she was sharing. The young girl desperately desired to meet her parents. Sonya waited a few moments trying to give her friend time to collect her thoughts.

"I'll start at the beginning." Sonya sipped her water and sat back down on the sofa. "I began my search at an orphanage in Kuwait. It took a lot of time and money, but I managed to trace you back to a hospital in Baghdad. I went through the records to see who was born in February, 1991. Forty-seven babies were born in that hospital during that month. I became suspicious of one baby in particular."

"Why were you suspicious? I mean, why the red flags?" Brianna raised her eyebrows.

"There were two infant deaths at the hospital during that time, but this particular one was on February 18th. The mother and baby both died."

Brianna interrupted, "If the baby died, why were you suspicious? After all, I'm alive and well."

"It gets pretty strange." She cleared her throat and continued with the bizarre, almost unbelievable story. "I asked to see... well actually, I paid to see, the records of both deaths. After carefully examining the birth and death certificates, I noticed something odd. There were discrepancies in the dates."

Brianna listened attentively.

"The certificates state that both mothers and their babies died during a bomb attack."

"So... why was that strange?"

"Military accounts reported no bombing occurred close to the hospital on those dates. I studied the death certificates of both babies, and noticed that on one of them the date obviously had been changed, tampered with. Going through tons of hospital paperwork, I discovered that one of the moms actually died during childbirth. The archived hospital records were different than the death certificate. Why the conflicting dates? I suspected a cover up of some type."

Brianna didn't even blink. She sat motionless, trying to absorb the information, and wondering where the conversation was headed.

Sonya continued. "I decided to pay a visit to the families of both mothers. I visited the first family and they said their daughter died during childbirth on February 14th.Her baby died from a bomb explosion on February 18th. Like I said, military records state that no bombs were dropped nearby on that day."

Brianna was on edge.

"The other family had close ties to Saddam Hussein and was known to collaborate with terrorists. I was warned by military authorities to stay clear of them. Of course that made me more curious, so I started investigating. You know me, I love a good challenge!" She grinned.

Brianna chuckled.

"I checked the records and discovered that their daughter, Mira Murat, was in France from January to June, 1990. She was attending school in Paris nine months before you were born. So I headed there to dig deeper."

Brianna's head was spinning. She watched her lawyer closely.

"I went to the school and asked questions, but did not get much information. Nobody remembered anything. However, I managed to get into the records and learned some interesting information about Mira Murat."

Brianna sat spellbound.

"Come to find out, Mira was not attending the school, but teaching there—Arab dialect. I obtained a list of her students, but most of them led to dead ends, except two. One was an older woman from Paris who desperately wanted to learn the Arab language. She didn't remember many specifics, only that Mira was a beautiful young woman with a sweet disposition. I asked her if she ever saw her with a man. She had not."

Silence hung between them for a moment. Brianna took another sip of water.

"Now, the second woman was a young college student at the time. She figured Mira had a man on the side because of the way she acted, but never knew who it was. She thought she may be dating a man outside the Muslim faith and was trying to keep it quiet. A few days before Mira disappeared she had asked this student, who knew the local area, where she could spend a couple days in seclusion. She told her about a small cottage outside of Paris; a place where a lot of young lovers spend the weekend—out of the way and private."

Brianna was impressed with how much information Sonya was divulging. Even though it was not what she wanted to hear, the attorney surely had done her homework. She knew Sonya was the best, which is why she came at a premium cost.

"I headed to the cottage. It certainly was secluded. It had a quaint wedding chapel. Not surprising, the people there did not remember them; after all, it had been almost twenty-three years. Fortunately, they kept a record of everyone who stayed there in the past. It cost you a few dollars, but they allowed me to look through the records. I knew I had my job cut out for me when I noticed Elvis Presley stayed there no less than twelve times in the last twenty-four years. Even he and Priscilla on a few occasions."

"Elvis is dead!" Brianna snickered.

"Precisely. Many patrons used fake names to hide their real identities. I managed to narrow the timetable to within a couple days. Finally, one couple stood out. They signed the guest registry with bogus names. She signed Maya Madiha. I immediately recognized that name. She was an Arab princess in a coloring book I had as a child. I believe Mira and Maya was the same person. The man signed Albert Einstein. I faxed the signatures to a friend in California, and he came up with a match to the woman at the hospital. Bingo! Yes, Mira Murat matched the signature perfectly. My theory proved right; she was your mother."

Brianna's face showed the intensity of the moment.

Sonya paused to take a drink and then continued. "His signature... well, we need something to match it with. At this point, we have nothing. Evidently, they secretly married before she went back home. Records from the cottage showed they were married in a private ceremony at the wedding chapel, but there never was a marriage license."

An ache settled in Brianna's heart. "I can't believe all this, Sonya."

"I'm not done yet, Brianna. There is more. I hate to tell you this... brace yourself. Your mother's two brothers physically abducted her, and took her back to Iraq against her will. Then the Gulf War hit. Iraq invaded Kuwait, which resulted in the coalition forces invading Iraq. Mira was not permitted to leave her country as it prepared for war. It was at that time, her family discovered she was pregnant. That alone was a disgrace, but when they found out she was secretly married it was even worse."

"Why would that be worse?"

"It all comes down to her religion. The man she married was a devout Christian. He led her to Christ, and she rejected her Muslim faith. That is a death sentence for the... should I say... more radical Muslims. They call it an 'Honor killing.' She managed to escape to Baghdad, but when complications with the birth occurred, she was rushed to a nearby hospital. You were born in February, one month prematurely. Unfortunately, it gave away her whereabouts. It was only a matter of time until her family found her."

Brianna sighed and shifted her position. "What happened?"

"I hung around the hospital for days talking to everyone. By the way, you made a substantial donation to the new birth ward of the hospital."

Brianna laughed, but it sounded nervous even to her. "Sounds like a good cause."

"Yes, it was. Because of it, an old Cuban cigar box mysteriously showed up one day." Sonya picked up the box from the couch and held it out to her.

Brianna walked over to Sonya and gently took the box, then sat down gingerly on the sofa next to her friend.

The entertainer clutched the box to her chest, blinking back tears. With hands trembling, Brianna opened the box and looked at the contents: A couple of faded pictures, a gold bracelet with a few Arab charms, a gold cross necklace, and a plastic, pink wristband with the handwritten name, "Mandy Dawn."

"In the box are two pictures of your mother holding a baby... that is you! Your birth name is 'Mandy Dawn,' with no last name. Your Arab name is 'Madiha.' I find that interesting, it means 'worthy of praise.'" Sonya gave her some time to digest all the information.

Brianna stared at the picture of a gorgeous young woman with jet-black hair, a radiant smile, holding an infant. The birthmark above the baby's right eye was prominent.

Sonya finally broke the silence. "The original pictures were old and faded, so I had them professionally restored." She handed her a couple eight-by-ten photos. "As you can see, the beauty mark is the same. It is definitely you and your mother."

Brianna closed her eyes and wondered what to do next. She took a deep breath. "Are there any other pictures?"

"I assume so. Notice the month stamped on the side of each picture." Sonya pointed to the date, which read February '91, and the numbers three and twelve. "We can assume there were at least eight unaccounted photos, possibly ten. However, these are the only two I could find. Who knows? They may have been destroyed during the war." Sonya shrugged her shoulders.

Brianna picked up the gold bracelet and examined it. With the other hand, she held the wristband. She read aloud, "Mandy Dawn." Her eyes grew wider, "It's written in English, not Arabic."

"I noticed that. By the way, that gold charm bracelet you're holding is eighteen karats, worth well over two thousand dollars. It seems to be very old."

Brianna studied it closely. "It's beautiful. This actually was my mother's?"

"I believe so."

Shifting her gaze back to Sonya, Brianna stated softly, "These are striking stones embedded in the bracelet. I wonder what the charms mean."

"Quick thinking, girl!" Sonya smiled. "I knew you would wonder, so I had it checked out. Apparently, they were good luck charms. They don't really seem to mean anything or hold great value, except the diamond."

"The stones are beautiful. I've never seen anything like them." Brianna kept her focus on the unique piece of jewelry.

"I thought so too, but the jeweler said they were just stones. He had never seen any like them. He thought they were probably marbles with no great value."

Brianna placed the items back in the box. She picked up the cross necklace to examine.

Sonya explained, "The twenty-four karat gold cross and chain is worth approximately three thousand dollars. It was the best clue I had to your father. The unusual etchings on the cross led me to a small jewelry store in Paris. The owner said it was his father's work, but unfortunately, his dad had died two years ago. They would have had a receipt for it, but all their records had been destroyed in a fire three years earlier. I asked if he had any idea what the numbers and letters, 1C1347 meant. He had no idea... so the trail ended there."

"You really have no idea what the etching means?" Brianna's face showed disappointment, confusion.

"None whatsoever," Sonya replied.

Brianna stared at the necklace, unable to take her eyes off it. "It's beautiful, so delicate, and unique. Do you think my father gave it to her?"

"Yes, I do. It's our only link to him."

Brianna started to return it to the box and then stopped. She walked over to the mirror and held the chain to her neck; her eyes were drawn to the cross. She gently touched it, and whispered, "It's my mother's... I can't believe it!"

Sonya did not rush her, allowing her to have the needed time to reflect. Finally, she walked over to Brianna, and quietly fastened the cross necklace around her neck.

Sitting back down at her makeup table, she looked at Sonya's image in the mirror. "You really believe my mother was killed by family members? Why do you think that?"

"Your mother had serious birth complications and was in the hospital five days. It was easy for the family to track her to the hospital. It just so happened, one of the nurses I visited with recalled being there the night of her death. She remembered it clearly. It was her third night on the job. It was a crazy time; bombs were dropping in the distance and sirens sounding. Many times medical personnel worked in the dark, or with just a little emergency lighting. I can't imagine. Anyway, the nurse recalled seeing two men in the hallway that chaotic night. They were causing a ruckus and were ordered to leave the premises. Another nurse took Mira's baby to be fed. The nurse I talked to said your mother was fine when she checked her, which was about the same time she noticed the two men in the hall. She found out later, they were your mother's brothers. When the nurse returned, your mother was dead. The hospital ruled it a bomb killing, so there would *be* no investigation, but no bombs ever hit the hospital. Several bombs had hit nearby on different days, so it did not create suspicion."

"How was she killed?"

"The nurse believed she was suffocated—smothered by a pillow."

"Why wasn't I killed?" Brianna raised a questioning eyebrow.

"You were... at least, your uncles *thought* it was you. From what I understand, there was a shortage of cribs. It was common practice to take one baby for feeding, and leave another infant in the same crib. The brothers evidently killed your mother, and the other baby whose mother had died at childbirth. It was the perfect cover-up for the hospital. That's where the discrepancies in the birth and death certificates come in. The nurse thought it strange when three days later those same two men returned asking questions about the baby with the birthmark."

"How did they know I had a birthmark?" Brianna asked.

"Evidently, they must have somehow got their hands on one of the pictures and noticed the birthmark. That's when they realized the baby they killed was the wrong one."

Brianna was mystified by the bizarre cover-up. "What happened to me?"

"You! That's a good question. You just disappeared, and the altered death certificate showed up. It appears someone was trying to protect you."

Sonya cleared her throat. "I contacted the nurse who took you away to be fed, but she would not say anything—no matter how much money I offered her. I believe she knew more than she let on. I think she was afraid for her life. Therefore, another dead-end."

"What would they have done if they found me?"

"I asked the same question. The nurse wouldn't comment."

Brianna crossed her arms and gripped her elbows. "Where's my father? Who is he?"

Sonya walked back to the sofa and sat down. "That question may never be answered. There is a possibility that he also is dead, killed by the same brothers. There were rumors of Americans killed in Iraq during that time. Of course, you never read about them in the paper."

"What about my mother's parents? Who are they?"

"Like I said, they are rich Sunnis from Saddam Hussein's ruling class. They are worth millions."

Without hesitation, Brianna directly stated, "I want to meet them."

Sonya blinked and sighed deeply. "Meet them... uh... why?" She knew the answer even as the singer made the request.

For the space of several seconds, Brianna turned and stared at Sonya.

The lawyer toyed with her water bottle nervously. "Well, I understand why, but there is one thing I have not mentioned."

Brianna swallowed back the lump in her throat, trying to keep the tears from her eyes. "What else could there be?"

Sonya searched for the right words. How can she tell her brokenhearted friend the truth? She paused. "The family... how should I say it? They have... they have a hit out on you."

"A hit? What do you mean a hit?"

"They believe you are alive, and consider you to be an infidel. Almost like a 'devil child.' They will kill you without anyone in their faith even questioning it."

"You have got to be joking?" Brianna almost had a smirk on her face.

"No, I'm dead serious. The authorities will look the other way. This family is powerful. If they knew where you were, they would kill you instantly—no questions asked. You are relatively safe in America and most of the free world, but over there you're marked for assassination."

Brianna's voice escalated. "Over there? You mean in Iraq? I have visited the troops, how many times, maybe a half dozen or more in the last few years. I feel safe there. The Iraqis have always welcomed me warmly."

Sonya added, "Yes, but they didn't know who you really were."

A slight grin came to Brianna's face. "Just out of curiosity, how much am I worth dead or alive?"

Without hesitation, Sonya replied, "One million dollars."

"No way!" She said, dropping her jaw.

Determined, Brianna pressed on. "That gives me even more of a reason to meet them. Besides they are my mother's parents—my grandparents. I need to ask them a few questions. I'd also like to visit my mother's grave. She was given a decent burial, wasn't she?" Staring into the mirror, she fixed her eyes on the cross necklace.

Sonya's face showed sadness before she got the words out. "She was buried, but had no tombstone, just a flat rock with her name inscribed on it. Unfortunately, it was vandalized."

Standing and facing Sonya, Brianna said emphatically, "Get her a tombstone with her name on it. Spare no expense." She picked up her guitar and lightly started to strum. She sat down again, looking off in the distance as if she was a world away. "Have this inscription on the granite. 'Mother of...'" She stopped strumming. Picking up one of the old pictures she had taken out of the small box, she placed it between the guitar strings, and stared at it. Sounding melancholy, she whispered, "Her eyes show love. She loved me, didn't she?"

"Yes, she did. The nurse said she was so happy. She would hold you until she fell asleep. The nurses would come by and place you back in the crib. She loved your father too, whoever he was. She talked to the nurses about him, telling them what a good man he was, but never mentioned his name. She must have been protecting his identity."

The star solemnly stared at the picture; silence engulfed the room. She started strumming again. "Inscribe on it... *The Lord's love never ends; his mercies endure forever.* Just put that. No, put the reference with it— *Lamentations 3:22.*" Her face lit up with approval. "Yes, that's perfect!"

"You do realize it may be vandalized again." Sonya hated to be the bearer of bad news, but it was reality.

"That's why I said, spare no expense. If you have to hire twenty-four hour guards, then do it. She was my mother, and that's the least I can do for her. She gave me life... and died for me. Did she not?"

"Yes, she did."

Brianna sighed. "On the other subject, what did you find out?"

Sonya continued sharing vital information with her client. "I have his address. No phone... he has none. He lives in a trailer park. It's a real dump, I may add."

"What else? What has his life been like?"

"Putting it bluntly, it's been a living hell."

Sadly, lowering her voice, Brianna replied, "I figured that."

Looking at Brianna, Sonya pushed on. "He spent six years in prison. He lives in Casper, Wyoming, in a small run-down trailer. He pays one hundred and thirty-five dollars a month rent, and works at a local truck stop washing dishes and doing odd jobs."

"What happened to his family?" Brianna straightened, her eyes fixed on Sonya.

"His wife took the three kids and divorced him. He has never been allowed to see them."

The mood was somber. Brianna started to strum again. She sang softly.

It's a story as old as the hills,
A story of lies for thrills.
Does it not matter who gets hurt?
As long as you don't get burnt.
A little girl of innocence,
In a world that's promiscuous.
It's a story as old as the hills.

"What is your plan?" Sonya interrupted, knowing Brianna was retreating into her music, her typical means of escape.

"I'm going to do what is right. For once in my life, I'm going to do what is right." She continued strumming softly.

"At what cost?"

With resolve, Brianna answered. "Everything I have!"

Sonya raised an eyebrow. "Even your reputation?"

"Reputation?" Her voice rose, and she strummed harder. "What reputation? What I did was the worst thing anyone could do to another person."

"You have a reputation for helping people, aiding children through adoptions and foster care. Your charity work and donations have made a world of difference to many less fortunate."

"What good is it if I can't sleep at night?" Brianna's gaze fell to the floor.

"He's only one person. If your career dies, everything you have created the last six years collapses in a heap."

Brianna winced. "So, the rights and lives of many, outweigh the life and rights of one. Is that what you're saying, Sonya?"

"Yes," she answered bluntly.

The singer looked in the mirror again, touching the cross necklace. "I don't see it that way. My lies put a good, decent, innocent man behind bars for six years and destroyed his life. What was his crime? Helping me as a frightened young girl and loving me like a father should?" Brianna's voice continued to escalate.

Sonya didn't speak, knowing when to remain silent.

Fresh tears stung Brianna's eyes. "Sonya, I thought you would support me on this."

"I am. I'm only warning you what everyone else will tell you. You are playing with fire, my friend. I'm afraid you'll get burned."

There was silence for a few seconds as Brianna reflected on the recent developments. She played a tune on her guitar. Finally, she spoke softly. "He taught me to sing. He taught me about God and His Word."

She stopped playing and stared at the floor. "It's funny, I... I keep thinking of the Scripture he told me the day he rescued me from the orphanage. It was *Psalm 57:7. My heart is steadfast, O God, my heart is steadfast; I will sing and make music.*"

Sonya's heart ached for her friend. Brianna had endured much already. Was there a breaking point for this vulnerable woman?

Brianna, sounding robotic, continued. "He predicted my singing and musical talent. He believed in me and taught me about God, but I just could not grasp it then. I just could not grasp it." Despondent, she shook her head.

She glanced into the mirror. Almost trance-like her mind began to drift to another time, another place... nearly twenty years before.

TWO

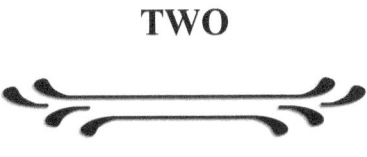

The Music and Discord

Do not remember the sins of my youth and my rebellious ways;
According to your love remember me, for you, Lord, are good.
Psalm 25:7

Twenty years earlier

For most people, memories are a way of holding on to things and people they love. For others, the ghosts of their past can destroy and sometimes haunt them for a lifetime. That's what happened to Brianna Bays.

In February, 1994, a beautiful, black-haired, three-year-old girl arrived in an orphanage in Iraq. That was the superstar's first memories. Although vague, the recollections of a dark, dingy room with a long line of beds and a musty odor were permanently etched in her mind. She recalled fighting for a place to sleep and food to eat in the over-crowded orphanage. It seemed she merely existed.

Her life prior to that point was unknown. Once in a while a face would surface in her mind. Other than that, she remembered nothing. She asked, but no one knew anything about her past life. There were no pictures of her as an infant, no accounts of her being held or loved. Nothing! It was almost as if her past was erased, or she had never been born.

Over time, perspective parents would visit the orphanage searching for the right daughter. Brianna believed it was her hideous birthmark that prevented her from being adopted. She tried her best to hide the spot. She attempted to paint the spot away, but for a five-year-old that was impossible. She tried to keep her long dark hair covering her face, but she was still the butt of jokes among the other orphans.

Brianna's life was in constant upheaval by being moved from one place to another. At age six, she was taken to a large house in Kuwait. With big hopes for a new family, she entered her environment excitedly; she thought she would finally have a chance at a better life. She soon

15

discovered it would be a temporary shelter, only for a few weeks, but did not know why. The child assumed it was because she was faulty merchandise—no one would ever choose to love her. The birthmark and deep blue eyes made her unadoptable; after all, none of the other orphans had either one of those rarities.

Brianna longed to live a normal life and play games that little girls played. Dolls, dress-up, and jump-rope were things she desired to do, but unfortunately never would. The games the people at the big house wanted her and the other girls to play were not children's games. Their caretakers had devastating plans for the youngsters. Within weeks they would be sold to a home in Asia, which used children to make adult movies.

Shortly before the move from the big house, an unexpected event changed Brianna's life forever.

The day started like any other—oatmeal, dry toast, and watered-down powdered milk.

After breakfast, she saw the man for the first time. To her, he looked like a giant. He came with a group of men carrying guns. A few women with shoulder bags and pads of paper followed behind. She clearly remembered the loud noises—people running and shouting. The chaos and fear were still vivid in her mind.

Hiding under the beds, the terrified girls were unsure what was happening. Paralyzed with fear, and hardly able to breathe, they listened to the sounds around them.

Brianna's heart was pounding so hard she wondered if the other girls could hear it. With shaking hands she moved the dangling blanket, peered out, and viewed the adults who worked in the house forcefully being removed from the premises in handcuffs.

The girls were located almost immediately. The man in charge asked them to stand in front of their beds. His voice seemed kind, non-threatening.

The orphans were trembling as the visitors strutted in front of them. Silently, the strangers eyed them from head to toe. Tensions began to ease slightly when one of the men smiled at a couple of the girls and offered them some candy, a rare treat.

The man with the kind voice announced to the orphans, "If you were taken from your family, you will be returned. If we can't locate your parents, you will be available for adoption. You won't be hurt anymore. We will protect you. Don't be afraid."

The announcement, intended to give the orphans hope, excited most of the girls. Not Brianna! Her hopes were shattered again. She believed with every ounce of her being that she was unadoptable and would end up in still another orphanage. No one wanted her—she was flawed—damaged goods. Nothing could change that... not ever.

Brianna stood frozen in time, terrified by the recent events, and fearful of the future.

As the visitors examined the children, Brianna noticed the same man again. He did not seem intimidating. He was tall, strong, and had a pleasant smile. Kindly, he questioned the other girls.

Brianna stared intently at the man as he went from girl to girl. She stood timidly at the end of the line.

The man smiled at each one, knelt down, and asked her name. A woman next to him wrote the information on a notepad. He assured each child that everything was going to be better. "These nice people are going to help you." The stranger handed each girl a piece of candy and a small toy. Before long, some of the children were smiling.

Eventually, he stood in front of Brianna. Kneeling, he looked into her eyes.

She hurriedly placed her hand over the birthmark, but it was too late. He had already noticed it.

Then, unexpectedly, he picked her up, and stood. She recalled his arms were strong, yet tender; she felt comfortable in his grasp. She noticed immediately that he was different, like her—he also had blue eyes.

He stared at her for a moment and spoke in Arabic. "What is your name beautiful girl?"

She put her head down, embarrassed. "Wesh-m," she whispered.

"Wesh-m?" Flabbergasted, he repeated the word in English. "Tattoo! Why are you called Tattoo?" He pushed her hair back to get a closer glimpse of the birthmark.

The conversation continued in Arabic.

"Please sir, don't look at that."

The man responded patiently, "What's the matter with it?"

"It makes me ugly."

He brushed a finger across her brow. "No, child, it makes you special. It's a gift from God, which means, 'You are my little angel.'"

"You really think it's special?"

"Yes, I do. It's in the shape of a heart. Do you know what Jesus would say about that?"

"Who is Jesus?"

"Jesus is the Son of God. He died on the cross to save us."

Brianna tightened up. She brought her lips together in a straight line, her voice grew louder. "Allah is the only god."

A sad smile played on the nice man's lips.

After a short time, the six-year-old crossed her arms, and her expression softened, "Save us from what?"

"From our sins." He smiled.

Brianna shrugged nervously, not understanding what he meant.

"Well, there will be time to talk about that later. The Bible says, *I will sing and make music.* Can you say that?" The man slowly repeated it.

After a few attempts with the help of the man, she repeated it in both Arabic and English.

"That's great. Now, Little Miss, your name is not 'Wesh-m,' anymore. You will be called 'Janna,' which means, 'God is gracious.'"

Then the man did something strange. She had never seen anything quite like it. He started to sing softly a song intended only for her. It was a simple melody, but it was calming. She had never heard the song...

Jesus loves the little children,
All the children of the world;
Red and yellow, black and white,
They are precious in His sight;
Jesus loves the little children of the world.

With the girl still in his arms, the man turned back to the people with him, and nodded his head. "Let's take these children home!"

She remembered the man had a song about everything. He would see a sign on the highway and make up a tune about it. He sang when he noticed a snake in the road, the color of the sky, or a beautiful sunset. It was sometimes sort of annoying.

Ethan Anderson was his name.

When Janna's paperwork was located, they discovered she had spent her entire life in different orphanages. She had no known parents.

For Ethan, the decision was simple. He would adopt the little girl who stole his heart.

Within days, Janna would arrive in a strange country to begin a new life with Ethan and his family.

Janna thought the flight to America would never end. One of the flight attendants told the timid girl how pretty she was. The child simply lowered her head and clung tighter to Ethan's hand, unable to make eye contact, or speak to the well-meaning woman. The girl noticed that not one person on the flight commented about her birthmark. It was unlike the orphanage where the other children teased her.

Janna felt secure with Ethan. She didn't understand why, but she trusted him. He seemed genuine, like he really cared about her.

They disembarked in Los Angeles.

Janna noticed immediately how different America looked from her native country—things were cleaner, brighter. It felt safer—there were no soldiers holding guns.

She asked in Arabic, "Is this where you live?"

"No, but it's our last connection. The next plane will bring us home." He raised his hand as if he was flying.

At the airport gift shop, Ethan bought Janna a fluffy teddy bear. She named it 'Deb Zghir,' which meant 'Baby Bear' in her native language. She clung tightly to her bear as they walked across the terminal to the next plane, her other hand firmly grasping his.

Janna noticed that Ethan continued singing and whistling, but it rarely ever was the same song. She could not understand the words at first. However, she was a fast learner and enjoyed learning new words in English.

They boarded the plane to their final destination. Janna sat next to the window. Rising above the clouds, they watched the city and ground disappear. She finally mustered the courage to ask a question. "Where are we going?"

"Mesa, Arizona."

"Will I meet my mother there?"

"Yes... and your little brother, Eric. He's one."

"Eric." She repeated it slowly. "Does he have black hair like me?"

"No, he has very blonde hair, almost white, like his mother."

"Does he have a mark on his face?"

"No, he doesn't."

"Does that mean he's not special?"

Ethan thought about the remark, and remembered what he said when he first met her. He nodded his head, chuckled, and wondered how he was going to get out of answering the question. "No, but he does have his mother's green eyes."

"Oh." She looked up at him. "I have blue eyes. My real mother must have had blue eyes, too."

He looked down at her, smiled, and gave her a slight hug. "Maybe so."

Janna pulled her teddy bear closer, and brought her legs up on the seat. She wasn't use to anyone hugging her, it felt strange, but comfortable. Her mind was racing. What would her life be like? Would her new mommy and brother be as kind as her new daddy was?

She enjoyed the man's humming and quiet singing. She was beginning to pick up some of the lyrics. The music helped the time pass.

Ethan looked down at her and smiled. "Hey, I have an idea. Let's learn another song in English." He began singing an old familiar children's song...

> *This old man, he played one,*
> *He played knick-knack on my thumb*
> *With a knick-knack patty whack,*
> *Give the dog a bone*
> *This old man came rolling home*

He smiled at the child and repeated the song, teaching her the words and motions. Before long some of the others on the plane sang along. By the time they landed in Phoenix, she and many of the passengers knew the words and actions by heart.

The flight attendants were humored by the antics of the passengers.

They finally disembarked. Ethan and Janna were both on edge as they walked through the terminal.

The girl was excited to meet her new family, but figured it would be temporary—it always was. She would try hard not to become attached to anyone; it was too painful to be separated from them. It would especially be hard to lose her new daddy... Janna was growing quite fond of him.

"Is my new mommy here?" The pace slowed as they walked.

"I'm sure she is. She will pick us up soon."

"Do you live in a nice house?" Janna's eyes sparkled.

"Yes, a very nice house."

"Do you work?"

"Yes. I'm a professor and counselor at school. I was on a mission trip helping some schools in Kuwait when I found you."

Janna was full of questions. "What does a counselor do?"

"I help people who are having a bad day."

"Will you be able to help me?"

Ethan put his arm around her shoulders. "I'm counting on it... with Jesus as my guide, I will help you."

Inquisitively, she spoke, her eyes widened. "Who is Jesus?"

In her language, he explained, "Jesus is my Lord and Savior."

"Jesus is bad."

He stopped, knelt, and looked directly into Janna's eyes. His training taught him that it is best to talk to a child at eye level. His tone was warm as if he understood her confusion. "Did the people at the orphanage tell you that?"

"Yes. They taught me that only Allah is good."

"Did they treat you with kindness? Did they feed you when you were hungry? Did they clothe you when you were cold?"

Janna let her gaze fall to the floor. The truth was so real it was suffocating. She shook her head, acknowledging that her care had been less than adequate.

"Jesus showed love, not just with words, but with actions. He set the example we should follow. Did you know he fed five thousand people at one time with just a couple fish and five loaves of bread?"

She looked at him, and her big blue eyes grew even wider. "Wow, they must have been big fish!"

Ethan laughed. It was a pleasant sound to the apprehensive youngster.

They walked a little further, and then a warm smile spread across Ethan's face. He spotted a woman, holding a young child, walking toward them. His eyes glistened as she neared him.

The approaching woman was tall and slender with long blonde hair. A former beauty queen, she had a way of capturing people's attention, both male and female. As Miss Arizona, just five years before, she came in fourth place in the national pageant. When she walked into a room, people took notice.

She was a college student, a business major, when she first met Ethan. After graduating, she landed a lucrative career at a large cosmetic firm. Advertising was her specialty. Her glowing face was often seen on commercials, billboards, or in beauty magazines.

As a child, Ethan spent eight years in Saudi Arabia with his parents. His father worked with the United States Embassy for several years, and then took a part-time position with Middle East Internal Affairs. That's where Ethan learned to speak the Arab language fluently.

Originally, Ethan planned to be a missionary in the Middle East. However, when he met Susan four years ago, his plans changed. He took a job as a counselor and professor at a private school in Phoenix. Many of the students spoke Arabic.

He enjoyed the job and his life, but there always seemed to be something missing.

Ethan sprinted to the woman, embraced her, and took the young boy from her arms. "How is my little boy today?" He pulled his son, Eric, close to his chest.

Unsure what to do, Janna watched the scene unfold. She paid close attention to the noticeably pregnant woman.

Finally, Ethan backed up and reached his hand out to Janna. She glanced at his hand and reluctantly took it, still clinging to her teddy bear.

Turning to Susan, he stated, "Honey, this is Janna."

Speaking in Arabic, he looked at the confused girl and said, "Janna, this is Susan. She is my wife... your new mother."

Susan's eyebrows lifted. She glanced at Ethan and then back at Janna. Reluctantly, she reached her hand out to the hesitant child.

Janna clutched Ethan's leg tight and turned her head away. When she did, her hair flew back exposing the birthmark. Without hesitation, the woman reached out and brushed the little girl's hair aside. Susan examined the heart-shaped birthmark just above her right eye and scrunched her face in disapproval.

Before his wife had a chance to speak, Ethan commented, "I guess she's going to be a little shy. She'll get used to you." He smiled weakly.

"I sure hope so. This is your idea, you know, not mine!" Her tone sounded harsh, cold-hearted.

Ethan brought his lips together in a straight line. He glanced at his wife and then at the apprehensive girl. The look on his face showed disbelief, betrayal, and most of all, heartbreak.

He forced a sad smile at Janna trying to hide the painful words, but he knew it was too late. Even though she could not understand the words— Susan's looks, her tone of voice, said it all. More rejection for the little girl who had been rejected all her life.

Susan's demeanor left the girl devastated. Janna inhaled a deep breath. Unexpected tears pooled in her eyes, but she blinked them away.

The powerful words of rejection, spoken by her new mother, began a downward spiral that would eventually result in disaster.

The former beauty queen's body language spoke volumes. She spun around in a huff. After walking a short distance, with a touch of condescension, she inquired, "Do we have to go to baggage pick-up?"

"No. I'm having everything delivered tomorrow morning," Ethan replied matter-of-factly.

"Good," she snapped. "I have things to do."

The walk to the car was silent. Ethan held his young son in one arm, and Janna's hand with the other.

There was an uncomfortable air between them—all of them.

Janna will never forget the sound of Susan's heals clicking the pavement loudly, intentionally. That sound would haunt her forever.

When they reached the car, Susan threw the keys at Ethan. "You drive. I've had a hard day."

Ethan buckled Eric in his seat. As he fastened Janna's seatbelt, his face was close to her; she scowled, lips tight, as she stared at him. He noticed her look of distress and attempted a grin.

Janna knew something was wrong. Where were the smiles and the music? She hoped for something better, yet why should it ever be any different? She was afraid nothing had changed... nothing would ever change.

Susan stood by her door, hands on hips, waiting for Ethan to open it. After the children were in their seats, he walked over and opened her door. She plopped down in the passenger seat, immediately pulling the visor mirror down, and began touching up her lipstick.

Ethan swallowed hard, trying to keep his composure. He exhaled; his frustration was evident.

Susan finally broke the silence. "When do you start back to work?"

"In another week," he replied curtly.

"Are you sure we're doing the right thing bringing her to America. I mean, she can't even speak English."

Ethan peered at Janna in the rear-view mirror. "Yes, I am. That little girl has been through a tough time. I had the opportunity to help her, so I did. I could not, would not, turn my back on her."

Susan's voice was cold and her expression anything but welcoming. She snapped, "Well, I guess if things don't work out we can always take her to the Christian Adoption Agency in Phoenix."

Ethan looked dejected, but not for long. "It'll work out. She is so sweet and very smart. I think she's picking up our language quickly—verbal and non-verbal, if you know what I mean." He felt the heat rising in his cheeks.

Totally ignoring his warning, Susan continued. "What about that hideous flaw on her face? The kids are going to tease her when she goes to school."

Ethan drew a deep breath and exhaled slowly. "Why are you so obsessed with beauty, Susan? She'll be okay. Most people are polite when it comes to things like that. Once they meet her, they will see what she's really like."

Susan retorted with another negative reply. "Yes, but there's always kids who make fun of people with disabilities. Kids are cruel, you know?"

Her words felt like daggers through his heart. How could his wife be so cold and heartless? He swallowed hard, trying to keep his cool. "Susan, it's not a disability—it's a birthmark. I prefer to call it a beauty mark. It's God's special mark, just for her."

"That is so typical of you. Of course, you would throw God in my face again!" Susan's voice was thick with anger.

For the space of several seconds, Ethan just stared, silent, hurt, and disappointed.

Susan took a compact out of her purse and reapplied her makeup, never taking her eyes off her image in the mirror. "You know, Eric and the twins are going to have to follow her through school. That will be difficult for them. Have you even thought of how they will feel about this?"

He could feel his wife's repulsive glare. "I said it will be fine." Ethan clenched his teeth and gripped the steering wheel even tighter, his knuckles white.

Susan's look showed her disbelief, but she chose not to respond. She knew when she crossed the line and believed she was getting dangerously close to it.

For a few moments, a cold hush filled the car.

Ethan shifted his position and glanced at her. His voice took a more optimistic tone. "Speaking of the twins, how are you feeling? How was your doctor appointment last week?"

"It went fine. Babies are good."

Making small talk, Ethan shook his head and smiled. "Twins—a boy and a girl. I still can't believe we are going to have two babies... I can't wait to meet them."

"That's easy for you to say. You don't have to get up all hours of the night to feed them and change their diapers."

Ethan was crushed. "Susan, you know I will help you. I did before."

"That was one, this is two. What about me and my career? The firm wants me to push their latest cosmetics as soon as the babies are born." She crossed her arms, glaring at him.

"I think you should wait until the babies are older. We don't need the money. We have a good size nest egg, and I make a good salary at the university." Ethan cautiously entered the freeway.

"It's not just the money... it's about my career. It's important to me. You should know that by now." Her voice grew louder.

With certainty, Ethan replied, "Susan, nothing is more important than raising our children."

"Oh, I see, a woman's place is in the home!"

Her words stung. Without backing down, Ethan glanced at her out of the corner of his eyes. "At this point in our lives, yes, it is."

With that, the conversation was over. Susan knew she had gone too far. The rest of the trip home was silent... and long.

Janna stared out the window as they passed a development of large, upper-scale homes. Finally, they drove up to one that had a circular driveway, and a long sidewalk to the front door. It was the biggest house she had ever seen. The car stopped in front of a three-car garage. Her eyes were wide with wonder.

Ethan stepped out of the car, and Susan hopped out from the other side. She opened the back door, unbuckled Eric, picked him up, and stomped inside.

He opened Janna's door and unbuckled her seat belt. "Honey, this is our house." Reaching for her hand, he said excitedly, "Come on! Let me show you to your very own room."

Janna clung to her teddy bear with one arm and Ethan's hand with the other. He led her through the giant doors. The entryway was immense with a ceramic tile floor and an elegant chandelier. Her jaw dropped when she viewed the giant staircase.

Ethan made eye contact with her and raised his eyebrows. He pointed in the direction of the rooms. "That's my study. Over here is the dining room."

Janna put one hand on her hip, stifling a smile as she looked around.

Trying not to push too hard, he paused, giving her some necessary time to take it all in.

He angled his head looking into her eyes. "Come and see the kitchen." Offering his hand to her again, she readily accepted it.

The little girl, enthralled by the size of the rooms, had never seen anything like it. As they walked past the staircase, Ethan pointed to a bathroom. "We have five bathrooms."

She stared, overwhelmed by the enormity of it all.

"Here is the kitchen."

Janna wondered what purpose all the appliances had, but didn't ask about it. She noticed the huge family room nearby. There was a large television on one wall and a fireplace on another.

Ethan noticed her reaction and lowered to his knees. His voice was soft. "This is your new home. I hope you enjoy it." He gently brushed her hair back showing the mark.

Janna flinched, obviously afraid.

He slowly bent forward and softly kissed the birthmark. He took a deep breath, staring at the little girl for the longest time, as if he were a thousand miles away.

Finally, picking her up, he announced enthusiastically, "Let's go see your room." He bounded up the stairs with her in his arms and opened a door.

Speaking in Arabic, he said, "This is your room. Later we can go to the store, and you can pick out some paint and decorations. You can decorate it the way you want. Teddy bears, dolls, or whatever—it will be your choice."

As she studied her new room, certain thoughts flooded Ethan's mind. This must be overwhelming to the young girl. Are things happening too fast? Why in the world did Susan act the way she did? She couldn't be jealous of a six-year-old girl, could she? He closed his eyes and uttered a silent prayer. Those questions quickly disappeared the more Janna was around.

It did not take Janna long to learn to speak English, but Ethan made sure she did not forget her native language. After all, she might someday get a job as a language teacher.

Susan barely tolerated Janna, always keeping her at arm's length.

Ethan felt helpless; nothing he could do would fix the relationship between his wife and adopted daughter. They seldom spoke to each other.

His relationship with Susan was weakening. For a short time, the couple was drawn together by the birth of the twins, Lonnie and Alana, but that was short-lived. They soon grew distant again, almost as if they were strangers living under the same roof. Sometimes he wondered what attracted them to each other in the first place—it saddened him.

Susan's parents came to help with the birth of the twins. They would take care of Eric, but it was as if Janna didn't exist. They never acknowledged her—no hugs, no gifts, not even any kind words. Nothing!

Hurt and bitterness began to simmer in Janna. When Ethan was around things seemed okay, but when he was gone, she was constantly in trouble. Janna could do nothing to please Susan.

At first, Janna brought home straight A's on her report card. Basketball, softball, and tennis were sports she loved. Proud to live in America, and well-adjusted in school, her social life boomed. Ethan supported her in whatever she tried.

However, nothing was more important than her music. Her music was a means of escape—Janna found solace in it.

By age eight, she was singing solos in church. Her beautiful, strong voice had a resonance far beyond her years.

When Ethan came home, he would listen or sing along with her. Often one of them would play the guitar while the other played the keyboard.

The adoptive father spent a lot of time with her, yet tried to be careful to never neglect Eric or the twins. Family meant everything to him—he loved all his children.

Many times Janna would ask, "Daddy, can we go see the ocean?" They would pack their bags and head to Ethan's parent's beach home near Corpus Christi, Texas. It was the favorite place for Janna and Eric.

Ethan treasured the time he spent with his children at their vacation home. They would talk for hours, strolling along the beach. They made a game of finding the most seashells.

Occasionally, when his wife was able to join them, Ethan and Susan would sit on the porch at sunset watching the siblings chase each other up and down the sandy beach. Somehow they felt more like a normal, loving family when they were at the beach house.

More than once, Janna overheard Ethan say, "One of these days, I'm going to move down here permanently."

When Janna was ten, her personality began to change. She began to lie to Susan. Ethan and his wife were already having marital problems that usually involved Janna. The rebellious girl's lies added to their already troubled marriage.

One night, Ethan came home from work and discovered Susan had disappeared with the other three children.

Janna was in her room sobbing. He knocked on her door and then entered. On the floor next to her bed, her guitar lay in ruins.

He sat on the bed next to her and hugged her. "What happened?" His kind voice was barely audible over her sobs.

After a few moments, Janna calmed down enough to speak. "Susan broke my guitar... she smashed it on the floor."

His voice was filled with fury. "Why would she do that?"

"She said she was tired of hearing the noise."

Ethan looked into Janna's tear-filled eyes. His heart broke. He blinked, and a stream of tears slid down his face.

Through sniffles, Janna said, "It wasn't noise... it was a song I wrote. I wanted her to hear it. I thought she would like it... if only she would listen."

Fighting to hold back unleashed rage, he replied in a soft voice, "I'm sorry. Will you play it for me on my guitar?"

She agreed reluctantly, still weeping softly.

Ethan returned with his guitar and handed it to her, forcing a sad, slight smile.

"Will I be able to get another guitar?" Janna pleaded.

"You can have mine. Keep it and treasure it."

She began playing a slow, melodious ballad. The lyrics rang true. It described a family who adopted a young girl. As Ethan listened thoughtfully, his heart melted. He knew the song was about him and Susan.

Who would have guessed that ten years later that same song would be a top hit, sung by a twenty-year old superstar named... Brianna Bays?

Susan came home later that night acting as if nothing happened. No one ever mentioned the incident again—not a word.

Ethan and Susan's marriage went even further downhill. Their fights were more intense and frequent.

They no longer went to church together. Susan didn't even attend church the day Janna was baptized. Neither did Susan's parents. Fortunately, Ethan's parents were present at that special service. They always supported their son and grandchildren.

When Janna turned twelve, she began drifting away from Ethan. It could have been her physical changes—that's what Ethan told himself. Perhaps she was trying to gain her independence. After all, she would soon be a teenager, and he knew how troubling those years could be.

It was a difficult year for Janna... and for Ethan.

Ethan's mother died of cancer.

At her grandmother's funeral, a heartbroken Janna sang a song she had written, entitled, *Coming Home.*

A couple months later, Ethan's world was turned upside down, shattered. The reason was unknown. Nevertheless, it happened.

THREE

The Shameful Arrest

May integrity and uprightness protect me,
because my hope, Lord, is in you.
Psalm 25:21

Late one afternoon, three police officers arrested Ethan at school. He was totally bewildered because they would not give him an explanation. Humiliated in front of his students, the officers read him his rights, handcuffed him, and led him to a patrol car. They drove him to the Maricopa County Court House where he was photographed and fingerprinted.

Before he stood in front of the judge, he met with Robert Cain, his attorney and close friend. They sat across from each other at a table in an interrogation room. His lawyer finally told him why the police arrested him.

"Ethan, you are being charged with child abuse."

His eyes grew troubled. "What? There has to be some mistake. I've never harmed any of my students."

"I don't know how to tell you this." Cain hesitated briefly and then blurted out the painful words, "It's not one of your students... it's Janna."

His heart stopped beating momentarily. Ethan stood and angrily replied, "That's not true. Who would make such horrible accusations? Of course, it had to be Susan. Nobody else would stoop that low."

The attorney continued, "Ethan, it was not Susan. It was... it was... Janna. She is the one accusing you."

Ethan's arms went limp at his side and he slumped into a chair. Confused, he shook his head. At first, no words would come. After a few moments, the despondent man spoke, "There has got to be a horrible mistake. Who put her up to this? Why would she lie about me?"

"Ethan, you tell me."

Obviously in the state of shock, Ethan repeatedly asked, "Why? Why?"

"According to Susan, you have been spending a lot of time alone in Janna's room..."

Ethan interrupted. He stood, angrily shoving the chair aside. "Of course I do. We play music together in her room because Susan hates hearing it. Janna is extremely gifted. She's been showing me the music she's writing. I really think she's a child prodigy, her musical ability is amazing." A small smile came to his face when he talked about her exceptional gift. "She can put a song together, both lyrics and score, in a matter of minutes. It just comes to her naturally. I bet she has written over a hundred songs already... I'm talking top-quality music. Do you remember last year when I gave you some music to send to that agent in Nashville?"

The lawyer lowered his voice. "Ethan, this is serious, extremely serious. I can't emphasize that enough. This is not the time to talk about her music!"

His smile disappeared as he was jolted back to reality.

In his usual optimistic way Ethan spoke. "I know. But, it will be okay. I'm sure Janna and Susan had another blowup, and she's taking it out on me. We will get it straightened out as soon as I can talk to my daughter."

Robert's voice showed the frustration he was feeling. "You don't understand. There is no talking to her... Janna's been taken from you. Furthermore, Susan wants nothing to do with her, or you, for that matter. Janna has been placed in a foster home. We have a sworn statement from her that on several occasions you beat her. The police report indicates there may even be possible inappropriate conduct in another way."

The atmosphere was charged with emotion.

"What? Robert, that's absurd. You know I would never do that."

"Ethan, you have to admit you have been very close to her. It seems you spend more time with Janna than with your other kids."

"She's had so many strikes against her. She needed more help, that's all. She's my daughter. I love her... as a father loves his daughter. Even the thought of this sickens me."

Ethan's mind drifted for no apparent reason. He seemed to be far away in another place.

"Is there anything you are not telling me? Ethan..."

"Oh, sorry, Robert. I was just wondering why she would do this. She's my daughter. Music is our special bond... that's all."

"The jury could see that special bond as an inappropriate physical relationship."

He needed air. Ethan took a breath, but it didn't seem to help. He began to shout, "For crying out loud, Robert. She's twelve years old... she's my child. I love her as a daughter... in a pure, wholesome way. I would never do anything to harm her. That is disgusting—only a monster would do such horrific deeds."

"Times have changed. Anything can be misunderstood and looked upon as inappropriate."

"This is all crazy, Robert. You know me. You've known me for years."

"Yes, I know you, but at the same time I realize you and Susan are on the outs. The jury is going to look at that as probable cause. The prosecution is going to bring in specialists who will take the child's side."

Ethan closed his eyes for a minute. Was this really happening? What could he say to make it go away? It must be a nightmare. Surely he'll wake up and everything will be okay. He opened his eyes. The attorney was still waiting for an explanation—anything that made sense. The only words he could muster were, "I would never do anything to hurt her. Never! She's my little girl."

Robert Cain's stern face showed his frustration. "You could in the eyes of a jury, and unfortunately, that's all that matters."

The broken man stared blankly at the wall.

"Ethan, I repeat... is there anything you're not telling me?"

"What's not to tell? It's just not true. I know it all boils down to the fact that it is her word against mine. If that is the case, you know I can't defend myself."

"What do you mean you can't defend yourself? If you don't, you will be admitting your guilt." Robert emphatically tried to make his point.

"I will not drag her name through the mud. I will take the fall in order to protect her," the desperate father insisted.

"Listen to yourself. She's going to ruin your life. Janna's almost a teenager and she's confused, rebellious. There is no telling what she went through before you rescued her. We can use that as our defense."

Ethan pounded his fist on the table. "And do what? Destroy her reputation, mess her up even more, and put her life in jeopardy." He hesitated. "Don't tell me you have physical evidence."

"She was pretty bruised. She has given the authorities dates, times, and places."

"Bruised? How?"

Cain shook his head. He had no answers.

Ethan's face showed defeat. "Dates, times, and places are easy to make up. It's your job to get me off. However, I will not defend myself—not if it means bringing Janna down or exposing her past. Furthermore, I'm not going to allow this to be a media circus."

"Ethan, please reconsider. Think about this!"

Still denying the seriousness of the situation, Ethan added, "There's nothing to reconsider. I don't believe this will go anywhere. I will have a talk with Janna and try to straighten it out."

Cain tried desperately to connect with the hurting father. "Ethan, I told you, you cannot talk to her. The judge has a restraining order against you. You can't come within fifty feet of her or you will be arrested."

The client stared at his lawyer. No words would come.

Ethan's heart was shattered. After a few moments, he spoke. "This is not real. This can't be happening."

"Believe me. It is real. It is happening."

Ethan sat up straighter. "Let me reiterate one more time. I will not allow this to hit the major newspapers. She was a Muslim and became a Christian. Some may see that as rejecting her faith, which could result in a death sentence to her. I cannot, will not, put her life in jeopardy. You know that!"

The attorney looked directly into his client's eyes, frantic to get through to him. "Ethan, it comes down to your freedom or hers. Let's fight this and get her the help she needs. Arizona laws are very strict when it comes to these cases. It's hard, almost impossible, to beat these charges in court in this state."

Ethan's face showed a certain resolve. His mind was made up. "I'm going to have to take the chance. She's confused, but she will come to her senses. I believe she looks at me as a father figure. I think she wanted to get away from Susan and this seemed to be the easiest way."

"She's going to destroy you and there is nothing you will do about it. Nothing!" Robert's voice sounded dejected.

Ethan looked at his lawyer with disbelief. "Surely this will not go anywhere."

His attorney knew there was no talking him into anything at this point. His only hope was that he would eventually come to his senses, and realize his best defense is to confront the wayward girl in court.

Ethan was released on bail and went home. There was no denying the loneliness; the quiet of the house suffocated him. The place that once was filled with laughter, happiness, and love was empty, quiet, and lonely... stillness everywhere.

Thoughts raced through his exhausted mind. Susan's love for him had died years before. He could not understand why she loathed Janna. She did from the beginning, but why?

Perhaps Janna was getting too much attention. Could Susan have been jealous of her? What could he have done differently? His concern was to provide a stable home for a little girl who had been neglected. He was not a monster. He had enough love for all his family.

As he walked around the large, silent house, he could not grasp the recent events. More questions flooded his thoughts. *What happened?* He loved his family—Lonnie, Alana, Eric, Janna, and at one time, Susan.

Ethan reached over to a shelf and picked up a family picture taken two years before. Happiness and contentment were obvious by his genuine smile. The twins and Eric looked like normal, well-adjusted kids. Even Janna looked happy. Susan's appearance seemed different from the others. Her smile seemed artificial—was she ever happy?

They were very much in love when they married... at least, he thought they were. He knew he was. Ethan prided himself on the fact that he was a good provider—Susan never lacked for anything. They lived in a luxurious home with no financial worries.

As Miss Arizona, she had the world at her fingertips. Susan was sought for television interviews, radio broadcasts, and had a lucrative contract with a cosmetic firm in Phoenix.

Both were in excellent health. In many ways, they were the perfect family.

Thoughts continued to jumble his mind. Perhaps his past had put a damper on their relationship. After all, he had a love before Susan—a strong love, his first love, maybe even to the point of obsession. However, she had been taken from him.

Ethan picked up the phone and dialed a number. "Hello, Tim. This is Ethan. Is Susan there?"

The voice on the line was Susan's father. "Ethan, give it up. It's over between the two of you. She never wants to see you again. Never! As far as your children, you never will see them again either. Stay away from them, or you will be arrested. Besides, it appears you like twelve-year-old girls better." His words stung.

Ethan tried to stay in control. "Sir, that's not fair. None of this is true. I'm innocent. You know that I'm..."

The voice interrupted him. "It's over, Ethan. Don't ever call again. The court has a restraining order against you. You can't come close to Susan or the children. You are a sick man. Take your punishment and leave them alone. Leave us all alone!" Then he heard a click and a dial tone.

Full of anger, Ethan threw the phone across the room, hitting a mirror and shattering it.

In the deepest pain he had felt in his life, he cried out, *Lord, why? I have followed You! I have loved You! I was obedient! Why? Why have You allowed this to happen?*

He waited for an answer, but there was none.

The devastated father stared at the family picture and tears began to flow. He dropped the photo, buried his face in his hands, and sobbed uncontrollably. He had lost everything. There was nothing to live for... his life might just as well be over.

FOUR

The Prosecution Rests

Though I cry, 'I've been wronged!' I get no response;
though I call for help, there is no justice.
Job 19:7

The old saying, "Justice is blind," has never been more true than in this trial.

A well-known professor married to a beauty queen created a huge buzz among the paparazzi. Ethan had hoped it would not be a big media event, but there was no denying it, the trial was gigantic news. No one could understand why the professor would risk everything and abuse a helpless twelve-year-old girl. It made no sense. After all, he was married to one of America's most beautiful, successful women.

Ethan's heart skipped a beat on the first day of the trial when he entered the courthouse and noticed Susan standing in the hallway. He was pleased she was there to lend support. He gave her a weak smile, but she hastily turned her head away. Within minutes, his feelings changed to sorrow when he found out his wife was there to testify against him.

Ethan was relieved that his children were not present; he did not want them to hear the sordid details that were bound to surface in the trial. Lies or truth—either would confuse them even more. Distraught, he shook his head. His children didn't deserve any of this.

The confident assistant prosecuting attorney, an energetic woman named Carol Moore, had a lot riding on the highly publicized event. It was her first major case, and she would make every effort to impress her superiors with a win. At any cost to Ethan!

Ethan and his lawyer learned that the judge was also a woman. The news troubled Cain who wondered if his male client even had a chance for a fair trial.

Everyone rose as the judge entered the courtroom.

Ethan's stomach was in knots. It seemed like another world, like something seen on primetime television... not his life.

The bailiff's voice echoed through the courtroom, "All rise. The Honorable Judge Sara Summers presiding."

Ethan glanced around the room. His heart was heavy, and his mind racing. He knew Janna had been confused about something, but still did not know what caused her to make the unfounded accusations against him.

Since she was underage, only her sworn testimony could be entered in the trial. That's the way Ethan wanted it. He still felt the need to protect Janna's reputation at all costs. He found some comfort in the fact that since she was a minor, the press could not legally print her name or photo. That would help her identity remain concealed. In spite of her accusations and the possible outcome for him, he still felt responsible for Janna's safety and well-being. He hoped that one day his daughter would realize how much he loved her.

He took a deep breath as more thoughts flooded his mind. He reflected on how Christ must have felt at His trial. Sinless, yet tortured, and hung on a cross to die a painful, agonizing death—the thought of such injustice almost brought tears to his eyes.

In the crowded courtroom, Ethan's thoughts wandered to Susan. He never wanted his marriage to fail. He had hoped his wife would accept the frightened girl into their home and be a mother to her. He wanted Janna to love him as a father. Tears began to fill his eyes, but he blinked them away. All of his dreams were shattered. Emptiness filled his soul.

He questioned why his life fell apart. No answers came to his hurting heart, only sheer confusion.

He switched his attention to the woman dressed in a black robe as she walked up the steps and sat behind the large mahogany desk. She appeared ready to judge and condemn him—at least, those were Ethan's first impressions.

"Please, be seated," the judge pronounced, glancing around the courtroom at the spectators.

The words stung as the bailiff read the accusations for the entire courtroom to hear. "Case A73289–The State of Arizona versus Ethan B. Anderson."

"Mr. Anderson, how do you plead?" The judge cast a look at Ethan that sent a shiver down his spine.

A wave of panic suddenly engulfed Ethan. Had the judge already decided his guilt? He swallowed hard. The drama must play out. How he wished he could open his eyes and wake up from the horrible nightmare he was facing! He knew it wasn't possible—this situation was far too real.

Ethan's attorney stood beside his anxious client and spoke with authority. "To the charge of child abuse, Your Honor, my client pleads, 'Not guilty.'"

"Very well, Counselor. Proceed." The judge shuffled some papers in front of her and then looked up.

Unexpectedly, Robert Cain said, "Excuse me, Your Honor?"

"Do you have something to add, Counselor?"

The defense attorney glanced at Ethan Anderson one more time for confirmation.

Ethan nodded nervously, signaling for his attorney to continue.

Cain cleared his throat. "Yes, Your Honor. My client will not be taking the stand in his own defense, nor does he want his adopted daughter to appear in court."

The judge's expression turned to astonishment and her mouth dropped. "Let me get this straight, Mr. Anderson. You are pleading 'Not guilty' to these accusations, and you will not take the stand in your own defense."

Ethan nodded his head slightly, lowering his gaze to the floor.

The judge glanced around the courtroom and eyed a group of reporters who were taking notes as the developments played out. Then she looked straight into the defendant's eyes and rose from her chair. "I would like to see the defendant and counsel from both sides in my chambers." She led the way into her private office and sat down behind her desk.

Ethan, the attorneys, and the bailiff followed.

The judge gestured to the chair in front of the desk. "Mr. Anderson, please be seated."

Judge Summers watched as the once-proud man sat directly in front of her.

Ethan hung his head, staring at the floor.

"Okay, Mr. Anderson, what is this about? I have tried many child abuse cases. The defendants are always innocent and they fight to the end. I sense this is different. What is your story?"

"Please Ethan, tell her the entire story," Robert Cain pleaded. The creases on his forehead showed the seriousness of the moment.

Ethan looked at his attorney. "Why? It won't change the outcome of the trial. The jury will still convict me, and the press will destroy Janna. You know I will not do that. I can't." His tone held a resolve, a determination that his decision was final. His mind was made up.

The judge stared at him. "I can see there is a piece of the puzzle I don't know and probably never will. Am I right?" She sat back in her chair and looked directly at Ethan, who still could not make eye contact with her.

He sat rigid in his chair, his sweaty palms locked together on his lap.

The judge paused for a moment and finally broke the awkward silence. She leaned her forearms on the desk, and her voice grew louder. "Understand this. I will not allow my courtroom to be turned into a media circus, and I will find the underlying cause of this entire drama."

Carol Moore immediately spoke up. "Your Honor, can we please get on with the trial? I will bring out any secrets this man is hiding."

The judge glared at the prosecutor. "Counselor, there will be plenty of time for you to make a name for yourself. So do not question me on how I run my courtroom. Do I make myself clear? I am in charge here. Don't forget it!"

The prosecuting attorney stiffened and quieted.

The judge studied Ethan. "Okay, if you won't tell me what this is about, let me ask you one question. Are you innocent of the charges?"

Ethan said nothing. He didn't move a muscle.

Robert put his hand on Ethan's shoulder for support and squeezed it gently.

The defendant finally looked at the judge and something changed in his eyes. He took a deep breath. "Yes, Your Honor... I am innocent."

Judge Summer's face perked up. "I want you to know that I read the police report and have personally talked with Janna. She told me the same story every time. Mr. Anderson, why would your daughter accuse you of such horrible things?"

Ethan hesitated. "I keep asking myself the same question. If I knew that answer, I probably would not be here. I haven't been able to talk with her. I don't know her feelings, and she doesn't know mine."

"Let me ask you this. How was your relationship with her?"

Again, silence.

The judge broke the tense quiet. "I know what you're thinking. You're accused by the State of Arizona of abusing a twelve-year-old girl. The prosecuting attorney and the judge are women. You have not been able to confront the victim. Let me rephrase that... you have not been able to confront the alleged victim—your own adopted daughter."

The judge cleared her throat and continued. "The fact that she is adopted certainly doesn't help your case. The majority of abuse cases involve a live-in boyfriend or an adoptive parent. How much more could this trial be stacked against you? Am I right?" She waited for a response.

Ethan drew in a slow breath. With a sullen voice he stated, "Your Honor, you are right on all those things. However, I cannot reveal all the details regarding my daughter. I won't hurt her."

"Okay. Speak to me. What is it? You may not believe it, but I do want the truth. If the child is lying, I want to know it. Is Janna lying?" Judge

Summers waited for an answer, anything that could help her make sense of the situation.

Ethan stared at the judge, uncertain how much information he should divulge. Cautiously, he proceeded, "Your Honor, I am innocent... that's all you need to know."

Judge Summer's voice grew louder. "No. If what you say is true, and you are innocent, why is the girl lying? What is her motive?"

Ethan defended Janna. "You know how it is. She's almost a teenager. Teens are rebellious by nature. They lie, cheat, and steal. Especially Janna... she came to us with a lot of baggage in her life, many unresolved issues."

The judge didn't break eye contact. "Mr. Anderson, this is more than cheating and stealing, and much more than a little white lie. What reason does Janna have to hurt you this way? Did the two of you have a good father-daughter relationship?"

A small smile came to his face as he thought about the good times he had with Janna and his other children. Janna and he had a special relationship, but he could not tell the judge that... she may not understand their unique bond.

"Mr. Anderson, you may know this is very unusual for a judge to do what I am doing. It's on the edge of breaking protocol. However, I feel there is something extremely important that you are not divulging to me, and you will not tell the court. Can you trust me... off the record?"

He stared into her eyes and swallowed hard, trying to keep his composure. "Trust is a difficult concept for me. You see, I trusted my wife, and I trusted Janna. How can I trust a justice system, which usually takes the side of the alleged victim—especially when a child is involved? I was guilty the moment the accusations came forth—my own father-in-law told me that."

The judge sighed noticeably. "Mr. Anderson, there is more to it than that."

"You have no idea." Ethan reluctantly continued in a shaky voice. "Do you know that Janna was adopted from Kuwait?"

"Yes, I do."

"Well, she came from a Muslim country and was raised in an extremist Muslim orphanage, and then she became a Christian." Ethan paused. "Your Honor, know what the punishment for that is? It's death!"

The judge, focusing intently, replied, "Mr. Anderson, Americans do not put people to death when they don't believe the same way they do."

"No, but some of the more radical Muslims do."

"I see. So you believe her life may be in danger." The judge leaned back in her chair and crossed her arms. "Mr. Anderson, Janna told me that she rejected her Christian faith. She said you forced it on her. She told me that she intended to find her real parents and her real faith."

Ethan looked shocked as more truth came out. His voice grew louder. "No! I led her in the prayer of salvation, and she was baptized. She was sincere. I know she meant it. That can't be true!" He shook his head in disbelief.

"Believe me, Mr. Anderson, what I said is true. The state placed her in a Muslim foster home, and the caseworker is currently trying to locate her birth parents."

Ethan's chin dropped, and his eyes welled up. He felt the fight seep out of him. With his voice choked with emotion and resolve, he added, "Then there is nothing else to say. Nothing else I can do. Let's get this charade over with."

The judge stared at him, seeing his dismay. "Mr. Anderson, I want you to know that everything you have said here will remain confidential. It will have nothing to do with the verdict, or the sentence that I impose on you... if you are found guilty."

Judge Summers faced the attorneys. "Counselors, nothing you heard in here will be used in the courtroom. If it is, I will call for an immediate mistrial. Am I clear?"

The judge turned back to face the defendant.

Ethan looked downward. He was finished. He had given up. There was no hope left for the grief-stricken father.

Judge Summers felt the weight of her responsibility. "Bailiff, take Mr. Anderson back to the courtroom. I will be there shortly."

Dejected, Ethan Anderson rose slowly from the chair and strode ahead of the bailiff, followed by the two lawyers. The door closed.

The judge watched as the depressed man left her chambers. She knew the pieces did not fit. At the same time, she knew it was not her responsibility to find out why—that was up to the attorneys.

Judge Summers couldn't let it go. She reached for the phone. "John, get everything you can on Janna Anderson. Who is she?" After a pause, she continued, "I know. There is just something not right about this one. Maybe with some pull, I can find out the truth, if only for my own sake. When he is found guilty... I guess I should say... if he is found guilty, at least I could give him a lighter sentence."

She listened to the lively voice on the other end of the phone line. "Yes, I know it's totally out of line on my part. Something isn't right, and I am not going to send a man to prison for thirty years for something he didn't do. This whole thing is not adding up. Thank you." The judge hung up the phone and sighed.

Her job was to listen to both sides, and give a fair sentence. She had a strange feeling that she would not be able to make the ruling as easily as she originally thought. One thing was certain—this was one trial she was not looking forward to.

Judge Sara Summers stood slowly and walked out of her private chambers into the busy courtroom to listen to the presentation of the unusual case.

She glanced around the courtroom. Most onlookers were media—all anxiously awaiting fresh details on the shocking story. Near the front, sat a row of women she believed was from a women's rights organization. She had seen them in similar cases. Her experience told her they may not be searching for the truth, but for their own idea of justice. She thought it sad that nobody except the lawyer from the defendant's side was present.

The cards continued to be stacked against Ethan Anderson.

The judge looked at the jury, studying their demeanor. The disdain on their faces was evident. The law clearly stated that Ethan was innocent until proven guilty. That is not how it appeared in this case. Anderson's attorney would have to prove his innocence. Judge Summers knew that would be nearly impossible. She was certain what the outcome would be, and unfortunately, she knew what her role would be. She would be required to sentence an innocent man to prison. After their discussion, she realized that Ethan, not Janna, would likely be the victim in this trial.

However for now, she must keep an open mind.

Judge Summers officially opened the trial—The State of Arizona versus Ethan Anderson.

She glanced at the twelve jurors—eight women and four men. "I would like to address the jury first."

The jurors sat stone-faced, ready to proceed, some of them glaring at the defendant. To others, Ethan was already guilty. After all, the young girl would not, could not, lie about something like this. Why would she?

The judge's message was clear and precise. "This is one of the most difficult cases you could ever hear as a jury. First, it pits one family member against another. Both sides may sound believable. It is your job to decipher the information and decide who is telling the truth. Therefore, I am pleading for you to be open-minded. Listen carefully to both sides, and be prepared to make an unpopular decision. Start right now, clear your mind. Remove all pre-existing stereotypes or judgmental opinions. Ms. Moore, please begin with your opening statement."

The young prosecuting attorney, dressed conservatively in black dress slacks and a cream-colored blouse, approached the jury. Carol Moore was quick and to the point as she directed the jury's attention to Ethan Anderson. "Ladies and gentlemen of the jury, meet the defendant, Ethan Anderson. He claims to have been a good role-model father." She over-emphasized the words, "role-model."

Ethan sat calmly. Dressed in a dark suit, with a white dress shirt, and blue tie, he looked like he could have been going to church.

Moore continued, "At first glance, Ethan Anderson is a nice looking, charming man. He looks like the perfect gentleman, doesn't he? Anyone would be proud to have this man as a father, right?" She paused briefly. "Wrong!" Moore's tone sounded poised, but cocky. "Ted Bundy was one of those good looking men, and look at the horrific crimes he committed. Ladies and gentlemen of the jury, I tell you, Ethan Anderson is the devil in disguise. Do not let his looks deceive you. When he should have been protecting his trusting little girl, he was abusing her. I will bring forth the evidence that Mr. Anderson is guilty of one of the most heinous crimes a man can be accused of. Be prepared to hear testimony to support that fact. Thank you." She sat down, glaring at the defendant with scorn.

Judge Summers asked, "Does the defense have an opening statement?"

"Yes, Your Honor." Ethan's close friend stood motionless for a short time, and then walked by the prosecutor as he neared the jury. For effect, he abruptly turned and stared directly into Carol Moore's eyes. "Ted Bundy—you have to be kidding!" He chuckled. "Ladies and gentlemen, you have heard the young attorney state that she will present evidence that my client, Ethan Anderson, is... how did she put it? 'Guilty of one of the most heinous crimes a man can be accused of.'"

He turned to face the jury. "I disagree. You will only hear what the prosecution wants you to hear," he said, pointing to the opposing attorney. "The fact is the only evidence you will hear from them will be circumstantial. You will not hear any evidence of crimes Mr. Anderson has committed, because there is no real evidence. There is no real crime!"

He paced the floor, speaking passionately. "Yes, Ethan Anderson is guilty of something. He is guilty of loving a little girl with all his heart. If that is a crime, I am guilty, also. What's more, I'm proud to be guilty of that. What about you?" He stared at the jurors one-by-one, giving them time for the statement to sink in. "Listen carefully to all the testimony. Please... a man's future is at stake. Be fair and open-minded."

He slowly walked by Ms. Moore, his eyes pierced her soul. He sat down next to his client and shuffled some papers that were stacked in front of him.

The judge eyed the jury. "If no one sees a reason to recess, I would like to begin the trial. Is everyone ready?" She looked at the two lawyers. No one objected, so she continued. "The prosecution may begin its case."

Carol Moore stood and faced the jury. She knew she would have to be alert and seize every opportunity to win them over. Although she felt confident that most of them, perhaps all of them, had their minds made up already. The result may be a foregone conclusion, but they needed to go through the motions. "Your Honor, we would like to call Doctor Alicia Burrows to the stand."

The bailiff went to the waiting area and called the first witness for the prosecution.

A young blonde-haired woman came through the door and confidently sauntered to the stand.

The bailiff asked her to put her left hand on the Bible and raise her right hand.

"Your Honor, I find this tasteless. Since the Bible is made up of lies and fairy tales, I refuse to abide by that rule."

The judge sighed, loud enough for all to hear. "Very well. Bailiff, remove the Bible."

The bailiff reluctantly placed the Bible on the table and turned to face the witness. "Do you solemnly swear that the testimony you are about to give will be the truth, the whole truth, and nothing but the truth."

"Yes," the doctor murmured.

The bailiff had a slightly annoyed tone. "Raise your right hand and say it again."

The woman raised her right hand halfway and then began to sit down.

The judge immediately took charge. "Please do not push my boundaries, Doctor Burrows. This is still my courtroom. I will bend the rules to fit your religion, or should I say lack of it, but you will raise your right hand high and say, 'I do,' not 'yes.' Surely you have watched enough television to know how it's done properly."

The woman sneered at the judge.

"Raise your right hand," the judge repeated, unwilling to back down.

Defiantly, the arrogant witness extended her hand high in the air.

The bailiff repeated the question. "Do you solemnly swear that the testimony you are about to give will be the truth, the whole truth, and nothing but the truth."

"I do!" The doctor responded coldly.

"State your name."

"Doctor Alicia Burrows." She over-emphasized the word "Doctor."

"Please, be seated."

The female prosecutor stepped forward. "Doctor Burrows, please state your occupation."

"I am a psychiatrist. I specialize in child development and provide therapy for victims of abuse." She sat straighter in her chair.

"Do you have a patient named Janna Anderson?"

"Yes, I did, but she is no longer in my care."

"Tell us about her. What did you observe while treating her?"

Dr. Burrows tensely shifted her position. "She suffered from severe mental instability brought on by continued physical, mental, and sexual abuse by her adoptive father."

Cain angrily jumped up. "Your honor. I object. What is this? Can she stick with the questions at hand and not let her own non-medical stereotypes enter in."

The judge faced the cynical witness. "Ms. Burrows, please just answer the question."

The doctor sighed loudly, obviously not in control of the situation like she wanted to be. "I'm telling the truth as I understand it."

Judge Summer's voice intensified. "No, you are not. You are saying what you feel. I'm not interested in your personal opinion. It is the truth that we are after, your professional opinion. Remember, the defendant is innocent until proven guilty. The jury will disregard Dr. Burrow's last remarks. Ms. Moore, please continue, but make sure your witnesses stick to the questions at hand. They are not the judge or the jury. Understood?"

"Yes, Your Honor." Carol Moore crossed her arms, looking directly at the doctor. "Doctor Burrows, continue, but without the accusations. Let's start with when you first met Janna Anderson."

"She was brought to me on April 17th of this year; she was a twelve-year-old with deep emotional problems."

"Who brought her to you?"

"A representative from child services."

"Please continue with what you learned. Tell the court her history." Moore gestured around the room.

The doctor cleared her throat. "She was born somewhere in the Middle East, and apparently was separated from her biological family during the Gulf War. At age six, she was adopted by the Anderson family from an orphanage in Kuwait."

"Did she say anything about her adoptive parents?"

"Oh yes, plenty." She peered at the judge. "Can I repeat what she said?"

Judge Summers nodded her head. "Please tell us what she said."

"She told me she hated living there. She especially hated her adoptive mother."

Ms. Moore continued without missing a beat. "Did she say why she hated Mrs. Anderson?"

"Because of her constant insults—Janna told me that she could do nothing right in her stepmother's eyes."

"Doctor Burrows, in your expert opinion, what do you think caused such hatred?"

"I would have to say their Christian beliefs. They were trying to teach her false teaching, and false hopes, in a false God. At the same time, they were trying to teach her to be perfect according to their beliefs." The doctor had a smirk on her face.

Cain stood up and quickly shot back. "Your Honor, what is this, some sort of a Christian-bashing session? I object to the doctor's tone and her insults of Christianity."

The judge's patience was growing thin. She erupted with a loud voice. "I agree, Counselor. Strike that from the record." She glared at the witness. "Doctor Burrows, I'll have you know that I am a Christian. You can think and believe what you want, but how dare you talk about Christianity, or any other religion for that matter, as being false teachings with false beliefs, and hopes in a false god! That is your opinion, not mine, not of this court, or the accused. This country was founded on freedom of religion, or in your case, freedom from religion. However, I already told you, do not give your opinions in my courtroom. Give facts! It is up to the jury to decipher the facts and make a judgment, not yours. I will not warn you again, Doctor."

Dr. Burrows looked at the attorney for help, but Moore was looking down, obviously uncomfortable with the situation.

Judge Summer's voice indicated frustration. "Now continue, but mind your tongue. One more outburst like that and you are out of here. Understand?"

There was no reply.

The judge persisted, "I said, do you understand?"

"Yes, Your Honor," the embarrassed witness mumbled.

"Counselor, proceed."

The prosecution resumed. "I will repeat the question. What do you think caused Janna's anger while living in Ethan Anderson's home?"

Determined, the witness cautiously said, "Their Christian beliefs."

"Why would their Christian beliefs cause anger in the child? There are millions of Christians in the world who have good, loving homes."

Doctor Burrows knew she must choose her words carefully. She was treading on thin ice with a Christian judge who was already frustrated with her. "Janna was conflicted because she was born and raised Muslim until she was six-years-old."

"Do you think the Muslim teaching stuck with her?"

"Most certainly. Muslims are known for indoctrinating their young. Once a Muslim, always a Muslim. According to some extremists, if they change religions, they can be killed by their family members."

"Have you ever dealt with this before?"

"Oh yes. Many times." The doctor sounded smug.

"So, let me understand this. Janna was there to see you because of a religious problem?"

"Oh no... she was sent to me because she had been abused."

"Abused by whom? Is he in the courtroom?" Moore stepped out of the way.

Cain quickly stood to his feet. "Objection, Your Honor."

Judge Summer's tone showed displeasure. "Sustained. Counselor, I'm really getting tired of this. I'm mighty close to calling a mistrial."

Without hesitation, Moore continued with her witness. "Sorry, Your Honor. Let me rephrase that. Who did Janna *say* abused her?"

"Her adoptive father—Mr. Ethan Anderson." The doctor pointed to the defendant.

"Did she say where and when the alleged abuse took place?"

"She sure did. It was in her room in April of this year."

Moore felt confident things were going in the right direction. "Did she tell you if it happened on other occasions?"

"She was too upset to talk about her previous experiences, so I didn't push her for more information." The doctor shook her head sadly.

"That's interesting. Doctor Burrows, what was the child's state of mind the last time you talked with her?"

"She is currently in a foster home. I can only tell you what I discovered while she was in my care as a state psychiatrist. She came to me extremely confused and frightened. It was obvious she had been traumatized. I would say she suffered from serious emotional problems, most likely post-traumatic stress disorder. In addition, I observed something strange with the girl. She relieved her stress with singing... I mean, she sang all the time."

"Singing? Why would that present a problem?"

"During our sessions, she would strum her guitar nervously. I finally told her to leave the guitar at home because I wanted to see how she would react without the instrument. The next time we met, she pretended to strum her guitar. One time she was moving her fingers like she was playing the piano. Poor girl, she could not distinguish reality from make-believe. I believe she resorted to music as a means of escaping the horrible events in her life."

The prosecutor looked at her notes. "Can you tell the court about child abuse? How prevalent is it in today's society?"

"Abuse is at epidemic proportions in our nation. It's out-of-control. Unfortunately, most cases are not reported. Child abuse includes neglect, as well as physical, emotional, and sexual abuse. The abusers were victims themselves in a high percentage of these cases. At least half of all child abuse cases involve some degree of substance abuse—alcohol or drugs. Sadly, most of the perpetrators are family members or friends—people the children trust most. It is becoming more common as the economy worsens. That's the most common trigger for abuse—family stress, particularly the disintegration of the family."

The doctor glared at Ethan. "In this particular case, Janna's adoptive father did not have a physical relationship with his wife. That is often when children are most abused."

Cain stood. "I object, Your Honor. What happened or didn't happen between a husband and wife in the bedroom is not relevant to this situation."

"Overruled... we are looking for the truth. You may continue with your line of questioning." Judge Summers motioned for them to continue.

Ethan did not look up. He showed no visible signs of emotion.

Moore paced in front of the jury. "So in your professional opinion, the defendant, Ethan Anderson, abused his daughter because he did not have a physical relationship with his wife?"

"Yes."

"No more questions. Thank you, Doctor Burrows."

Judge Summers inquired, "Does the defense counsel have questions for the witness?"

"Yes, Your Honor." The defense attorney, Robert Cain, neared the witness stand. He looked sternly at the doctor. "So... let me make sure I understand you, Doctor Burrows. You are saying that singing all the time is a psychological problem?"

"It certainly is."

"I see. Could singing indicate someone is happy, contented?"

"Not in her case." Burrow's reply was short and cold.

"Come now, Doctor Burrows. I have read her files and talked with her father. Mr. Anderson considers Janna extremely talented musically. Could she be a child prodigy? Could her musical ability be a gift from God?" Cain stepped closer to the witness.

The doctor snickered. "It could be a gift, but I don't believe it is from God. It's something you are born with." It was another smug, conceited reply.

"Born with. I see." Cain walked closer to the jurors.

All eyes in the courtroom were on the defense attorney.

"Let me ask you a question, Doctor Burrows. You believe that Janna Anderson was physically abused. Do you believe she had been sexually abused?"

The witness eagerly responded. "Yes I do, but if not, it certainly was leading down that path."

"Why do you believe that?"

"Janna fits a profile for a sexually abused child. She was clingy and withdrawn."

Cain continued his line of questioning. "During your sessions, did she talk about her alleged abuse?"

"Not to me, but she gave the police details."

"Do you find it strange that she gave details to law enforcement, but refused to talk to you about it in therapy?"

The doctor's voice sounded defiant. "No. It is perfectly normal for a traumatized child to withdraw into her own world."

"What is your prognosis for Janna Anderson?"

"I believe she's going to have mental problems all her life, even if she comes to terms with the abuse. Many foster children have similar issues. Then there's the religious aspect, which alone could be devastating to the young girl."

"Doctor, could she have made up the whole story?" Cain watched the jurors' reaction.

The doctor's face displayed shock. "Make up the fact she was abused? No, I am certain about that. Why would she do such a thing?"

"You tell me! After all, you're the professional." Cain snickered.

"We professionals know children don't lie or make up stories of abuse... contrary to many people's beliefs. While children have active imaginations, young children do not have a reference point for abuse or sexual behavior. They are unable to make up details of abuse... especially staying consistent."

"Come now, Doctor Burrows. Are you telling this court that children are not capable of concocting stories and conniving to get what they want?"

"Not in abuse cases," the doctor replied smugly.

"Do you expect the court to believe that some children are not capable of manipulating people and the system to get something they want?"

"In my professional opinion, no, not in cases like this."

"I see. Doctor Burrows, has Janna Anderson been sexually molested or not?"

"Well... um..." She nervously shifted her position in her chair.

"Doctor Burrows, you and the prosecuting attorney have alluded to it. I want a direct answer from you, and remember I have the hospital report right here," Cain said, waving a paper.

The doctor knew she was under oath. "No, she had not been sexually abused, but as I said earlier, it was headed there."

"How do you know that? Do you have evidence to confirm that?"

"I'm a professional. I have years of experience. I just know. I have the ability to read between the lines."

"How can you know for sure that Janna told you the truth?"

"Again, my years of experience speak volumes." She continued in her arrogant manner.

"I see. Let me ask you this. Has Janna ever given details about her relationship with her adoptive father?"

"She's twelve-years-old, underage. It is child abuse pure and simple. Furthermore, I think sexual abuse was also involved. Is that what you want me to say?" Her words were sharp and caustic.

Cain faced the judge. "Your Honor, please."

Judge Summers sighed. "Doctor Burrows, you did not answer the question. The question was about their relationship as a father and daughter."

"I'm sorry, Your Honor." There was a smirk on the doctor's face because she realized she successfully planted the idea in the minds of the jurors.

Cain rephrased his question. "Did she ever talk about the relationship between the two of them?"

"No, she did not."

"Did the subject ever come up?"

"I never asked her about it. I was more concerned about her physical and mental condition from the abuse, not about the two of them going to the zoo together." She lashed back in a derogatory tone.

"Then it seems to me you did not do your job very well. How much do you charge an hour?"

The doctor snapped, "Your Honor, do I have to take that?"

"No more questions, Your Honor." Robert shot back, "But I would like... on second thought, I would not like to hear from this witness again."

Judge Summers realized things were escalating out of control in her courtroom; the mood was tense. "You may step down, Doctor Burrows."

The witness glared at Robert Cain as she left the courtroom.

"Call your next witness," Judge Summers said to the haughty assistant prosecuting attorney.

"I would like to call Detective Anthony Hastings to the stand, please."

A middle-aged man was led in by the bailiff, walked to the stand, and was sworn in.

Carol Moore wasted no time. "Detective, can you tell me when you first heard about this case?"

"I was called to a local school to investigate a complaint. When I arrived on the scene, I went to the principal's office where I was introduced to a twelve-year-old girl by the name of Janna Anderson. The poor child had been physically and sexually abused by her father, Ethan Anderson."

Cain reacted angrily. "Your Honor, I object."

The judge stepped in quickly. "Sustained. Detective Hastings, how many times have you testified in a courtroom?"

"Sorry, Your Honor."

The judge glared at the detective, then glanced around the courtroom and focused on the jurors. She waved her arms in the air in frustration, and her voice grew louder. "This country was founded on the principle of being tried by peers and being innocent until proven guilty. I want to make it perfectly clear in this courtroom, my courtroom, that Ethan Anderson is innocent until he is proven guilty beyond any reasonable doubt." She emphasized the words "innocent" and "guilty" to make her point. "It would be good for everyone in here to remember that. Understood? You are exhausting my patience. Counselor, please continue."

"Detective, what happened after you arrived at the school?"

Hastings let out a breath. "I was introduced to a girl, Janna Anderson, who claimed to have been beaten, possibly molested. I took her aside and asked her a few questions."

"Was anybody with you?"

"Yes. Detective Debbie Osborn was with me. I always have a female officer with me when I question girls in cases like this."

"What did Janna Anderson say?"

"She said she had been beaten by her adoptive father."

"Did she give specifics?"

"At that time no, she did not. She was too upset."

"What happened next?"

"We took Janna to the hospital for an examination. Detective Osborn stayed with her. I drove to the girl's home. Her adoptive mother was there. I informed the mother about the situation and the accusations."

Moore glanced at the jury and then back to the witness. "How did she react?"

"She was a little shocked."

"A little shocked? Detective, did you say a little shocked? Was the mother crying, screaming, or what? Please elaborate."

"No, Ma'am. She just looked confused."

"Did that seem strange to you?"

"Yes. Usually mothers go into the state of disbelief, get angry, or hysterical."

"Then what happened?"

"I continued asking questions while the mother took me to Janna's bedroom."

"Why her bedroom?" Moore's eyes widened.

"That is where Janna and Ethan spent a lot of time together. Janna had said that is where the abuse occurred."

"What evidence was found?"

The detective shrugged his shoulder. "None. No real evidence, anyway. We saw nothing unusual. The adoptive mother substantiated that her husband and Janna would spend hours in the bedroom with the door closed."

"What else did you find?"

"Nothing at the house. However, when we talked with the girl, her story was always the same. It stayed consistent."

The prosecutor stepped back, positioning herself closer to the jury. "What did she say?"

The detective pulled out the police report. "Janna reported that on numerous occasions she was beaten by her adoptive father. The hospital reported she had bruises all over her body."

Carol Moore closed her eyes, indicating her horror of the mental image. "How terrible... poor girl. Did she go into details?"

"No, she would not. Like I said, she was too upset to say what happened."

"Was she sexually attacked?"

"She would not comment on that. She only insinuated."

"Why didn't the girl tell her mother what happened?" Moore persisted.

"Adoptive mother," the detective corrected. "The two did not get along. Neither spoke highly of each other."

"Let me ask you this question. Compared to other cases like this, do you believe Janna Anderson had been sexually molested?"

"Judging by the bruises on her body, her testimony, and her absolute terror, yes, I do."

"Thank you. No more questions." Moore seemed pleased with herself. She could see her idea had taken root.

The judge turned to face Robert Cain. "Does the defense have questions for this witness?"

"Yes, Your Honor." The defense attorney neared the witness. "Detective, let me get this straight. Janna said she was abused by her adoptive father?"

"Yes." The detective spoke with certainty.

"Do you find it strange that she did not give any details?"

"No, I don't. That often happens. Many victims try to forget what happened. They block it out. It's their way of dealing with the trauma. It is too painful. Sometimes they blame themselves."

"Did Janna give any indication of what happened?"

"Hitting, slapping, a few times he tried to sexually abuse her."

"You say he tried... how did he try?"

"Like I said, she wouldn't go into great detail. Every time she started, she broke down crying. It was too agonizing for the girl."

"In your professional opinion, could Janna have fabricated her story, just acting upset?"

"If she did, she deserves an acting award for her performance." The detective chuckled. "No, it was not acting! Janna Anderson was deeply affected by the trauma of abuse."

"I'm curious about one thing, Detective. The prosecution did not elaborate on the physical findings. She was given an examination by a medical doctor, wasn't she?"

"Yes, of course she was."

"Where?"

"At the local hospital."

"What did they find?"

"They found bruises and marks."

"What kind of marks and bruises? Where were they located?"

"There were bruises around her throat, shoulders, and ribs."

"I see. What about on her legs or thighs—were there any marks there?"

"Yes, on the outside of her legs."

Robert Cain walked closer to the jury. As he eyed the twelve jurors, he noticed one of them smiling at someone in the courtroom. Another was scratching her head and yawning. Obviously, some of the jurors were not paying attention to the testimony.

He turned to look at the witness. Then suddenly, trying to capture the jurors' attention, he yelled, "Detective!" His action startled everyone in the room. "Was Janna sexually abused or not?" He shifted his gaze to the jury, all eyes now fixed on him. He moved his hand in the direction of the detective, signifying for the jurors to pay attention to the witness.

The detective hesitated, "Everything pointed to the fact..."

Cain interrupted, "Detective, please answer the question without speculation. Was Janna Anderson sexually abused or not? I have asked a simple question, so please give me an answer."

Moore quickly stood up. "Your Honor, the counsel is badgering the witness."

Judge Summers instantly shot back, "He sure is, and I'm waiting for an answer from the detective."

Moore sat down, noticeably displeased.

Everything quieted.

The detective looked around the courtroom. "No sir, she was not sexually molested. Fortunately, we intervened before that happened."

The defense attorney turned from the detective and approached the judge. Cain pointed to the court reporter. "Your Honor, I demand the last part of his statement be stricken from the records. It was a mere assumption."

The judge nodded her head, "I agree. Please strike the last part of the statement from the records. The jury will disregard it. Please, continue."

Cain shook his head. "So everyone in the courtroom can hear this... Detective Hastings, was Janna molested or not?"

The detective lowered his head, "No sir. She was not."

Cain continued, "So... you really have only a confused twelve-year-old girl's word about the whole thing. Is that true?"

"Yes, that's true, but why would she lie?"

Cain turned to face the judge, "Your Honor!"

The judge brushed a finger across her eyebrow. "Detective, you were asked a question. You are to give us the answer. You know that. Strike that last statement from the record." She addressed the jury. "Members of the jury, you will disregard that statement."

Robert Cain approached the bench. "Your Honor, I would like to call for a mistrial. The first two witnesses have tainted the minds of the jury making it impossible for my client to get a fair trial."

"I agree somewhat, Counselor, but not enough for a mistrial—not yet." The judge shook her head.

The defense attorney continued. "Your Honor, look at the jury. Most of them are more interested in tonight's high school ballgame than in this case. I believe the only things they will remember are the remarks that have been stricken from the record. There is no way my client can get a fair trial."

"Counselor, I understand your concern, but this is my courtroom, and this case will continue. Your client has the best chance for a fair trial in my court. Now proceed. I will listen carefully to the rest of the prosecution's witnesses. However, if they step out of line one more time, I will call for a mistrial."

Judge Summers glared at the prosecuting attorney, "Do you understand, Ms. Moore?"

She rose. "Yes, Your Honor."

The judge spoke again to the jury. "Like I said at the beginning, this is not a game. I will be watching each of you, and if I find anything out of the ordinary, I will release and reprimand you. Understood?"

The jurors responded with murmurings of agreement and head nods.

"Continue, Counselor." Judge Summer's voice indicated she meant business.

Cain answered, "No more questions for this witness."

"Does the prosecution have any more witnesses?"

"Yes, Your Honor. We would like to call Susan Johnson to the stand."

There was an instant hush in the courtroom as Ethan's wife strode into the room.

Cain stood. "Your Honor, the prosecution must be aware of the fact that in a court of law a wife cannot be forced to testify against her husband."

The prosecution quickly responded. "Your Honor, she came to us, we did not seek her out. She asked to testify."

Robert bent over, speaking softly to his client. "Ethan, why would your wife testify against you?"

The only words a despondent Ethan could speak were, "I don't know."

He watched the woman, who once was the love of his life, approach the stand. She was dressed in a tight, short skirt, and a low-neck fitted sweater. Her heels clicked—a sound all too familiar to Ethan. She raised her hand and with the other hand on the Bible took the oath.

To Ethan, it was like a bad dream getting worse.

"Ms. Johnson, you came to us to share your story. Why?" Carol Moore's confident look demonstrated satisfaction.

"This is very hard for me." Susan reached for a tissue.

"What is hard for you?"

"To testify against someone I once loved." She wiped her eyes, but there were no visible tears.

"Continue."

"I need to tell the court what happened in my house."

Moore decided to take advantage of the moment, playing on the sympathy of the jurors. "Take a deep breath. We know this must be extremely difficult for you. Take your time."

Ethan had enough! Impulsively, he jumped to his feet, shouting, "No, Susan. No! If you ever loved me, don't say anything."

Robert subdued his client until the bailiff forcibly sat him down.

Susan turned, and for the first time looked into her husband's eyes. A stray tear rolled down her cheek. She wiped it away quickly. Did her demeanor change for a moment? It happened so rapidly it was difficult for Ethan to tell.

The judge banged her gavel a number of times. "Order, order in the court. Counselor, keep your client quiet, or I will have him cuffed and removed from this courtroom. Understood?"

"Yes, Your Honor. It will not happen again."

He sat down by his hurting friend. "Ethan, settle down, or they will come down on you even harder. You have to control yourself."

"She knows." He mumbled to his attorney. "She knows the truth."

Cain nodded his head and put his arm around his friend.

"Well, that was interesting," Carol Moore chuckled. "Ms. Johnson, please continue."

Susan stared at Ethan, choosing her words wisely. "My husband would spend much of his free time in Janna's room, sometimes for hours at a time. Janna was very beautiful and physically mature for her age. Many times I would enter the room and the bed would be messed up. I would ask Janna what was going on... she would just shrug her shoulders and say, 'Nothing.'"

"Did you suspect your husband was having a relationship or was abusing your adopted daughter?"

Cain's voice rang through the room, "Objection. Mere speculation!"

"Objection sustained," the judge hastily replied.

"I will rephrase the question. What did you suspect?"

"I was beginning to think there was a physical relationship between the two."

"You say physical, could you be more precise?"

"I believe they were too close. I had never seen two people with such a close bond in my entire life. I would watch their relationship and compare it to our friends. I even asked some other mothers if their husband had a close rapport with their daughters, and they all agreed it was too much. It was just uncanny how close they were. I talked to Ethan about it and got nowhere. One day, I finally came out and asked him if he was having an inappropriate relationship with Janna. He laughed... he just laughed."

"Why do you think they were so close if it wasn't for, shall we say, physical gratification?"

Susan's eyes wandered around the courtroom and finally rested on Ethan. After a long moment, she lowered her eyes to the ground, closed them, and shook her head, "I don't know."

"What kind of marriage did you and your husband have?"

"It used to be great, but something happened. There was no intimacy the last few months we were together."

"Give us a time frame from Janna's accusations. When you say the last few months, what do you mean?"

She exhaled hard. "I'd say three months or so before he was arrested."

"Thank you. I have no more questions."

Judge Summers was fatigued. She could only imagine how emotionally spent the defendant must be. "Does the defense have any questions?"

Ethan gripped the edge of the table and leaned in. "No," he shouted.

Robert reprimanded his client. "Ethan!"

The lawyer faced the judge. "Your Honor, may I have a minute with my client?"

Judge Summers responded hastily, "Yes, please do. I have many questions I would like to ask the witness, but that's not my job, it's yours."

Cain bent over, placed his hands on the table, and looked directly into Ethan's eyes. Softly, he said, "There are holes throughout her testimony. It's my job to show them to the jury."

"But if the truth comes out, Janna's life will be in danger. Susan knows the truth... the whole truth," Ethan whispered.

"I will bypass any questions about your daughter. I just need to get one more thing across."

"Go ahead, but nothing about Janna's past."

Robert turned to face Susan. "Mrs. Anderson."

"It's Ms. Johnson," she corrected him.

"Oh yes, I'm sorry. Ms. Johnson, I see many discrepancies in your testimony. However, I couldn't help but notice, as I'm sure everyone else in the courtroom has, you certainly are dressed to the hilt today. Do you think it may be a bit too much? I mean, this is a trial, not a beauty pageant."

"I object. Your Honor, can we proceed with the questioning?" The prosecuting attorney's face showed a flush of anger.

"Please do, Mr. Cain. Let's get on with the questions, not a discussion about Ms. Johnson's wardrobe." Judge Summers frowned with displeasure.

Cain studied the journalists in the courtroom. "Yes, Your Honor. I was just noting all the reporters from women's magazines. I guess this is a very important story for them. Would you not think so, Ms. Johnson?"

She didn't respond. Her face showed no emotion.

"Tell me, did you ever observe Ethan touching Janna inappropriately or abusing her in any way?"

"They were always touching each other."

"In what ways?"

"He would tickle her, and he hugged her often. When she was younger, he swung her around by her arms." Susan's voice sounded sort of stiff.

The defense attorney inched closer to the jury. "Ladies and gentlemen, I'm sorry for the shocked look on my face, but... well, perhaps I shouldn't admit it, but I do the same thing with my two daughters. I believe most fathers do... most loving fathers. Am I guilty of child abuse, also? Are you?" He made eye contact with the four male jurors who appeared stunned by Susan's words. It was obvious a couple of them were visibly shaken.

Cain turned to face Susan. "I believe if we called Doctor Burrows back to the stand, she would agree that good fathers have close relationships with their daughters, which often involves hugs and appropriate touch."

Anger came over Susan in a flash. "She's not his daughter... she's his adopted daughter, there's a big difference"

The attorney, surprised by her comments, pressed on. He walked to the table and picked up a paper. "Ms. Johnson, I hold in my hand a copy of Janna's birth certificate. If you look at it closely, you will see your name and your husband's name listed as Janna's parents. It says nothing about an adoption. When you adopted her, you became her parents in every sense of the word." He handed it to Susan.

She skimmed over the paper and returned it to the lawyer.

"Let me ask the question once more. In what inappropriate ways did Ethan touch Janna?"

Susan cleared her throat nervously, and drew in a slow, cleansing breath. "Well, sometimes they... um..." She cast a look at Ethan, and then shrugged her shoulders. "I guess I never saw them touching inappropriately."

"I see. You say the bed was messed up?"

"Yes, it was."

Cain continued. "Could you be more specific? You see, I have two teenage daughters and their beds are always in disarray."

"Well... it was neat during the day, but when they came down for dinner..."

Cain interrupted. "I see. Ms. Johnson, when they played their music where did they sit?"

"I don't recall. I never really watched them. I suspect when they played the keyboard... I don't really know." Susan made a strange face.

"And the guitar?"

"They probably stood."

"Could they have sat on the bed?"

Susan hesitated and shifted nervously in the chair, "I guess they could have sat on the bed."

"Could they have messed up the bed when they played the guitar?"

"Um... well yes, I suppose." Susan ran her fingers through her hair.

"How much time did they spend playing music together?"

"Almost every waking hour," Susan responded sarcastically.

"It sounds like you are resentful of that?"

"Resentful? Actually, it disgusted me. My husband spent all of his time with Janna making music."

Cain's piercing eyes seemed to look right through her as he spoke. "Did he neglect you and the other children? Now, really think this through before you give your answer. Remember you are under oath, Ms. Johnson. Did Ethan ever neglect you or the other three children?"

Susan sat motionless, pondering the question. "No, not really. He spent a lot of time with all the kids."

"Was he a good father?"

"Was he a good father?" She repeated his words slowly. Reluctantly, she answered, "Yes. Really, he was a very good father."

"Was Ethan a good husband?"

She scraped up the courage to look at Ethan face-to-face. "Yes, he was. But things changed when that girl came into the house."

"That girl? I assume you mean Janna, right?"

"Yes."

"Let me ask you a question. Is it possible that you were jealous of Janna and the time your husband spent with her?"

Things were not going as Susan had imagined. She felt like she was on the verge of losing control. Her answers were rehearsed, why was it so difficult? She paused, trying to form the right words in her mind. She finally blurted out words that shocked even her. "Yes, I was jealous from the beginning!"

"Was it her beauty, or the bond that Janna and your husband had that upset you most? Or was it both?"

Unexpected tears streamed down Susan's face.

"I withdraw that question." Her facial expression was all the defense attorney needed to make his point... he was satisfied.

Cain proceeded with his questioning. "You have filed for divorce. What is the reason for that?"

Moore protested. "Your Honor, that question is not relevant to the case."

Cain quickly responded, "Your Honor, I would like to further pursue the question to see if it is."

"I agree, Counselor. The witness will answer the question." The judge sighed.

Cain restated the question. "Ms. Johnson, what is the real reason you filed for divorce?"

Susan waited for a second. Then she breathed long and loud. "I missed my career. I missed doing what I did before I got married. I was tied down, trapped."

"I see... so you missed your past life. What about the children?" The attorney cast a look at the jury.

"They are being taken care of."

Relentless, Cain pushed on, "By whom, Mrs. Anderson, I'm sorry, Ms. Johnson. By the way, is that Ms. or Miss?"

"Your Honor, that has nothing to do with the case," Moore protested.

Judge Summers urgently wanted answers and would not back down. "I disagree, Counselor. She came to you to testify, and I would like to know why. So far, I have not heard a legitimate reason. I'm curious why someone would testify against her own husband. The defense can continue with the cross-examination."

Cain breathed a sigh of relief. "Thank you, Your Honor."

The defense attorney rephrased the question. "Who is taking care of your three children?"

"My parents... and it's Miss Johnson."

"Miss, I see." Cain put his hand to his chin. "So your parents are taking care of your children." He let the thought pass.

The experienced attorney returned to the table, picked up a paper, and waved it. "You have a restraining order against your husband. Why?"

"I don't know. I just don't think it's a good thing for him to be around my children. It would confuse them even more."

"Miss Johnson, could it be you are trying to distance yourself from Ethan and your children to further your career? Isn't that why you are here... for free publicity?"

"No!" Her heartbeat doubled, and a layer of perspiration broke out across her forehead.

Cain pointed to the back of the courtroom. "I mean, look at this... radio, television, cable, newspapers, magazines... this could be big for you."

"Your Honor," Moore stood protesting urgently. "The defense is badgering the witness."

"Your Honor, I have no more questions." Robert Cain felt a faint glimmer of hope as he sat next to the defendant.

Judge Summers tone was subdued. "You may step down. Ms. Moore, please call your next witness."

Susan walked slowly by Ethan, turned slightly toward him for a split-second, and paused, unable to make eye contact. A faint look of sorrow crossed her face, and then a small teardrop fell to the ground.

Suddenly, the former beauty queen lifted her head, and strutted down the aisle and out of the courtroom, head held high. Her walk resembled a stride on the stage of a beauty pageant. Her lips rose slightly showing a hint of a smile as she snapped her high heels against the wooden floor. She looked straight ahead at the reporters, never altering her gaze. Her stride never wavered.

Moore spoke to the judge. "Your Honor, the prosecution will not call any more witnesses. Frankly, Your Honor, we are afraid if we do you will call a mistrial. We also believe that we have no need for any more witnesses. We have effectively presented our case."

Judge Summers blew out a lengthy breath. "Ms. Moore, does not the defendant have the right to face the accuser—either by video tape or sworn statement? Based on the United States Constitution, all alleged offenders have a right to face their accuser. Am I to understand that will not be happening?"

Moore replied, "Your Honor, Janna Anderson will not be here to testify. We were informed by the defense that they would not cross-examine her. We made the decision based on her mental condition to bypass her testimony. The defense has waived their right. Only her sworn statement is admitted as evidence. Since Janna is a minor, for her protection, no pictures or video will be used."

Judge Summers turned to face the defense attorney. "Counselor, the defendant has the right to be confronted by the accuser. I need to ask Mr. Anderson a question."

The judge looked directly into Ethan's red, moist eyes. "You have agreed not to confront the accuser, is that correct?"

Cain spoke on his client's behalf, "Yes, Your Honor, that is correct."

"Counselor, I want the defendant to answer that question directly."

Confused, Ethan stood. Stammering, he replied to the judge. "Your honor... I... I do not wish to drag my daughter through this any more than is necessary."

The judge stared at Ethan for a long time trying to understand his reasoning. "I see."

Judge Summers glanced around the courtroom. "I am going to stop the proceedings here. It's been a long, grueling day. The defense will present its case tomorrow morning at nine-o-clock. The defendant is still free on bail."

She banged the gavel, stood, and walked out, as the bailiff ordered everyone to stand.

The courtroom emptied quickly.

Ethan slowly paced to the crowded hallway. He heard a ruckus, turned his head, and noticed the reporters gathering around his wife.

Susan eyed Ethan, and for an instant it looked as though she wanted to talk to him. She pursed her lips to speak, and then the cameras began flashing. She raised her head high, smiled, and then turned and strode out of the courthouse, followed by a number of reporters, her heels continuing to slap the ground.

An ache settled in Ethan's heart. His mind went back to the day he proposed to Susan at an intimate restaurant. It was their special place. They were madly in love. Since then the restaurant had been torn down to make room for a giant convention center. A sad smile crept across his face as he realized the similarities. His marriage, once strong, was torn down and replaced by Susan's career. In the same way, the family he loved more than life was split, perhaps forever.

Heartbroken, Ethan wondered if things could get any worse than they were at that moment.

FIVE

The Defense

As a father has compassion on his children, so the
Lord has compassion on those who fear him.
Psalm 103:13

Ethan returned alone to his empty house. Most of the furniture was gone. A thin layer of dust covered the few scattered pieces that remained.

Dazed, he wandered through each room where his children had played and laughter once filled the air. He recalled the way he used to throw his kids high and catch them. He could almost hear them giggling and they would yell, "More, Daddy, more."

He let the images in his mind fade.

Ethan felt as empty as the emptiness of his house.

Where was God in all this? He prayed with his children every night, led a good Christian life, gave generously to charities, and tithed regularly to the church. Ethan helped people in need, and served as a deacon. What went wrong? It seemed the God of former times wasn't there when he needed Him most.

He opened Janna's door slowly and peered in; her bedroom was the only room that remained almost untouched. The guitar he gave Janna after Susan smashed hers, and the music notebooks were missing. Everything else seemed intact.

He sat on his daughter's neatly made bed and picked up a case that held a new guitar. The plan was to surprise Janna with it, but he never had the opportunity. Life had changed too quickly. Removing the guitar from the case, he began to strum it, but no tune came. It sounded only like noise. Did even the music leave him?

He stood and a sudden rage consumed him. Trembling, he shouted, "Janna, why? Why?" In his wrath, he shattered the guitar on the piano.

Emotionally spent, the broken man fell to his knees and wept. The first hour blended into the next, then another, and another. Sometime in the early morning hours, he climbed onto Janna's bed, pulled her pillow close, and drifted to sleep.

A few hours later, his father woke him. "Son, you look awful."

"What time is it?" Ethan asked groggily.

"It's 8:30. Robert called and wanted to know where you were. You have to be in court in thirty minutes."

Ethan's appearance revealed his distress. As he sat on the side of the bed, he shrugged his shoulders. "What difference does it make? The verdict has already been decided."

"You don't know that. Think positive. Come on. Let's get you shaved and into some fresh clothes. I will call Robert and try to get him to stall the proceedings."

Ethan showered and shaved while his father took a set of clothes from his closet and placed them neatly on a chair. He was dressed and out of the house in fifteen minutes.

The ride was silent as Allen drove Ethan to the courthouse. What could he say to help his son?

Finally, Ethan broke the silence. "Dad, what do you think will happen to Janna?"

"Son, you continue to amaze me. You are still defending that girl."

"Could I do any less?"

"I don't know. I just don't know. We have to face the facts, Ethan. This thing could destroy your life. You've already lost your wife and kids."

"I lost Susan long ago. I thought we had something special. As the years passed, I didn't like what she became. It was pitiful to see her so wrapped up in herself."

They stopped at a traffic light. Each man deep in his own thoughts.

"I know you're right, Son. Have you thought of what could happen if you have to spend time in prison? They say you could get up to thirty years."

"You don't think that scares me? Am I prepared for that? No, I'm not. At the same time, I just can't turn my back and throw Janna to the wolves. She's too important to me, Dad."

Allen didn't hesitate. "I know. That's why I petitioned the court to get custody of her, but that was refused. It's out of our hands now."

"I'm worried about her."

"I understand, but we must stay focused on your future now. Just know I am here for you. If your mother was still alive, you would have her full support too."

"Thanks, Dad. You've been such a help all along. I could not have done any of this without you."

There was numbing quietness; neither man knew what to say.

Ethan stared straight ahead. Finally, he spoke in a raspy tone, "I dropped by Mom's grave the other day and left some flowers." He paused. "She was too young to die."

"Cancer knows no age limits."

There was nothing more to be said.

Allen parked the car. The father reached over and in a show of support squeezed his son's shoulder. How he wished he could do something to ease Ethan's pain, but there was nothing he could do. There was nothing anyone could do!

An exhausted Ethan rushed into the courtroom late.

"Did you oversleep? The prosecuting attorney was about ready to put out an all-points bulletin on you," Robert joked.

Ethan nodded tersely, "I'm here... don't make such a big deal about it."

Within seconds, the bailiff announced Judge Summers. "All rise. The honorable Judge Sara Summers presiding."

The judge gestured for Ethan to be seated. "Mr. Anderson, I'm glad you could join us."

"I'm sorry, Your Honor. It was a bad night."

"I bet it was. Just don't let it happen again." Judge Summers narrowed her eyes.

Addressing Robert Cain, the judge continued, "Counselor, are you ready to present your first witness?"

"Yes, Your Honor. My first witness is Allen Anderson."

The bailiff went to get the witness.

Ethan's father walked toward the front, stopped momentarily, and patted his son's back.

He was sworn in and the defense attorney began his interrogation. "Mr. Anderson. If you would, please, for the record, tell the court what your relationship to the defendant is."

"I am Ethan Anderson's father."

"Do you have any reason to believe that your son is guilty of the crime of which he is being accused?"

"Your Honor, I object," Carol Moore hastily protested.

Judge Summers cast a questioning look at the prosecutor. "For what reason, Counselor? He asked him to make a character evaluation."

"Yes, Your Honor, but he's his father, of course he wouldn't have anything negative to say about him."

The judge retorted, "Counselor, that is about the lamest excuse I have ever heard. He is under oath. The witness may continue at his leisure."

"Thank you, Your Honor." Robert Cain showed a hint of a grin.

The attorney continued. "Mr. Anderson, tell me about your son."

"I'll be happy to tell you about my son. Ethan never gave us any problems. He is honest, dependable, and kind. He stayed away from drugs and tobacco, and was an honor student in school. Church was important to him. Everyone always enjoyed being around him. He has an incredible musical gift. I always thought someday he would become a musician."

The courtroom was quiet.

The father continued, "Ethan had a knack for learning foreign languages. He knew Arabic, German, Spanish, and even a little Russian. When he went to college, he could already speak several different languages. He often was asked to be the interpreter for overseas mission trips." He beamed with pride.

"How did he put these languages to use?"

"He taught at a private school for children of foreign diplomats. He loves children. If he could save them all he would... he would never hurt a child."

Carol Moore drew a loud breath. "Objection, Your Honor."

"There's no objection, it's the truth," Allen yelled back at the arrogant attorney.

Moore continued, "Your Honor, please."

The judge rolled her eyes dramatically. "Counselor, sit down."

Moore sat, and the judge spoke directly to the witness. "Mr. Anderson, it's not your job to object, or to set the counselor straight. However since you did, I stand by what you have said. Now please, continue, Counselor."

Cain resumed his pose in front of the defendant's father. "Mr. Anderson. Why would this young girl accuse your son of such horrible things if they were not true?"

Allen Anderson stared at the members of the jury. "If I had the answers to why children do half the things they do, I could solve the world's problems. The one thing I know for sure is that my son is not guilty of any of these ridiculous accusations. If he is guilty of anything, he is guilty of loving his family too much."

"Thank you, Mr. Anderson." Cain sat next to his client.

The judge glanced at Ms. Moore. "Your witness."

"Your Honor, I have no questions for this witness."

Surprised, Judge Summers stated, "The witness may step down." She turned to the defense. "Mr. Cain, you may call your next witness."

The defense attorney stood. "Your Honor, the defense has no more witnesses. My closing statement will summarize our case."

The judge's eyes widened. She stared at Cain for a second, and then shifted her focus to the defendant. She paused, and then made a surprising move. "Both attorneys and Mr. Anderson, please approach the bench."

Speaking only to those in front of her, she cautioned, "Mr. Anderson, you do realize that the only testimony you had was a character witness. That can help in some cases, but unfortunately, most cases like yours are decided by emotions, not facts."

Ethan remained silent.

Judge Summers turned to face the prosecuting attorney, "Do you wish to recall any witnesses?"

Carol Moore smiled, feeling smug. She was confident she had her first win and bounced back with an overzealous reply. "No, Your Honor, we do not."

The judge angled her head and stared at Ethan for a short time. She wished she could understand him. What was he thinking? Dreading the outcome, she redirected her thoughts. "Then please continue with your closing arguments."

Ethan and his lawyer returned to their seats.

Moore drew in a deep breath as she positioned herself closer to the jurors. This was her big chance to make a name for herself. She sounded powerful, certain, as she spoke. "Ladies and gentlemen of the jury. We have here a classic parental abuse case. It is unfortunate, but true that most cases of child abuse and molestation come from adoptive parents, live-ins, or foster parents. It is also characteristic in cases such as this to pit family members against each other. Here it is... an innocent child against... this man." She boldly pointed to the defendant. "Thankfully, we do not have to put this young girl through the horror of telling us what happened in her bedroom. A room that should have been a place fit for a princess... her castle... her safe place... not a dreadful chamber of horrors."

Moore began pacing as she continued passionately. "Here we have a man who looks like he would be the poster boy for innocence. The defense testified that Ethan Anderson is a great father. We know better! He was a man who... well, let's be honest, he got too emotionally and physically involved with his beautiful daughter and let things go too far."

Ethan felt nauseated over the thought. He looked as sick as he felt.

"You heard the testimony of the psychiatrist, the detective, and even the adoptive mother. Isn't it strange that Ethan Anderson won't even defend himself?" She shook her head. Focusing on the men and women who were waiting to decide the man's fate, she stated, "That alone should convince you of his guilt." She turned and pointed to the defendant who was sitting with his head down.

Moore went on. "Members of the jury, this man, Ethan Anderson, is a menace to society, and should be locked away for a very long time. He abused his own adopted child. What would stop him from doing it to your child, or yours, or yours?" As she spoke, she pointed to different members of the jury. "His little girl needed to be protected, not violated."

Everyone in the courtroom sat spellbound.

Moore sounded like a professional with years of experience. Her confidence was contagious; her enthusiasm couldn't be ignored by the jurors. She continued, "I have met Janna Anderson. She is striking with jet-black hair, and bright blue eyes—her beauty is beyond comparison. The poor girl will be scarred for the rest of her life. She will always have memories of what took place. Thank God she had the courage to step forth."

The jury sat mesmerized as they listened. A couple of them wiped away tears.

"There is only one possible verdict in this case." Her voice grew louder and more forceful. "Guilty! Guilty! We need to put this man away for many years. I'm sure in prison he will get what he dished out. Thank you, ladies and gentlemen of the jury."

Her walk, her demeanor, told the story. She knew she had successfully presented her case. She sat down and felt the victory.

The judge called the defense to present its closing arguments.

Robert Cain glared at Ms. Moore as he walked past her. He felt she had gone over the line in dismantling his client's character. He forced a smile. "Wow! Thank you, Ms. Moore, for your final thoughts." He cleared his throat. "What was it you said? In prison he might get what he dished out. I would have thought you were more professional than that." He scowled at the prosecutor.

Moore sat pompously with her hands folded on the table, showing no remorse.

Cain continued fervently. His words came straight from his heart. "You see, I have an advantage over all of you because I know Ethan Anderson personally. I know he is innocent of these preposterous charges. We have known each other since we were children. He is kind and decent, a man of integrity, faith, and self-denial, always putting the needs of others before his own. I can testify to Ethan's character."

Robert felt the weight of his responsibility. "I assisted him with the adoption of Janna. I was there when she was baptized, and noticed the tears in her grateful dad's eyes. I was at her first piano recital, and was there when she pitched her first softball game. Ethan was a proud father. I saw the way he respected her, as well as his other children—loving them, caring for them, and being there for them. In today's world, too many fathers are absent from the home, or are too busy to take an active role in their children's lives. Ethan was always available, even his wife testified to that."

The room was so still you could hear a pin drop.

Cain proceeded, "Why would Janna accuse her father of such a repulsive crime? I'm not sure I have the answer, but I have a couple theories. Could a young adolescent's search for identity be the motive? Imagine if you had no idea who you were, or where you were born. You didn't know if your natural parents were dead or alive. Do you have brothers or sisters? The list of questions is endless. These thoughts and others haunted Janna Anderson day and night."

Ethan had a renewed sense of hope. It seemed that Cain was hitting the nail on the head—surely that must have been Janna's motive. It seemed logical.

Cain leaned on the railing in front of the jury and looked into the eyes of some of the jurors. "However, there is another strong possibility. How many of you have had a rebellious child?"

A few of the jurors seemed uncomfortable with the question. Did Robert Cain hit a nerve?

"Imagine this. Your clean-cut son came home late one night with a giant tattoo on his forearm. Or, what if you discovered your daughter was doing drugs? Have you ever known a teenager who faced an unwanted pregnancy? How can you explain the behavior of a teenager? You can't! Psychiatrists have been trying for centuries."

His eyes didn't leave the jury. "Ladies and gentlemen... why, is not the question we need to ask. The question should be... what... what should we do in this case? Should we condemn an innocent man to prison? No! Instead, I plead with you to do the right thing. End this travesty. Find Ethan Anderson innocent of the bogus charges that face him. Give him the respect he deserves. After all, there is no physical evidence against him. Only bruises, which could have been self-inflicted, and a troubled teenager's testimony, which could have been concocted."

Cain paced the floor. "Your Honor and members of the jury, look at him. He was... no... he is a good man. He is an outstanding citizen and has a record for service to others. Many times he went on mission trips to assist the needy, the helpless. This poor man has lost everything—his wife, family, career, and his future. Even if he is found innocent, as he should be, he will forever be branded a child molester. His reputation has been destroyed—where is the justice in that? Ethan Anderson is innocent. You hold what little future he could have in your hands."

The defense attorney stopped pacing. He positioned himself directly in front of the jurors and evened out his tone. "So I ask you, no... I *plead* with you, do what is right. The evidence is not there. This whole scenario is about the emotions of a young, lost girl in search of her identity. I am confident of one thing—someday, Janna will look back at this day with regrets, but it will be too late. At that time, the accused will have paid the penalty."

The lawyer straightened and cleared his throat. "Ladies and gentlemen, if you bring back a verdict of guilty, it may haunt you the rest of your lives. But if you come back with the right verdict, not guilty, Ethan Anderson will be able to make some attempt to rebuild his life, and Janna will not have the guilt that someday could consume her."

The jurors were attentive, seeming to connect with the polished attorney.

"Members of the jury, think! Think this through. Is the evidence there? Does the evidence prove guilt beyond a shadow of a doubt?" Cain's voice rose, the inflection demonstrating his loyalty to his friend. "No, it does not! A guilty verdict will destroy this man's life. Come back with the straightforward verdict of not guilty. Thank You." He sat down next to his client.

Judge Summers studied the faces of the jurors as Robert Cain stunned the courtroom with his thought-provoking closing statement. She deliberately paused, giving time for the summary to sink in.

Finally, she spoke. "Thank you, Counselor. The jury now will go to the deliberation room to decide the fate of this man. I remind you once again, Ethan Anderson's future lies in your hands. Weigh the evidence carefully, and remember the key words—beyond a reasonable doubt."

She hit the gavel a final time. "Court dismissed."

"All rise," the bailiff announced as the judge exited the courtroom.

The bailiff led the jury to the room where they would decide Ethan's future. Would he be free to have a life outside prison bars, or be confined to years of imprisonment?

Ethan and his father went home to await the verdict. As they sat somberly in the cold, empty house, fear rippled through them. They had no appetite, little hope, and not much faith—despondency and loneliness consumed the pair.

It was early afternoon when the phone call jarred them. Allen answered.

"Allen, this is Robert. Come on back, the jury has already made its decision."

"So soon? It has only been a couple hours... is that good or bad?"

"It can go either way. Hurry back, and be prepared for anything."

They rushed back to the courthouse. Ethan looked around, thankful the courtroom was not full yet. He noticed Susan's absence immediately.

The women who had been sitting in the front earlier had returned to their same seats, eagerly awaiting the verdict.

Reporters were setting up their equipment—a quick verdict could be a big story.

The bailiff escorted the jurors into the room.

Robert noticed right away that the members of the jury would not make eye contact with the defendant. His years of experience taught him that was a bad sign. Cain was as ready as he could be for the verdict. He was confident that he did all he could do without Ethan's testimony.

"All rise," the bailiff's voice resounded.

The judge walked in and took her seat. Wasting no time, she asked, "Has the jury reached a verdict for the defendant, Ethan Anderson?"

The jury foreman stood. "We have, Your Honor." He handed the bailiff a paper, who in turn gave it to the judge.

Summers read it, shifted her gaze to Ethan, and then to the foreman. "What is your decision?"

The man stood confidently. "Your Honor, we find the defendant guilty as charged... on all counts."

Some of the spectators in the courtroom exploded with applause.

A woman in the front row shouted, "I hope you get what you deserve in prison! See how you like it!"

The judge stood, hitting her gavel repeatedly. Her voice grew loud, and her face displayed rage. "Order in the court. Order!"

She looked directly at the row of women in the front. The same one that shouted was still celebrating the verdict with her arms folded and a broad smile.

Judge Summers drew a loud breath. Without breaking eye contact, she spoke to the woman who was still carrying on. There was no denying the fact, the judge was furious. "Young lady, stand up!"

Nobody moved. The woman remained seated and shifted her gaze to the floor.

Judge Summers was not about to let the action go unnoticed. "Bailiff, the woman in the blue blouse, have her approach the bench."

The bailiff walked to the woman who had yelled the condemnation. "Come with me," he demanded.

In a huff, she strode forward with the bailiff to the bench. The other three women rose and joined her in support.

The judge peered at them. "I see. You all want to face my wrath, right?"

In front of the judge, they locked arms, arrogantly silent.

"Okay... we can all play this game. In my courtroom, I do not allow this sort of behavior. I hereby fine each of you fifty dollars, and you will be immediately escorted from the courtroom." Judge Summers scowled; her voice was harsh.

"This is outrageous," one of them contested. "How dare you!"

Judge Summers banged the gavel one more time and shouted, "Okay, make it one hundred dollars." Her eyes displayed fire.

One of the others protested, "You can't do that. We're Americans!"

Judge Summers again banged the gavel, "Two hundred dollars... each of you. I can fine you all day long. However, if I were you, I would leave this room as silently and quickly as possible."

They quieted, spun around, and stormed out of the courtroom.

Judge Summer's voice was clear and forceful. "This is my courtroom and there will be no insulting or name calling. We are to be civilized."

With that, order was restored.

The judge took a deep breath and faced the defendant and his lawyer. "Now, getting back to the case. Mr. Anderson, the jury has found you guilty. They have made their final decision, and I must now make mine. It is my duty as judge of this court to sentence you. I have weighed this carefully, and already decided what I would do if the verdict came back guilty."

The news reporters were scribbling on their notepads. To them it was just another story, but to Ethan, it was his life, his future. He was numb. It was almost as if he was a spectator watching someone else's life being played out.

The judge gave the defendant a grim smile.

Fear played in Ethan's eyes. His chest tightened.

Summers faced him and spoke to him like no one else was in earshot. "I have always been honest when dealing with these decisions, and many times I have not been popular. Mr. Anderson, I personally talked with you, and last night I learned your history. I looked at many things... even made a few calls of my own. Only good things were found in your life. I searched, but could not find even one skeleton in your closet."

Ethan felt a wave of panic.

"What I have to say and do here is difficult. You see, I believe you are innocent, but I have to abide by the decision of the jury. Unfortunately, my job is to sentence you. My dilemma is what type of punishment should I confer on someone who has been found guilty by his peers, but I believe to be innocent. The maximum sentence for this crime is thirty years; the minimum is six."

Ethan stood straight, barely able to breathe.

"Therefore, I sentence you to six years. Two of the years will be in a state medical facility here in Arizona. There, you will be able to give back to society by helping others. I refuse to put you in a state prison because I do not believe you are a hard-core criminal. I am recommending, Mr. Anderson, that if you are a model prisoner, the remaining four years will be spent under house arrest supervised by your father. In other words, you will be in your father's custody, and never be permitted to leave the house without your father, or unless there is an emergency."

The prosecuting attorney's face showed disgust. "Your Honor, may I say something?"

"No, you may not... my sentence today stands. As for you Mr. Anderson, maybe one day you will tell me the whole story. I pray that I have done the right thing, and you do not prove me wrong."

"Thank you, Your Honor," Ethan responded with a weak smile.

"Mr. Anderson, I trust you have your business in order." Judge Summers couldn't disguise her disappointment—it showed in her voice and on her face.

"Yes, Your Honor. I am ready now. I would just like to have a few minutes to say goodbye to the man who has always stood beside me, my father." Ethan's voice cracked.

"Very well, take as much time as you need. Then bailiff, take Mr. Anderson and begin proceedings to turn him over to the proper authorities." The eyes of the judge portrayed her sadness.

The looks on the jurors showed surprise at the lenient sentence. There was murmuring among them.

Judge Summers redirected her thoughts. "Members of the jury, it is obvious that you disapprove of my decision. Let me explain something. While you were running on emotions, I was working with facts. I could have thrown everything out. I almost did. For the sake of true justice, I made this decision. However, for the sake of American justice, I abide in what you said. This system is not perfect, but it's still the best that society has to offer. This trial is closed." She banged the gavel one last time.

It was over.

"All rise," the bailiff announced. The few remaining people rose, and the judge exited the courtroom.

The father hugged his son. "I wish your mother could have been here for you."

"I don't. I would not have wanted her to see her only son go through this. It's bad enough you had to."

"I'll be here when you're released. We will see this through together, Son. Hang in there."

"Thanks, Dad. I love you. You know, I tried to pattern my life after yours. I'm sorry if I failed you."

"You didn't fail me. Your downfall was that girl."

Confused, Ethan stepped back, staring at his dad.

The father noticed his confusion and tried to clear the air. "Not Janna, definitely not Janna... I meant Susan. She was your downfall. I saw her self-centeredness from the beginning, but for some reason you loved her. If she would have welcomed Janna into your home with love and understanding, none of this would have happened. I noticed her disdain for the child from the beginning. I believe that's where the problem was, but now it's too late to fix any of it."

Allen's eyes welled up and soon tears streamed down his cheeks. "I will pray for you every day. Please Son, don't hold any bitterness toward Janna—bitterness will destroy you. One of these days she will return to us, and she will need our forgiveness. Then you must give it to her. We all must."

"I know, Dad. I hope you're right. As much as she hurt me, I still love her." He shook his head in sorrow. "But forgiveness, that's a different story. I don't know if I will ever be able to do that."

"With God's help you can. That's the only way, Son. There comes a time when you must forgive. Remember, God has not abandoned you. He didn't cause this. He's still in control of your life, and He still loves you... don't ever forget that."

Ethan mustered a small, but sincere smile. "Thanks, Dad. Thank you for the words of encouragement and for always standing by me."

"I love you, Son."

"I love you too, Dad."

The two embraced as the tears flowed freely for both of them.

Alone, Allen watched his son being escorted away in handcuffs.

Ethan carried out his sentence at a rehabilitation hospital for prisoners, where his devoted father visited him regularly for almost two years. Ethan taught college courses to the inmates, hoping that they could return to society better prepared educationally.

With only days left on the first part of Ethan's sentence, tragedy struck. One afternoon, Allen Anderson walked across a parking lot and was hit and killed by a speeding truck. The driver in the black truck was never apprehended.

Ethan received special permission to attend the funeral. At this point, Ethan did not care if he lived or died. At least in death he could be with his dear father.

Feeling as if he could not sink any deeper into the pit of despair, things quickly became even worse for Ethan. Immediately following Allen's death, his father's identity was stolen. Before he knew it, his father's estate was depleted.

Ethan was penniless and alone. His only supporter, the man who was always there for him, was gone forever. He sunk to the lowest point in his life.

He not only lost his father, but his only way out of prison.

The last four years of his sentence were to be served in his father's custody. With Allen dead, Ms. Moore, now the district attorney, wasted no time in returning to the courts.

Judge Sara Summers was now a federal judge and could not hear the case.

The new presiding judge ordered Ethan's sentence to continue in the state penitentiary.

Living behind bars was not really living at all, but merely a miserable existence. Ethan was beaten on numerous occasions because prisoners show no mercy to a convicted child molester. Even though he was not a hard-core criminal, the guards treated him badly.

His attorney tried to get his friend's sentence overturned more than once. He even petitioned Judge Summers, however her hands were tied.

At the beginning of his second year in the penitentiary, while eating lunch, Ethan was stabbed multiple times. It appeared to be a random attack. Hanging on the verge of death, he stayed in intensive care for ten days.

After Ethan's lengthy recovery, Judge Summers stepped forth and put in a good word for him. He returned to the clinic for prisoners. There, he served the rest of his sentence.

Ms. Moore was not happy with the decision.

Finally... six years after his conviction, a destitute Ethan Anderson was released from prison. His friend and lawyer, Robert Cain, was there to meet him the day he was released.

Ethan had no home or family to return to. Even the pastor and church where he had once been active would have nothing to do with him.

Robert tried to help, but realized Ethan was mentally ill. His hands shook and paranoia was at its peak. He believed everybody was out to get him.

The year in the hard-core penitentiary destroyed him emotionally. He no longer took time to get a haircut, shave, or even shower. He had lost everything, and prison took the last thing in life he had—his dignity.

He needed to get away. A grubby-looking Ethan hitchhiked through Colorado and stopped at a truck stop in Casper, Wyoming. He met the woman who owned the place, and asked if he could work for a meal. Before he knew it, the woman had hired him as a handy man. He fixed broken doors, changed light bulbs, cleaned bathrooms, and washed dishes.

He lived in a broken-down trailer next to the truck stop.

Ethan kept to himself. He never sang, played the guitar, or attended church again. After all, he now was considered a pedophile. The people at a nearby church and the neighbors all were aware of it and stayed clear of him. He would get off work, walk home, lock the door, and stay there until it was time to do it all over again.

Working for his room and board, Ethan had little extra cash. What he did have bought treasured keepsakes of a popular singer named Brianna Bays. He had followed her from her first CD, when she was just seventeen.

SIX

The Much-Needed Friend

My days are swifter than a runner:
They fly away without a glimpse of joy.
Job 9:25

During the trial Janna was taken to a foster home in Phoenix, and her life returned to the way it was before she met Ethan Anderson.

In the next couple years she was shuffled from one foster home to another, never having a place she could really call home. Some foster parents showed compassion and treated her well—others did not.

Sadly, the search for her birth parents by the authorities never took place.

At age fourteen, Janna's most dreaded fear became reality. Her latest foster father abused her in the worst way possible, leaving the teenager even more blemished and rebellious.

Somehow Janna found the strength to survive, but was afraid to report her abuse to the authorities because of the charges she had made against Ethan. She thought no one would believe her, which caused her to further internalize her problems. She never spoke to anyone about the horror she endured. No one!

Janna's radiant smile was gone and her eyes no longer sparkled; her face displayed only sadness and remorse.

No extracurricular activities were allowed. With no friends, she was a misfit in school. No longer was she a tennis star or softball champ.

Depressed, Janna would spend hours staring out the window. She longed for something that could take away the emptiness inside her.

Her beautiful voice and incredible musical ability were silenced by her foster parents. She no longer sang in church or school choir. Janna was not permitted to play the guitar or piano.

She created music in her mind at a rapid pace, and sometimes she felt like her head would explode. Song after song flowed freely. Late at night under a dim light, she would put her musical compositions on paper, hardly able to capture them fast enough.

She hid the notebooks containing her creations, afraid that if her foster parents found them they would destroy them.

Janna would return home from school and for the next several hours complete her daily chores. Sometimes she recalled the story, Cinderella, which Ethan used to read to her. She wondered if a handsome prince could ever rescue her. No, that was only a fairytale, make-believe. Certainly not real life!

Just before her fifteenth birthday, she devised a plan to escape her misery. She went to school, but never returned home. She fit everything she owned in her backpack—her notebooks filled with dozens of songs she had written, and a few personal items. Everything else had been pawned by her foster parents, even Ethan's guitar.

Her foster parents had no need for the notebooks—they were of no monetary value to them. Little did they know how valuable they would be someday.

Janna found a job on the other side of Phoenix in a small diner, flipping burgers, and doing odd jobs. At least it was a steady paycheck.

She lived anywhere and with anyone who would give her shelter, mostly men, until she saved enough money to make her next move.

One day as she walked past a pawnshop on her way to work, Janna was astonished to see the guitar Ethan had given her on display in the front window. He had painted a red heart on the instrument with the letter "J" in the center, which made it easy to identify.

At that moment... her life's purpose became clear.

The next morning, she grabbed her backpack, music, and a few pieces of clothing. She took all the money she had stashed away, walked into the pawnshop, and bought the guitar. Then she hitchhiked to Los Angeles, in hopes of pursuing a music career.

The road to L.A. was rocky, but she survived, and quickly landed a job as a waitress in a small restaurant.

The runaway did what she thought she had to do to survive, things which she later would regret, just for a place to lay her head, or the opportunity for a gig. Many of the men she lived with offered her a chance to sing or produce a CD. She finally realized the lies men would tell and stopped accepting their advances—all empty promises.

By age sixteen, Janna had enough! She decided never to get emotionally involved with anyone. Men were off-limits. As far as she was concerned, they were good-for-nothing.

Janna Anderson was tired of living the life she was living, and wanted a fresh start. She took a bus to Nashville, Tennessee. The young girl decided on a new name... Brianna Bays... it had a certain ring to it.

A new name... a new town... and a new life.

While in Nashville, sometimes the lonely teenager slept on a park bench or in a back alley. Guilt consumed Brianna day and night. The gnawing fact that she knowingly hurt the one person in her life that cared most about her began to take a toll. Ethan Anderson was never far away in her thoughts.

Brianna landed a job as a waitress in an upscale dining establishment. Tips were good. Elevated in the center of the ritzy restaurant sat a baby grand piano. On the weekends local talent provided entertainment for the customers.

One afternoon before her shift, she wandered to the piano. It had been four years since she had last played. When she reconnected with the instrument, it was as though she had never stopped. Her hands glided across the keys producing a sound that was breathtaking. She began to sing a melody she had written in her mind, but never actually heard aloud.

> *I used to sit and watch the sunrise,*
> *Never by myself*
> *I used to run along the sandy beaches,*
> *Enjoying the sun*
> *I used to love without regretting,*
> *But those days are done*

There were only a few customers dining at the time, but her singing immediately commanded their attention. They stopped talking, listened, and watched intently as this young, dark-haired beauty continued the haunting melody.

> *Now I sit and cry all alone,*
> *Now I walk the streets of this city*

Now I question if love was ever real,
Before there was rain
Yes, before there was rain

The owner of the restaurant walked in and stood next to one of the waitresses.

Brianna continued her poignant tune.

I look to the time of no more heartache,
I look forward to that time coming
I remember the time of happiness and love,
The time I felt a part of life
A time made just for us
Now I see that time has ended
I feel no need to remember,
I feel as if I'm all alone

"Who is that?" The owner whispered to the waitress, never taking his eyes off the girl at the piano.

"That's Brianna. She's one of our new servers."

He walked over to the amplifier, flipped a switch, and turned on the microphone, so all could distinctly hear the amazing voice of the singer.

Are you there?
I'm calling to you
But I just hear silence
Nothing coming from anywhere
There is no hope
Only sorrow

The owner continued watching with interest as Brianna stunned the patrons with her vocal ability. "She's beautiful... and listen to that crystal clear voice."

Those in the restaurant obviously were awed by the young girl's talent.

What can break me from this pit of despair?
I used to hold him in the moonlight
Look deep into his eyes
See the depths of wonder
It was a dream I surmise

"I've never heard that song before. Listen to the words. They're sad, yet, captivating." The waitress wiped away a tear.

"Her voice is amazing, beautiful, and full. It sends chills down my arms." The owner inquired, "What do you know about her?"

"Not much. She's sweet, very quiet, and always singing."

"What else do you know? What does she talk about?"

"It's interesting. She never really complains about anything, but it's obvious she has been hurt many times. She doesn't have anything good to say about men. She's a good little waitress though—hard worker."

"She's not a waitress anymore." The owner continued to stare, mesmerized by Brianna's stage presence. She was composed, self-assured, and presented a song in a way that everyone in the room took notice. He walked over to the piano and stood silently, as she continued to enchant the small audience.

> *Why did you leave me?*
> *Where did you go?*
> *Did I ever mean anything to you?*
> *Or was it all for show?*
> *Are you there... are you there?*
> *Before there was rain*
> *Before there was rain*
> *Yes, before there was rain*

Lost in her music, Brianna was oblivious to her surroundings. When the song was finished, she stood slowly, turned, and came face-to-face with the owner. Startled, she nervously remarked, "I'm sorry, sir. I got carried away. It's been so long since I played the piano. I... I... I'm sorry!"

Putting his hand gently on her shoulder to calm her down, he looked into her bright blue eyes. "No apology needed. That was beautiful. Where did you learn to play and sing like that?"

With sadness in her eyes she replied, "I guess it just came naturally."

"What was the name of that song? I have never heard it before."

"I think I will call it, *Before There Was Rain*. This was the first time I ever played the tune; it's just been bouncing around in my head."

"You mean to tell me that you wrote it? Do you have others?"

She laughed. "Oh, I have hundreds. I never sing anything but my own songs. I'm not up on today's music. In fact, I haven't even listened to the radio for years."

"I'd like to hear more."

"Thank you, sir, but I don't have time right now. I have to wait on customers. It's time for my shift to start."

The enamored boss replied, "You no longer have a job as a waitress."

Her smile faded quickly with the remark. She could not afford to lose her job.

The man looked around at the enthralled audience. "I want you to play your music instead. That's your gift. This is what you should do." He pointed to the piano.

"I don't understand," she said, bewildered by the events.

Suddenly, a middle-aged couple who had been listening to her walked by and placed a twenty-dollar bill in the tip cup on the piano. "Miss, when will you be singing again? We want to come back and hear more."

She didn't know what to say.

Immediately the owner stepped in, "She will be singing nightly six days a week from six to ten. Tell all your friends."

"We'll do more than that, we'll bring them. Young Lady, you have the most incredible voice I've ever heard." The couple shook the owner's hand and left.

That was the end of Brianna's career as a waitress. Her new career as an entertainer was launched.

The restaurant's business began to boom, packed with patrons who wanted to hear the budding entertainer. Every night the lines grew longer. Before too many evenings, the line stretched out the door and down the sidewalk.

The owner of the establishment enjoyed the business the singer attracted and paid her accordingly. In addition, the tips were lucrative.

The night before her seventeenth birthday, something extraordinary happened.

She finished her last set with one of the songs she and Ethan had written years earlier. As she walked to the back, the entire crowd gave her a standing ovation. Many people reached their hands out to shake the young woman's hand. Sometimes there would be a large tip in their extended hand.

After she finished, she sat down at a table that was reserved for her between sets. During the day, she would sit at that same table and compose music for hours at a time. The lyrics and notes flowed endlessly.

A waitress brought Brianna a small meal and a glass of water. She smiled and thanked her.

Brianna noticed a woman with an open laptop at a table nearby. She smiled at the stranger who returned the favor.

A man she had never seen before approached her as she began to pick at her food. She was used to being hit on by men, so she became quite efficient at giving them the brush-off.

Brianna was not interested in a relationship. She was finally in control of her life, and she would keep it that way.

Primarily, she would stay focused on two things—her music and her identity.

Her music career was extremely important. When she sang, she felt like she was a person of worth—a feeling she had not had in recent years.

But something else kept surfacing in her mind. Who was she? Who were her natural parents? And why did they abandon her?

As the middle-aged man neared her, she was prepared for any line he would hand her. She would reject his offer nicely, but in polite terms tell him to take a hike.

"Excuse me. My name is Randy Burns. I work for Petrichor Music, the number one music company in the world." He reached out to shake her hand.

Brianna shook his hand, smiled slightly, but didn't comment.

"You have an unbelievable voice. I was especially interested in your last song. You sang it with such... such emotion."

"Thank you," she said taking time to accept his compliment. He seemed nice enough. "I always close with that song. One of these days, I hope to record it."

Burns chuckled. "Ma'am, where have you been? Don't you know that song has already been recorded? It was written and performed by Sandra Porter two years ago. It went platinum."

"You're mistaken, Sherlock," Brianna said with a touch of sarcasm. "That is my song. I wrote and sang it for my grandmother's funeral six years ago."

The man's face showed surprise. "You mean you arranged it, right? I happen to know for a fact that Sandra Porter wrote that song. She is one of the artists represented by the recording studio I work for. I know her well."

Perturbed by the stranger's remarks, Brianna argued, "Excuse me, but I wrote both the lyrics and the music to that song."

Burns folded his arms. "You're telling me that you wrote that song. You must have been... what, thirteen or fourteen? Come on."

"No, actually, I was just eleven." She said matter-of-factly.

"You're joking, right?"

Brianna glared at the man, insulted by his line of questioning. "No. I remember it very well. My father helped me with it."

The man raised one eyebrow. "What is your father's name?"

Her voice dropped. "Well, he really was my adoptive father. His name was Ethan Anderson. Why?"

"Do you have any proof that you wrote that song?"

"I certainly do. I have the original in my music book. I was with my father the day he gave a copy to his lawyer. Why do you ask?" A frown accompanied the question.

The young woman with the laptop had overheard the conversation. She approached Brianna. "Did I hear you correctly? Did you claim to have written a song that Sandra Porter released?"

"Yes, I did. I never listen to the radio, so I had no idea." Brianna studied the woman.

"Did you ever give permission for her to sing it?"

"Ma'am, I have no idea what you're talking about. All I know is that my father and I wrote the song, *Coming Home*, six years ago." She sighed, frustrated.

The woman spoke directly to the man. "Mr. Burns, if what she says is true, you have a major problem." She pointed her finger at him.

The man straightened his shoulders. "I'm sorry. It seems you have an advantage over me... I have no idea who you are."

The young woman reached in her purse and pulled out a couple of business cards. She handed one to Brianna and the other to Burns. "My name is Sonya Ellis. I saw you about a year ago in a Los Angeles courtroom. At that time, I was representing Petrichor Music."

Brianna read the card and questioned the woman. "You're a lawyer?"

"Not just any lawyer. I work for Boarder and Simms. We specialize in media lawsuits. When a song is recorded without permission, we represent the artist. When a movie is reprinted without consent, we represent the company."

"I remember you!" Burns retorted. "You're the law firm that won the case against the rock group, Mansanto, aren't you?" He grew slightly pale.

"I work both sides—my firm was the front-runner of the internet download case. Millions of songs were downloaded and sold on the black market." Sonya spoke with confidence, never missing a beat.

A bewildered Brianna asked, "What happened?"

Burns stepped in. "Songs were downloaded by a group of Americans and sold to fans in Asia as originals. Over one hundred people in eleven countries were tried and convicted. You saved Petrichor Music millions."

Sonya didn't blink. "Thanks for the compliment. Let's stick to the subject at hand. Mr. Burns, if this young lady can prove what she says, you and Sandra Porter will be facing me in court soon."

Burns face reddened with anger. "Now wait a minute. I came across that music legally."

He turned to Brianna, "Where is your father now?"

"He's out of the picture." Brianna stood.

"You say you came across that music legally?" Sonya asked, believing Burns knew more than he was letting on.

Avoiding the question, Burns drew in a deep breath. "Miss... um... Brianna, right?"

Brianna nodded her head, unsure of what was happening.

"You have a great voice. In fact, you do a better job with that song than Sandra did." He smiled smugly.

Sonya grabbed her laptop. "Don't try to change the subject," the attorney snapped, as she researched the song Brianna had just sung.

For a minute time stood still. Brianna's heart began to race.

Sonya looked through questioning eyes. "Excuse me. According to the CD credits, Sandra Porter indeed wrote this song. Who is telling the truth?"

Brianna grew rigid and took a step back. "I wrote that song when I was eleven-years-old. My father sent it with some other songs to a Nashville agent."

Sonya spoke with fervor. "If that is true, then you have grounds for a suit against Sandra Porter, her agent, and the recording company, as well as the man you sent the songs to. Do you have any idea who that was? Do you have any proof that you really sent the songs to someone?"

Brianna sighed. "No Ma'am. I have no idea who my father's lawyer sent them to."

"What are the other songs?" Sonya asked, unwilling to back down.

Burns had enough. He voice sounded cynical. "Wait a minute. You can't be serious. You really think an eleven-year-old girl could write a powerful song like the one Porter did. Oh, come on! You must be joking! Listen, I came here to give this young lady a recording contract."

Burns turned to the singer. "Miss, you are great. You're fresh and extremely talented, to say nothing of gorgeous with that black hair and those blue eyes." Then he caught a glimpse of the birthmark. "I'm not really partial to that tattoo, but we can hide it, or have it removed."

"That's a birthmark, not a tattoo," Brianna snapped, not at all surprised by his comment.

"Well, we can still hide it," the man responded rudely.

A determined Sonya leaned on the table, looking directly into the man's dark eyes. "Mr. Burns, I have a feeling you know more about this than you are letting on."

Brianna could imagine how tough Sonya Ellis must be in court. She liked what she saw and heard.

Burns glanced at the pretty lawyer and then at Brianna. His tone was calmer. "I'm just here to see how good this girl is. I'm not the enemy. You claim to have written that song... we can talk about that later. If the rest of your music is like this, you could be a star. After all, it did make Sandra Porter famous, and you make her look like a frog sitting next to a princess." He smiled, trying to lighten the tenseness.

"I guess that's a compliment." Brianna snickered.

He removed a card from his billfold and handed it to her. "Here's my information. Be at this address tomorrow morning, ten-o-clock sharp. We will offer you a contract."

Sonya stepped in taking charge of the conversation. "We will be there. Meanwhile, I'll be making phone calls about this song. If necessary, we will consider filing a suit against all parties connected with it."

Her words were barely out when Burns took Sonya's arm, tugging her away from Brianna. He swallowed hard trying to keep his composure, but his voice indicated belligerence. "Knock yourself out, lady. You may think you're powerful, but I represent the biggest recording company in the business. You're out of your league. You have no real proof of anything. It's that little tramp's word against mine. And lady, I can make yours and Miss Tattoo's life really miserable... just wait and see!"

Sonya took a step backwards, and her voice grew louder. "Don't you dare threaten me, and take your hand off me right now! If I were a man, I would deck you for grabbing me, and insulting my client like that. But since I'm a lady, I will resort to other tactics." She yanked her arm away from him.

Burns turned back to Brianna. "Just be there in the morning. I'm sure you will be happy with the deal we offer you."

The two women watched as the man stomped off angrily.

"Wow!" Brianna said, "What was that all about?"

"How old are you?" Sonya asked, rubbing her arm where the man grabbed her.

"Nineteen."

Sonya looked at her with suspicion. "If you were eleven six years ago, you can't be nineteen. The numbers don't add up."

"Okay, okay... just don't tell anyone. I don't want to lose this job. I'll be seventeen tomorrow." Brianna looked around nervously.

"Seventeen... and you have really been around, haven't you?" Sonya typically got straight to the point.

Brianna whispered, "Yes, and I'm not proud of that. Unfortunately, it is what it is. It is part of my life. I had to survive... somehow."

"It doesn't have to be that way anymore." Sonya pointed to the table. "May I join you?"

"Sure, have a seat. I have a few minutes. I'm finished for the night. I was going to eat my dinner and then turn in." She sipped her water. "I love singing, and I love entertaining these people. They're great!"

Sonya sat across the table from the singer. "We have not been formally introduced. My name is Sonya Ellis," the woman said, extending her hand.

"Brianna Bays," she said, shaking the attorney's hand.

"Nice name. I take it that's not your real name, is it?"

"It is right now," Brianna replied.

"I see. I'm an attorney for a law firm in California. It just so happens this is one of my specialties. I represent many well-known artists. Plagiarism is a huge problem, but usually not by the popular artists. I have met Sandra Porter. If it is copyright infringement, she will be in big trouble. The fact is, if the other songs were stolen, and you have proof they are yours, the recording company will be facing some serious consequences."

"Oh, I have proof. My adoptive father filed a copy with his lawyer when he sent them off." Brianna sounded wiser than her years.

"Interesting... that means he may have already had them copyrighted. Where is he now?"

"Do you mean my father or his lawyer?" Brianna questioned.

"Your father."

"Like I said, he's out of the picture, and I want it to stay that way." A chill came to her.

"What about his lawyer?"

"I don't recall his name. I could probably get it for you."

Sonya didn't break eye contact with Brianna. "Tell me your story."

"There's not much to tell. I was abandoned as a baby, spent some time in an orphanage, was adopted, and here I am now." Brianna halfway smiled.

"Looks like I need to fill in the blanks."

"Good luck. I can't even do that." Brianna chuckled apprehensively.

"Do you want to tell me about it?"

Without hesitation, Brianna quickly responded, "Tell you about it? Why would I want to do that? I don't even know you."

"No, you don't, but if those songs are yours, you could become a millionaire overnight, and you need a good lawyer to make that happen. I'm a good lawyer, and I want to help you."

Brianna leaned closer. "Oh, they're mine all right. There's no doubt about that."

"How many other songs were there?"

"As I recall, I think there was a total of four songs."

"Please, give me the names of the other songs."

"I could give you the names I used, but they may have changed the titles."

"True. Can you give me a line from each of them?" Sonya picked up her cell phone and dialed a number.

"Who are you calling?"

"Someone I work with. His name is Simon. He is a walking music encyclopedia. If the song was recorded, he knows who sang it, and when it was released. While I talk to him, you try to remember the other songs your dad sent to the lawyer."

Brianna corrected her. "I'll try, but remember, he's not my dad."

She began to recall the songs she had written years ago and a slight smile came to her face.

"What are you smiling about?" Sonya questioned.

"I was just thinking of my life a long time ago."

"A happy time?"

Brianna hesitated. She finally replied, "Yes, a very happy time."

"Do you wish you could have those times back?"

"With him? Yes, but that is gone forever." Her eyes displayed sadness.

"Him? Somebody you were in love with?"

There was silence for a few seconds as Brianna seemed lost in her past. "Well, there was somebody who loved me."

The conversation stopped when Simon answered the phone. "Hello, Simon here."

"Simon, this is Sonya. Are you near your computer?"

"Yes, what's going on? It's after hours."

Sonya chose her words carefully. "Not for you. Listen to me closely. I need you to get your song-writing brain working overtime. I'm going to give you some lyrics, and you need to find the titles. They were all probably released within the last four years."

"This is some sort of a game, right?"

"No, I'm dead serious," Sonya impatiently answered.

"Wait a minute. If I don't know them, my computer will. Okay, shoot. I'm in."

"Let me start with Sandra Porter's song, *Coming Back to You*. What are the specs on that song?"

"Let me see... it was released in 2005, and sold four million copies."

The attorney jotted the information down. "Who wrote it?"

"She did... Sandra Porter."

"Simon, I'm going to give you some lyrics. See if you can find them."

"Okay. Go for it!"

She nodded for Brianna to begin.

"I'll have to sing it. Is that all right?" Brianna smiled.

"Sure. Go ahead. I'll put on speaker phone."

Brianna began to sing effortlessly...

> *I'm finding a new way to love,*
> *A way I've never done before.*
> *Could it be with you?*
> *Or could it be without you?*
> *I'm finding a new way to love.*

"Who is that singing?" Simon inquired. "My goodness, her voice is beautiful. It's so full and crisp... it's hard to explain. It's unique... it's... I can't even describe it."

"She's the young girl who claims to have written these songs."

Simon instantly replied. "Well, not that one. That song is called, *Could It Be You?* It was a big hit by, 'The Seventh Son'. The lead singer, Don Jameson, wrote it. That song sold three million copies."

"Are you sure of that?"

"Positive. Same exact lyrics."

"Okay, Simon, listen to this one." Sonya nodded to Brianna.

> *It was a time to love,*
> *It was a time to reflect,*
> *Where will it lead me?*
> *When will it start?*

"She can stop. It's a little bit different tune, but that song is, *A Time to Love*. It sold over five million copies, and was written by Sam Case, from the group, Baron's Leaf. What's the next one?" Simon asked eagerly—he loved a good challenge.

Sonya signaled Brianna.

"Okay. Okay." Brianna began singing.

I'm thinking of a time,
A time for happiness
A time for new mornings
I am thinking of a place,
A place of forgiveness
A place where love never ends
I am praying for someone,
Anyone who can change me
Someone to love.

Recognizing the song, Sonya's face lit up.

"This is all a joke, right?" Simon said sarcastically.

"No, Simon, I told you this is serious, and I know what you're going to say."

Her partner jumped in. "That song is, *I'm Thinking of a Time*, and is the biggest song in America, in fact, the world. It has sold over nine million copies and won three awards so far. It was written by Judd Stevens. It was his mega hit on his latest CD, *My Time*, and also was in the movie, *Time*. And guess what! It has been nominated for a Motion Picture Award."

"Did it win?" Brianna asked eagerly.

"The Motion Picture Awards are in two weeks, and this song, your song, is the front runner." Sonya confirmed.

Brianna's head was spinning. Things were happening too fast. She had dozens of questions.

Sonya tilted her head. "I need to ask again. How many songs did you send in?"

"I believe it was four."

"You said you have the originals. Can I see them?"

"Sure," Brianna stood up, looking around nervously. She walked over to the piano and grabbed her backpack. She brought it back to the table, and opened it. Sonya sneaked a peek and saw a dozen or more notebooks of various colors.

"My dad... I mean, Ethan, taught me to be meticulous with my music. I have a different color music book for each year."

Brianna scanned through the backpack and pulled out a blue notebook. "This was my first year's music. I used blue because it matches the color of my eyes. Ethan always told me I had the most beautiful eyes in the world." She smiled, remembering.

The young girl thumbed through the notebook while Sonya continued her phone conversation. "Simon, let me guess... Petrichor Music was the company that released the songs, right?"

"That's correct."

Sonya looked up as the girl handed the music to her.

"I have more upstairs," Brianna said excitedly.

Sonya's eyes brightened and a broad smile lit up her face. "Simon, these look legit. They are handwritten with a date on them. This one says, October 13th, 2002. Get a hold of Harry, and tell him it looks like these four songs were stolen."

"You're kidding me right, Sonya?"

"No, Simon! For the umpteenth time, I have never been more serious. Let's see where this all leads. I know what I'm asking, but I think it's true. Just do it. Send Harry out on the redeye flight. I need him here by ten in the morning to meet with us at Petrichor Music. I think these people are going to try to pull a fast one on this unsuspecting girl. I'll get back with you later tonight."

"Sonya, if this is true, it will be big. I mean huge! I'm talking mega bucks. Off the top of my head, that's twenty million copies stolen from this girl."

"I know, I know. Just get everything ready. Tell Harry I'll call him in a little while." Only then did Sonya breathe a sigh of relief as she hung up the phone.

The attorney looked at her hand-written notes and shook her head in disbelief. Could this really be happening? Could Petrichor Music have really used this young girl's musical talent for their own gain?

Sonya looked at Brianna and smiled. "If this all pans out, you will be a very rich young lady."

Brianna's eyes sprang up. "What do you mean?"

"Did you ever hear any of your songs on the radio?"

"I haven't listened to the radio for years. I tend to keep to myself, just trying to survive. What does all this mean?" She rephrased the question.

"Like I said, if what you say is true, and we can prove it, you are going to become very wealthy."

Brianna, still in shock from the surprising news, shook her head in disbelief. "You're saying someone stole my music?"

"Stole it, yes, and they didn't even have the smarts to change the lyrics, only the titles." Sonya continued skimming through the notebook.

"Ms. Ellis, you said, I could be a very rich person. How much are we talking about? Help me understand." Brianna leaned forward, her elbows on the table.

Sonya let out a deep breath. "For example, say a songwriter gets two cents for each copy sold. Your four songs sold twenty-one million copies... so, at two cents each... that would be almost a half million dollars. There would be bonuses for awards, especially if they won. There would have been money made from sheet music and royalties from other artists who recorded your music. If you had recorded those songs yourself, you would have made over four million dollars. In other words, those four songs could have made you a minimum of five million dollars. That's not taking into consideration concerts and advertisements you lost."

"Five million?" Brianna couldn't contain herself any longer. She stood up and shouted, "Five million dollars!"

Her words drew the glances of virtually everyone in the restaurant.

Sonya nodded, her face beaming.

Brianna looked into Sonya's eyes attentively. "I've been living on the street, giving in to the whims of men, just to survive, and these people have been making millions with my music." Her expression sobered. She brushed away a tear, recalling her devastating teenage years.

Then as anger took hold, Brianna slammed her fist on the table. "What?" She glanced around and noticed some of the patrons watching her. She sat down, leaned across the table to get as close to Sonya as she could, and spoke softly, "What can I do about it?"

"We can sue, but that could be a long drawn-out process since four of the biggest names in the music business are involved. Petrichor has unlimited funds, and it could take years to get anything."

Brianna cast a look of discouragement. "I'm not really happy with that. Are there other options?"

"We can approach it as a threat. If we prove they are your songs, we can offer them an out-of-court settlement. If it goes to court, the names of the artists will be dragged through the mud. The artists may be innocent; it's not unusual for someone to buy a song from an unknown writer and put his or her name on it. That is perfectly legal. In this case, you did not give them permission and were never paid anything. There is the possibility they have a fake contract. We will have to get as much evidence against them as we can. Fast! Is there a possibility that your father or his lawyer waived the right to the songs? Can we get any testimony from your father?"

"Adoptive father, and no, I told you he's out of the picture. He wouldn't have sold my music... I know he wouldn't have!"

Sonya noticed how touchy the topic of the girl's father was. "Okay, Okay. Just let me research your music. You said that your father's lawyer may have information?"

"Yes, that's a possibility. But I don't want my adoptive father involved at all. Do you understand?"

"I understand, but if his name is on any documents, he will have to be involved. I can probably find his attorney, if I know your adoptive father's name and where he lives."

She thought about it for a short time and then blurted out, "His name is Ethan Anderson, and he lives in Mesa, Arizona. At least he did. I have no idea where he lives now."

"Okay. I will contact his lawyer and get as much information on this music as he will divulge."

"Why are you doing this?" Brianna asked, confused by Sonya's actions.

"Why? It started when I saw a young girl who needed help. You would have been no match for that man, and certainly no match for his highfalutin lawyers."

Sonya noticed the uncertainty on the teenager's face and realized she needed to explain what Burns was plotting. "When you walk into Petrichor tomorrow, you will see a large table with about six to twelve classy-looking people. Most will be lawyers looking for any possible weakness in you. They will threaten you, and make you feel as though you are the guilty party. When you leave, you will have signed your life away, and have only enough money to buy a bus ticket to the next town. I'm going to make sure that doesn't happen."

"And now, why are you doing this?" Brianna's eyes widened as she waited for a response.

"I still am doing it to help you, but also there's the money. Whenever we can go after the big music companies, we will. There's good money in these cases for the firm I work for."

"Why were you here tonight, Ms. Ellis?"

"Probably the same reason Burns was—to hear you."

"What do you mean?"

"The owner of this restaurant is my uncle. He called me a few weeks ago and told me about his new singing sensation. He said you had the beauty of a goddess and a voice of an angel. I asked him to send me a recording. When I heard your voice, I was impressed, so I decided to come and listen for myself."

Brianna smiled.

"Now that I am here, I know he is right. You do have the beauty of a goddess, and I have never heard anyone with such a crystal clear voice. I'm considering going on my own and getting a few artists to represent. I love the music industry and find it exciting."

Boldly, Brianna asked, "Ms. Ellis, do you really think I can make it big?"

"Hon, you've already made it big. You have four bestselling scores... and please, call me Sonya."

Sonya stared at Brianna, still a child, who had grown up much too fast.

Suddenly, Brianna's mood changed. "By the way, yes, I did."

"Excuse me." Sonya gave her a curious glance.

"I did love him." Brianna looked down.

Sonya's mind reflected on the conversation of the past hour. "How long have you been thinking about that question?"

"Since you asked. I've known the answer, but couldn't find the right words. Actually, I really didn't want to answer," Brianna confided.

As Sonya studied her, Brianna continued. "Ms. Ellis... I mean Sonya, I'm sort of worried about that meeting in the morning. What's going to happen?"

"Leave that to me. I have Simon and Harry working through the night. By morning when we walk into that office, we will have a list of demands. Don't worry about a thing. I'll have your back, Brianna Bays!"

"Will my adoptive father have to know about this? I really want to leave Ethan out of it."

"Did he help write the music? Is his name on the scores?"

"He helped write them. In fact... in fact..." Brianna's mind disappeared into the past. She recalled the times she and Ethan would create music. No, the music was hers, but the inspiration was his. He had always been there to motivate and encourage her.

Sonya watched Brianna, realizing she was a million miles away. "Hey girl, are you with me? You're not high on anything are you?"

"Oh, I'm sorry. I was just thinking. No, I'm not high on anything. Believe me, I've done some stupid things in my life and had bad relationships, but I've never taken drugs or alcohol. I don't even smoke. My body is very important, and I like to keep in shape."

"Do you run?"

"What?"

"Jog? Do you jog?"

"Yes, every morning. I used to run track in school."

"Used to? Did you finish school?"

"No, I dropped out a couple years ago."

"Bad grades?"

"No Ma'am... bad circumstances. I couldn't make a living if I had to go to school."

Sonya took charge in her lawyer-like way. "Okay, first things first. We will take care of your schooling later. Where do you live?"

Brianna pointed up.

"Upstairs? In the loft?" Sonya questioned, eyebrows raised.

"I guess you can call it that. Otherwise, I would probably have to live with some guy somewhere. They promised me recording contracts and music gigs. You name it, I was promised it. I was too naïve to realize they didn't really care about me or my career, just my body, and their own selfish desires."

"Welcome to the world of adulthood." Sonya crossed her arms.

"Is that what you call it? I've been doing this since I was fourteen. Ever since I... I..." Brianna became withdrawn, sullen.

Sonya decided not to push her; she would find out what this fascinating entertainer was about in due time.

The lawyer took the girl's hand and patted it. "You don't have to talk about it now. Show me the other music. I'd like to see what else you've written."

"Follow me." Brianna signaled for her to come. They bounded up the stairs and walked into a quaint room. The room was neatly kept with a single bed in the center. By the only window was a small electronic keyboard. In the corner was a guitar standing alone. No television. No radio.

Sonya picked up the guitar and commented. "What a nice guitar. What is this heart on it?"

"It's nothing. It's just a keepsake, which was painted by someone I once knew."

Brianna sauntered over to the nightstand and took out several thick music notebooks. Next to her bed were more.

"What does the J in the heart stand for?" Sonya set the guitar back in its stand, questioning the mysterious girl.

"Nothing." Brianna handed her a few of the notebooks, trying to redirect the conversation.

Sonya skimmed through one of the notebooks. Her knowledge of music told her the contents were something special. The only word she could muster was, "Wow!" She flipped over a few more pages. "These are good. Good tunes, good lyrics. It's interesting..."

"What's that?"

She was slow to reply. "Never mind. I'll talk to you about it later. Can I borrow these tonight?"

"I guess so. I think I can trust you. You seem to be on my side."

"You can be sure of that. If these are as good as they seem to be, I will not be looking for any more clients. You're all I need."

"You really think they're that good?" Brianna picked up her guitar and gently began to strum a melody Sonya had never heard.

"Better than good... much better. In fact, I'd say phenomenal." Sonya stared at her prospective client.

Brianna stilled, letting the words settle in her bones.

After a time Sonya spoke, "You are gifted on the guitar and piano. Anything else you have mastered?

"Violin... and I enjoy drama; I love acting."

"Did you act in school?"

Brianna stopped strumming and instantly froze. Her voice grew soft and uncertain. "Yes, it was in school."

Sonya watched the girl. She was curious about her story, but instinctively knew it was time to stop asking questions.

"Honey, get some rest, I will come by about 5:30 to run. Is that okay?"

"Sure. I'd love to have some female company." Brianna began strumming again. "Most of my offers come from guys wanting to run with me."

"You seem down on men."

"Down isn't the word. If I never have another relationship in my life, it will be all too soon."

Sonya asked, "How old did you say you were?"

"I'll be seventeen tomorrow. Why?"

"I've never seen a seventeen-year-old down on men as much as you are. Usually girls your age are gaga over guys."

"If you have been mistreated by them the way I have, you would feel the same way."

Sonya looked sad. "Oh, I have many times. I've had my share of bad relationships."

No one spoke for a moment.

Sonya eyed the young girl–beautiful on the outside, but hurting on the inside. She hoped she could help her—maybe in more ways than one.

"Okay, Brianna. We will run, shower, change our clothes, and get to our meeting by ten. Deal?" With a genuine smile, Sonya extended her hand.

Brianna stopped strumming, and shifted her gaze to Sonya. Did she dare trust this seemingly kind lady who was offering her the world? Her mind flashed back to Burns, the man who approached her in the restaurant. After a pause, she lightly took Sonya's hand, "Deal." She took a deep, steadying breath, and returned the smile.

"No, no, no. When you shake someone's hand, you grab hold firmly. You don't have to squeeze hard, just hold it firmly." Sonya demonstrated it to Brianna. "You will be going into the world of business tomorrow. Many men think they own that world. You need to be strong and direct. Watch me, and please observe Harry. He is a master in negotiating. Oh, I have a word of warning—be leery of Harry. He loves beautiful women. He's a nice enough man, but he loves to hug." Sonya rolled her eyes.

She gave Brianna a quick hug and left. As the door closed, she heard guitar music and a beautiful voice begin to sing.

Sonya smiled and shook her head. "This is too good to be true!"

She hurriedly called Harry. "I've been waiting for your call, Sonya. I'm all ears."

"Harry, find out the name of the lawyer for an Ethan Anderson from Mesa, Arizona. I need to reach him tonight. He may have an answering service, which can get him an urgent message. And this is extremely urgent! Tell him the music that Ethan Anderson and Brianna Bays wrote when she was... on second thought, just have him call me right away. I'll explain what's going on."

Unknown to Sonya, Harry was already doing a search on the Internet.

"There's something else, Harry. I met Randy Burns from Petrichor Music today. Gather as much information as you can on him. I have to meet with him at ten in the morning, and I want to be prepared for whatever he is going to throw at us. Find out what his angle is. I just don't trust him."

Harry interrupted her. He was efficient and always one step ahead of the game. "Sonya, please quit talking, and listen for a minute. Ethan Anderson's attorney is Robert Cain. According to what I have found, the girl is about sixteen or seventeen, right?"

"Yes. In fact, she'll be seventeen tomorrow. What do you have?"

"It looks like her real name is Janna Anderson. She accused her adoptive father of abusing her when she was twelve. He was sentenced to six years in prison."

Sonya listened carefully as more facts were disclosed.

"Anderson's wife was an Arizona beauty queen. The girl was placed in foster care when she was removed from the home. That's all I know at this point."

"Poor girl. She's been through a lot. No wonder she has such a tough outer shell. What's the lawyer's phone number?"

Harry recited the number and e-mailed her an article he found about Ethan Anderson.

"Thanks, Harry. I owe you another one. Can you get out here by ten?"

"I've got a flight leaving in four hours. I've already talked to the boss. He's sending me in his private jet. This can be big. How about dinner tomorrow night?"

"Harry, when you see this girl, I'm not the one you'll be chasing anymore."

"I look forward to meeting her. See you tomorrow morning."

Sonya hung up the phone and glanced back at the door. On the other side was an amazing, brave, talented teenager. She whispered, "I hope we can win this, girl. For your sake, I hope we can win this. You've been through so much."

She bounded down the stairs as she phoned Robert Cain. It was almost eleven, well past office hours. An answering machine picked up and a woman's voice was heard. "Robert Cain Law office. I'm sorry, we are closed. Please leave your name and number and the reason for your call. If this is an emergency push the star key, and your call will be transferred to the operator. Thank You."

Sonya pressed the star key.

A woman answered. "Robert Cain Law Office, may I help you?"

"Yes, this is Sonya Ellis. I am with the firm, Boarder and Simms, and I represent Brianna Bays. I need to reach Mr. Cain tonight. It's urgent. Is there any way I can talk to him immediately?"

"I'm sorry Miss, but unless this is a dire emergency, I won't be able to reach him until morning. Perhaps you can call back then and make an appointment."

"It's of the utmost importance that I talk to him. It won't take long—it concerns Brianna Bays."

"I'm sorry, but I'm certain he does not have a client by that name."

"Let me correct that." Sonya looked at the name she scribbled on the paper. "It's about Janna Anderson, Ethan Anderson's daughter. Does that ring a bell?"

There was a brief pause. "Pardon me, who did you say you were?"

"Sonya Ellis. I represent Janna Anderson."

"Just a moment, please."

Almost a minute passed before a man answered the phone. "This is Robert Cain, who is this?"

"Hello, Mr. Cain. My name is Sonya Ellis, and I represent Brianna Bays. You may remember her as Janna Anderson."

"Is this some sort of a sick joke or what?"

"No sir. It's not a joke. I work for the law firm, Boarder and Simms. We specialize in recording and motion picture pirating. It seems you sent a few songs to Nashville about five years ago. Sir, those songs have done quite well—unfortunately, under the name of other artists."

"I'm very familiar with Boarder and Simms. I went to law school with Fred Simms." Cain paused briefly. "You say the songs have done quite well. How could that be? Those songs have copyrights on them. I sent the paperwork in myself."

"Mr. Cain, I don't know how involved you are with Brianna, or should I say Janna. All I know is that I have to go with her tomorrow morning to Petrichor Music. We will meet with Randy Burns and all his lawyers to discuss a contract with Brianna. They are trying to defraud her."

A puzzled Robert Cain asked, "Did you say Randy Burns?"

"Yes."

"Hold on a minute." It felt like an eternity before he returned to the phone. "Well Miss Ellis, you have quite a track record for being so young."

"I've done pretty well, thanks."

"Just what I thought... Randy Burns... I *knew* that name sounded familiar. I talked with him five years ago about four songs that Ethan Anderson and his daughter brought to me. I had them copyrighted and sent them to Randy Burns at Petrichor Music. Never did hear back from him. Of course, things exploded about then, and Ethan's life fell apart. My secretary later called about them. Burns told her they were trash and that's where they ended up."

Sonya chuckled. "Mr. Cain, that trash has sold more than twenty million copies. One song has been nominated for a Motion Picture Award."

"You don't say. Ethan said they were masterpieces. What do you want from me?"

"I suspect the meeting in the morning is nothing more than a trap. They will try to convince Brianna to sign her music over to them by way of a promised CD, so they can get out of the predicament they are in. If I could get some proof that the songs are hers and they had a copyright, I can end this quickly—in Brianna, or should I say, in Janna's favor."

Robert Cain cleared his throat. "If I may ask, how is Janna doing? I have not heard from her since she disappeared four years ago. We were afraid she was dead."

"She's amazing and multi-talented. She's doing all right for a girl who had been abused and tossed from one man to another just to survive. If she would have had the father a girl deserves, there's no telling how much better her life could have been."

Cain's voice was stern, "Ma'am, it's obvious you do not know the whole story. You probably never will. But the fact of the matter is... Ethan never abused her."

Sonya interrupted, "That's what they all say."

"You know, we could get into an argument like lawyers do, but the truth is Ethan was innocent. That's all water under the bridge now. His life was totally destroyed. Let's deal with the problem at hand. I can send you the copyrights for the music; I know Ethan would want me to do that. When do you need them?"

"Tomorrow morning at ten, Nashville time," Sonya answered.

"I see. I can't get the originals to you that quickly at this late hour, but I can have my secretary fax you copies. I have them on the computer at the office. We will fax them to your firm to make it legal. If you need the originals, let me know. Ethan and Janna brought them to me just months before everything fell apart."

Sonya asked boldly, "Let me ask you this. Whose name is on the copyright, and will Mr. Anderson have to be brought into this?"

"If I remember correctly, Janna's name is. Ethan never wanted credit for any of it, even though he helped write the music. This was for her... most everything he did was for her."

"You said Ethan would want you to do this. Why would he want to help a girl who destroyed his life, if he's innocent?"

"Oh, he's innocent all right. I can't go into the details. All along he's just been protecting her."

"I don't understand." None of this made sense to Sonya.

"No. You probably never will, unless Janna decides to tell the truth. However, that's not likely to happen. I'll get this stuff out to you within the hour. Do you have a fax number I can send it to?"

"Yes. Let me get it for you," Sonya said stiffly.

Cain added, "Does Janna need any money? I could wire her some."

"No, I don't think so. If she does, I can take care of her."

As she gave Robert the number and said goodbye, she wondered what secrets the young girl holds. Does Brianna even know the answers? Would Sonya ever know the truth?

Meanwhile, Cain was making a call of his own. "Ethan Anderson, please. Yes, I know it's late. This is Robert Cain, his attorney."

After a few minutes, a voice answered. "Hello, Robert. How are you doing?"

"I'm doing all right. I figured you'd still be awake."

"Yes, I'm watching an old movie with some of the patients—it seems to be a nightly ritual."

"How are you?"

"Okay, considering where I am. Of course, I've been in worse places." Ethan moved to a quiet table to talk.

"Ethan, I just received an interesting call. Janna is alive, and about to hit the big time. Remember the songs we sent to Nashville five years ago? They were recorded by other artists without our permission and have become big hits."

Ethan's voice showed no inflection. Calmly, he replied, "I see. I'm glad to hear she's still alive. What are you going to do about the music?"

"I'm going to fax the copyrights to her attorney in Nashville. Ethan, you were right about those songs being phenomenal. They have all been million sellers, and one of them has been nominated for a Motion Picture Award."

"You're kidding me." Ethan smiled slightly.

"No, I'm not. You might get to see Janna on stage. I think she will be performing that song at the Motion Picture Award ceremony in a couple weeks."

Ethan's heart started beating faster. "What makes you think that?"

"If I was her lawyer, and that was my client's song, I would demand the original artist sing it at the awards. Or, I would file suits against everyone from the janitor all the way to the top. Ethan, I understand she's a beauty. Her name is Brianna Bays now."

"Brianna Bays. Good name. I don't know if I can watch it or not. I'll have to talk the patients into it. They can sometimes be pretty testy. But you are doing the right thing, Robert. Those are her songs—she deserves the success. Do you know how she is doing?"

"She's had her ups and downs. Hopefully from here on, it's all uphill."

Ethan didn't know what to say, how to respond, what to feel. He was numb. "Keep me informed," he struggled to get the words out.

"Are you sure you are doing okay?"

"Yes, I'm better, now that I'm out of the joint."

"Can I do anything for you?"

"No, Robert. I must fight my own battles. I'm where I'm supposed to be for now. Nobody knows what the future holds."

Cain sighed. He wished he could say something to uplift his friend. "I understand, Ethan. Just remember, I'm doing everything I can to get you out of there. If there is anything you need, give me a call."

"Thanks, Robert."

Cain added, "By the way, how is the shaking, and mood changes?"

"As long as I keep on my meds and keep the stress level down, I'm all right. You know, prison can destroy a man."

"Especially an innocent man." Robert's voice dropped.

Ethan paused. What could he say? "It was my decision. I had to do it."

"I know."

"Goodbye, my friend."

"See you in a few months. I'll be there to pick you up when you're released."

"Okay. The first thing I'd like to do is visit my parents' graves."

"We'll do that. See you then, Ethan." Robert hung up the phone thinking of the time when Ethan was at the top of his game.

Now, he was just trying to survive... one day at a time.

SEVEN

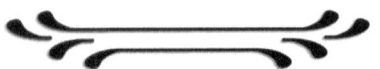

The Showdown

He holds success in store for the upright, he is a shield to those whose walk is blameless, for he guards the course of the just and protects the way of his faithful ones.
Proverbs 2:7-8

True to her word, Sonya showed up at the designated time to run with Brianna. The attorney was impressed with the teen's endurance—she certainly was physically fit. A healthy lifestyle was a noticeable priority.

As they ran, Sonya couldn't help but feel sad for the girl who had so much potential. Brianna was never allowed to be a child, and unfortunately seemed to have been tossed into the streets to find herself. Did she even have the capability of making it in the dog-eat-dog entertainment industry? Could she find herself though her music, or would she end up going down an even worse path like many who hit success at an early age?

Sonya also wondered if God placed her in this young girl's life for a reason. Perhaps it was to help show her the way to true contentment. Maybe the reason was to protect Brianna from the evils that awaited her in this crazy business. Sonya did not believe in coincidences. Yes, for some reason God orchestrated it all. But, why? Whatever it was, she was up to the task. She firmly believed God would not call her to do something without enabling her.

Sonya thought about Brianna's music. There was something strange with the lyrics she read the night before. It hit her! Every song had the same theme—even the hits that had been stolen from her. In every song, she was searching: searching for herself, searching for love and acceptance, searching for her parents, and searching for God. It reminded her of many of today's troubled youth who fall into the lairs of drugs, illicit sex, and gangs. They're all searching—searching for that missing piece of the puzzle in their life, which only God can supply.

Sonya was jolted back to reality. They had run nearly six miles and were back at the loft. Brianna's stamina and strength was impressive. She hoped the girl was strong enough to handle whatever her future held. Sonya was tired, but had previously made up her mind she would not quit as long as Brianna ran... she was in it for the long haul. Sonya felt she had passed her first test in gaining trust and respect from the complex teenager.

Brianna went to the refrigerator and grabbed two water bottles. They sat relaxing at the rickety dinette set.

At first it was small talk, but the conversation deepened as they discussed their past lives. Sonya had to keep reminding herself how young Brianna was. Her maturity level and life experience made her seem much older than her actual age.

The lawyer shared her life story. She married an army officer at the age of eighteen; he was only twenty-two. They were inseparable. Unexpectedly, her husband was deployed at the onset of the Iraq war. The devastating news came on the fifth day of his second tour when his vehicle hit an explosive. He and three fellow soldiers were killed. A widow at twenty-one, she wanted to die. How could she continue without the love of her life? Somehow, she kept living one-day-at-a-time. She threw herself into her studies at law school and then her practice. She has not dated anyone since.

Somehow Brianna felt she could trust her new friend and shared some of her sad story. Men used her. However, while men used her for their satisfaction, she used them for survival—a place to live, money, food, or a job. She was not proud of it, but it was a way of life with her, just like many of society's runaways.

"Our most precious commodity—our young people, need our help and understanding, and often society neglects them," Sonya said.

With that, the conversation ended. Both beauties lived through heartbreak—they had a common bond.

Sonya lowered her head and prayed a quick, silent prayer for their newfound relationship. She asked God to reveal His plan, and believed He would in His time.

Sonya broke the silence, "I will pick you up at nine. By the way, I have some good news for you."

"What is it?" Brianna asked before she took a long swig of water.

"I'll tell you on the way. See you soon."

"You're going to keep me hanging? Okay, I'll be ready." Brianna grinned.

"Oh, I almost forgot... happy birthday." Sonya reached into her tote and pulled out a wrapped box.

Brianna's eyes showed her surprise. "What is it?"

"It's a birthday gift."

"A birthday gift?" Tears began to form. Her mind raced back to a time and place when she was part of a family. That was the last time she had a birthday present. Ethan bought her a new guitar, and she was thrilled because her favorite artist had signed it.

Brianna held the neatly wrapped gift. "Thanks." A few tears slid down her face.

Noticing her reaction, Sonya asked, "What is it? Have I done something to offend you?"

Brianna looked at her. "Oh, no. This was the nicest thing anyone has done for me in a long time. It brings back memories of the last time I had a birthday gift. It was five years ago. My dad..." she stopped. "I mean, Ethan, gave me a guitar which was signed by Tammie Allen."

"The Christian recording artist?" Sonya asked excitedly.

"Yes. I still remember what she wrote on it. 'To Janna, hope this guitar brings you joy and success.'" Brianna sniffled. "Then she wrote a Bible verse... Psalm 144:9."

Sonya noticed the teen's big blue eyes move back and forth as she tried to recall either the words or the occasion. The girl seemed oblivious to everything around her.

Familiar with the verse, Sonya recited it. *I will sing a new song for you O God; I will make music for you.*

Brianna snapped out of it, looked up at Sonya, and exclaimed. "Yes, that's it!"

As Sonya observed Brianna's actions over the last several minutes, a thought occurred... what if Robert Cain was right? Is there a chance that Brianna's adoptive father was innocent?

"Well, open it up girl," Sonya voiced.

A big smile came to Brianna's face as she tore off the wrapping. It was special for Sonya to see an innocent child-like side of this girl, something she had not witnessed.

She opened the box and pulled out a stylish new outfit.

"I thought you should look glamorous when you meet those high-society people this morning." Sonya tried to sound upbeat.

A big smile lit up Brianna's face, and she could not contain herself any longer. Jumping up, she threw her arms around Sonya, and held her tight. "Oh, thank you. Thank you."

Sonya sensed how desperately Brianna needed love. She could hardly stay composed as she held the teenager for the longest time.

Again, Sonya was prompt.

Brianna was dressed in her fashionable new outfit. She was stunning; her long black hair blowing freely in the wind as she walked. As always, she made sure her birthmark was covered. When she smiled, the entire world seemed to notice.

The sidewalk was busy with people rushing to work. Sonya could not help but notice the eyes of the men turn as they walked to the car.

Sonya was beautiful in her own right, but nothing like Brianna—there was just something about her. The lawyer was almost jealous of the heads turning, but Brianna seemed oblivious to the gawking men.

In the car, Sonya began telling her about the conversation she had with Ethan's attorney. She purposely left out sensitive details pertaining to Brianna's past. She said Cain knew Ethan would want her to pursue this.

Sonya watched for any reaction from Brianna when she mentioned her father's name, but there was none. What was she hiding?

Sonya boldly asked, "Brianna how is your spiritual life?"

"My what?"

"You know, God. Do you believe in God?"

Emotionless, she stared straight ahead. "The big man upstairs?" She said more like a question than an answer.

"Well, that's one way to put it, I guess."

"I don't talk about that." Brianna sounded definite.

Realizing there were some hidden secrets in her life, Sonya wisely backed off. One of these days, they will have to come out. At that time, the girl will hit rock bottom. She had seen it happen before.

Sonya broke the quiet. "Let me explain to you what's going to happen at this meeting. I'll do the talking. You just agree and act polite. I'll take care of everything else. Understand?"

"I understand. Let me ask you something."

"Okay."

"What are you going to get out of this?"

Sonya appreciated her honesty, her boldness. She certainly would not be a pushover. "Me? Well, three things: I hope to get a percentage of the settlement, I hope to retain you as my client permanently, and I hope to keep you as a friend."

Brianna looked at her wise advisor and smiled. "I think all three are a possibility. How much money do you think I... we, will get?"

"It's like you said. Your father..."

"Adoptive father," Brianna interrupted.

"Sorry... adoptive father had all his ducks in a row. His lawyer sent all four songs to the copyright office in Washington D.C. and then sent them to Mr. Burns in Nashville."

Brianna turned quickly and faced Sonya. "You mean the guy at the restaurant last night?"

"Yes."

"No wonder he was so defensive."

Sonya nodded her head in agreement. "The proof is overwhelming. I can't believe Petrichor didn't check it out."

Brianna didn't comment.

Sonya continued to prep her for the meeting. "They will try and say that you purposely gave the music scores to them. They might even say that they could not locate you, or they never heard back from you. We have ways to battle all of these excuses. As for the money, if they go to court, they risk bad publicity for themselves, as well as the musicians. Bad publicity is sometimes good—many celebrities seem to thrive on it. After all, the American public loves reading about celebrities' misfortunes. Some believe that more people listen to the entertainment news than all the other news combined. It's kind of sad."

Brianna felt out of touch with the subject.

Sonya pressed on. "Most young people in America can tell you the name of last year's winners of the music awards, but not the name of the vice president, or their own U.S. Senators."

Brianna chuckled. "That's true. I don't know who it is. I don't even know who is president. What's more, I don't care."

Those bits of truth saddened Sonya.

Brianna turned to face the attorney. With a tear in her eye, she said, "I'm sorry."

"Sorry for what?"

"For your loss—your husband. I can see you loved him very much. I don't think I am capable of loving a man like that."

Stunned by her reaction, Sonya asked, "How long have you been thinking about that?"

"Since you told me."

"Well, thank you for your thoughts."

"How did you get through it?"

Sonya straightened. "That's easy... God."

"God. Which god?"

A small grin came to Sonya. She was happy for the opportunity to share her faith. "Yes, there are many gods, with little g's, but there is only one true living God."

Brianna snickered. "Don't say it... Jesus Christ!"

"Yes, do you know Him?"

"I know of Him. I was baptized seven or eight years ago."

"Was it real? Did you mean it?"

She glanced at Sonya. "You know me pretty well. You don't beat around the bush, do you?"

"No, I know the routine. Many make the decision, but few follow to the end."

"And have you followed it to the end?" Brianna questioned.

"Oh my, no! I'm still walking the path."

"Are you looking forward to the end?"

"I know what the end is, if that's what you're asking. Am I looking forward to it? Forward to the end of pain, disease, hate, and strife. Yes, I am. But at the same time, I can enjoy knowing and serving a living God... big G. He loves me unconditionally, and cares about every detail in my life."

"If God loves you so much, why did He kill your husband?"

There was an awkward silence.

Brianna resumed the conversation. "I'm sorry. I really didn't mean to say that."

"That's okay. It's one the most difficult questions posed to Christians. There is no easy answer—except sin."

"Sin? What's that got to do with anything?"

"I don't want to get into a long Sunday school lesson, but because of Adam and Eve's disobedience, sin entered the world and everything changed. God desired the perfect world for us, but did not create us as robots. He created us with the power of choice. Our choices cause all the problems in the world. Sin separates us from God. Therefore, God sent His son to die for all our sins. That way we can come before God, through his Son, Jesus Christ."

"Sorry I asked," Brianna replied skeptically.

"I'm not. It seems complicated, but it really isn't. You wonder how I can continue loving God after the death of my husband. Please understand that God didn't kill my husband. A man did. Sin did!"

"A Muslim must have killed him!" Brianna blurted out.

Sonya shot an astonished look at Brianna. Perhaps it was the way she said it. Maybe it was her black hair or dark complexion. Could the girl be of Arab descent?

"No, it wasn't because the man was a Muslim; it was because he was misinformed about life and how important it is. It's the inability of mankind to get along with one another, regardless of what race, creed, sex, religion, or political party they are associated with."

Brianna snapped, "Don't you blame the Muslims for his death?"

Sonya quickly responded. "Never! You see, there was also a time when a Muslim saved my husband's life. During his first deployment, Jim was assigned with an Iraqi—a Muslim, and they became best friends. They were in an awful firefight one night. The result was Jim's friend, Aahil, saved his life. A couple years later when my husband died, Aahil came to his funeral, and wept with me. He helped me get through the hardest time in my life. I still occasionally hear from him. The point is... I know God loves me and cares about me."

"He doesn't care about me." Brianna's response came swiftly.

"Oh, I'm not so sure about that. I think in the next few days, weeks, and months you will have a series of miracles come your way."

"There's only one miracle I want."

"And that is?"

Brianna's words surprised even her. "To find my birthmother and father."

"What happens then?" Sonya raised a questioning brow.

"I'm going to ask them why they dumped me."

"Do you have any idea what happened?"

"None whatsoever."

"You may never discover the truth. And Brianna, somehow, you will have to let it go, bitterness will destroy you."

"Watch me!" Brianna spoke defiantly.

"You don't know if they got rid of you... let me rephrase that. You don't know why you ended up in an orphanage. Perhaps your birth parents were killed. Maybe they were poor and wanted something better for you."

"Yes, an orphanage is better." Brianna snickered. "I was in an orphanage in Kuwait, and almost sent to Asia to become a child porn star at age six. Can you imagine the life I would have had on the big screen?" She shaped her fingers into a square and emphasized the word "Big."

This part of Brianna's life, Sonya was unfamiliar with, but nothing really surprised her about her new friend. She knew her life was complicated, heartbreaking. "You don't know what really happened, and I doubt you ever will. There are too many miles in between, and too many wars! Do you think your adoptive father might know the truth?"

"No!" Brianna snapped.

"He's out of the picture," Brianna and Sonya said simultaneously.

Sonya stared at Brianna. "Do you want to talk about it?"

"I'd rather talk about the flu I caught last year."

"S-o-r-r-y," Sonya deliberately drew the word out long.

Again there was an uneasy quiet with only the soft hum of the car engine.

Brianna finally spoke. "I'm sorry. I didn't mean to belittle you. That's part of my life I never want to talk about and won't. Do you understand?"

"No. I sure don't, but there's someone who does. I will abide by your wishes."

Silently, Brianna stared out the window. She spoke softly. "You never finished."

"Finished what?"

"Telling me what was going to happen at the meeting."

Sonya drove into a parking lot directly in front of a large ten-story building. The giant gold letters on the front spelled the words, "Petrichor Music." She turned the car off and looked directly at Brianna. "Right... and you never answered my question."

"Which was?"

"Was it real? Your baptism... your relationship with Christ."

Brianna tried to avoid eye contact as she pondered the question. "You don't give up, do you? Well, I... I thought it was. A lot was happening at the time. Some things in my life seemed perfect, yet so much was wrong. Just wrong." She turned her head, looking at Sonya. "Please, can we talk about something else?"

Sonya could see the pain in the teen's eyes and changed the subject. "Yes. Let me explain to you what's going to happen. We will be meeting Harry in a few minutes. He has everything ready to present to them. There will be men and women of all ages looking professional. They will try to butter you up first, and then go in for the kill, portraying you as the guilty party. They will offer you a pittance of what you're worth. It will seem like a lot of money, but we will reject the offer. Then they will offer you a contract, which we will also turn down. At that time, I will show them what I have. They will likely begin arguing with each other. The CEO of the company will not be happy. The fact is, they could have bought the music from you legally and avoided all this, or gave you a percentage of the sales."

"What are you going to ask for?"

"We're going to ask for a couple things. First, an open-ended contract. That means Petrichor will have to release all the music you write, perform, and produce, including the four stolen hits."

Brianna could not believe what she was hearing. Could success be at her doorstep?

Sonya continued. "You will be paid the premium amount, the top price for recording artists. There will be a press release stating that you are the original writer of these four songs, and the artists that released the music were actually the arrangers. You will be paid a flat settlement of one million dollars."

Brianna nodded slowly and let the details sink in.

"Last, but not least, you'll be the one who sings your song, *Time*, at the Motion Picture Awards in two weeks."

Brianna's eyes widened and her heart beat faster. "You're joking?"

"No, I'm dead serious."

"You think they will go for that?"

"Petrichor will have no choice. I can file a motion in court to pull that song from the shelves and from the award ceremonies."

A confused Brianna shook her head as if she understood.

"You have to realize that many artists are on a rampage because their music is being pirated and sold worldwide. Most top musicians write their own music. They can put themselves in your place and understand where you're coming from. Once they hear this, they will not stand idly by."

Sonya noticed a man standing in front of the building. "There's Harry, let's go meet him."

They walked to the front entrance where a man around thirty met them. He was good-looking, well-built, and dressed in a suit with no tie. He stood still, eyes glued on Brianna, his mouth wide open.

"Harry, you're drooling." Sonya rolled her eyes.

Eyeing Brianna, he blurted, "When you said she was beautiful, you weren't kidding. She's drop dead gorgeous. She's... she's a goddess. Look at those eyes."

Brianna smiled a sheepish grin.

"Earth to Harry, come in Harry." Sonya laughed.

"Can I give her a hug?"

"No, Harry, you can't. Stay on task. Do you have everything we need?"

He smiled and glanced at Sonya. "Oh, hi, Sonya, I didn't know you were here."

"Obviously!" Sonya chuckled.

Harry and Sonya had a comfortable relationship. They kidded with each other, but both knew when to be serious. Their work ethic was identical. They worked together on some important cases, and now it was almost like they could read each other's minds. That would prove beneficial.

"I have everything here in my briefcase." He turned his gaze back to Brianna. "This is amazing Sonya, but are you sure you want to do this on your own. I mean, shouldn't we go through the firm? How old are you?" He asked Brianna, changing the subject. He realized he was rambling.

Sonya came to his rescue. "She's seventeen... in fact, today's her birthday."

"Well, happy birthday. Can I give you a birthday kiss?"

"Harry... hello, Harry." Sonya elbowed him gently.

Brianna smiled as Sonya tried to get Harry to focus.

Sonya clarified the situation. "I've already talked with Charles. He said Brianna Bays is my client because I found her. Unless it goes to court, the firm will step aside."

"Are we ready?" Sonya asked, standing at the door.

"Yes," Brianna whispered. Her pulse was racing.

Harry opened the door.

"Let's do it!" Sonya motioned for Brianna to lead the way. Sonya stayed close behind her.

Harry looked at Sonya and mouthed the words, "Wow." He had a huge smile as he traipsed behind the young women.

When they entered the building, they observed the expensive decor. Framed plaques containing gold record albums and CDs adorned the walls. Autographed photos of several well-known artists were displayed. One in particular caught their eye. In the center of the wall was the CD, *My Time*, with a large picture of Judd Stevens. Below the photo was the inscription, *I'm Thinking of a Time*—nominated for best song from the motion picture, *Time*.

They all stared silently at the plaque.

Brianna gently rubbed her finger over the inscription. No one intruded on her thoughts.

Music was playing softly in the background. Suddenly, something happened that Sonya would remember forever. *I'm Thinking of a Time*, began to play through the sound system. Immediately recognizing it, Brianna said, "That's my song!" She shook her head. "He's butchering it."

At that moment, a guard approached them. "May I help you?" He gawked at Brianna, a typical male reaction.

"We have a meeting with Mr. Burns at 10:00," Harry responded.

"Oh yes, they are waiting for you. Here take this elevator." He escorted them to a private elevator and opened it for them.

The guard reached into the elevator and pushed a button. "There. It will stop at the private meeting room. It's sort of intimidating when you step out." He winked at Brianna, hoping to calm her down. He assumed she was nervous, but she was actually quite calm, maybe still in shock over the fast-moving events.

"Please turn your cell phones off. Have a great day." The guard stepped aside and motioned for them to step in.

"Cool!" Brianna said, "A private elevator."

The elevator door closed. As it began to rise to the top floor, Brianna's song played through the speakers. She softly sang along for a few measures. "There is too much drum and not enough bass. The words are almost unrecognizable, and the piano sounds like it's in another room." She turned to face Sonya. "They totally destroyed my song. You say it's nominated for an award?"

Sonya nodded her head.

Harry interrupted, "It's the fan favorite of the five songs nominated. I happen to agree with Brianna. In my opinion, it would have been better with a female lead."

Sonya abruptly changed the subject. "Like the guard said, the elevator will open directly at the meeting room. They do that as a psychological ploy. When the door opens, a young person like you may feel overwhelmed by the enormity of it all. The power and money can make you feel like you have to bow to their every whim. So be prepared. Do not get caught off-guard. Just do your best to look normal and pleasant. Above all, be yourself."

The elevator came to a stop.

Sonya gave one last word of advice. "Remember Brianna... don't say a word, unless they talk directly to you. Do not talk business. Let us do that."

Brianna nodded her head.

The doors opened, and they stepped into the busy meeting room. Large picture windows overlooked the city of Nashville; the sight was breathtaking. Just as Sonya predicted, there were a number of professionally dressed men and women seated around the giant mahogany table in the center of the room.

All eyes focused on Brianna.

Mr. Burns stepped forth to greet them.

"Come in, Come in. Have a seat over here. I didn't know you were bringing someone else."

The three guests were seated.

Burns walked to the end of the table and motioned to a distinguished looking woman. "This is Barbara Evans. She is the president and CEO of Petrichor Music."

In a take-charge way, Barbara led the conversation. "Please introduce yourselves, if you would." She assumed they were there to take advantage of her company.

Sonya had predicted they would be hardnosed until the evidence was presented. "I am Sonya Ellis and this is my partner Harry Stillman." Sonya pointed to Brianna. "This is Brianna Bays, the writer of four songs, which your firm has released without her permission."

"You are direct, aren't you?" Evans was not amused with her forthrightness.

"There's no reason to beat around the bush," Sonya stated assertively.

Evans readily replied, "You believe in the old adage, the longer you are here, the more you'll lose, right?"

"Right." Sonya didn't like the small talk, but she expected it—a formality.

Evans spoke, like she was thinking out loud, "Sonya Ellis... that name sounds familiar... and you look familiar. Have we met?"

"I represented your company in a music download suit last year."

"Now, I remember. Thank you. You saved my company millions of dollars. Well, Ms. Ellis, we will get right down to it. Mr. Burns, tell Ms. Ellis what we have to offer."

He walked over and handed Sonya and Brianna a folder. "I'm sorry, I'm a copy short. You will have to share." He cast a snide look at Harry and then walked back to his seat.

Burns continued. "You'll see we have been extremely generous. There is a check here for twenty-five thousand dollars. In addition, note the legal document, which simply states that the music in question belongs to the rightful artists who are listed. Furthermore, we offer a contract to the young lady, Brianna Bays, for one CD to be released in the near future." He paused, giving time for everyone to review the papers.

Sonya had predicted that this is where the game would turn ugly. Even though they hadn't had much time to prepare, she was confident they were ready.

Burns interrupted the quiet. He leaned forward, both elbows on the table. "Let me warn you, if you do not accept our offer, we will be forced to sue you for defamation of character. You know that will be tied up in the courts for years, and you most likely will end up with nothing." He chuckled. "Beside thousands of dollars in legal bills that is."

Sonya gave him a half smile, not the least bit amused with his antics.

Burns glared at Sonya with a look of confidence. He believed he had the upper hand.

All eyes stared at Sonya watching for her reaction as she skimmed over the document.

Evans waited, trying to read the well-known attorney's body language.

Sonya finally spoke, calmly, matter-of-factly. "It's interesting," she said, still reviewing the document.

"What's that?" Burns questioned.

"You have all four of her songs listed by name."

"Yes. So what?"

"We never mentioned the song titles, and we never said there were four songs." Sonya studied Burns and Evans response to her comment.

The CEO had a look of perplexity.

Without showing a hint of emotion, Sonya silently eyed each person at the table, and then moved her gaze directly to Burns, and then to Evans.

Sonya placed her cell phone on the table and turned it on.

"Ms. Evans, it seems like you have everything in order. Harry, what do you think?" Sonya handed the settlement papers to Harry.

He skimmed over them, mumbled a couple things, and nodded his head. Harry held the check up to the light to examine it. "Wow, twenty-five thousand dollars! That's a lot of money for a young girl. Of course, we would get forty percent, which would mean that Brianna would get about fifteen thousand dollars, and a CD contract. Sounds generous, but I believe that music sold over twenty million copies. Quickly figuring it in my head, that would be less than half a cent for each copy sold. If I recall, these songs won more than a dozen music awards, not to mention, one is the front runner at the upcoming Motion Picture Awards."

Harry winked at Sonya. "In my opinion, I believe they are trying to take advantage of this young lady."

Sonya nodded her head, still showing no emotion. "I agree, Harry. Now it's time to show them what we have."

Harry pushed their check and folder to the center of the table. He bent over the side of his chair, opened his briefcase, and drew out a couple files. He walked around the table passing out the papers from one of them.

With the sureness of a professional, Harry took command. "Good morning, ladies, and gentlemen. You are all looking well this morning. I trust many of you are lawyers, so you know the routine. I am handing each of you copies of the legal information of this young woman's music. I only made twelve copies, so some of you will have to share." He glared at Burns when he emphasized the word, "share."

"Pages one through seven are copies of the original handwritten scores with dates on each of them. Pages eight through eleven are the official documents issued by the United States in accordance with all legal statutes. Please notice the date on each of them. Each is stamped by the official United States Copyright Office."

All heads were down as the people around the table scanned through the legal documents.

Harry continued. "Notice that pages twelve through fifteen are copies of your clients' music. You will see that the copyright dates are three or four years later than Ms. Bay's music. Let me remind you, she was formerly known as Janna Anderson."

When he got back to his chair, he gave the executives some time to study the documents. "Now, please note the lyrics, which match our client's lyrics—I highlighted them for you. Oh, look how strange. Every page is completely highlighted," Harry fanned the pages. "Usually when one steals music, it is done piece by piece—perhaps some of the lyrics, or some of the tune. In this case, everything is the same. Everything!"

Evans and the others were stunned, yet impressed that the opposition could be so well prepared in such a short time.

Harry pulled out a small CD player. "Let's see now. This song is sung by Sandra Porter, entitled, *Coming Back to You* with the copyright date, 2005." He hit the play button and played an excerpt. In his take charge, confident way, Harry sang along, pretending to conduct the music. "Wow, nice song, isn't it?"

He gave a wry smile and held up another CD. "This one was hard to come by. Let me see." He read the cover. "Interesting, it says, *Coming Home*. It's by Janna Anderson, and the date is April 12, 2002." Harry picked up the CD and waved it around. "Oh, the miracle of technology." He put the CD into the player and played a segment. "Wow, she sounds good. Sounds a lot like Sandra Porter, doesn't it?" After a few seconds, he stated, "I personally like Janna Anderson's version better. What do you think?" He continued playing the melody.

Sonya took over the conversation. "As you can see, there is not only a similarity, but an exact replica of Sandra Porter singing the song an eleven-year-old girl had written and sung nearly three years before."

Harry put in Judd Stevens' CD. "Let's see, here is Judd Stevens' version, *I'm Thinking of a Time*." He listened for a few seconds. "Beautiful melody and amazing lyrics, but the drums seem to overtake the melody, and the words are difficult to understand. I think it will grow on you. It would make a great motion picture song, don't you think? Wait a minute... it has in fact been nominated for a Motion Picture Award." Harry had the gift of sarcasm, and knew how to use it to his advantage.

He put in another CD. As it played, Harry began to speak. "Wow! Awesome! Listen to the beat and the lyrics. Hard to believe the singer is Janna Anderson at just eleven-years-old."

Scorn was written all over Barbara Evans face. She scowled at Burns, and then faced Sonya. "What do you want?"

Harry stood to his feet as the music continued to play. He handed out the contents of the other folder. "This is the contract we are presenting. Once again, I have only twelve copies... some will have to share." He sat down. "The first page is self-explanatory. It simply states that these four songs are the sole property of our client, Brianna Bays, alias Janna Anderson. The second page is also very simple. Brianna Bays will receive from Petrichor the sum of one million dollars. In other words, you will be buying the music outright. It is noted in the contract that the four songs in question belong to her."

He continued effortlessly. "In order that the artists who released the songs are not embarrassed, it will be noted on all music and CDs that the person who wrote the music and lyrics is Brianna Bays. The artists can have credit for arranging a song—that will give them some sort of ownership, and they can continue to receive royalties for the songs. Janna, or should I say Brianna Bays, will not ask for any more monetary gain from those four songs done by these artists, but if anyone else releases them, she will receive all royalties. If someone breaks the contract and this goes public, Petrichor Music will be open for another major suit."

Harry pressed on. "Now, the next page gives Brianna Bays an exclusive contract naming Sonya Ellis as her sole manager. Brianna, alias Janna, will write, perform, and produce as many CDs as she wants at the premium rate. In other words, she will be paid top dollar for every CD she sells, and a bonus every time she is nominated for an award. This starts with the upcoming Motion Picture Awards."

"What do you mean by that?" Burns interrupted.

"Very simple," Sonya stated. "Brianna will sing her song, *Time*, at The Motion Picture Awards ceremony in two weeks."

"No way is that going to happen!" Burns shouted rudely, looking to Evans for support.

The others in the room agreed with him, murmuring their displeasure.

Burns continued in an elevated voice, "She's a nobody! Judd Stevens will have a fit if we suggest that!"

"Not to coin a phrase, but is that your final answer?" Harry asked, calmly.

Standing, an irate Burns pointed to Brianna. "There is no way that tramp is going to sing at the Motion Picture Awards."

Evans scowled at him.

Harry jumped up angrily.

Sonya pulled Harry back to his chair. With her other hand, she reached for her cell phone. Without picking it up from the table, she pushed a number, and the phone rang. A voice sounded through the speakerphone. "Yes."

"Simon, do it." Sonya disconnected the call.

"Harry, continue." Sonya said to her partner in her typical straightforward way.

"All right." Harry handed another paper to those anxiously watching. "We thought that's what would happen. What we did not expect was for anyone to treat a girl as talented as Brianna Bays the way you have. I would have enjoyed pounding your face in Mr. Burns." He stopped pacing behind Burns and scowled at him. "But then again, I'm going to enjoy watching you squirm."

Harry resumed walking. "Again, I only have twelve copies so a couple of you have to share. This is a copy of the cease-and-desist order. The FBI and Los Angeles Sheriff Department have been camped outside Mr. Judd Stevens' home for the last thirty minutes and are at this moment issuing the same summons to him. He will never be permitted to play or sing that song again or he will be breaking the law. He is also being summoned to appear in court, here in Nashville, on Thursday, for unlawful plagiarism. By the way, stealing another artist's copyrighted material is an FBI offense, punishable for up to two-hundred and fifty thousand dollars, and five years in prison. He is also being sued by Brianna Bays, alias Janna Anderson, for the sum of twenty million dollars."

The entire room erupted in discord.

Evans shouted at Burns, "You told me this morning that you paid for that music. You said they were just trying to get more money from us."

"The statute of limitations is up," Burns yelled in self-defense.

In the chaos, another lawyer spoke. "Seven years is the statute of limitations, this copyright was six years ago. Besides it would not hold up in court."

Speaking above the roar, Sonya tried to regain control. "You can be as hardnosed as you want. The fact is you stole this young lady's work. You have two choices. You can accept the deal we have presented and make millions, or you can reject the offer. Mr. Burns knows Brianna Bays is a gold mine. The publicity at the Motion Picture Awards alone can cost you millions or make you millions. The choice is yours."

The lawyers around the table whispered to each other.

Sonya stood and spoke directly. "Listen up, ladies and gentlemen. Look at her. She will be singing at the Motion Picture Awards in two weeks. Will she not be the talk of the night? I guarantee she will be. Her beauty, you can see for yourself. Mr. Burns can tell you about her compelling stage presence. Her voice is one of the best, no, it is the best, I have ever heard. Look at her again. She's only seventeen; she'll be a teen idol. Backpacks, clothing, perfume, shoes, hats. Her earning potential is unlimited. She can be the biggest star you have ever represented. I've seen her perform, and I've heard her music. She has written hundreds of songs—all of them are available for recording. She will be sought for commercials, television, movies, and fashion magazines. She's bound to be the biggest prize ever found... I guarantee it!"

All eyes stared at Brianna, and then fixed on Ms. Evans awaiting her reaction.

Suddenly the door flew open, and a woman burst into the room. "I'm sorry Ms. Evans, but there is an emergency call for Mr. Burns from Judd Stevens." She handed the phone to him.

Burns flashed a look of distress. "Hello, Judd."

"Put it on speaker phone," Ms. Evans ordered.

Burns ignored the order and began to strut out of the room.

"Put on the speakerphone, I said!" Evans commanded much louder.

Burns obeyed her reluctantly.

Uncontrolled obscenities echoed from the phone. "Burns, what is this all about?"

"What do you mean?"

"I was just served with a warrant. It seems I have to appear in court in Nashville, and I got a call from my manager saying I won't be able to sing my hit song at the awards. What's going on?"

"Settle down, Judd, settle down. I'll take care of everything. It's a little misunderstanding." Burns turned off the speakerphone, and slowly backed toward the door.

"Put the speaker back on now," Evans ordered. "Now!"

Burns knew better than to cross Evans when she was enraged. He pushed the speakerphone button as more swearing and threats erupted.

Judd continued with his ranting, "You assured me that song was written by a nobody, who would never be a problem. Well, look at me now. I've been summoned and have to appear in court at some Podunk town in Tennessee."

"Cool it. I told you that I will take care of this."

"You had better. I need to sing that song at the awards. That would be the best publicity I could ever get. Burns are you there?"

"Yes, I'm here." Burns scowled.

"Make that problem go away, or I'll have one of my goons do it. Get rid of that nobody, now. Understand?"

"Give me the phone," Evans shouted.

Reluctantly, Burns complied.

"Mr. Stevens, this is Barbara Evans. I am the President and CEO of Petrichor Music."

Judd was still out of control with his vulgar language.

She turned off the speaker. "You watch your language, young man. I don't care who you are, I can pull your contract quicker than you can blink. And don't you threaten me or swear at me ever again. The decision is final. You will not be singing that song at the awards; it is not your song. The person who wrote the music will perform it. Judd, Brianna Bays makes you look like the nobody."

Judd continued his tirade.

Evans interrupted, "Go ahead, and sue me. I'm going to be suing you myself. Call your lawyers. You're going to need some good ones. I'm finished with you."

She threw the phone at Burns. "You're fired. Get out of my sight. Get out of here before I find something else to throw at you."

A shocked Burns stammered, "I..."

The CEO pointed to the door, screaming, "Not another word. Get out of here now... and out of the building!"

Burns stormed out.

Evans called the guard desk. "Richard, Randy Burns is coming down the elevator. Escort him out the front door immediately. Under no circumstances allow him back in. If you have to throw him out, then do it."

Barbara Evans looked around the table and took a deep breath. "I will not tolerate the stealing of a musician's music, no matter who he is." She glanced at Brianna. "Or she is."

The others around the table sat in stunned silence. This is not how they expected their morning to go.

Evans was not finished. "And stealing such quality work from an eleven-year-old. If Burns had been smart, he would have signed the child up. We have wasted six precious years of talent, and I'm not going to miss another moment."

She approached Brianna, who had not yet uttered a word.

"Young lady, please stand up."

The teenager looked at Sonya who nodded her head for approval.

Brianna rose to her feet.

Evans studied her from head to toe and motioned Brianna to turn around. "Wow!" She exclaimed. "Young lady, if you can sing half as good as you look, you are going to be famous... and very rich."

Sonya moved closer to Brianna and put her arm around the future star's shoulders. "She has the most powerful voice I've ever heard. You're looking at America's newest music sensation."

Evans faced Brianna. "Miss Bays, can you sing, _I'm Thinking of a Time_ at the awards ceremony? You have less than two weeks to get it together."

Smiling, Brianna finally spoke. "It's my song. I know how to sing it."

"Remember, this is not a small restaurant. Millions of people will be watching you perform. This will be the launching of your career."

"I can do it!" Brianna's voice showed resolve, pure determination.

Evans stared at her for a moment impressed with the young girl's fortitude. "I believe you can."

She returned to her seat. "You do realize that if your song wins, you will receive a Motion Picture Award—the most prestigious award presented to an entertainer."

Brianna didn't know what to think, feel, or say. She grinned, "I never thought about that. I haven't had the time to process any of this. Wow!"

Sonya embraced Brianna. "It's your beginning, and you'll be starting at the top."

Evans face turned serious, and her tone unwavering. "Ms. Ellis, we will abide by all of your requests. I believe your client will be an investment well worth it."

Shifting her conversation to the board members around the table, Evans spoke. "I want an internal investigation on these four artists. Call them all in... I want to have a talk with each one of them personally. They will be dealt with. I don't know if we can keep this from the media. However, we'll do our best. If it does go public, we will be forced to deal with it."

"Thank you," Evans said to Sonya. "My office will be getting back with you later this week to sign the necessary papers. You have my word on it. Does anyone have anything to add?"

The room was silent.

The CEO smiled. "Good. Young lady, I think you had better get a move on. You have a lot of work to do to get ready for the awards. I'll walk with you to the elevator."

"We'll get right on it!" Sonya said, motioning for Brianna to follow.

"Thank you," Brianna replied as they walked toward the elevator door.

Evans shook Sonya and Harry's hands. "I was impressed with your presentation. If either of you ever need a job, give me a call."

When she shook Brianna's hand, she commented, "You have a great handshake, Miss Bays. That's a sign of a true professional."

Brianna's radiant smile shone.

They entered the elevator and looked at each other. When the door closed and the elevator began it's decent, Harry broke out laughing, and gave Sonya a high-five.

"We did it! We did it!" Harry said excitedly, doing a dance that only he could do.

"No," Sonya replied, "Brianna did it."

Brianna was overwhelmed. "What just happened in there?"

"What happened?" Harry repeated. Putting his hands on her shoulders, he looked into her blue eyes. "You just became a millionaire, and are going to be singing at the Motion Picture Awards, live on television, around the world to millions of people. Your life has turned around. You are going to be a superstar... that's all!"

EIGHT

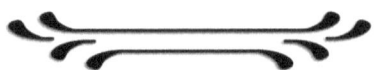

The Busy Preparation

Though my father and mother forsake me,
The LORD will receive me.
Psalm 27:10

Preparing Brianna for the Motion Picture Awards (MPA) was Sonya's highest priority. She knew this was a make it or break it chance, a once-in-a-lifetime opportunity for the teen. Her singing and voice were flawless, but Sonya was not as confident in Brianna's choreography. Sonya concluded that she needed professional help with that skill.

Sonya called an old friend, Derek Peterson, a choreographer from Las Vegas. He had the reputation of being one of the best in the business. Without giving many details, she explained the potential they had in an unknown teenager. Trusting Sonya's instincts, the choreographer was on the next plane to Nashville.

The budding star enthralled Derek. After he worked on a few dance steps for less than an hour, he reported to Sonya. "She's a natural, one of the most talented dancers I've ever seen. You said she sings, too?"

"She sings and writes her own music; she also plays guitar and piano exceptionally well. She is the full package... the real deal!" Sonya searched Derek's face. "Will you help her?"

"All she has to do is stand there, and she'll be a hit." Peterson laughed. "Yes, I'd be thrilled to help her. She has the moves already... she just needs to put them all together. Fortunately, that's my area of expertise."

"That's why I called you—I know you're the best, my friend." She smiled. "Can you have her ready for the Motion Picture Awards?"

"MPA? That's less than two weeks."

"Yes, it is." Sonya replied, batting her eyelashes.

"Well, I will do my best. As I said, she's a natural. Who will be in charge of her stage set-up?"

"She will be."

Surprised by the answer, he continued. "That's a big responsibility for a seventeen-year-old. Does she have her dance routine planned?"

"She has an idea how she wants to perform it. It's your job to see that it all comes together. You will be compensated well!" Her tone was reassuring.

"I love a good challenge! I will get a group together to dance with her. I think we can be ready. What song is she dancing to?"

With eyes locked on her friend, she answered, *"I'm Thinking of a Time."*

Derek's face showed his astonishment. "She's going to be dancing to Judd Stevens' song?"

Sonya realized Derek deserved to know some pertinent information. Composed, she went on, "I know I've been sketchy on the details. We're still trying to keep this under wraps. Brianna is going to sing and dance to that song."

He nodded confidently. "Oh, she is one of the back-up singers. That sounds interesting."

Sonya's eyes shone a little brighter. "Not back-up. She'll be singing solo."

His face went blank. "What? That's Judd's song... what's he going to do?"

Sonya smiled weakly. "Actually, it's her song, not his. As far as I know, he's going to be knocking his head against the wall somewhere. She will be performing it instead of him at the awards."

Derek chuckled. "You're kidding? Judd's not one of the nicest people in the music business. I bet he isn't too happy about any of this."

"No, he's not, but he didn't have a whole lot to say about it."

Still confused, Derek announced, "I'm not going to keep asking questions. I trust you, Sonya. Sounds like we don't have a minute to waste... we better get busy!"

The next four days were grueling. Brianna worked twelve hours a day trying to perfect her routine—she rarely took a break. A perfectionist by nature, Brianna even practiced when the choreographer returned to his room.

She would be ready to meet the world, but would the world be ready for her?

Rumors were flying about Judd Stevens being pulled from the awards. He was powerful and would not go down without a fight.

Sure enough, with less than a week before the awards, news broke that the song from the movie, *Time*, would be sung by an unknown singer at the awards. Judd Stevens had been replaced at the ceremony.

Less than twenty-fours later, the MPA officials announced it was only a rumor. The spokesperson said, "Judd Stevens will perform, *I'm Thinking of a Time*, since it is his hit song. If he is unable to perform it for any reason, the soundtrack from the movie will be played in its place. There will be no live performance from anyone else. There will never be a substitute for the one and only Judd Stevens."

The theft of Brianna Bays' songs had surfaced despite Petrichor Music trying to hide it. Apparently, Burns broke the news to the press for monetary gain and then fled the country.

Sonya was not caught off-guard. Fully expecting a fight, she immediately called a press conference. Hundreds of reporters gathered for the announcement in front of the MPA building. All the entertainment media were present, as well as the major networks; no denying the fact, it was big news!

Alone, Sonya stepped to the microphone. A true professional, she wasn't easily intimidated standing in front of a mass of people. Her plan was to handle the press as if they were a jury. "Good morning. We had hoped to keep this out of the news, but since Judd Stevens and the MPA wanted to push the issue, we have no other option than to use force."

Sonya waved a paper in the air. "I have in my hand an order barring Judd Stevens from singing, *I'm Thinking of a Time*. By court order, the movie clip from *Time* cannot be shown at the awards without my client's permission. My client, Brianna Bays, is the rightful owner of this song, as well as a number of other hits that were stolen from her. If the song is performed by anyone other than Brianna Bays, or the movie clip is played, the MPA officials will be held in contempt. If Brianna is prevented from singing at the ceremony, MPA will also be held in contempt of this court order. I would suggest that those making decisions at the Motion Picture Awards stop playing political games, and be prepared for the debut of one of the greatest talents ever to set foot on their stage."

A reporter in the front yelled, "That's a bold statement."

Sonya's voice was certain. "Yes, it is, but it's a true statement. I have never seen such incredible talent. You will agree when she performs."

Another reporter shouted, "What do you think your chances of getting her on the stage are?"

Sonya looked directly at the reporter who asked the question and smiled. "With the help of you and the rest of the media, plus the American public, I believe it will happen. Brianna and her dancers will be arriving shortly. She will be practicing on the stage this afternoon. If they lock her out, we will be forced to pursue other options, possibly even an injunction against the MPA. Make no mistake... we could shut the awards down completely, if necessary. We could even file a suit against the producer of the movie and everyone associated with it."

The press was scribbling down the news and murmuring.

Sonya was not quite finished. "Frankly, I'm mystified. Those who run the MPA are always the first to protest when their movies are illegally copied and sold. Here is a girl whose music sold over twenty million copies... that music was pirated. She deserves her due as any other singer, songwriter, movie producer, or actor would."

A reporter with a caustic tone shouted, "Ms. Ellis, what are the songs she supposedly wrote?"

"Not supposedly. It has already been proven, and justice has already been served. The fact is we wanted to settle out of court quietly. We did not want to hurt anyone's career. We just want what rightfully belongs to my client. The artists themselves could have been innocent in singing the music. Unfortunately, a couple people involved thought they were bigger than the system, and decided to make something out of it by going public. It will destroy their careers—I will see to that! When I'm done with them, they will be finished in the music industry."

There was no denying the fire in her eye, the passion in her demeanor. "Please, no more questions. I need to meet my client at the airport. The outcome of this soap opera lies in your hands—the media. Will you stand up for what is right, or will you back the power-hungry establishment? Thank you." Sonya exited quickly.

The paparazzi were doing everything possible to get a good photo of the girl in question. So far all that had surfaced were old pictures from restaurants where she had entertained in the past. The pictures that were released were not very clear, but were being shown on every television and cable news show.

Who was this mystery girl? They knew her name was Brianna Bays, but there was no other information available anywhere. It was as if she appeared overnight. Her past was unknown. Where was she born? Who were her parents? What school did she attend? The only people who seemed to know anything about her were waitresses she had worked with. They spoke highly of her—she had a good work ethic, was a kind person with a beautiful voice, but usually kept to herself.

Sonya's press conference piqued the curiosity of the media. Overnight, their opinion of the unknown girl changed. They did not understand why Brianna could not sing her song at the awards. The publicity was overshadowing the other entertainers, and movies, which were nominated for awards. The Middle East news, the war in Iraq, even the presidential race was put on the second page of the newspaper. The number one news story was, "Who is this mystery girl?" Suddenly, all of America was supporting the young girl. In time, the audience would judge her for themselves.

The MPA could no longer ignore the growing disapproval and announced their change of heart. After seeing the worldwide publicity over the teen, they realized the monetary gain from advertisers around the world would be huge. The ceremony would draw an enormous audience.

Sonya was there to meet the private plane that brought Brianna and her dance team to Los Angeles. Of course, the press was also there.

As Brianna's limo neared the entrance of the awards theater, the police were there to hold back the press and the curiosity seekers. The only current photos caught showed a mysterious figure with hat and sunglasses, which heightened curiosity even more. The world would have to wait until tomorrow night's awards ceremony to catch their first actual glimpse of Brianna Bays.

The practice went smoothly. Sonya and Derek felt confident that Brianna was ready.

Afterwards, backstage in her dressing room, Sonya and Brianna finally had a chance to chat. "How are you holding up?" Sonya asked.

"I'm doing just fine. Fame is easier to take than living on the streets. People are willing to help me now. They all want to get a piece of the action." Her demeanor changed, she lowered her head. "People, especially men, used to help me just to get... to get me."

Sonya's heart went out to her friend. She listened, not sure how to respond. After a lengthy pause, Sonya spoke, "Those days are gone. You are a very brave, strong woman. I've been impressed with the way you have dealt with the stress of everything the last couple weeks. Don't underestimate yourself."

It felt good to have Sonya in her corner. She felt like she had a true friend!

For the first time all week, they both enjoyed some quiet time together.

Brianna sat in the chair in front of the mirror. They discussed Brianna's life during the past five years. Whenever Sonya would mention Ethan Anderson, the teen would immediately stop the conversation and redirect it. She made it clear that he was still a topic off-limits. Maybe he always would be.

Sonya was thrilled to have the opportunity to talk with Brianna about her spiritual life and explained what it meant to be a Christian.

Brianna stared past her. "I know all the answers. I know all the Christian answers, I know all the Muslim arguments, and I don't need either." Brianna picked up a guitar and began strumming. "I have my music—that's all I need."

Sonya's face looked pained. She knew what Brianna needed, but she couldn't make that choice for her. Obviously, the teenager wasn't ready for a discussion on spiritual matters.

Sonya wisely changed the subject. "How about a man in your life, you know, a romantic relationship?"

Brianna giggled. "If there is ever a man in my life, the next one will be the right one. However, I don't think he's out there. I have too much of a bitter taste in my mouth for men. I refuse to be used by them anymore. I don't need one to take care of me—I'm strong enough on my own."

Sonya's phone rang. "Hello. Yes, let them in, and bring them down here."

Brianna wondered about the call, but didn't ask questions.

Sonya smiled, "Speaking of men... I have one I would like you to meet."

"Why?"

"Bodyguards. You are in the spotlight, and you need protection. I've hired three men and a woman. The female will be used not only for your protection, but also as a decoy. I only know one of them, but he highly recommended the other three. He is my husband's little brother. They were in the Marines together. In fact, he was in the vehicle behind Jim when it exploded. My husband died in his brother's arms." Sonya closed her eyes and then blinked them open.

Sonya's words stirred Brianna. "That must have been difficult for him."

"It was. The last thing they did together was pray for me... that I would be strong, and not turn away from my faith because of what happened." Sonya's eyes were moist.

The mood was somber.

Brianna continued, "Isn't seeing your husband's brother hard on you? And Sonya, why do I need four guards? Isn't one enough?"

"My, you always have so many questions." Sonya grinned. "No, it's not hard on me. In fact, it makes me feel closer to Jim. And yes, you need four, just trust me on this. I don't think you realize the enormity of the situation you are in."

Listening intently, Brianna stilled.

Sonya cleared her throat. "There will come a time when you just want a few minutes alone... just to do nothing. The press will hound you; photographers will take pictures of you wherever you are. Fans will want to meet you, touch you, or have you listen to them sing. They may even stalk you. It will be impossible to have a few minutes to yourself. You will find it difficult to go out to eat, go on a date, or even to the powder room. Their job is to protect you, and see to it that you have a few minutes to yourself. You will like them." Sonya smiled reassuringly.

There was a knock on the door. Sonya opened it. A well-built young man in his early twenties entered. Two other men and a woman around the same age followed him.

Brianna stayed seated as the four stood at attention.

The young man in front greeted Sonya with a long, heartfelt hug.

Sonya didn't hesitate. "Conrad, thanks for coming."

"It's the least I could do for my sister-in-law. Thanks for the opportunity to help."

He eyed Brianna. "And this is the young lady that needs our protection?" The first thing he noticed was how mature she looked. Just seventeen, but everything about her, looked older than her years.

Brianna finally stood and faced the visitors. She was immediately drawn to Conrad. His good looks and muscles caused her to take notice. She wasted no time in moving closer to him. At the same time, she cautioned herself—men are off-limits. She was finished with them... at least for now.

Sonya raised her brow. "Conrad, may I introduce you to Brianna Bays."

He reached his hand out to his new client as he lost himself in her eyes. "Wow, she has a strong handshake. When Sonya said you were gorgeous, she wasn't kidding. I can see why you need protection."

Brianna smiled, not knowing what to say about these new people in her life. It surprised her that she didn't know how to respond; she usually wasn't at a loss for words.

"Sonya told me I needed to have a firmer hand shake if I was going to make it in the business world." Brianna's voice sounded dry.

"Well, you're doing a good job. I think you can stop now." Conrad smiled.

She looked at her hand in his and quickly released it. She stepped back, almost embarrassed.

Conrad introduced the others. "This is Cathy and Jonathan Turner. We have known each other a long time. They served in the Marines, like me. They went in together as friends, and came out as husband and wife." He laughed.

Brianna smiled. She immediately noticed some similarities between her and Cathy. They were about the same height and weight, even had the same color hair.

Brianna was caught off-guard when Cathy gave her a warm hug.

"It's an honor to meet you." Cathy smiled.

"Thank you."

"This is the love of my life," Cathy said, pulling Jonathan closer to Brianna.

Jonathan reached out his hand to Brianna.

The prospective star grabbed his hand and shook it. "How tall are you?"

"Six foot six."'

Brianna could tell Jonathan was a man of few words.

"Cathy affectionately put her arm around her husband. "He's still growing, too. He was a star basketball player in high school, and was offered a full scholarship to Duke, but joined the Marines instead. He said he wanted to defend his country instead of the basketball hoop." She whispered to Brianna. "The guy won't admit it, but he just wanted to be near me." Cathy's eyes sparkled.

Brianna continued to watch the couple, obviously, they were much in love.

Cathy added, "A little advice from another girl. If you want to get the right man, run from him... eventually you will catch him!"

Brianna listened politely, but her eyes kept drifting to Conrad.

Conrad interrupted, breaking up the girl talk. "And this big guy is Bruno Strauss. He is German inside and out. I met him in Berlin, when he was serving in the German Army."

Bruno clicked his heals, snapped to attention, and spoke with a strong German accent, "Glad to meet you, Ma'am." He raised Brianna's hand and kissed the back of it.

She smiled... it reminded her of a scene from an old movie.

Bruno was 6'2" and well over two hundred pounds of pure muscle. His thick neck and broad shoulders, coupled with bulging biceps indicated he must spend hours a day in the gym.

"Conrad, explain your job to Brianna." Sonya said.

"Sure. We'll be spending a lot of time with you. Basically, we will be with you everywhere you go. Sometimes it may be uncomfortable for you. If it is, let us know. We will weigh the options and make a decision on what we should do."

Bruno smiled, staring at Brianna.

She returned his smile and then studied each of the new visitors, not knowing what to think about the entire situation.

Conrad continued, "You have to realize you're going to be in the limelight. If Sonya's predictions are right, and you hit the big time, we will have our work cut out for us. Rest assured we have a lot of experience. Since we left the military, we have protected actors, singers, politicians, and other important people. That's our job. We'll be close to you when you perform, dress, sleep, and even when you go to the bathroom. We work twenty-four hours a day. For security reasons, you will never be left alone."

Brianna put her hand up and stepped back. "Uh... people, I'm not ready for all this. I don't think I need it, Sonya. It's overkill. They'll be with me when I sleep and go to the bathroom? I suppose when I take a shower, too. What if I decide to go on a hot date?"

"They'll be nearby 24/7 for your protection," Sonya shot back with a look of pure determination.

Conrad's face showed the gravity of the situation. "You may not understand it now, but you will. I'm not trying to scare you, but many famous people are assaulted every day. People will try to touch you, hug you, kiss you, and get your autograph."

"What's wrong with that?"

"Nothing, it's where they want to touch you, and how they want to hug or kiss you. Some psychos may want to kidnap you, or harm you physically just to get in the headlines. Sadly, there are some who will hate you just because you are rich and famous. There have been a number of celebrities killed by stalkers. This is very serious. If you're as talented as you are beautiful, reporters from every newspaper, magazine, and television network in the world will pursue you. Makeup, hair, teen, and even X-rated magazines may be after you. Just let us do our job, and you can do yours. That's all we ask—your safety is our only business."

Brianna stared at the handsome ex-Marine and grinned. He was an interesting man. For some reason she was drawn to him. "Well, I can see there is no talking you out of anything. You're all business." Brianna stepped closer to Conrad, and brushed her finger down his chest in a flirtatious gesture. "Do I have to be afraid of any of you coming on to me?"

Without even a glimpse of a smile, Conrad spoke. "No Ma'am, you said it—we are all business."

"Pity," she said, spinning around. She sat in her chair, picked up her guitar, and began strumming it again.

Finally, she looked at Conrad. "Very well... when does this all begin?" Brianna realized arguing with any of them would be futile.

"It already has," Sonya said. "Tomorrow night will be the biggest night of your career. It will make or break you. I would suggest you concentrate on your dance steps and voice. Get your sleep when you can. Stay away from drugs, alcohol, tobacco, and men."

"Okay, Mom." Brianna brushed her hair away from her face. "Seriously, you don't have to worry about any of that—especially the drugs and men. I have something much more important in my life, and now I think I can finally achieve it. I need all my senses to accomplish it. And don't worry about tomorrow night—I intend to give the performance of a lifetime—one that will get the world talking about a new star, and hopefully attract the attention of somebody."

"May I ask who?" Conrad asked as he folded his arms.

"My real parents—they're out there somewhere, and I'm going to find them."

Conrad replied swiftly. "I take it you were adopted and never met your biological parents. What will you do when you find them, or if they find you?"

Brianna was deep in thought, miles away, as she softly strummed her guitar. "I don't know. I guess I hope it will be a huggy, kissy time when I find them." She smiled a sad sort of smile at Conrad. "You know, I've been searching for you my whole lifetime, kind of thing. I don't know. It's just something I need to do. I've done some horrible things to get to this point. I have... I've lied, cheated, stolen, sold myself and my talents. I have... I've destroyed people's lives. I can't stop now, or it will be all for naught." A sick feeling hit her like a freezing winter wind, taking her breath.

Conrad cast a questioning look. "What if you don't find them? Maybe they don't want to be found. Have you considered that? You may want them in your life, but they may not want you in their lives. And once you do find them, you may not like what you see."

Brianna studied her new bodyguard thoughtfully. "It's my understanding that most parents get rid of their child for one of two main reasons."

"What are those, if I may ask?" Conrad questioned.

Brianna paused, her voice suddenly sounding nervous. "Either they don't want them, or they could not care for them. The parents who don't want their children, you wouldn't want in your life anyway. However, for those who give their child away because they were unfit, or they couldn't give them proper care, it's possible they were looking out for the child. There are several variables, but there could be some hope. Time brings forth healing on both sides... at least, that's what I've read."

Brianna stopped her strumming and stared at Conrad, almost oblivious to the others in the room. "I can't believe I'm talking to you about this. Who are you anyhow? You're just a bodyguard."

She began strumming and with a voice of an angel, the lyrics flowed— words she had never penned. No one knew if the message came from her heart, head, or an experience from her past.

> *Who are you, but just a man?*
> *You can't possibly understand*
> *The heart of one searching,*
> *The love that I'm bringing*
> *This is the story,*
> *I'm going to keep singing*

Conrad didn't blink, or break eye contact. "I'm not too different from you. I spent much of my childhood in foster homes. I could tell you horror stories about some of them, others were good. I thought I'd never have any real parents. However, at age eight, my last foster parents adopted me and showed me what life and family was all about. They showed me what living in a family with two loving parents and a big brother was like— Sonya's husband, Jim, was that big brother. He was two years older than me. I taught him what it was like to be tough and what it was like in the real world. More importantly, my family taught me that God loved me. Yes, maybe my real parents did not love me, but God loves me unconditionally. Unlike people, His love never changes."

Brianna looked up, her eyes darkened. "Back to another Bible lesson... I just can't get away from them!"

The warmth in Conrad's voice grew. "That's the one thing that is constant—God's love for us." He thought it heartbreaking that Brianna was so turned off with spiritual truths and wondered why.

Brianna listened, not sure what to say. After a pause, she questioned the guard, "What about your real parents? Weren't you interested in finding them?"

"Yes, I was persistent, like you. I guess it's just something that many adopted children feel they need to do. When I did locate them, it was not a happy sight, or a joyous reunion like the one I had hoped for. They were druggies—both of them. I located my mother in a drug rehabilitation ward, and found my father drunk in the gutter. When I told my dad who I was, he laughed at me, and called me a loser." Conrad shook his head. "But I wasn't a loser—God helped me make something out of my life."

Brianna's breath caught in her throat.

Conrad didn't hesitate. "But they were not my parents. My real mother and father are Ben and Cindy Thompson, from Tulsa, Oklahoma. Every time I get a chance, I let them know how much I love them. I've always tried to make them proud of me."

"My, aren't we on a roll? Am I going to have to listen to his lectures the whole time he protects me?" Brianna smiled at Sonya to help lessen her sarcasm.

Sonya answered. "I'm afraid so. Conrad has been many places and done countless things in his short life on earth. His knowledge far exceeds one's expectation. You may want to learn from him."

Brianna stilled, letting the truth settle in. She looked dejected, but not for long. "You may be right, Sonya."

Laying her guitar down, Brianna approached Conrad. Playfully, she stuck her hand out. "Hi. My name is Brianna Bays... and yours is?"

He smiled, reaching for her hand. "Conrad Thompson, at your service, Ma'am."

"No... not Ma'am... Brianna. My friends call me Brianna. The four of you are now my friends." She silently placed her guitar in the case.

Everyone watched her, intrigued by the teen's words and actions.

Lightening the mood, Brianna asked, "Where are we going to stay tonight?"

"My house," Sonya replied.

"Your house?" Brianna questioned, her voice sounding sort of bewildered.

"Yes, I figured it would be the safest place for you."

"Is it big?"

"Big and gated—nobody can get in or out without going through the guard station."

"Wow! I'm impressed."

"Don't be. Both of my neighbors are politicians." Sonya's face was serious.

Brianna thought about it for a few seconds and started to laugh. "Poor you!"

Sonya joined in the laughter—it felt good.

Brianna announced, "I'm tired. I'd like to take a shower and get some rest." She angled her head, looking at her bodyguards, and jokingly asked, "Will I be taking a shower with one, or all four of you?"

Conrad's voice was ripe with teasing. "We drew straws, and Bruno got dibs on the first shower with you."

Brianna looked at Bruno who had a big grin on his face.

Suddenly, Brianna stopped smiling and looked at Sonya. "They are kidding, right?"

"Let's go home." Sonya said, patting Brianna's arm.

Grabbing her guitar case, Brianna said, "Now wait a minute, you guys were kidding, weren't you?"

Bruno stepped forth with his huge smile. "I'll carry that for you," he said in his broken English.

"Wow, such a gentleman. Thank you, but this is my life. I can carry it—I am quite capable. I'll tell you what... you can open the door for me."

"My privilege," Bruno grinned.

"Now, let's get back to that shower thing." Brianna continued the kidding, realizing she had met her match with her new friends.

All of them erupted into laughter.

Sonya handed a hat and pair of sunglasses to Brianna. Bruno opened the door, and she slipped them on.

Conrad led the way past some curious onlookers who took a second look, but had no idea who she was. No one knew!

The six quickly piled into an SUV, and Bruno drove to Sonya's house. The ride was quiet. Each of them consumed with thoughts of what the next day would hold.

Nearing an elegant home at the end of a long driveway, Brianna turned her attention toward Sonya. "What did you say you did for a living?"

"I'm a lawyer."

"Wow! Nice house. How many bedrooms?"

"Six."

"Bathrooms?"

"Six."

Brianna scrunched up her nose. "Are you sure you're single?"

"Yes, I'm quite sure," Sonya responded.

"You live by yourself?"

"Yes. I have a housekeeper who comes in a few times a week to clean."

With wide eyes, Brianna asked, "If I may ask, why do you have such a big house?"

"I got a good deal on it... and I have three cats." Sonya had a sheepish grin.

"Oh, that explains it," Brianna murmured. "You have three cats—they must be very spoiled!"

Brianna stepped out of the vehicle and looked around. The quiet street and the massive homes with their manicured yards caught her immediate attention. As she inhaled, she noticed the scent of freshly mown grass. The scene was peaceful. "Do you think I'll ever own a house like this?"

Sonya lifted her chin. "Like this? No, you'll probably have a dozen homes, ten times this size, all over the world."

Brianna shook her head. "I don't think so. I have better things to do with my money."

"Like what?" Conrad's eyes were wide, curious.

"Like helping people, especially orphans." Brianna's voice sounded casual.

"That's an honorable thing. Don't ever lose that," Conrad replied.

The guests walked through the giant double door entryway. The home was elegant on the inside, yet, comfortable, homey.

Sonya led Brianna up the stairs to a guest room. When she opened the door, Brianna could barely breathe. Speechless, she stared at the room.

"Is something the matter?" Sonya asked, confused by her reaction.

"No. It's... just that this room brings back memories."

"Good or bad?" Sonya asked.

"Just faint recollections... I can't really tell if they are good or bad."

Concerned, Sonya offered, "Will you be okay? I can give you another room."

"No, no. I have to face my ghosts one of these days. I might as well start now."

"I'm going to get some rest. Will my bodyguards be staying in your home, also?"

"Yes, they will be. I heard that Cathy and Jonathan are great chefs. They are going to cook us an Italian dinner."

"Good. I'll look forward to it. Call me when dinner is ready." Brianna shut the door.

Sonya stood motionless for a moment, not knowing what to think of Brianna's strange behavior. Then hearing the familiar sound of the guitar strumming, Sonya smiled and walked away.

Evening came soon, but the short nap seemed to lighten Brianna's mood.

The gang gathered around a large table and Conrad led them in prayer. He prayed for protection for Brianna, and then boldly petitioned God in a way that caught the entertainer off-guard. He asked God to help her find what she was looking for. He ended the prayer asking for protection for the military troops stationed around the world—for safety and a quick return to their families.

Brianna was overwhelmed with his prayer. Raising her head just high enough to take a glimpse of these new people in her life, she realized she had gained a new respect for her protectors. This would be the beginning of her desire to help the military troops in any way she could. At that moment, she decided she would love to visit and entertain the troops around the world someday.

Cathy and Jonathan lived up to their reputation as great chefs—dinner was superb.

All of them enjoyed the food and laughter.

After the meal, they all took a part in cleaning the kitchen, and then retired to the family room where they conversed for hours. They each shared stories, which led them to their present paths.

Conrad's job in the Marines was similar to what he was currently doing—protecting influential people. He and his brother were guarding a senator when the explosion killed his brother, Sonya's husband. He commented that the senator never should have been there, but was for political reasons. He always thought it ironic, that he could protect the politician—someone he didn't even know, but he could not protect his brother. Sometimes guilt still plagued him.

Cathy and Jonathan started kindergarten together and remained best friends through high school. They were inseparable as teenagers. Both were stars on the basketball court and in the school dramas. Their senior year they played leading roles in the school play, "South Pacific." That was when they shared their first kiss.

After graduation, the couple joined the Marines. Ironically, they would not kiss again until their second year in the Marines—at their wedding.

One day they decided since they spent so much time together, they might as well get married—they made a lifetime pledge of love and loyalty.

Conrad knew the couple from school, and when Sonya approached him about this job, he immediately thought of them.

Bruno had a much different history. Conrad was in Berlin protecting the President of the United States when they met. Bruno was the personal military bodyguard of the Chancellor of Germany. Conrad was impressed with his wit and personality. Now, together again on this assignment, they resumed their friendship.

Leave it to Bruno to make a person laugh—and that he did, all evening long. He would tell jokes about things he saw as a bodyguard for world dignitaries. Bruno loved to impersonate well-known people. He did not do a very good job of it, which made it more comical.

Brianna laughed until she cried. It was the first time Sonya had seen that side of her.

Still, Brianna would never comment on certain parts of her life. Sonya wondered if she would ever be able to open up honestly about her past. She uttered a silent prayer for her friend.

Fascinated by Brianna, Conrad's eyes focused on her. She was complicated. Only seventeen, she had experienced much more life than any child should have. In spite of her dark past, she still seemed to be able to keep things in perspective. He enjoyed being around her. However, he knew in order to fulfill his responsibilities, he must not become emotionally attached. He would stay focused on the job at hand—her protection—nothing more!

Brianna took a liking to Conrad as well. At times their eyes would meet, and then one would change the subject and quickly look away. Her pulse quickened.

When Bruno asked Brianna to play the piano, at first, she hesitated. With the coaxing of the others, she sat down at Sonya's piano and began playing a classical piece she had arranged as a child. The five friends looked at each other with disbelieving eyes, awed by her talent. Brianna completed her song, and the small group gave her a hearty applause.

"Wow!" Bruno exclaimed. "Can you play other instruments?"

"Almost any stringed instrument, but my favorite is the violin."

"You've got to be kidding," Cathy interrupted. "Violin is difficult. I played the violin in high school. You're one gifted girl."

Sonya had to break the party up at eleven. "The biggest day of Brianna's life, in fact all of our lives, will be tomorrow. We all need to get our beauty sleep."

They said their goodnights and went their separate ways.

Sonya could not sleep. She had great expectations for this young talent, and stepped on some big toes to get where she was. She hoped it was worth it. Tomorrow night at this time... she would know. In fact... the world would know.

The halls echoed with the soft voice of Brianna singing and strumming her guitar for what seemed like hours until the music stopped.

Sonya quietly walked to the room and opened the door. The light next to Brianna's bed was still glowing. She stared at the dark-haired beauty as she slept. Exhausted, Brianna had fallen asleep, still holding her guitar. Sonya gently removed the instrument and placed it in its case. She tenderly covered her with a blanket.

She gazed at the sleeping beauty. What secrets does she hold? Who are you really? She lovingly whispered, "I hope I can help you face your fears, and find what you are searching for. For your sake, I hope it's worth it."

Sonya touched her face lightly, brushing her hair aside, and accidently exposing her birthmark. "I wonder if that beauty mark holds any secrets."

Pulling the cover up further, Sonya said softly, "Sleep well, my child. Tomorrow is your big day." Sonya bent over and gave Brianna a soft kiss on her forehead, similar to that of a concerned mother with her daughter. She hoped she was up to the task of helping this vulnerable girl—who, for some reason, had captured her heart.

Sonya whispered a prayer, and then tiptoed out of the room, quietly closing the door behind her.

NINE

The Shining Star

For we are God's handiwork, created in Christ Jesus to do good works,
which God prepared in advance for us to do.
Ephesians 2:10

Before sunrise, preparations for the big day began. First, there was a five-mile run for Brianna, Sonya, and the bodyguards. Exercise was essential in beginning the day, followed by a nourishing hot breakfast.

Conrad noticed how Brianna pushed herself to the limit in whatever she did—he admired her resilience. At the same time, he realized that one day everything she held inside would need to come out. He knew she had been internalizing her problems far too long. He prayed he would be with her to help see her through that day.

He had known Brianna for less than a day and realized he was already becoming emotional involved. To what extent, he didn't know—it was too early to tell—maybe he thought of her as a sister, perhaps a close friend, maybe more. Whatever it was, it certainly was more than he expected. Something, he, as a professional, swore he would never do. He could already tell that she was not just another body to protect. No, she was more, much more, and it frightened him.

As Brianna prepared for the night's festivities, Conrad took time to talk with Sonya by herself. He didn't know how to explain what he felt toward Brianna, but whatever it was, Sonya had noticed it already.

"Conrad, I sense that you have been bitten by Brianna mystique," she said, pouring a couple cups of coffee and handing one to her friend.

"Is it that noticeable?" He took a sip of the hot brew.

"Not just with you, but all of us."

"What is it about her that pulls us in?" Conrad sat at the small kitchen table.

"I'm not certain if it's her physical appearance, her mysterious life, bubbling personality, or what. I just know that she captured me on the first day." Sonya shook her head.

There was a comfortable silence between them as each pondered the situation.

Conrad sighed, "Poor Bruno's beside himself. I pity the person who tries to touch her. He will show no mercy." He laughed. "Sonya, what do you know about her past?"

Sonya stared out the window. "Not a whole lot, but probably more than I should. I really don't know what to believe about what I've heard." She joined Conrad at the table.

"Can you tell me about it, or would you rather not?" Conrad wore a look of empathy.

She rubbed her temples, unsure how to respond. "I feel that on one hand I shouldn't, but on the other hand I need to tell you so you know what you're up against. It is confidential information, but I know I can trust you with the few details I have."

Conrad shot her a strange look.

"I know that her real name is Janna Anderson."

"I suspected that Brianna Bays was a made-up name." The bodyguard crossed his arms, listening intently.

"Yes. From what I gather, she was adopted at age six. She was physically abused, possibly molested, by her adoptive father at twelve. She was placed in foster care and ran away when she was just fifteen. Sadly, she lived on the streets for over a year, worked anywhere she could, and did some things young girls do to survive."

Conrad nodded his head with a sad expression, understanding what she was talking about.

"She doesn't talk about it. Her father... adoptive father, as she says, is off-limits. So don't talk about him if you can help it."

"What happened to her family?"

"Her adoptive father is in prison. I have no idea what happened to her mother, or any siblings she might have. She won't talk about it. She may not know. I feel there is a sense of regret, or more precisely, guilt."

"Guilt about what?"

"I talked with her lawyer, Robert Cain. He was up-front with me, even helped me get that matter settled with her music. He made the comment that her father was innocent. When I asked him for the truth, all he would say is, he did it for Janna—she knows the truth."

Conrad didn't break eye contact. "You mean she's lying about her story? She had her adoptive father sent to prison for something he didn't do. I don't buy it. What was her motive?"

"I don't know. The entire story is strange. A piece is missing from the puzzle."

Sonya lightly grabbed Conrad's arm. "Hey, be careful. She could be a lioness in a kitten's outfit. She may come back and bite you... and bite hard. She could have us all fooled."

Conrad took another sip of coffee. "I don't believe it."

"What don't you believe?" Sonya asked.

"I think she's in great turmoil. As a foster child myself, I know what she is going though. I feel her pain."

Sonya cleared her throat. "She has a strong desire to find out who her biological parents are."

"That's not unusual. Most of the foster kids I knew had that yearning, and many would do anything to find out who their parents were."

"You said that your true parents are Ben and Cindy Thompson."

"Yes, that's true. That's what I chose to accept as truth, but first, I went through the same process... searching. I recall a number of kids running away to discover their answers. I guess there is always the hope that they may be looking for you, too. Unfortunately for most, they aren't."

Loudly, Bruno burst into the room. "I smell coffee. Wasn't that a great run this morning? What a way to start the day." He poured a cup of coffee and sat down next to Conrad.

Sonya and Conrad said nothing as Bruno commanded the conversation. "My, that girl can run. I think I'm going to like this job."

"Another one of her many skills," Conrad replied.

Sonya and Conrad glanced at each other as they finished their coffee—both reflecting on their conversation. They knew the future was uncertain. Neither knew where Brianna would end up—all they could do is face it one day at a time.

As the morning wore on, Sonya tried to keep everybody relaxed and calm.

She and Brianna had previously picked out what the performer would wear for the awards. That morning, the outfit was delivered to the house.

The hairstylist spent hours getting her hair ready; the style needed to be full, yet flowing enough to fly in the wind for special effects.

The make-up artist covered the birthmark. Brianna really wasn't self-conscious about it anymore; she just had made it a habit to cover it up. Ethan had always made sure it was covered, but assured her he was not embarrassed about it. He would tell her how cruel kids can be about those things. So, she continued with the practice.

It was early afternoon when the group piled into their vehicle and started toward the entertainment center, hopefully, early enough to beat the crowd.

Sonya called ahead to let security know they were on their way.

Conrad and the other guards were edgy, but Brianna seemed extremely calm—too calm. Did she realize the impact the evening could have on her career, her life?

When they arrived at the theater, a larger crowd than they expected had already gathered hoping to get a glimpse, a picture, or maybe an autograph of their favorite star.

Tabloid and news media lined up rows deep—all eager to capture the first photo of the mystery girl who had managed to bring the Hollywood elite to their knees. At least, that's what some media reported.

As the SUV inched its way through the crowd, fans would press their faces against the tinted windows to try to get a clear look, but without success.

Bruno parked in the back, close to the entertainer's door.

Brianna stepped out of the vehicle, disguised in her scarf and sunglasses.

Without warning, paparazzi broke through the barricades with cameras flashing. Working as a team, one member of the paparazzi snapped pictures, while two others tried to rip Brianna's scarf off.

Fortunately, the teen was standing between Cathy and Jonathan.

Brianna was new at this. She was not sure what to do—it all happened so quickly. She let out a light scream as she tried to resist the man's hand tearing at her scarf and glasses.

"Put your head down," Cathy shouted, shielding Brianna.

Jonathan knocked the man's hand off her.

Then a large fist came to the head of one of the men. Bruno wasted no time in knocking the attacker out cold.

Conrad grabbed the other man, bending his arm, and forcing him to the ground, just as three police officers arrived.

The officers grabbed the third man, and then proceeded to arrest all of them for trespassing, and confiscated the camera.

The guards circled Brianna, rushing her into the dressing room. Once safely inside, she removed her sunglasses and head covering.

Sorrow and relief took turns with Brianna.

"Are you okay? They didn't hurt you, did they?" Conrad put his hands on her shoulders and bent over looking directly into her frightened eyes.

She noticed the strength in his hands, and found comfort knowing he genuinely cared about her. "No, I'm okay. It just caught me off-guard; it happened so fast." She looked at the expression on his face and reached for his hand. "Thank you for your protection and concern. I mean it... if you and the others wouldn't have been there... no telling what could have happened." She felt her heart racing, and wasn't sure if it was because of the attack, or the touch of his hand.

Conrad could barely concentrate.

Unexpectedly, she put her arms around the guard's neck, pulling him close. She wasn't sure what was happening, but neither was Conrad. Without resisting, he put his arms around her and pulled her into a warm embrace.

Quickly, Conrad came to his senses and released her. Without making eye contact, he distanced himself. "Miss, you had better get ready. We'll be right outside if you need us."

He turned to face Sonya, who had silently watched the entire scene. "Is she all right?" Sonya asked, not knowing what else to say, but noticing the heat between them.

"Yes. She's one brave cookie."

Sonya watched Brianna's eyes track him as he opened the door and left. It was unlike Conrad to act on emotion. No doubt, Brianna's magic, her passion, had captured his attention.

The terrifying experience with the paparazzi showed Brianna firsthand how quickly things could escalate out of control, and why she needed her bodyguards. If they had not been there, she certainly would have been accosted, manhandled, just for a picture. She grew pale as she replayed the scene in her mind.

Until it was her time to perform, she would remain safely in her dressing room. She glanced at her watch. There were still six hours until show time.

Cathy and Sonya would remain with her. The other three took their place outside the door not letting anyone unauthorized enter.

While waiting, Brianna practiced her song. Derek came in to work on her dance steps. She knew she was ready, but it helped the time go faster.

The make-up artist and hairstylist did their last minute touch-ups. Even though the stylist said, "I'm wasting my time here; I can't make you look any better than you already do."

Brianna looked closely in the mirror for her birthmark. The makeup artist did a great job—it couldn't even be seen close-up.

As Sonya watched her, she boldly stated, "If you hate your mark so much, you could probably have a plastic surgeon remove it."

"I've often thought about doing that if I had the money. However, something in the back of my head keeps saying not to... it's a gift from God." Her mind drifted to the time Ethan told her those exact words when he rescued her from the orphanage. He mentioned that she was God's special child. She shook her head and the memory faded.

Sonya responded, "Well, you can afford to do it now."

"I guess I can. What time is it?" Brianna asked, deliberately changing the subject.

It occurred to Sonya that the girl had no intention of removing the birthmark. The birthmark must serve a purpose—possibly a bridge to her biological parents. It could be uncovered or shown, if it ever needed to be. Brianna knew exactly what she was doing.

Throughout the day, celebrities attempted to meet her, but were not permitted.

Word came that the ceremony had begun.

Brianna strummed her old guitar. Sonya had bought her a new guitar for the ceremony, but she refused to use it. "I sing with this guitar and no other."

The choreographer had suggested she perform without a guitar. He felt the orchestra was all she needed. She would have none of that. She finally compromised. She would put the guitar down halfway through, when she began the dance routine.

The sounds of voices and applause resounded through the hallway as celebrities received their awards. Brianna was not concerned with that—she had no idea who was nominated since she had not seen a movie in years, and paid no attention to Hollywood happenings.

Finally, there was a knock on her door. A voice sounded, "Fifteen minutes."

With the announcement, Brianna's face lit up. Staring into the mirror, she peered past her image to Sonya, who stood behind her massaging her shoulders. Sonya's voice was calming. "You look gorgeous."

"Beauty is not what's going to win this crowd."

"You're right. You'll be making your debut in front of the most beautiful, sought after, people in the world. Let's hear your voice."

Brianna started low, working up the scale, and then effortlessly went back down. "What do you think?" Brianna questioned, "Am I ready?"

Sonya faced her friend and gently fluffed her hair. "I think it's time. Let's do this. Break a leg."

Brianna's radiant smile encompassed her face. She walked through the door Cathy held open for her. Sonya followed.

In the hall, the budding star took a deep breath and winked at Conrad, who was standing outside the door.

"Wow!" Conrad said, as his jaw dropped. "You look smashing!" He stared at her for a second, and then turned his head looking both directions. "The hallways are jammed. There are hundreds of people here waiting to get the first glimpse of the girl who stole the show from Judd Stevens, and brought the Motion Picture Awards down."

"Not his show, it's mine." Brianna grinned.

"You go get 'em girl," Bruno said with his German accent.

"I love hearing that accent. It's... it's kind of sexy." Brianna giggled.

Bruno looked at Conrad who was rolling his eyes.

She had dreamed of this moment her whole life. Brianna took a deep breath and started down the long hallway. Bruno led the way.

The dancers were already in place, waiting behind stage.

During the first part of the ceremony, many jokes were about Brianna, which was another reason Sonya tried to shelter her.

The emcee made a tacky one-liner about the noise backstage. One insensitive attempt at humor was about a nobody taking the place of one of America's hottest talents. "Well, ladies and gentlemen, I can tell by the commotion in the back that we are about to get a show. I'm not sure what to expect. I hear that the young girl, Brianna Bays... you may have heard about her on the news..." He paused until the laughter died down. "Apparently, she looks like Dorothy from the Wizard of Oz—the cartoon that is."

The audience broke out in more laughter.

The emcee continued, "Okay, without further ado. Here to announce the last song for the night is two-time female vocalist of the year, Billie Snow."

The well-known entertainer walked to the microphone to read the card. "Nominated for best song from the motion picture, *Time*, is, *I'm Thinking of a Time*, by Judd Stevens, and written by Brianna Bays."

Sporadic applause rippled through the audience when Judd Stevens' name was announced; some booing and hissing occurred when Brianna's name was mentioned.

Snow continued, "Tonight the song will be performed by Brianna Bays... whoever that is. America, we are about to find out. Ladies and gentlemen, meet the mystery girl, Brianna Bays!"

The dancers moved into formation.

Brianna took her place onstage. She glanced at her new friends, shooting them a quick smile.

This was it! The spotlight turned on the silhouette of a woman center stage. The curtain rose and the lights flickered. The dancers gathered around the lone figure. As the lights expanded, the awed crowd finally saw the mysterious, Brianna Bays.

The audience hushed.

The orchestra began.

Suddenly, the voice of an angel filled the auditorium. The strong, clear voice of the young lady, not only caught the ear, but the emotion of those in the house, as she hit with precision the low notes and jumped to the high soprano notes in one breath.

As the camera zoomed in for a close-up of Brianna in her splendor, the audience watched spellbound, anxious to take it all in.

When Bays handed the guitar to one of the dancers, the show really came to life. Her dancing was spectacular.

The music was melodic and meaningful; the message in the lyrics heart wrenching. The choreography, lights, dance, song, all were flawless!

The finale was astounding, as the singer displayed her vocal acrobatics. When the entertainer hit the last note and held it longer than anyone would expect, the audience jumped up in standing ovation.

Yes, it was her song and everyone knew that now—there was no more denying the fact. Brianna Bays proved herself beyond any doubt.

Brianna stood center stage. Only one light shone in the entire theater, and it was on her. It was her stage—she was the center of it—and she commanded it.

The houselights brightened. Brianna clearly viewed the audience for the first time—standing, whistling, and clapping in approval. Even the greatest entertainers in the motion picture industry were applauding.

She glanced at Sonya, whose smile said it all, hands clutched together as if she were praying. Brianna noticed the radiant faces of Conrad and Jonathan, who were shaking their heads in disbelief cheering her on. She chuckled to herself when she saw Bruno jumping up and down, shouting words of affirmation.

Rushing off the stage, she melted into Sonya's arms and hugged her tight. "You did it, girl!" Sonya exclaimed through misty eyes, which came from a combination of relief, nerves, and pure joy. "You did it! You won them over. The stage is yours."

Surrounding her were her dancers, all smiling and congratulating her.

"Young lady—Brianna Bays, come out here, please." The emcee said waving his arm. "I'm supposed to tell a joke now, but I'd rather have the honor of meeting you."

Sonya motioned with her head for Brianna to return to the stage.

Slowly, Brianna returned. The audience was still standing and cheering in thunderous applause.

"Wow! You are a knockout!" The host put his arm around her shoulders. "You think she looks good from down there; you should see her up close."

The crowd grew even louder.

The emcee paused, wandering from the script, searching for the right words. "Brianna, I owe you an apology. I spent all evening making jokes about you, and it seems you've had the last laugh. The joke is on us! You're one talented young woman. I've spent years dancing. I watched you carefully and your dance steps were perfect. Most entertainers cannot sing and dance at the same time the way you did. And your voice is fabulous... that last note... wow! You have star qualities! What do you have to say for yourself?"

"Nothing for myself, but I do wish to thank the orchestra for the great arrangement, and Derek Peterson, my choreographer. My dancers... aren't they incredible?" She turned smiling, applauding her dancers.

"Nice move," Sonya whispered, watching from the side of the stage.

The emcee continued, "You keep amazing us, Brianna Bays. That is something you don't see too often—a star that's not bragging about herself. Next thing you know, the Republicans will thank the Democrats for voting against them."

A few laughed at his attempt at humor.

"Brianna, sincerely thank you." He applauded with the rest of the excited crowd.

She ran off the stage and again into the waiting arms of Sonya.

"Young lady, don't go too far." The emcee announced, "With any luck you'll be coming back up here."

The host continued, "Ladies and gentlemen, to present the award for best song in a motion picture is Billie Snow, returning with Manny Sullivan, winner of seven music awards."

The two veteran singers paced to the microphone as the audience stilled.

"What do you think of that last act?" Billie asked Manny.

"I was going to give the little lady a hug and ask her out, but did you see the size of her bodyguards?" Manny leaned back, trying to catch a glimpse of Brianna off-stage.

"Manny, shame on you... you're a married man. Open the envelope." Snow laughed.

"Right." His eyes widened as he opened the envelope and showed the result to Billie.

"Do you want to announce it, or should I?" Billie asked.

"Here. You can announce the winner. I'm going to get ready for a hug."

Billie broke out laughing and the audience went wild.

"The winner for best song from a motion picture is... *I'm Thinking of a Time*, written and performed by Brianna Bays, from the motion picture, *Time*." Billie shouted enthusiastically, clapping at the same time.

Brianna stood frozen as two girls came to escort her onstage.

She glanced at Sonya who proudly had tears streaming down her face. Her new friends, her bodyguards, were beaming.

Turning her attention to the center of the stage, Brianna walked out to receive the coveted award as the crowd erupted. The tears came unbidden as she stood there for what seemed like an eternity. Finally, she gained some composure, and the applause died down. Brianna's shaky voice cracked, "What do I do now?"

"You thank those who helped get you here. You want me to do it?" Sullivan joked.

"No, thank you. I think I can handle that." Brianna smiled.

Reaching for the award, she glanced around the massive theater. "Thank those who helped me?" She repeated his words, sounding a little confused. "I can think of only one person and that is my good friend, Sonya Ellis."

She spoke to Sonya. "Thank you. Thank you for believing in me. I was a risk, yet you took me from the streets and gave me this opportunity."

The emotional entertainer shifted her gaze from Sonya, to the trophy she held in her hand, and then to the audience.

Complete silence engulfed the theater.

What happened next stunned Brianna as well as the hushed crowd. She swallowed hard, trying to calm her emotions, but it wasn't working. Struggling to keep her focus, she continued. "There is another person... and if he is watching tonight... I want him to know that this award is just as much his as it is mine. If it had not been for him, I definitely would not be here tonight."

She returned her gaze to the floor, and then to the ceiling, desperately fighting tears. "He took me in as a child and taught me everything I know about music. I recall a verse he taught me when I was a little girl. *My heart is steadfast, O God, my heart is steadfast; I will sing and make music.*"

She searched to find the right words. "And I want him to know..." she took a deep breath, "...that I'm sorry."

She could no longer control her tears. Looking directly into a nearby camera, she was talking to one person, one man. Through sobs, she continued her heartfelt message of pain and regret, hoping that the one person, who needed to hear, was somewhere, somehow listening. She took a deep breath, "I just want you to know from the bottom of my heart... I'm sorry for hurting you."

Many in the audience had wet eyes, obviously touched by the emotional scene.

Wiping her tears, Sonya realized that the mysterious girl was one step closer to revealing her past.

Raising the impressive trophy in the air, Brianna's smile returned. "Thank you."

She sprinted off stage toward her friends, collapsing into the strong arms of Conrad. He held her tight as years of pent up emotions flooded her soul. She wept tears of joy, relief, and regret... and there seemed to be no end to them.

Over the next four years, Brianna Bays would consistently be on the top of the charts—the number one entertainer in the world.

Her career included starring roles in two motion pictures, and singing around the world in front of hundreds of thousands of fans. Her dream of entertaining the American troops in Iraq, Afghanistan, and other places in the world came true. Brianna was the first entertainer in years to do a worldwide tour for the American troops. She performed at the White House on numerous occasions, and entertained kings and leaders throughout the world. Her resume included a half-time Super Bowl show, which left the massive crowd awed. In her showcase were over a dozen prestigious music awards and another Motion Picture Award as an actress.

To the public, Brianna seemed to be on top of the world—outgoing, caring, and exuberant. However, on the inside, her past was eating her up. What she had done, and what she knew she needed to do, haunted her both day and night.

While many stars deal with success through drugs and relationships, Brianna escaped through her music, which had been her coping mechanism since she was young—her ultimate escape. She would sing, play guitar, piano, or violin, for hour-upon-hour, trying desperately to recapture the happy moments of her past, but to no avail.

Brianna gave of herself until the day came when there was nothing left to give.

TEN

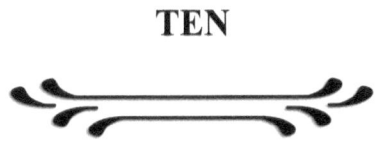

The Truth Revealed

*"Who can hide in secret places so that
I cannot see them?" declared the LORD.
"Do not I fill heaven and earth?"
declares the LORD.
Jeremiah 23:24*

Through the years, Brianna held her secret inside her. What happened a decade ago had taken an emotional toll on her. She could no longer get a good night's sleep; the nightmares became more frequent.

Sonya and Conrad talked to Brianna many times about getting back in church, but she always told them the same thing—she was not ready. She might never be ready. She did not believe even God could forgive her for what she had done.

One morning before a concert, the moment Sonya and Conrad had feared most, occurred. The famous entertainer hit rock-bottom.

Brianna and her staff were in upstate New York preparing for a show near Buffalo. It was an unseasonably warm spring day. One-hundred-thousand screaming fans would attend the afternoon concert.

It started like any normal day.

The guards and Sonya had become like a close family, inseparable. The group was staying at a friend's mansion near Niagara Falls. That sunny morning they decided to chance a visit to the Falls, and take in the sights and splendor of the famous landmark.

Dressed like a tourist, Brianna tucked her long black hair under her hat, and put on her sunglasses. It was one of her many disguises.

The young idol had become a favorite of the paparazzi. The photographers had cleverly discovered that they didn't have to look for Brianna—they had to look for her bodyguards who were easy to spot. Ingeniously, the guards also began to disguise themselves with hats and glasses, but still their size often gave them away. Several times, Conrad and Bruno had to get tough with the reporters, part of the job they didn't enjoy.

Viewing the majestic falls, tears began to stream from Brianna's eyes for no apparent reason. That was most unusual since she prided herself on her inner strength. Keeping her feelings bottled up inside, she rarely, if ever, shed a tear, certainly never in front of anyone.

The concerned friends gathered around her at a nearby picnic table.

Conrad confronted her with a barrage of questions. "Brianna, what's going on? You haven't been yourself for a while. What are those nightmares about? What is happening with you?"

Unable to contain her inner conflict any longer, Brianna poured her heart out to her small circle of friends.

Why on this day did the superstar's life come crashing down?

At age twenty-two, Brianna remembered that it had been ten years to the day since the lie began. The date was the catalyst to push the enormously successful star over the edge.

Brianna couldn't shake the cold, helpless feeling in her heart. It was dominating her life. Her tearful eyes stared straight ahead as she retraced her bitter past, a time she never wanted to relive. "I can't forget that day, no matter how hard I try. I looked like I was happy on the outside. Ethan had been such a good father to me. It wasn't his fault... it wasn't him!"

She let out a huff of breath. "The problem was my hateful stepmother, Susan. She was making my life miserable. I could do nothing right in her eyes. She would berate me constantly. 'Why can't you do anything right Janna?' Once she said, 'Life was so much better before you came.'" Brianna paused, her voice broke. "The clincher was when she told me, 'I wish you didn't live here—just go away.'"

Unable to make eye contact and choked with emotion, she continued her heartbreaking story. "Susan and I had a fight that morning. Dad... Ethan, always seemed to set things right. I knew things were bad between the two of them, and I knew I was the main cause. Susan's last statement was the final straw... she wanted me to go away."

Sonya handed Brianna a tissue.

"I arrived at school, deeply upset. It was then that I recalled a conversation with a friend. I knew this girl was trouble from the word go, but I still hung around her, not really sure why. She had been in a few foster homes, and each time she was in a bad one and wanted to leave, she would report the foster parents for child abuse. She never got in trouble for it. She told me that the authorities always believed her—at least, it seemed that way. In the end, she always got what she wanted and was moved to a new home."

Brianna's friends, feeling helpless, listened intently. Conrad and Sonya prayed silently.

"I wanted to find my real parents. In order to do that, I knew I had to escape. I certainly didn't want to return to that house, not to Susan. When Ethan was there, things were good as long as we played our music, but that was only a couple of hours every night. I thought it through very carefully, and I knew I must make my story believable and be consistent. I had even watched a show about child abuse. A teen-age girl had done the same thing, accused her adoptive parents of abuse. Therefore, I followed that girl's lead and copied her every move. I was already a pretty good little actress, so I put my acting skills to work."

Sonya's eyes began to fill. She could hardly believe Brianna had carried such a heavy weight for so long.

"I went into the girl's restroom and slammed the door on my hips and legs, basically anywhere I could cause bruises. I was still sexually pure so I could not, would not, claim anything like that—besides, the thought of that was disgusting to me. But, I could make up other lies, and I did... a lot of them."

Sonya leaned forward cupping her hands together.

Brianna proceeded with the painful details. "That horrible day, ten years ago today, I went into my counselor's office sobbing. I told her the awful story I had concocted, and said I never wanted to go back home. I had no idea what I was saying. I was only following the lead of the girl at school, and the one on that television show. I thought I would be removed from Susan's home, which I believed in the long run would be best for all of us, especially Ethan."

Conrad shifted his position. He could not believe what he was hearing.

The tears were flowing freely as she told about the tale she had fabricated to the authorities. "I knew I had hurt Ethan. However, I didn't know the extent of the damage until a couple years ago when I got the courage to search for him on the Internet. I never once thought of the consequences to my actions. I never dreamed I would have destroyed Ethan's life. That's when it really began eating me up. I haven't been the same since."

Motionless, her friends listened, oblivious to the roar of the cascading water in the background. The only thing that mattered was Brianna and the words she was sharing—her painful, bitter regrets.

Glancing around the table at Conrad, Sonya, and the others, Brianna could see the disappointment written on their faces, but knew she must finish her story. "The police and child welfare people were called in, and I was taken to the hospital to be examined. They took pictures of my bruises, which I had caused that morning. The sad thing is, whatever I said, the authorities kept taking it a step further—they just kept pushing—and then things spiraled out of control. The officers believed every word I said... and a lot more. They kept putting words in my mouth. What started out as physical abuse turned into something much worse. I just nodded my head and cried. I now know that the tears were not because of a bogus beating, but because deep down I knew what I was doing to Ethan—a man who loved me unconditionally. The rest is history. I think you already know everything else."

It took a while before anyone could speak, each of the friends visibly moved.

Sonya reached for Brianna's hand and took a deep breath. "Yes, I had heard some of this. The night I talked with Ethan's lawyer, he told me that your adoptive father was innocent. He said you knew the truth. I didn't really believe him—criminals always say they're innocent. I never told anyone except Conrad. I didn't think it was my place to tell anyone else. Much of your story I've never heard before, you just filled in the missing blanks."

"You accused your father of something so horrendous just to get out of the house?" Cathy countered, shocked at the thought.

"He wasn't my father," Brianna sounded irritated by the question.

"What's the difference? You still lied. Whatever happened to the poor man?" Cathy let out a groan.

Brianna remained silent as Sonya wove her way through more details. "He was arrested, tried, and convicted—sent to prison for six years, and then he dropped out of sight."

Conrad resisted the impulse to touch Brianna's cheek and wipe away her tears. His heart broke for his despondent friend.

"I only thought I would be removed from the home and get far away from that witch."

"What happened to his family? Were there other children?" Jonathan boldly inquired.

Sonya's tone suggested the worst was yet to come. "I'm sorry to say, his wife divorced him, and he was never permitted to see his other three children again."

Brianna felt her heart racing within her, and anger overwhelmed her. "I didn't know that." The dam of tears broke again at the startling news. "I didn't mean for any of that to happen. I just thought I could get out of that house, be free, and search for my birthparents."

"What happened to him after that?" Conrad waited, barely able to stand the suspense.

Sonya knew she must come clean and reveal all she knew. There would be no more secrets! "I don't know all the details, but I heard his father died two years into Ethan's sentence, and lost everything he owned."

Brianna sobbed, "Grandpa died? He was so nice—always kind to me. Grandpa would bring me gifts from all over the world. He always treated me special, telling me that I was his little princess." She took a moment to let the news sink in. "How could he lose everything? He was worth a lot of money."

"I don't know that answer," Sonya answered truthfully.

The pain of her grandpa's death, coupled with the news about her father, was more than the broken woman could bear. Grieving, she cried, "What am I to do? How can I live with what I've done?"

Sonya, still holding her friend's hand, spoke straight from her heart. "Brianna, I've told you many times what you need to do."

"Oh no! Not that Jesus thing again!" Brianna looked doubtful.

Leaning closer to her friend, Sonya inhaled a deep, composing breath. "Yes, that Jesus thing! You know the answer; you have been through it. But in order for it to become reality, you have to put your total trust in God. He is your only hope."

Brianna sounded worn out, exhausted emotionally and physically. She pulled away from Sonya and shouted, "Then what? Does that make everything good again? Does Ethan get his life back? Do I sell another million CDs? No! Not even Jesus can fix this mess. He can't undo it. I have to pay the consequences for all of it."

As the Falls thundered in the background, silence reigned around the table.

The superstar didn't move. She didn't even seem to be breathing. She just stared at Conrad, feeling like she was caught in a trap.

Without warning, Brianna jumped up, and took off running full force, leaving her small purse and cell phone on the bench.

Sonya grabbed the purse and phone and ran after her. Conrad and the others sprinted behind, but they lost Brianna in the throng of sightseers.

"I didn't see that coming." Conrad said, as they stopped to catch their breath and regroup.

"Neither did I," Sonya replied.

"Boy, she sure can run fast," Jonathan said.

Without further delay, Conrad dished out the orders. "Okay, let's split up. That will give us a better chance to find her quickly. Bruno, you head back and wait at the table. She may remember her stuff and come back there. Jonathan, you and Cathy head in the direction we last saw her running. Sonya and I will go into the center of town. Keep in contact with your cell phone. We have to be at the concert in less than three hours."

Frantically they searched thirty minutes, unsuccessfully. It was as if she simply vanished.

"Where would she go?" Conrad faced Sonya.

"She could have caught a cab back to the house or gone to the stadium." Sonya's voice demonstrated her concern, her anxiety.

Conrad was at his best in situations like this. His instincts were keen. "Not likely... she didn't have any money with her. Just in case, you call the house and have security search the area. Meanwhile, I'll call the stadium and have the security team look for her." Quickly they made the calls.

"Where could she be?" Sonya's voice cracked with concern.

Conrad flashed a look of worry. "She was very upset; maybe she'll just walk around until her head clears. No! It just hit me—I know where she'd go."

"Where?"

"Think about it. What does she always do when she gets upset, or wants to change the subject?"

"She plays her guitar," Sonya shot back.

"Right!" Conrad stopped a man walking by. "Excuse me. Is there a music store close by?"

"Music store? Do you mean a place that sells music or instruments?"

"Instruments," Conrad answered, still slightly winded.

"Um... that would be Music Sales, USA. Two blocks down, turn left. You can't miss it." The stranger pointed in the direction of the store.

"Thank you." Conrad took off running full-speed.

Sonya sprinted closely behind the bodyguard, praying on the way. *God, please help her to be there.*

Conrad did the same thing—a quick, urgent prayer.

Within minutes, they neared the store and could see a large crowd of people milling around the entrance.

Conrad looked over the crowd, but could not see Brianna. His curiosity ended when an excited voice in the crowd shouted, "I can't believe it—Brianna Bays is in here playing with a local rock band. Awesome, man!"

The business was packed with people, and music was heard from the back of the store.

"I think we found her," Sonya said, breathing a sigh of relief. "We need to get her out of here... fast!"

With adrenaline pumping, Conrad shouted, "Sonya, call Bruno and have him pick us up out front. Get a hold of the other two and tell them to meet us at the stadium. I will get Brianna."

Conrad urgently pushed his way into the store.

"Hey mister, get in the back of the line," a voice in the crowd shouted.

"Yeah, we were here first," yelled another.

When the mouthy teenagers turned and saw the size of Brianna's personal bodyguard barreling his way through, they quickly backed down.

Continuing to push his way through the store, Conrad stopped when he saw the band. Sitting in the center was Brianna, serenely playing a guitar she had picked up—her hat and sunglasses removed.

Dozens of people crowded around her as she strummed. The mob roared with delight. Many were phoning others, reporting the events as they unfolded. Cameras and cell phones were snapping pictures. After all, who would believe that superstar Brianna Bays was at a local business, playing music with a small band?

Glancing up, Brianna noticed Conrad. Shooting him a quick smile, she continued to play the song to the end, oblivious to the danger, lost in her music.

The crowd was going wild. Some folks were trying to touch the famous star, which angered the band members. Therefore, a couple of them began shoving the fans away, which resulted in some serious pushing. Expensive store equipment and instruments were knocked over. Things were escalating out of control.

Sirens sounded in the distance. The police were on their way to break up a possible riot.

A man standing next to Conrad, shouted over the noise, "I like having her here, but this crowd is destroying my equipment."

During the craziness, Conrad stepped forward, grabbed Brianna's hand, and shouted, "We need to go. We're late!"

"Hey mister, leave her alone," a boy in the front of the crowd yelled.

"You don't have anything to say about it, kid." Conrad scowled at him. "She has a concert to perform in two hours, and it's my job to see she gets there on time."

Pulling Brianna by her hand, he forced his way through the chaotic crowd.

"Wait!" Brianna commanded, "I want to buy this guitar. It has a great sound."

Reaching into his pocket and pulling out a credit card, Conrad handed it to the man behind the register. "You work here, right?"

"You bet! I'm the owner."

"Here, this is for the guitar. Put the store damages on it, too. The card has a limit." Conrad halfway smiled.

The manager held the card up examining it, and then glanced back at the bodyguard. "Thanks... I think."

Most fans stepped out of the way in a hurry when they saw the serious look on Conrad's face. He wasn't in the mood to talk.

Speaking into his cell phone, Conrad asked, "Sonya, where are you?"

"I'm in the front... Bruno is just pulling up."

"Open the car door—we're coming out!"

Still smiling, Brianna shook the hands of a few well-wishers as her bodyguard whisked her away. She yelled back to the manager, "I'll mention your store at the concert tonight—free advertisement."

"Thanks!" The storeowner shouted, looking confused.

When the police arrived, Sonya quickly briefed them on what was going on, and asked for their help controlling the crowd for their getaway.

Just then, Conrad and Brianna came barreling out of the store. After pushing Brianna into the SUV first, the others quickly piled in. Bruno was behind the wheel.

As the vehicle sped off, Brianna laughed. "Wow! That sure was fun. Hey, listen to the sound of this guitar. I'm going to use it at the concert this afternoon."

"Young lady, don't you ever pull a stunt like that again," Sonya scolded Brianna, and sliced her with a glare.

"You could have been hurt badly," Conrad reinforced.

"Chill out. They were my fans—they treated me good. Besides, I can take care of myself—you taught me that." She batted her thick eyelashes at her concerned bodyguard.

He was not the least bit amused with her antics.

Brianna could always find comfort in her music, but lately it was different. As soon as the music stopped, her mood changed—usually to regret and guilt.

Without warning, Brianna's demeanor altered as she bounced back to reality. Her arms began quivering. Fresh tears stung her eyes. Within seconds, she buried her head in her hands weeping.

Sonya reached over and touched her shoulder gently.

Brianna collapsed into her arms. Desperate for answers, the girl cried, "What can I do? It's killing me. This feeling inside—I just can't shake it."

Sonya didn't know what to say, but Conrad did. "I have been around you for five years." His expression softened. "I have eaten with you, watched you as you slept, punched people out for you, and even taken a few hits myself. I know what I'm talking about. This way of life will not get any easier for you. You can buy anything you want. There's no limit to what you can do, or where you can go. Even though you have the world at your fingertips, you're missing the most important thing."

She wasn't prepared for the flash of fire in his eyes, or the intensely serious expression that had settled over his features. Brianna pleaded, "Why do I have this feeling of emptiness? Why am I never satisfied?"

"It has to do with trust... trust and love... and God."

Bruno and Sonya listened attentively as Conrad and Brianna had a heart-to-heart talk.

"I do trust and love."

"Yes, but not the right things. You trust and love the things of the world, but they are temporary."

"I can trust you and Sonya."

"Yes, but we're not enough. We can't fill the void in your life. Our lives are like the wind... we come and go. Jesus is the only one who remains forever."

"We're back to Jesus again. Why does it always come back to Jesus?"

"Because He is the answer. He is the beginning and the end. He will be with you forever, if you let Him. I think you know the answer, but are afraid to face it. You know how painful it will be to come to grips with your past, but if you do, you will finally be free. Free to live your life with no more regrets and sadness."

"It hurts so badly! The pain never goes away!" Her head dropped and sorrow choked off her words.

"It all has to do with forgiveness. You must meet the Forgiver before you can find forgiveness from all that has stained your life."

"How can anyone forgive me for what I've done?" Barely able to speak through intense sobbing, Brianna cried, "Ethan Anderson was the most wonderful, gentle man in the world. He was innocent of all those trumped up charges. The only crime he was guilty of was loving me as his daughter. In return, I paid him back by lying and having him sent to prison. He lost his wife, his children, his father... because of me... all because of me. I destroyed his life."

Fighting the impulse to hold her in his arms, Conrad turned to face Sonya. "She can't perform today. She's having an emotional breakdown."

"Yes, and you know how she feels about taking drugs—even to calm her nerves," Sonya responded.

Oblivious to their talk, Brianna curled up in a fetal position, crying uncontrollably in Sonya's arms.

"It's your decision, Sonya. As I see it, we have three options—home, hospital, or the concert."

"The concert is out. She's not in any condition to perform."

Brianna prided herself on the fact that she never had to cancel a show. At age twenty-two, she had performed hundreds of live concerts, and never canceled one. What about her fans who were already on the way to the stadium?

Brianna continued to cry hysterically.

Sonya's eyes looked to Conrad for an answer, but no answers blew across his hurting heart.

ELEVEN

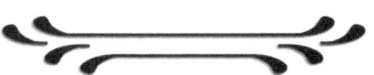

The Defining Moment

The churning inside me never stops;
Days of suffering confront me.
Job 30:27

Sonya knew that being in the high-stress entertainment industry Brianna was at an increased risk for an emotional breakdown. That, coupled with the secrets of her past, made it inevitable that a personal meltdown would occur someday. That day was here!

Brianna could run, but could no longer hide from what she had done. She had unwillingly come face-to-face with her past, which had haunted her for many years. She knew there was no way of correcting it; the damage to her loved one's lives was beyond repair. That's what made it unbearable. The horrific consequences of her lies were far worse than her darkest nightmare.

Through the years, Conrad and Sonya spoke to Brianna openly and honestly about her need for God. They knew what she had to do.

No doubt, Brianna also knew what she needed to do, but she alone had to decide if and when she would take the necessary steps.

At this moment, Brianna was in no shape to make any decisions. Still scrunched in fetal position in Sonya's arms, with tears flowing, everyone in the car felt helpless. No one knew what to do next.

The tears finally subsided and Brianna's cold eyes stared, almost in a hypnotic state, at the busy streets of Buffalo. Hordes of pedestrians were walking down the crowded sidewalks, each focusing on his or her agenda. Cars and taxis flooded the noisy streets. The broken woman stared out the window at the neon lights flashing on businesses. The stoplights turned from green to yellow to red, then back to green again.

Inside the vehicle, the superstar's life was spinning out of control—for the people outside, life continued as normal.

Suddenly, a bright, flashing light broke her trance and Brianna shot upright. "Stop the car, stop the car," she shouted.

Unsure what to do, Bruno pulled the car over. In an instant, the door flew open, and Brianna jumped out running toward the blinking sign.

"Not again," Conrad muttered as he took off running behind the woman he had grown to care deeply for. He would protect her at all costs, but this time was different. What could he do to help his dear friend? He can't protect her from herself. What could anyone do?

Conrad noticed the blinking sign in front of a block building. It simply read, "Jesus Saves."

Brianna sprinted past the sign and entered the front door of the old building. She had no idea what she was doing, operating on pure adrenaline. Instinctively, she ran down the hall into a large room, oblivious to the praise band practicing for the evening worship service.

A couple dozen young people sat in the front rows, obviously in silent prayer. They paused, looked up at the frantic woman, and then quickly resumed praying.

Stopping near the center of the auditorium, the room seemed to be spinning, and Brianna could see nothing. Blackness swirled around her. Unable to understand her actions, or feelings, she rubbed her eyes, hoping it would help her focus. What was happening?

For the last five years, she depended on Conrad and Sonya to keep her going. How could she find control for a life that had spun out of control? Brianna finally came to a startling realization—she must give full control to the only One who could truly help her.

Still unaware of anyone else in the room, Brianna closed her eyes and began to spin around, crying out to God Almighty. "God, why? Why?" Falling to her knees in the middle of the aisle, her eyes finally focused, and immediately fixed on a wooden cross hanging on the wall behind the altar.

While a few in the group continued to pray, most were staring at this woman's bizarre behavior.

One of the band members asked, "Isn't that Brianna Bays? I know she's doing a concert this afternoon at the football stadium."

Conrad and Sonya ran in and knelt beside Brianna, hoping to bring some comfort to their confused friend.

"Why? Why?" That was the only word that poured from Brianna's trembling lips.

Sonya knew it was a moment of emotional and spiritual crisis. She leaned close and spoke straight from her heart. "Let it go, Brianna. Let it all go. Give it to God! You have shut Him out of your life for too long.

Talk to Him, that's all He asks. He is there for you. He is the help you desperately need!"

It took a while, but Brianna finally regained her composure. Standing, she noticed the people around her, all at a loss for words.

Embarrassed, she looked up and noticed a tall, nice looking young man holding a guitar. "May I help you?" The man smiled and handed his guitar to one of the band members. He stepped off the platform and neared Brianna. "I'm Jeremiah, the worship pastor here."

Unable to speak, Brianna stood motionless for a time. Finally, she slowly meandered past Jeremiah and stepped up to the altar.

All the people in the room were bewildered at the strange happenings.

Brianna turned full-circle. She stopped and stared at the large cross. The cross was the focal point of the church—why was the Christ of the cross not the focal point of her life? Was it time to give God control and make Him the center of her life?

Falling on her knees at the altar, she sobbed uncontrollably. Pent-up tears of pain, regret, guilt, and sorrow flooded her soul.

Conrad and Sonya knelt beside her, one on each side, protectively putting their arms around her.

Jeremiah motioned for the band members to pray. They immediately formed a prayer circle around her. Before long, the altar was packed. None of them knew the details. They just knew that God was working in the life of this young woman, and they needed to intercede for her.

"Brianna," Conrad whispered, "Just let it go. Talk to Jesus."

One more time, through her tears, Brianna eyed the cross. "I don't know what to say."

"Just say what's on your heart." Jeremiah's tone was kind, warm, and understanding. His face showed a look of genuine concern.

A little girl with blonde curls walked up to Brianna and handed her a box of tissues. Forging a small smile, Brianna thanked her.

Brianna turned and looked directly into the pastor's eyes. "I spent six years in church. Ethan taught me all about Jesus. I heard about what He can do in my life. It's only now I'm beginning to understand it." She looked at Conrad, and then at Pastor Jeremiah. "Why is that? Why has it taken so long for me to see the truth?"

Seeing the doubt and sadness in her eyes, the pastor spoke. "The Holy Spirit prepares a person's heart in His time. However, ultimately the decision is yours. Perhaps you weren't ready, maybe you didn't understand. Possibly, you have been shutting God out because you knew the pain you would have to come to grips with. God gave us the privilege of choice. We can choose to keep Jesus out of our lives or let Him in." The look on his face and the light in Jeremiah's eyes were an outward expression of his warm, caring heart.

Brianna sniffled.

Pastor Jeremiah shared his story. "I was a drug addict for eight years. I came from a Christian home, but rejected Jesus. It took my parents' death in a car accident to break my will so I could see the truth. Like you, I had to hit rock bottom. The accident could have turned me further from God. In fact, in the beginning it did. I knew I needed God in my life. Only when I got honest with Him, and did what you are doing now, did the change begin. A peace came to my heart. He carried me through the pain and anguish of losing my family. Although, I did battle with guilt and regret over the pain I caused my parents. But God had the victory, and here I am today... singing for Jesus, and preaching in His name."

The pastor's testimony helped her gain a better understanding; even though the details were different, the solution was the same.

Brianna tilted her head, trying to grasp it all. "Do you think there would be forgiveness in your parents' hearts if they were alive today?"

Without hesitation the pastor spoke, "Beyond a doubt. They were my parents and they loved me, no matter what I did. They forgave me, even though I'm sure they were disappointed with some of my bad choices."

Jeremiah looked at the cross. "He died for you and me on the cross. John 3:16 tells us that God gave his Son to save the world. He did it because He loves us unconditionally. And you know what?" He turned and faced Brianna as she wiped her tears. "He did it willingly. What a loving God we have!" The pastor turned his gaze back to the cross.

"But what I did was unforgivable." She lowered her head.

"Nothing is too big for God's forgiveness."

"You don't understand. I have hurt, no, destroyed, so many people. Even if God forgave me, they could never forgive me." Brianna's voice cracked.

"We are to go to those we have wronged and ask for forgiveness. Even if they do not accept it, we did our part. As far as Jesus is concerned, He will forgive anything. He forgives us, and we forgive others."

"What do I do?"

"Do you mean concerning your obedience to Christ and His forgiveness, or asking forgiveness from those you have hurt?"

She thought for a second. "Are they not one and the same?"

Jeremiah gave her a weak smile and gently took her hand. "In a way yes, asking for forgiveness is obedience. Forgiveness is not only for you, but also for those you have wronged. If there is hurt, there needs to be forgiveness. Forgiveness from Christ has already been provided over two thousand years ago on a cross on Calvary. Because God forgives the inexcusable in us, it is our duty to forgive others. The first step, however, is to confess our sins and ask for God's forgiveness."

Pondering his words, Brianna noticed that the people surrounding her were still praying—not staring at her, or judging her. She realized with certainty, she was ready for a change—a heart change. "Pastor, show me the way, please."

Jeremiah put his arm around her. Together they bowed their heads.

Teary-eyed, Conrad and Sonya embraced her from the other side.

The pastor prayed, not wasting any words. *Lord, we thank You for Your love and wisdom, and above all, for Your grace and forgiveness. Lord, help this woman who desperately needs to find her way back to You. We ask You to show her the way to true happiness, true freedom. Father, she is hurting so much from something in her past. Lord, You know what it is. You know what she must do in the future to accept it, and if possible, correct it. Give her strength to do what is right in Your eyes. We ask this in Christ's holy name. Amen.*

Brianna's prayer followed. It was simple. *God, I don't deserve forgiveness for what I have done, yet, You offer it. Father, I confess my sins. For all the terrible things I have done, and all the people I have hurt, please forgive me. God, I want to make You the center of my life. I want to serve You. Give me the strength and wisdom to do what I have to do. In the name of Jesus, Amen.*

She stayed kneeling, basking in His glory.

The people at the altar continued to pray, many wept.

Finally, she stood. The same little girl walked over to her again, pulled out a few tissues, and handed them to Brianna.

"Thank you, Honey," Brianna responded to the kind gesture.

Silence settled over them for a moment.

Sonya eventually spoke. "Brianna, how do you feel?"

The well-known singer realized that the weight on her shoulders was gone. "I feel... I feel free! Sonya, I know what I have to do. God revealed it to me. I must right the wrongs in my life, so I can continue to live like God wants me to live." She looked around, then straight into Jeremiah's misty eyes, "To live for Christ."

"What happens if those wrongs can't be corrected?" Conrad asked.

She thought for a second. "I have no control over other people's actions. I only know what I must do. If it is not accepted, then I have done all that was asked."

"Right," Pastor Jeremiah agreed. "Jesus wants your obedience. In 1 John 1:9 it states, *He is faithful and just to forgive.* Luke 6:37 says,

Forgive and you will be forgiven. He did not say forgive and you *may* be forgiven, He said you *will* be forgiven. The enemy will continuously attack you with feelings of guilt, trying to steal your joy. Don't ever forget that no matter what you did, you are forgiven. However, that is not to say there won't be grave consequences to your past sins. You will have to face them head on."

She reached for a nearby guitar. "May I?"

"Sure, we would be honored." The Pastor smiled.

Brianna picked up the guitar. "I find music eases my soul. Ethan... my father, said I have the talent to make music by the way I feel, which reminds me of a certain song."

Sonya was surprised by her comment because she had never heard her refer to Ethan as her father, only her adoptive father. She was glad he was getting the respect he deserved.

Brianna began strumming the guitar and then broke out into a song, which had been one of her first hits. Ironically, it was called, *The Truth.* The ballad reflected a past love she once had.

The band members and the rest of the crowd joined her. When the song was finished, they looked at each other in awe.

Brianna commented. "Wow! I never realized the power in the words of that song. The message sure fits today."

Sonya grinned. "Brianna, all your songs are like that. They are songs of love, searching, looking for that one special relationship. It's almost as if you have been subconsciously writing music about yourself and your experiences. The reason those lyrics touched your fans is because they can put themselves in the same place in their own lives."

Sonya inched closer. "Brianna, we have to go. I don't think you are in the state of mind to perform this afternoon, so I think we need to cancel your concert."

Brianna shook her head decisively. "If ever there was a time to perform, it's now." She asked Conrad, "How long before my press conference?"

"Um... twenty minutes," he said, glancing at his watch.

Brianna acknowledged with certainty. "We can make it!"

She faced Pastor Jeremiah. "I've always loved that song. It fits all relationships, but especially the one I entered today with Jesus. I have never had a close relationship with a man. Oh, I've had plenty of men, but not the way I should have. I've known about Jesus, but always fought Him coming into my life. Now that He is, I know that I should have made Him Lord of my life years ago. I also realize that I must right the wrongs that I have done..." she paused, "...and apologize to those whose lives I've destroyed."

She held out her hand to Jeremiah. "Thank you for your wisdom and your help. You have a great church here."

"Thank you," he said taking her hand and cupping it with the other. "Please come back."

"I'll do that," she smiled and turned to go.

When she reached the door, she turned one more time to view the cross. Brianna's heart thudded hard in her chest. Somehow, she knew her life would never be the same. She was restored to her Heavenly Father. Softly, she uttered a prayer... *I will do whatever You ask of me. I won't let You down, Lord... not this time.*

TWELVE

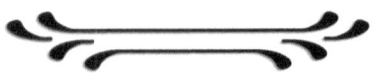

The Radical Change

My heart says of you, "Seek his face!"
Your face, LORD, I will seek
Psalm 27:8

The day wasn't going the way Brianna anticipated it would when she woke up that morning. She felt like a new person, alive, with a renewed sense of hope, and an indescribable peace. Her heart felt like it might explode with joy, and she could not wait to share the news with others.

Conrad and Sonya had never seen such radiance on Brianna's face. The transformation from darkness to light in a matter of hours was an answer to their persistent prayers. God had come through, in His timing, and His perfect way. Why did they ever doubt Him?

They sped to the press conference. As Sonya applied Brianna's makeup, she asked the singer what she planned to tell her fans.

"I don't know what I'll say. I guess I'll let the Lord speak through me."

Sonya shook her head and tried to comment, but she couldn't. Feeling extremely grateful that God answered her prayers for Brianna, a rush of peace swept over her. Of course, God would give her the words to speak.

Arriving a few minutes late, eager fans and photographers were already waiting to welcome the mega-star to their city, and hear what she had to say. They hoped she would announce the release of a new CD, or motion picture she was going to star in.

She strode toward the microphone, shaking hands with her admirers as she worked her way through the crowd. She always tried to be in reach of her fans. At the same time, her bodyguards never left her side. When she reached the microphone, she paused for a moment. She was at a loss for words, a rare occurrence for the star who was a natural among her fans.

The crowd hushed, waiting anxiously.

Finally, a shout broke the silence. "When's your new CD coming out?"

She smiled, looking into the vast sea of young people. "In about three weeks."

A reporter piped up, "Which is your favorite song on the new CD?"

"They are all my favorites! That's why I wrote them." She laughed.

The media had grown to love her wit and charm.

"Is there one that stands out among the others?"

"I would have to say the first and last songs. The CD begins somewhat in a fantasy world, but the last one ends in total reality." Brianna paused again, searching her mind for the right words. "Much like real life."

A different reporter inquired, "What was your motivation behind this project?"

"My first reason was to give my fans more music—something different, uplifting, and refreshing." She envisioned what just happened in the church. She was still in the fresh afterglow of her rendezvous with God, and a smile lit up her face.

A familiar-looking reporter asked, "I understand that the CD is a one-of-a-kind combination, and the recording industry is predicting this is going to be your best-selling CD, possibly the biggest selling CD of all time. Why is that?"

"I think it's because of the powerful message behind it. The double-disc collection consists of twenty-one songs and is almost a story. Although it did not start out that way—the more I wrote, the more personal it became. The result was me facing the reality of my own life. I guess that's what makes it unique. It is real life—everyone's life." She hesitated for a moment and then repeated herself. "Everyone's life... no matter who you are... rich or poor, black or white, Muslim or Christian." Brianna's voice faded, reflecting on a different time and place.

A journalist she couldn't see voiced the next question. "You said, first it was to give your fans a new CD, obviously, there must be a second reason. What is it?"

There was absolute silence as Brianna reached for something profound to say—she could think of nothing witty, just the truth.

After all the crying she had done that day, you would think no tears remained, but her eyes began to well up. "It's interesting that the last song on the CD relates to what happened in my life about an hour ago. You see, I was on a collision course with my past. I have done things that I am ashamed of. There are people I have hurt deeply. Today I realized I needed to come face to face with my past—no more running! There are people I need go to and ask for forgiveness."

"It sounds like you found religion or something." An unknown voice caught her attention.

A sincere smile came to her face. "No, not religion... I found Jesus."

Murmurings and distinct laughter were heard in the audience, but Brianna was unscathed by it.

On the sidelines, Sonya pointed to her watch, indicating the need to wrap things up.

"My manager just signaled that I need to get ready for a concert."

The crowd went wild.

"Thank you for coming. I hope you enjoy the new CD. It will be in music stores in about three weeks. I'll be kicking it off with a live concert, followed by a nationwide tour."

"I thought the tour didn't begin until next year?" Someone in the crowd shouted.

"Today my plans changed. In fact, my manager does not even know about the change. I decided the tour would begin immediately. This is something I need to do. And I want to visit the troops in the Middle East again. Thank you." She turned to walk away, and then quickly returned to the microphone. "God bless you all!"

She hurried off with her bodyguards surrounding her.

As soon as she entered the dressing room to prepare for the concert, Sonya began bombarding her with questions. "What was that all about? You know we don't have a concert tour planned until next year. What's going on?" Although Sonya was surprised at the announcement, the air between them was easy, it always was.

Brianna's eyebrows lifted. "Well, we do now. Today our plans changed. I have some things I need to do, and people I must see. I need you to do me a big favor."

"What would that be?" Sonya sighed.

"I'm going to right some wrongs in my past, which means you will have to do some traveling to find the answers I need. As for the concerts, get a list of major cities throughout America, Canada, and Mexico. Set up dates, and get all the preliminary arrangements started. I will put Conrad in charge while you're gone. I'll explain more later. Right now, I have a concert to perform."

"Are you sure you're okay?"

The star threw her arms around Sonya. "I have never been better. I finally have seen the light, and I know what I must do."

Brianna shot a smile at Conrad. "Thanks to you two, and the fact that you never gave up on me." She released her grip on Sonya, walked over to Conrad, and gave him a kiss on the cheek.

Conrad's heartbeat was anything but normal, yet he forced himself to focus on the job at hand—protecting Brianna Bays, superstar.

The concert was astounding with nearly one hundred thousand exuberant fans.

True to her word, Brianna showed off her new guitar, and gave a plug for the music store she had visited earlier.

After the last number, the energized fans burst into a lengthy applause for an encore, longing for their young idol to perform one more hit. The crowd cheered when the band returned to the stage. Brianna returned in a different glamorous outfit, with vigor and excitement, to give her fans what they wanted... more! One of the ways she pleased her fans was with several wardrobe changes during a concert—this performance, she had seven.

A stagehand brought her old guitar to her—the instrument Ethan gave her years ago had fresh significance today. "I would like to conclude with the last song on my new CD. This is the first time I have performed it in public. Call it a sneak preview of my next tour, which will begin in a couple weeks. I just asked my band if they would be willing to begin a tour immediately, and they all agreed enthusiastically." She looked back and smiled at her band members. "I will be calling it my 'Redemption Tour.'"

As the sun set behind her, hues of orange, crimson, and yellow, she acknowledged the beauty, which only God could create. It was the perfect backdrop for an incredible day.

Brianna shared openly with her fans in a way she had never done before. "Just a few hours before this concert, my life was spiraling out of control. Haunted by my past, I could not move forward. I was on the verge of a breakdown. My manager almost called off the concert today, and was ready to admit me to the hospital. No, I wasn't high on drugs. I have always talked against drugs, alcohol, and tobacco, and I always will. I guess I could say I was low on life itself. Suicide has one of the highest death rates among our youth today. I was not suicidal, but many in my predicament are. You see, I have a very private past... a dark past. Few people know anything about who I really am, or where I came from. In the coming days, I will be revealing more about my life. By doing so, I hope to help others who feel like I did earlier today."

The audience listened intently.

"Hours ago, I lay in my manager's arms weeping like a baby. I was at the end of my rope—physically and emotionally exhausted. I've always found comfort in my music. I guess you could call my music my drug of choice. However, when I stopped singing, stopped the music, the pain and emptiness engulfed me. My life had become futile in spite of all my successes as a performer."

She continued, "This afternoon, in the depths of my despair, a flashing light caught my eye. It said, 'Jesus Saves.' Why did it attract my attention? I would say it was providential. What I did next was pure instinct. I jumped out of the car and ran into an old church building. As I stood in the auditorium, I noticed a large cross. The world seemed to be spinning around and it always came back to that cross. Suddenly, I knew what I had to do. I fell to the floor at the altar and poured out my heart to God."

There was complete silence in the stadium.

Brianna looked at Conrad, Sonya, and her other friends for support. Conrad gave her a confident nod, encouraging her to go on.

"As a nine-year-old girl I gave my life to Jesus, but somewhere along the path I became a wayward seed. No longer will I be. I intend to be a blossom in a world of weeds, and I am starting here. I realize there are many things in my past, which I must confront. I have to come face-to-face with them. My past is not going to run my life any longer... Jesus Christ is."

She took a swig of water. "This last song will be a preview of my next CD and my next tour. I pray for each of you here today because I know many of you are facing your own demons, addictions, or secrets, which are weighing you down. Possibly, you do not even realize it. For some, it maybe bondage to drugs or alcohol. You may be in an inappropriate relationship. Perhaps you have hurt people in your past, and guilt and regret are consuming you. All of these lead down the path of destruction. With this song, I pray you will come to terms with things in your life, which either already have or will bring you to the point of brokenness. There is only one way to victory, and that is to have a personal relationship with Jesus Christ."

There was sporadic applause that grew into a rumble as she began the song. At first the band didn't play. It was just her and the guitar—exactly how she began five years before. Halfway through, the band joined in as she performed the vocal performance of her career.

Brianna believed God wanted her to share her story. She was aware that all people have baggage in their lives, and she firmly believed that Jesus was the answer for them, also. What an opportunity, her first opportunity, to tell her fans in suburban Buffalo about the saving grace of Jesus.

When the concert was over, she raised the special guitar into the air as she received a thunderous standing ovation. She waved to her fans before rushing off-stage with Conrad and the other bodyguards.

Sonya handed her a towel as she quickly raced by. "The dressing room is this way."

"I don't have time for the dressing room," she said, grabbing Conrad's hand, and dragging him towards the back door.

"Where are you going?" Sonya asked.

"Going? We're going to church—they have a Saturday night praise service."

"Church?" A confused Bruno inquired, "Church? Why church?"

Brianna faced Conrad, "Let's go to church!" She burst out laughing.

A chill ran up Conrad's spine. "Yes, let's do it. Come on Bruno, you don't want to miss this."

Bruno stood there scratching his head, watching Jonathan and Cathy enter the limo.

"Have the driver go to the church we were at this afternoon," Brianna said excitedly to Conrad.

He acknowledged her request and instructed the driver where to go.

"Well, I'm going, too." Bruno shouted, getting into the front seat with the driver.

As they settled into the seats of the spacious limo, Brianna spoke. "Sonya, I have a job for you... it will take a lot of time and money. As I said before, Conrad can take over managing for a while. However, you're the only one I trust with this task."

"What do you want me to do?" Sonya asked curiously.

"I need you to find my real parents... and I need you to locate Ethan Anderson."

"Well, Ethan Anderson will be simple to locate, but as for your parents... any idea where to start?"

"Kuwait. Start at the orphanage in Kuwait." Brianna stared off into space, clearly lost in the past.

"That was sixteen years ago. You think they will have records that far back?" Sonya sounded somewhat doubtful.

"You'll find a way. I told you, all my money is at your disposal; I have noticed money can buy almost anything you want. I'm just asking for what is rightfully mine—my real name and the whereabouts of my biological parents."

Brianna watched out the windows. Daylight had disappeared and was replaced by the lights of the city.

Soon she saw the familiar flashing "Jesus Saves" sign. The service was already in progress when the limo pulled up.

Stepping out of the vehicle, Brianna turned to face her bodyguards. "You won't be needed here... unless you plan on worshipping with me." She grinned.

Nothing more was said. They all knew better than to question Brianna when she was determined to do something.

After they climbed out of the vehicle, Conrad shot a big smile at Sonya, giving her the thumbs-up sign. He softly whispered, "Yes!"

Sonya instantly knew what he meant. God had answered their prayers! Both of them had waited for this day, the day that Brianna would come to grips with her past, so she could move on to a new life. What a day it had been! And to end it in worship at a local church—how could it get any better? Sonya's heart swelled and a smile lit up her entire face.

She already noticed a difference in Brianna; she possessed boldness, and had a burning desire to share her joy. No doubt her life would change tremendously!

The group quietly entered the church. The auditorium was full, probably about three hundred people. It was obvious this old church building had grown beyond its capacity. A few people looked back and noticed who had entered. The news spread fast! Within seconds, the entire church knew the famous Brianna Bays was in their service.

They walked up the aisle looking for a seat. The congregation was standing in worship, many raising hands in praise. The song ended when they were mid-way up the aisle.

Pastor Jeremiah noticed them. "Hello," he said. "There are plenty of seats up here. Come on up. Young lady, we have a place especially for you."

Brianna, Sonya, and Conrad walked to the second row where there were available seats.

The entertainer began to sit, but the Pastor called to her. "No, I mean up here." He offered his guitar to her.

Brianna glanced around the crowded room and then back at Jeremiah. "I'm sorry, but I don't really know the music you're doing."

"Yes, you do. You always have. Much of the music we do is actually yours."

"Mine? Why would you use my music to honor Jesus?"

"Think about it. The lyrics are the message. Many people can make a tune, but few can put words together to bring a truth that warms the heart, like you did in *My Father's Love*."

Almost as if the two of them were alone in the room, the dialog continued.

"That was a song saying how much I miss my father and his love. You know, *I'm searching for him. I need his love. I want his love.*"

"That's right. Now, think of it in terms of your Heavenly Father."

She blinked and a chill ran down her arms. "I never thought of it that way. But, you're right. You're telling me that my music signifies that not only have I been searching for my earthly father, but my Heavenly Father, too."

"Isn't it obvious?" Jeremiah smiled.

Unable to speak, she returned the smile, nodding her head.

He held out the guitar. "Come... and sing to your Heavenly Father."

Brianna noticed the room full of people were encouraging her through kind faces and warm smiles.

What happened next was much more than a coincidence. Brianna would never forget the special moment. Standing in the aisle next to her was the same girl who had given her the tissues hours before—the sweet child with the bright green eyes, blonde curly hair, and huge smile. Her hands were clasped together as if she was praying. Brianna saw the girl bring her hands below her chin and mouth the word, "Please."

The star tilted her head and smiled at the child, wondering how she could refuse her.

It began as a single clap. Within seconds, everyone in the church had begun applauding, including Sonya, and Conrad. By then, Bruno, Jonathan, and Cathy had joined them for the service and were clapping also.

Brianna approached the pastor, graciously accepting his guitar. She started quietly strumming a few chords, but within seconds, the full band joined her.

Pastor Jeremiah picked up the microphone. "Okay... let's worship!"

She was composed, self-assured, presenting the music in a way that everyone took notice. They were songs she had written, which many churches were now using as worship music. As always, her voice was amazing, beautiful, and full. However, this time was different. Closing her eyes, she worshipped in a way that was new to her. The message was clear—it was all about Jesus!

When the music segment was over, Brianna shook hands with the members of the band, hugged a couple of them, and then sat next to Conrad. Unexpectedly, Brianna gently took her hand and placed it on Conrad's hand. Her handsome bodyguard looked at her, and she faced him. As their eyes locked, her deep blue eyes showed something he had never seen in her before—hope! He squeezed her hand.

All sat motionless as Jeremiah began his sermon. "I had a message planned for tonight—a message on redemption. Jesus Christ's precious blood obtained our release from sin—He redeemed us. However, moments ago, God revealed to me that He wanted me to speak on forgiveness instead, something which goes hand-in-hand with redemption. Yes, the blood of Christ redeems us, but that wonderful gift also includes forgiveness and restoration."

He looked over the full congregation. "I had the honor of talking with a young woman today about this subject."

Brianna smiled at him.

"Do you have a situation where forgiveness seems impossible? If you do, then ask yourself, am I willing to be forgiven my offenses, but not willing to forgive someone who has wronged me? You see, forgiveness works both ways—giving and extending."

Many in the congregation nodded, understanding what he meant.

"The woman wondered what to do if you ask for forgiveness, and the person refuses to forgive you? The only thing you can have control over is your own actions."

There were a number of hearty "Amens."

"Recently, I read an article about a man who had savagely murdered two young girls. I know the inside story of this tragic event. A pastor friend of mine led this young man to Christ in prison. The prisoner admitted his guilt and asked forgiveness for his horrible actions. God forgave him, but there still were consequences. Society would not, could not, forget the heinous crime he committed. The guilt consumed him. He could not forgive himself. At the coaching of my pastor friend, the prisoner wrote a letter to the families of the two young victims. There were two daughters, who would never graduate from high school, never know the love of a husband, or never be able to hold their newborn baby. The man's sole intention was to ask for forgiveness."

Sniffles rippled sporadically through the congregation.

"I asked my friend how they responded. He told me that one of the girls came from a deeply spiritual family and the other did not. The mother from the non-religious home wrote a bitter note to the young man. It ended with these few words of hatred, 'I look forward to watching you die.'"

The entire congregation sat spellbound.

"The other response was quite different. The parents were Christians. The mother took time to write a three-page neatly handwritten letter. She shared things she did with her little girl—baking, shopping, and concerts. Sometimes they would stay up late at night watching romantic comedies and eating popcorn."

Pastor Jeremiah unfolded a piece of paper and began reading the last part of the letter. "I can never do any of these things again with my little girl because of what you did. You asked me to forgive you. I reflected on Calvary, when a man called Jesus hung on a cross for my sins. When I confessed my sins to Him, they were forgiven—no questions asked. Can I do any less with you? No! I must forgive you. Actually, I already have. If I hadn't, bitterness would have destroyed me. However, it does not mean I have forgotten. I can never forget the phone call I received the night she went missing. I can't forget the night the police stood at my door, with their heads held low, dreading to tell me the horrific news of my child's inexcusable murder. I will never forget the memory of her funeral. And I cannot, will not, ever forget the special times we had together. Yes, I forgive you. For the sake of my little Jessica, I do forgive you. But sin has consequences, repercussions, and I am not the final judge."

Jeremiah's voice cracked. He paused, trying to keep his emotions under control. "There were two mothers whose young daughters were murdered by this man. There were two decisions with very different results. The one who was unwilling to forgive will have a lifetime of bitterness, which will spread to everyone around her. While the one who has forgiven, can, and will continue with her life. There was nothing the killer could do to make things right. What he did was clearly wrong, and he paid the price for it. Just a few months ago, he paid the penalty and was put to death in the electric chair."

Pastor Jeremiah continued. "Jesus commands us to forgive. Forgiveness should be a part of our daily life, but it cannot erase the past. There are still repercussions from our bad choices. You can't change what has happened, but you can put the past behind you, begin a new life, and grow from the painful times. Life is full of learning experiences. Unfortunately, some are more difficult to get past than others. You cannot fix your life yourself. Jesus Christ is the only way to full forgiveness. So be careful what you say and do. Be prepared not only to ask for forgiveness, but also to grant forgiveness to those who ask it of you. We have a sinful nature, but Jesus died on a cross over two-thousand years ago. He took all our sins and provided forgiveness for us—for you, and you, and you." He pointed to random people in the congregation. "All we have to do is ask... He is faithful to forgive. Praise God!"

Pastor Jeremiah bowed his head. "Let's pray." *Lord, thank You for the cross, for the forgiveness, which You provided through Your agonizing death on the cross. We acknowledge the cross was real, Your suffering was real, and Your death was real. Likewise, our sin is real, but because of*

Your death and resurrection, You provided the way of forgiveness. Thank you! Amen.

Pastor Jeremiah smiled. "Let's remember these truths as we go into the world and face real pain. And the next time someone cuts you off in traffic, smile at him. Go that extra mile in everything you do. Remember to forgive and accept forgiveness."

The pastor continued with his closing remarks. "Thank you for coming tonight and worshiping with us. I would like to invite anyone who has questions about what I have said, or would like to know more about a personal relationship with Jesus to come talk with me, or a staff member. Have a blessed evening. And don't forget about tomorrow morning's service."

Pastor Jeremiah stepped down to greet the guests. He made his way to Brianna and extended his hand.

In return, she grabbed him around his neck, and warmly hugged him. "Thank you," she said. "Thank you for that message. It is near to my heart."

Brianna noticed dozens of people standing around her. She smiled, and greeted each of her fans, often signing autographs.

Sonya stepped beside Jeremiah, and together they watched the star interacting with her fans.

"She seems to sincerely care about her fans." Jeremiah grinned.

"Oh, she does. She's the most giving entertainer I've ever met."

Jeremiah's expression changed. "I spent a couple years in Egypt and got to know the people very well. If it wasn't for those deep blue eyes, I'd say she is of Arab descent."

"Yes, she is."

"Where did she get those blue eyes?"

"I would suspect her father."

"I don't know a lot about her life—only her music. I would like to know her story sometime. I think it would be fascinating." Jeremiah kept his tone upbeat, warm.

"So would I. She has locked her past inside her. Now, hopefully she may be able to release it."

Their eyes watched her as she knelt down and hugged the little girl who coaxed her into singing. "What's your name, pretty girl?" Brianna asked.

"Amanda," she answered, giving the star a crooked, shy grin.

Brianna looked up at a young couple standing close by. "Is this your mommy and daddy?"

The child glanced at them. "I think they are... for now. I've had a lot of mommies and daddies."

Brianna's heart dropped. She felt an instant kinship with the girl, because she too had many mommies and daddies by that age. For a moment, the entertainer held her breath, unable to speak. She again pulled the little girl close to her, holding her tight.

"She's been in a lot of foster homes. We're thinking of adopting her," the foster mother said, noticeably moved.

"Please don't just think about it. Do it! Her life is wasting. This sweet girl needs good parents," Brianna pleaded.

"But it costs so much, and we can't really afford it right now." The young woman choked back tears.

The husband put his arm around his wife's shoulders in a show of support.

Brianna spoke to the young girl again, "Do you see that strong, good-looking man over there?" She pointed to Conrad.

"Yes."

"I want you to tell him who you are. Give him your name and address. Tell him I am going to send you something."

"Your new CD?" Amanda said, a huge smile spreading across her face.

"Yes, my new CD, and a few other things. But I need you to pay me."

"I don't have any money." The girl frowned.

"All I want is another big hug."

The little girl giggled. "I have lots of those." She swung her arms around Brianna's neck, and held her tight, not wanting the moment to end. Neither did Brianna.

Finally, the two backed apart. "Now, go and tell Mr. Conrad your name and address."

They all watched the little bundle of energy run over to Conrad. He lowered to his knees. Listening to what the little girl had to say, he took out a pad and pen and wrote down the information.

Brianna inched closer to the foster parents.

"She's going to love that CD." The foster mom was still trying to fight the tears.

Jeremiah came close and officially introduced the couple to Brianna. "This is Toby and Sheila Newman. Toby plays the drums, and Sheila sings with us. Unfortunately, Toby lost his job a few weeks back. The company closed its doors after fifty years of operation."

Brianna searched the young couple's eyes. "Will you make good parents for Amanda?"

"Good parents," Jeremiah stepped in. "These are two of the best people I've ever met. Yes, they would make great parents! However, it costs so much to adopt with court costs and lawyer fees. All the preliminary things are complete, but unfortunately, it's tied up in the courts. Since Toby lost his job, everything is in limbo."

"She's a sweet girl. Take care of her. Show her your love every day."

Meanwhile, Conrad and Amanda had hit it off. Conrad had lifted her up with his strong arms, and was holding her, teasing her. Both of them were laughing.

Brianna couldn't help but smile at the scene.

The foster parents and Brianna resumed their conversation. "I am going to send you a few gifts. Accept them with my love. Use them to take care of that little girl. Promise me that."

The young couple looked blankly at each other and then back at Brianna. "We promise."

As the fellowship began to wind down, Sonya told Brianna it was time to leave. With an early flight in the morning, she needed to get some shuteye. Brianna said good-bye to Amanda and her newfound Christian friends.

Before she left, Brianna took Jeremiah aside. "Pastor, Sonya is going to write you a check. I can never repay you, or this church, for what you did for me."

"It wasn't me or the church. It was Jesus." He smiled.

"I know, but if that blinking sign wasn't there, or you would not have been available, there is no telling what would have happened to me. I would like you to take the gift and use it to build the church. Please help needy families in this church and community."

Sonya handed Jeremiah a check.

The young preacher looked at the amount on the check, and couldn't speak. Tears filled his eyes. With his voice breathy, beyond excited, he managed to get out a few words. "That's um... um... that's a lot of money. Are you sure about this?"

"When I was eight, I remember my father telling me I should give at least ten percent of what I earned back to God. I'm pretty far behind right now, so this is a start. I know you will put it to good use."

He looked at the singer and said with a gleaming smile, "Thank you! God bless you, Brianna."

"Oh, there is one more thing," Brianna added. "You'll be getting a package in a couple weeks. When you open it... you'll know what to do with it."

Jeremiah held out his hand to thank her. Brianna again ignored the hand and went for a hug.

The pastor was grateful and couldn't speak.

Brianna and her friends walked to the door. The star looked back to view the church one more time. She stared again at the cross. She would never forget Pastor Jeremiah, this church, or this day.

The next few months would be busy for Brianna and her staff.

Within a couple days, Sonya would soon begin the seemingly impossible task of trying to locate Brianna's birth parents. Little did she know, she would be gone for almost seven months.

Conrad would have his hands full managing, as well as protecting, Brianna on her concert tour. It was a tour to promote her newest CD. It would take her to over one hundred cities, and she would entertain over five million fans.

A couple weeks after Brianna visited Jeremiah's church, he received a package to give to Amanda and her foster parents. Inside was not one CD, but an entire collection of Brianna's music.

Also in the package, were three tickets to Disney World for Amanda, Toby, and Sheila. The family would stay at one of Disney's five-star resorts with all expenses paid. To top it off, they would be the guests of honor at one of Brianna's three concerts that she would be performing at the famous theme park.

Yet the biggest surprise, the most meaningful gift of all, came in a large manila envelope. Inside were the final documents stating that Amanda was legally Toby and Sheila's daughter. Brianna had petitioned the judge, who made it happen quickly. The adoption was final!

Brianna also contacted the music store she played at that day, and secured a job for Toby as assistant manager of the store.

The star never knew she could find such peace and contentment. Her life had taken on new meaning.

Brianna's *Quest for Forgiveness* had begun.

THIRTEEN

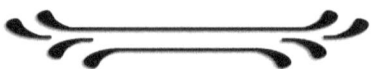

The Time for Decisions

See! The winter is past; the rains are over and gone.
Song of Solomon 2:11

"Brianna, can you hear me? Brianna!"

The entertainer opened her eyes, finally snapping out of the deep trance she appeared to be in. Remembering her past and her dramatic conversion had drawn her away from the discussion with Sonya.

"I was worried about you. Did you doze off, or were you daydreaming? You were really out of it," Sonya said, her voice expressing concern.

Dazed, Brianna glanced around the room, trying to collect her bearings. She realized she was still in her dressing room after the concert. The memories of the past had overcome her. She tried to clear her head, wondering how much time had elapsed. Looking at the clock, she realized only minutes had passed.

She looked at her friend Sonya in the mirror, and realized how much she had missed her the past seven months.

"Are you okay?" Sonya asked.

"Okay... um... yeah, I think so. It was strange. I don't know if it was a dream or what. It was like a flashback." She shook her head. "I relived the lies I told, the people I hurt. Sonya, how can I ever fix it all?"

"As your lawyer, I would recommend you say and do nothing."

"As my lawyer?" Brianna crossed her arms.

"Yes."

"How about as my friend—my Christian friend?"

"As your Christian friend, I believe the only thing you can do is the right thing. You must own up to your past. You were only twelve... that will be in your favor."

"I'm not concerned about me. What can I do about those I have hurt?"

182

"Remember what Pastor Jeremiah told you. You can't make the consequences go away. All you can do is ask for forgiveness... God will take care of the rest. If the one you have wronged forgives you, great, then you have gained a friend. If he or she chooses not to, you know Jesus will stand by you. That's all you can do."

Brianna looked straight into Sonya's eyes. "Because of the information you have brought me, I have changed my mind about what I will be doing in Iraq."

"You mean on our Freedom Tour for the troops?" Sonya raised a questioning eyebrow.

"Yes. I also want to visit my mother's family. Please make the necessary arrangements with the authorities, but don't let anyone know what my intensions are. Who I am, or I should say was, must remain a secret. One more thing, I want to visit my mother's grave."

Sonya continued making notes for herself. "Because of the information we have learned about who you are, you will need extra protection. I will contact my husband's friend, Aahil. He should be able to help—protecting visiting dignitaries is his specialty."

"That's a good idea," Brianna said.

Sonya questioned her friend, "I'm curious... why are you so intent on meeting your mother's parents?"

The entertainer chose her words wisely trying to make her purposes clear. "I want to meet those who murdered my mother. I want to face them, and ask them why they did it. Then... then, I will let God show me what to say and do. I also want to find out what happened to my father."

"They may not know anything."

"I realize that, but I must do what I can to learn his identity. There has to be a reason he never came back for me."

"There could be a couple explanations. First, he might have attempted to, and someone killed him. Also, you're talking about Iraq during the Gulf War. Americans were not permitted in the country during that time. It would have been hard for him to get in unless he knew people high up in the government. We can only speculate. I tend to think he was killed."

"If that's the case, I would like to know where he is buried."

"Brianna, you may not like where this leads you."

"I know. But, you don't understand, my friend. I have these gnawing thoughts. I believe God is leading me to do this regardless of how it all ends up."

Sonya gave her a weak smile.

Brianna blew a wisp of hair. "Look at me. I have so much money that I don't know what to do with it. I own seven mansions throughout the world. Why does anyone need seven houses, anyway? I have my own plane, my own yacht, my own personal island in the Caribbean. I have everything... except a mother and father to love." A lone tear rolled down her cheek.

She looked up at Sonya who had started massaging her shoulders. "I don't want to end up like other entertainers, and have the tabloids report all that negative stuff. I want to be known as a person who helps others—someone who makes a difference."

"You've been doing that."

"Yes, but it was not just for the recipients. It was more for my ego... because it made me feel good. Since I became a Christian seven months ago, my motivation for doing things has changed."

"The world has seen that. It shows in both your words and deeds." Sonya's words were reassuring to the star.

"I can do nothing less."

There was silence for a moment.

"We need to find you a man," Sonya joked, trying to lighten the mood.

"I've had plenty of them." Brianna blew out a long breath.

"No, I mean a first-class man. The ones in your past weren't good for you, they used you."

"I did my share of using. I'm not proud of that. It embarrasses me."

"That's where God's love and grace comes in. He knows your past, and His grace is sufficient to forgive it."

"Yes... and I am so thankful for that."

"I wouldn't be surprised if the man of your dreams isn't right in front of your eyes, but you're too busy to notice." The teasing faded from her eyes.

"Anyone in mind?" Brianna smiled.

Sonya winked at her. "Just a thought."

Brianna giggled at the idea. "I told you when we first met that I may never be ready for a relationship."

"Never is a long time."

"I read an article that said the first man a girl should fall in love with is her father."

Sonya smiled. "I can understand that. My father means everything to me. He's my role model, and what I looked for in a soul mate. When he walked me down the aisle at my wedding, I didn't want to let go of his arm. I know he didn't want to release me, either. However, he knew Jim would take care of me and make me happy. Dad was heartbroken the day I called him with the news of Jim's death."

Brianna looked at Sonya and felt her pain as she picked up her guitar. "Maybe it's you who needs a man."

"Great. I had to open my big mouth." The light mood continued.

"How about Harry? I think he's got the hots for you." Brianna grinned.

"Harry?" Sonya rolled her eyes.

"Yes. I think he's perfect. Good looking, rich, successful. I see how he looks at you... and he's always asking you out."

"He asks all the girls out."

"Don't sell him short."

Both women laughed heartily.

Brianna pulled her hair back and removed the makeup covering the birthmark. "I've always hated this thing." She moved her finger around the edges of the mark, angling her head to get a better glimpse of it.

"Have you ever thought that your birthmark could possibly lead you to your father?"

"Yes, I have. That's why I've never had it removed. My doctor wanted to remove it, but a little voice in my head always told me not to. At the same time, for some reason, I've always kept it a secret. I don't know why. I guess it all goes back to my adoptive father. He was never ashamed of the birthmark, but kept it covered so other children wouldn't make fun of me."

Dismayed, Sonya shook her head.

"It embarrassed Susan though—she thought it was hideous, and made sure I knew she felt that way. Ethan tried to make it as inconspicuous as possible to help keep peace between him and Susan. I recall every night when he tucked me into bed he would kiss it lovingly."

Sonya could tell she was reliving the memory in her mind.

"Right after that, he would sing a song, read a Bible verse, and then pray." She continued to stare at her image. "I have kept this mark for the purpose of finding my real parents. Ethan always said it was a gift, a sign from God. Maybe it was his way of telling me that it could be a link to my biological parents. After all, it was the photo of me with the birthmark, which found my mother. All that remains is to find out about my birth father. Maybe once I find the answers, the door can be closed, and I can live my life knowing they loved me."

Sonya raised one eyebrow. "Perhaps this will all end soon, and you will find the answers you have sought for so many years."

Brianna turned the old guitar around and stared at the hand-painted heart.

Sonya asked, "Brianna, there is something I'm curious about. With all the money you have, and all the guitars you own, why is this guitar the only one you use at your concerts?"

Brianna sighed. "At first, it was all I had. Now, for some reason I treasure it. I'm not sure if it's because it's what got me here, or because it belonged to Ethan—you know sentimental reasons. I really don't know."

Sonya tried to understand, but there were too many unanswered questions.

Brianna boldly said, "Sonya, when I get back from Iraq, I want a face-to-face meeting with Ethan Anderson. I hope he will agree to it."

"That's going to be very hard on you, and probably him too."

Brianna stood. The memories felt achingly real. "I know. Ethan was right all along. I see that clearly now, he showed me the truth. He saved me from becoming a child harlot in Asia, and he showed me the way to Jesus. It took ten years until I came full circle and found where I needed to be. The whole time, it was right in front of my eyes, but I was too blind to see."

Brianna quietly began singing an old familiar hymn, a song Ethan used to sing to her.

> *Amazing Grace, how sweet the sound,*
> *That saved a wretch like me...*
> *I once was lost, but now am found,*
> *Was blind, but now I see.*

With a renewed sense of hope and an upbeat tone, Brianna spoke. "My, how those words are true to my heart. I just thank God that you came along when you did."

Sonya smiled. "I was only His instrument. You know God's hand of protection was on you your entire life. He had big plans for you. There were many Christians you came in contact with along the way who helped you."

"You mean like Conrad?"

"Yes, like Conrad."

"He has been good to me; I don't know why he puts up with me."

"Well for one, you pay him pretty well." Sonya laughed.

"Not enough. How many times has he had to fight to protect me? Or the way he hides me so the piranhas can't get any pictures. I have really grown to care about that guy."

"He's a good man and has a good staff. Your security is their number one priority."

Sonya felt it might be a good time to change the subject. "Brianna, about your meeting with Ethan Anderson... there is something I haven't told you. He's considered a sexual predator. Legally, he can't get within fifty feet of you without being arrested. Do you realize that?"

Brianna's face looked pained as she blinked back some tears. She had always been strong... she had to be, just to survive after leaving the Anderson household. "I have to right that wrong... somehow."

"I know. I just want you to be prepared—it won't be easy."

"Sonya, after I talk with Ethan, no matter what the outcome is, I am considering going to Mesa to turn myself in. I will throw myself on the mercy of the court. Whatever happens, I will accept the punishment, even if it's a prison sentence. It's time for me to face the consequences of my actions."

"We'll cross that bridge when we come to it. I will see that everything you asked of me is done. Is there anything else?"

Brianna picked up the picture again, staring at her mother. "She sure was beautiful. Wasn't she?"

"Yes, she was. That's where you got your beauty. You look very much like her."

"Except the birthmark."

"If it wasn't for the birthmark, I never would have found out about your mother."

"You're right. The birthmark was the key." Brianna stared at the photo. Hopefully, it will lead me to my father too."

Brianna inched closer to her image in the mirror, studying the birthmark, then her bright blue eyes. "If I am of Arab ancestry... where did I get these eyes?"

"I would suspect from your father."

"But aren't dark eyes dominant?"

"Usually, but we don't know your background."

"Sonya, will I ever find my father?"

"Honestly?" Sonya's gaze fell to the floor.

"Yes... honestly."

"I haven't given you the bill yet. When you see it, you will understand why I don't think we will ever find your father. I believe he is dead. At any rate, maybe, just maybe, your mother's family can give you some answers. Hopefully, we can find out what happened to him, or at least find where he's buried."

"Yes. Then I'll be able to put that part of my life to rest." Brianna traced the birthmark with her finger again. "I hope and pray that day comes, and I finally will have the answers I have wondered about all my life."

Brianna whispered a heartfelt prayer asking for guidance and wisdom, but mostly for answers.

FOURTEEN

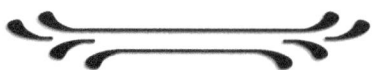

The Mysterious Stranger

God will call the past to account.
Ecclesiastes 3:15b

Hundreds of soldiers waited for Brianna's private jet to land in Baghdad. The roar of the crowd was deafening as the troops welcomed the entertainer with cheers and whistles.

Many stars performed for the troops, but none was more popular than Brianna Bays. This was her sixth visit to Iraq. The troops agreed Brianna was their official poster girl.

The plan was for Brianna to spend three weeks in Iraq and Afghanistan, not only entertaining the troops, but also visiting her mother's family, and gravesite. She would keep her expectations low, feeling quite certain that her family would not welcome her warmly. In fact, she had convinced herself that it didn't even matter. Still, she believed it was necessary to meet her grandparents. After all, she had things she wanted to say to them. The visit might give her closure to some of those painful chapters of her life.

Brianna knew her family was extremely wealthy and powerful, but believed her own money and fame could get anything she wanted in this country. She had peace about her visit, which she knew came from God.

The troops came out in droves to support their favorite female pop star; all the concerts were at full capacity

During her off-hours, Brianna spent her time visiting military personnel in the field and in the hospitals, never hurrying a discussion with a soldier. Photos, autographs, and uninterrupted time were the least she could give those who had sacrificed so much for their country. Many times, she prayed with them. She had the highest respect for these men and women in uniform... and it showed.

Even dressed in camouflage apparel much of the time, her beauty—both inside and out was dazzling. At the concerts, the troops went crazy when she came out sporting a camouflage dress.

Photographers were having a heyday filming her driving a tank and marching in formation with the troops. They also filmed her in the cockpit of a Super Hornet.

One of the highlights of her trip was the visit to an aircraft carrier. She performed to about five thousand men and women on the deck of the massive vessel. Conrad was the only bodyguard who accompanied her on board—she knew she would be well-protected.

When the concert was over Brianna walked into the crowd and unhurriedly greeted as many troops as she could. These men and women who stand in harm's way every day protecting freedom treated her with the utmost respect. The entertainer would stop and pose for a picture with anyone who asked.

A weeping Marine who had not seen her seven-year-old daughter in eight months captured Brianna's attention. Her devotion and sacrifice to her country warmed the entertainer's heart. After chatting with the hurting mother, she posed for some photos with her. The entertainer asked the woman for her daughter's address. "I want to send your daughter an autographed picture of us."

"She would love that," the Marine said genuinely.

When Brianna returned to the states, she would do more than that. She would personally deliver her latest CD and the picture to the daughter. It was a big surprise for the little girl. It was an even bigger surprise weeks later when the mother received a picture of the superstar hugging her daughter.

Before Brianna left the giant aircraft carrier, she went to the mess hall to eat with the troops. She personally thanked all the cooks; most were not able to attend the concert because they were working, but watched it live on the ship's monitors.

Too soon, her visit was over. She boarded the helicopter, waved goodbye to the troops, and flew back to Baghdad.

In just ten days, she had performed eight concerts, and entertained thousands of troops. Her time in Iraq was almost done.

All that remained was her personal business... the part she dreaded and feared the most.

The first step was to return to her place of birth.

The scene was surreal as she entered the hospital in Baghdad. Bittersweet emotions were running rampant—excitement, fear, sadness, and remorse. Brianna was trying desperately to capture a faded memory, or anything, of her long-lost mom. In a strange way, she realized this would be the closest she could ever be to her mother. She longed to sense her presence, her spirit, anything to make her feel closer to the mom she never knew.

As far as the public was concerned, her primary reason for going to the hospital was to dedicate the new birth wing, which was almost completed. Sonya had donated the money in Brianna's name, months prior.

The ceremony was memorable.

Afterwards, the entertainer enjoyed visiting the mothers and their newborns. As she held the infants tenderly, Conrad watched. It was a side of her he had never seen. Although she had held many babies before, this time was different. The love, the special spark in her moist eyes—perhaps it was sorrow because of what she never experienced as a child. He wasn't sure, but obviously his friend was deeply affected by the experience.

Previously, Sonya had told Brianna the room number where her mother had died. The staff allowed her some private time there, nobody knew why, nor did they ask. What Brianna wanted in that part of the world, she got... no questions asked.

Sitting in a chair next to the empty bed, she squeezed her eyes closed, sensing God's presence. Choked with emotion, in a desperate, honest prayer she poured her heart out to her Savior, the One, the only One, who could truly understand her wide array of emotions.

Conrad stood outside the door watching her, filled with empathy. Because of his similar past, he understood in a way most people couldn't, and he felt her pain.

An older nurse who had been watching the ceremony strode by. She smiled at Conrad, and then noticed the young woman sitting beside the bed in the empty room. She thought it strange at first, but resumed her duties.

A few minutes later, with tears running down her face, Brianna opened the door, and slowly walked out of the room.

Conrad immediately enveloped her with his strong arms.

Her words were muffled against his chest as she whispered, "Thank you for always being there for me."

Standing in the hall, Conrad consoled Brianna. "I'm here for you."

Finally, arm-in-arm Conrad and Brianna turned to walk down the long corridor. As they spun around, they almost collided with the same nurse, startling her. The woman gasped as she stared directly into Brianna's brilliant blue eyes. For what seemed like an eternity, their eyes locked. Then the woman shot Brianna a half-smile and scurried away.

Brianna spoke in Arabic. "Please wait. What is your name?"

The woman looked at Brianna. "I'm sorry. I have to get back to work."

"I only want to talk with you. You know me, don't you?"

The anxious nurse looked around to make sure no one was watching. "No. Well, yes... everyone knows you. You're Brianna Bays, the American entertainer."

"I sense it's more than that. You know me, and I know you. Your face looks familiar to me. Why? Did you know my mother?" Brianna tipped her face and looked deeper, studying the nurse in a way that was unnerving to both of them.

"Who is your mother?" The nurse's response was quick.

"Her name was Mira. She had a baby twenty-three years ago in this hospital. She died in that room." Brianna pointed to the empty bed. She walked closer to the nurse, and took her cold, trembling hands.

The frightened nurse wanted to run. "That was a long time ago. I don't know anything." Her answers seemed rehearsed.

"Please," Brianna pleaded, "I need to find my father. Do you know who he is?"

The woman looked in different directions. It was obvious she was terrified, afraid she might be seen. "I know nothing," she said, breaking Brianna's hold and walking away.

In a desperate voice, Brianna begged, "Were you the one that took me from the crib? Were you the one that returned the box of my mother's belongings?"

The woman froze.

"Please, I need to know." Brianna's voice softened. She knew she should watch her tone; nothing good could come from her getting frustrated with the woman.

The nurse looked straight into Brianna's piercing eyes and pursed her lips to speak.

At that precise moment, a group of military men came storming in, rushing toward Brianna. Aahil shouted, "We must go quickly. There's a bomb scare. A suicide bomber was shot and killed outside the hospital entrance. You're not safe here."

As they whisked Brianna away, she watched the nurse disappear from view. "Conrad, she knows. She knows!"

Conrad gave her a sad shrug. "I agree. She knows something, but now we must leave. Later we will come back and find out who she is. Right now we need to get you to safety."

That night, Brianna didn't get much sleep. She tossed and turned—her thoughts locked on the nurse. Who was she? Did she know her father? Why did she look familiar?

She wanted to go back to the hospital, but security kept it off-limits. She hoped in a few days she could return and finish her conversation with the nurse. "She was going to talk to me. I know she was," Brianna whispered in the darkness. "What was she going to say?"

Eventually, Brianna drifted into a couple hours of light sleep.

FIFTEEN

The Dangerous Visit

Do not hold against us the sins of past generations; may your mercy come quickly to meet us, for we are in desperate need.
Psalm 79:8

Even though Brianna was groggy from her lack of sleep, she was excited. She had waited all her life for this day—the day she would meet her biological family.

The military commanders had given her special permission to go to Fallujah to visit the Murat family. At this point, Conrad and her other bodyguards were the only ones who knew they were her grandparents.

The Iraqi city was still in deep turmoil, so the star had a company of hard-core troops around her, in addition to her four personal bodyguards.

Three helicopters circled the Murat compound as the caravan of military vehicles came to a halt in front of the large gate. A guard stood protecting the fortified home.

A colonel stepped out of the lead vehicle and marched over to the armed guard. Speaking in Arabic, he said, "Good morning, sir. We are here to see Emir Murat."

The guard grunted, "What for?"

"It's just a friendly visit. Brianna Bays, an entertainer from the United States, would like to visit with him."

"Why?" The solemn guard moved his gun in front of him, a silent reminder to the visitors that he was in charge.

"She did not tell me." The colonel kept an eye on the man's weapon.

The guard slowly backed up to a small building. He picked up a phone, never taking his eyes off the colonel, or lowering his weapon, and pushed a button.

"Brianna Bays is here to see you." The guard spoke in Arabic.

A voice sounded over the intercom. "Brianna Bays, the American entertainer? Why does she want to talk to me? And why the helicopters?"

The guard's voice dropped. "I don't know. They will not say."

The guard spoke to the colonel. "Mr. Murat wants to know why all the helicopters and military vehicles are here."

"It's for Brianna Bay's protection," the colonel answered swiftly, as if he was expecting the question.

The guard repeated his answer over the phone. "They said it's for her protection."

"I heard." There was silence for a few seconds while the man on the other end weighed his options. "She can come in, but nobody else." He announced in Arabic.

"That's not going to happen, and you know it," the colonel loudly announced, without even waiting for the guard to relay the message.

Even so, the guard began to repeat what the colonel said. "He said..."

Murat quickly answered. "I heard what he said. All right... tell them only her vehicle can enter the compound." The voice on the other end of the phone sounded agitated.

"Right. Only her vehicle." The guard looked directly at the colonel making sure he understood.

The colonel nodded his head acknowledging the message. He walked back to the vehicle where Brianna, her four bodyguards, and two other military personnel, sat waiting for the go-ahead.

The colonel explained, "He said he will only let your vehicle enter... and he's not budging on it."

"That's fine," Brianna said, without hesitation.

"I don't like it. These people are not on our side," the colonel replied.

"I'll be all right. I'm not afraid of them." Brianna's reply was straight to the point, decisive.

"I know you're not, but you should be. You don't know these people— they can't be trusted." The colonel cautioned.

"Yes, I do. Believe me! I do know who they are." Although her tone was forceful, deep down inside, Brianna couldn't shake the cold feeling in her heart.

The colonel could tell her mind was made up as he watched the guard open the massive steel gate to the mansion. "Okay." He looked at the driver. "Any sign of trouble and we will storm the compound." He made sure his voice was loud enough for the guard to overhear him.

Brianna was not afraid—she believed God would protect her, and she had confidence in her highly trained bodyguards.

After the vehicle passed through the gate, the guard slammed it shut. Two other armed men rushed to the gate for reinforcement. They watched as the helicopters continued to circle the compound. The pilots were careful not to go inside the perimeter of the massive estate.

The army had fitted Brianna with a tracking device. If something were to happen to her, the military could locate her quickly. Every conceivable precaution had been taken for her safety.

The Humvee stopped in front of the house. One of the military personnel jumped out of the vehicle. He faced the house, standing guard with his rifle, prepared for anything that might go wrong.

Inside the vehicle, Conrad held Brianna's hand. "Are you sure you want to go through with this?"

"I've come this far, I can't give up now. I will meet them, tell them who I am, and go from there." Brianna stared at the house, ill at ease, knowing that inside were members of her family who most likely want her dead.

"Are you ready?" Conrad asked.

"Oh yes! I have been looking forward to this day for years. I want to meet my relatives. In some ways I am excited, in other ways very sad."

The hummer's doors opened. Conrad, Bruno, Jonathan, and Cathy stepped out.

At the same time, two Iraqi men stormed out the front door with rifles. Another man followed them. The third man was older, about sixty, and well dressed. Behind him were three young children, who were trying excitedly to get a glimpse of the famous American entertainer.

Brianna Bays stepped out of the vehicle cautiously.

The older man greeted them in English. "To what do we owe this visit?" He extended his hand in a courteous gesture. His voice was pleasant, polite.

She stared at his hand. Thoughts raced through her mind. Should she shake the hand of the man who probably ordered her mother killed? After a split-second, she made the decision, and extended her hand, and smiled. She would be polite. She would not tip her hand... yet. One thing in her favor was that she spoke their language. The odds were that they did not know she did—she planned to use that to her advantage.

In English she voiced, "Mr. Murat, I have heard many things about you and your family. I have a few questions I would like to ask you."

Emir did not feel threatened by this woman. He was civil, even though he did not approve of the way she was dressed, especially since her head wasn't covered. Although, he didn't like it, he knew times were changing in his war-torn country.

"Come inside. I will have my wife get us some tea. You do like tea, don't you?"

"Yes, very much," Brianna answered. Her stomach churned.

Emir stopped at the entryway. He glared at Conrad, sizing him up. Then he eyed her other bodyguards, still following her. "They will have to stay out here," he said, nodding to Conrad and the others.

Without reservation, Brianna responded. "Conrad goes where I go." She pointed to her bodyguard, who stood alert and ready to protect her, whatever it took. "If you want to know why I am here, he comes in. If not, we will leave. But I believe you need to hear what I have to say." Brianna said directly.

The man could not believe such forceful language came from a woman. He cocked his head, scrutinizing her face, trying to figure her out. He could tell she was serious. "Very well, but his weapon stays out here," he said, pointing to Conrad's pistol.

Brianna nodded to Conrad. Reluctantly he removed his gun belt and handed it to Bruno.

The man turned and spoke to Brianna in Arabic, "Did you have a nice trip?" She didn't respond, knowing it was a trap, a trick to see if she knew his language. Knowledge of his language was her biggest asset— something she was not going to divulge at this point.

"Excuse me?" She said in English, looking confused. Her acting skills were being put to the test.

"I'm sorry. I forgot my manners. I was just talking to my guards," he responded slyly.

He spoke to his men again, now confident that it was safe to speak in Arabic. "You two stay out here. Assad, Doma, come with me. Keep an eye on the big one."

Conrad was listening to the conversation. He also understood everything they said, unknown to them.

The children ran past, glancing at the star and snickering. Brianna smiled at them.

"These are my grandchildren. They know who you are." His tone kept upbeat. "But then, who doesn't? Your photographs, movies, and music are everywhere."

Brianna was quite surprised how good the man's English skills were.

She followed the man she believed to be her grandfather into a foyer, then into a spacious room. The modern home was immaculate.

"Please sit down." He gestured toward the pricey furniture.

Brianna consciously sat in a low-backed chair facing the doorway, wanting to be aware of everyone's actions. Through the years, Conrad had taught her how to defend herself, and how to be alert in a crisis.

The older man sat across from Brianna on a large sofa, his two bodyguards stood directly behind him. They kept an eye on Conrad, who was standing at attention in the corner just a few feet to the side of them. Unknown to the host, Conrad carried two small pistols inside his sleeves, which he could get his hands on in an instant. He was a sharpshooter and never missed his target.

Emir spoke in Arabic, directing his words to his guards. "I'm not sure what this is about, but be ready. Keep an eye out for the bodyguard; I can take the girl."

"Is something the matter?" Brianna asked, playing along in their game of deceit.

"No, I just told them who you were. They don't speak English."

She knew that was a lie, already noticing the expressions on their faces when she talked. They understood every word she said, she was quite sure.

An older woman entered the room with several other people, one of them carrying drinks.

Emir made the introductions. "This is my wife Miridia, and my two daughters—Malak, and May. These are my two sons—Odel and Adel." He pointed at each as he introduced them.

Brianna forged a weak smile. She knew these were probably her mother's killers, and she felt the blood drain from her face as hatred and anger filled her heart. She reminded herself to stay calm, realizing the importance of not giving anything away through her body language.

Just then, the three giggling children returned to join them. They were ordered to sit quietly on the floor in front of their grandfather, which they did, no questions asked. They sat in amazement, staring at this world-renowned idol.

The conversation resumed in English. Making small talk, Emir said, "I read about your concerts in my country. You are very popular among the Iraqi people. To what do I have this honor of you being in my home?"

There was no expression on the face of either Brianna or Conrad.

"I love performing for the American troops. I have a lot of respect for them," Brianna said honestly.

"Dogs," Odel muttered in Arabic.

"Mind your tongue," his father shot back in Arabic.

Brianna asked, "Is there a problem?"

"No, No. He said you were beautiful." Emir lied, trying not to alarm his guests.

"Why thank you. I have been told I look like my mother." Brianna ran her fingers through her hair, looking calm on the outside, but churning on the inside.

When Brianna made that statement, she noticed the eyes of the older woman widen, and methodically examine every part of the entertainer's face. She deduced the older woman's mind was probably racing back to the memories of her own daughter, Mira, who had died years before. Brianna wondered if her grandmother even knew that her sons killed their own sister.

"I bet you do look like your mother. Does she live in America?" Emir continued.

"No. She is dead," the entertainer said, sipping her tea, but not taking her eyes off Emir.

His wife continued staring at her. Brianna wondered if her grandmother's strange reaction could be because she noticed the similarity between her and Mira.

"I'm sorry to hear that. Was she sick?" Emir took a sip of his beverage, acting interested in her story.

"No, in fact, she was murdered." She answered calmly.

"Murdered? When did it happen?" Emir's voice sounded dry.

"I was only a couple days old." Brianna put her cup down on the table beside her, carefully placing it on a coaster.

"My, how tragic! The violence in America is well-known. Who would do such an awful thing?"

Things were moving quicker than Brianna anticipated. She silently asked God for help.

"Actually she was not killed in America, she was killed in Baghdad. I believe her brothers killed her... but it was called an accident." She looked scornfully at both of her uncles.

Emir seemed to have no idea where the conversation was headed.

"Her brothers? Why would they kill her?" Emir slanted his head. Suddenly, he was interested... very interested.

"It's funny you should ask... why don't you tell me? I come from a country that respects life. We respect people's opinions, and accept them regardless of what color or nationality they are, or what religion they embrace." She emphasized religion, and her voice began to escalate.

"I understand, but why did you say, 'You tell me?' How would I know why your mother was killed by her brothers?" It was obvious the grandfather was becoming irritated.

"She was a Muslim, but she married a Christian, and she converted to Christianity."

Emir's stomach tightened. He glanced at his sons, noticing their expressions changed.

With all eyes fixed on Brianna, Conrad had quietly moved behind the two guards, and slipped his pistols out of his sleeves. Both weapons were ready to fire if he needed them. For a few moments the room was silent.

Surprising everyone in the room, the older woman suddenly jumped up, crying uncontrollably in Arabic, "Allah, forgive me!"

"Shut up, woman," the man yelled. He stood.

"Children, leave this room quickly," he shouted to his daughters and grandchildren. The younger women and children ran out of the room, looking back, wondering what was happening.

By this time, the man's voice was calmer, but his face showed fear. "I see. We Muslims believe that you can be a Christian if you want. We accept all people, just like we have accepted you into our house today." He began pacing the floor.

Brianna's heart beat faster, and her voice grew louder with each word. "You did not, would not, accept Mira, your own daughter." She reminded herself to exhale.

The grandmother fell to her knees, covering her face with her hands, and began weeping.

Anger came over Emir. "Look what you have done. You have upset my wife."

Just then, Emir noticed Conrad was no longer in the corner. "Take him out!" He yelled to his bodyguards, but Conrad's guns were already pressing against their necks.

"Drop the weapons," Conrad yelled in Arabic. "Drop your weapons, now!"

Emir's guards quickly obeyed the command.

The two unarmed brothers turned to see what was happening, and Conrad swiftly pointed a gun at them. "Stand down," he ordered.

Brianna stood, shouting in Arabic, "Look at me. Grandfather, look at me. Look at your granddaughter."

The older woman looked up with tears coursing down her face.

Brianna pulled back her hair to expose her birthmark, the evidence of who she was.

One of the brothers shouted, "Mira's child!"

"Mira! Mira! Mira!" The grandmother wailed, rocking back and forth on her knees.

"What is the meaning of this?" Emir demanded.

"You tell me." In despair, Brianna asked, "Why did you have to kill her? Why not just let her go?"

"Kill who? What are you saying? Nobody killed anyone," Emir insisted, still denying the truth.

"She was an insult to our family. We had the right to kill her," Odel interrupted, speaking in English.

"You had no right to kill her. You did not have the right to take an innocent life," Brianna shouted back.

"Allah said we are supposed to." Odel defiantly stepped forward.

"What kind of a god tells someone to take a life because of his or her beliefs... not a loving God." Brianna challenged her uncle's beliefs.

"Blasphemy!" The grandfather bellowed. "How dare you infidels come into my home and make these accusations against my family. How dare you talk about Allah that way."

"They are not accusations. Your son admitted the truth." She glared at her uncles.

"Get out of my house!" Emir thundered, pointing to the door.

"Get out of your house... *your* house? I'm your granddaughter. Look at me," she yelled in Arabic, walking up to him, and standing face-to-face. "We have understood everything you've said since we walked into this house. Look at me, Grandfather. You have made my life miserable. My mother... your daughter, did not deserve to be murdered because of her beliefs. In the same way, Muslims in my country should not be harassed and killed because of their beliefs."

"She rejected her family—our faith. We have the right... Allah says we do," her angry grandfather insisted.

"Is it true?" Miridia stood, looking directly into her husband's cold, dark eyes. "Is it true?" The usually mild-mannered woman demanded an answer.

"Mind me woman! I'll take care of you later," he scorned.

The heartbroken wife glared at her husband. "You did kill her. You knew. You told me American bombs killed our Mira. You knew all this time that our own sons killed her. You had my sweet Mira murdered?"

"Yes, I did! She married an infidel. The penalty is death. Death!" He screamed into Miridia's face.

Brianna's grandmother again dropped to her knees, covering her face with her hands, and sobbed uncontrollably. It was the sound of a mother lamenting the death of a child, a cry like no other.

"Does Allah say it is okay to kill an innocent baby?" Brianna persisted.

"She was the devil's child... the offspring of an infidel," Odel yelled.

At that moment, the astonished grandmother looked up at her son. "You killed the baby, too?"

"Yes, they killed a baby. The *wrong* baby... it was me they were after," Brianna shouted.

Even Emir was shocked with the news. He had no idea they had killed the wrong infant. All this time, he thought they had killed Mira and her baby. No wonder he was stunned to see Brianna at his home. Only now did he begin to realize that the beauty before him actually was his granddaughter.

"You killed the wrong baby, an innocent baby!" The father admonished his sons.

"We didn't know we had killed the wrong one until Mira's funeral. That's when we saw the picture taken at the hospital of Mira holding her baby. When we noticed the birthmark on the baby's forehead, we realized our mistake. We have looked for this devil child since that day, but couldn't find her." Odel angrily pointed to Brianna.

"Silence! This entire thing should have ended that day. You two bungled everything!" Emir was livid.

He glanced down at his wife, who was still on the floor crying hysterically, and then turned his focus to Brianna. "What do you want from me?" The grandfather's voice was calmer.

"Want from you... what does your devil granddaughter want from you?" She walked over to him and slapped his face full force, almost knocking him off his feet.

He raised his hand to strike her, but stopped.

"Try it, just try it. I would love to put you down right where you stand. I have a black belt in Karate and could kill you in one blow," Brianna threatened, meaning every word.

Looking somewhat remorseful, he said, "I deserved that. I have done things I regret—ordering Mira to be killed was one of them."

Returning to his question, Brianna shouted, "What do I want from you? I want my life back. I want my mother and father... that's all I want. You didn't even give my mother a proper burial." Years of suppressed wrath were unleashed. The rage in her voice, the hatred on her face said it all.

"No, we did not," her grandfather confirmed regretfully.

Odel took a menacing step forward. "Look at her, Papa. She has the devil's mark on her face. She must die!"

"You make one more step toward her, and you're the one who will die." Conrad pointed his pistol at Odel.

The angry son glared at the bodyguard, but silenced himself.

"Who was my father? Did you kill him too?" Brianna pushed further.

Looking distraught, Emir dropped onto the couch, burying his forehead in his hands. After a time, he looked up at his sons, then to Brianna.

Shaking his head he spoke, "We could not find him. We thought he was dead like my daughter and her baby. You think I wanted to do that? I loved Mira. But I love Allah more. We are expected to deal with infidels harshly and quickly." Emir clenched his fist in rage.

"Who was my father? What happened to him?" Brianna kept pressing for answers.

"We could not find out who your father was. We went back to Paris to search for him after we found out Mira was pregnant." Emir finally spoke the truth.

"That means you tried to kill him, too." Brianna blinked back the tears, she was too angry to cry.

"Yes, we tried. We would have, but could not find him. We only had a first name, which Mira accidently mentioned once. I don't even remember what it was." Emir lowered his head. He could not look at Brianna.

"Why kill him?" She clenched her jaw, waiting for a response.

Emir raised his voice again. "Because he was guilty... they were all guilty."

"Guilty... guilty of what? Loving my mother... your daughter? How does love make a person guilty?" Brianna was trembling.

The grandmother continued her wailing.

"She married outside the Muslim faith," the grandfather stood yelling.

"That doesn't make it wrong. It does not change the fact that they loved each other. That was their decision, not yours." Brianna's voice cracked.

Finally, the grandmother stood. She looked directly into her husband's eyes, confronting him, something she had longed to do for many years. "I suspected for over twenty years that you killed her, but I wouldn't allow myself to believe it. You are a devil!" The furious mother glared at her sons, then walked over and slapped each of them hard across the face.

"Woman, leave this room now!" Emir ordered.

Refusing to take orders from her cruel husband any longer, she glared at him defiantly, and walked over to Brianna. With tears still running down her face, she spoke honestly, straight from her heart. "My child, I did not know. I did not know." She gently touched her granddaughter's face, and then kissed her on both cheeks.

She started to walk away, but suddenly stopped and spun around, then walked back to her husband. With all her pent-up anger unleashed, she slapped him across the face with such force that he fell backwards.

Quickly regaining his balance, he raised his hand to hit her, but Brianna sprang into action grabbing his arm, and twisting it behind him.

An Iraqi guard heard the commotion and ran into the room with his gun raised.

Conrad sliced his right arm across the man's neck knocking him out cold. He fell to the ground forcefully.

The brothers and guards saw this as their opportunity to act. Stepping forward, ready for a fight, Conrad quickly reminded them he was still in charge. With weapons drawn, Conrad shouted, "Go ahead... just give me a reason to use these."

Brianna continued twisting her grandfather's arm. She wanted to inflict pain on him. However, she knew in her heart, no matter what she did, she could not get her mother back. Her lifetime of foolish choices and heartache stemmed from that one truth—her family cruelly robbed her from having a mother. Nothing could ever replace what she missed, but it was time for it to be over.

Brianna loosened her grip, but still held her grandfather's arm behind his back. She screamed in Arabic, "The one living God will be the judge. My God will judge all of you."

She glared at her relatives. Blood relatives... that's all they were. She realized that her real family was Conrad, Sonya... and Ethan, the man who raised her as his own.

She pushed Emir forward and he fell onto the couch grabbing his hurting arm. "What about my father? You said you got a name. What was his name?" Brianna pleaded with her grandfather one more time.

"We have no idea who he was. He was like a ghost who disappeared; it was like he never existed." He looked at his sons. "What was the name Mira mentioned?"

Neither son responded, not a word. Their silence confused Emir.

Brianna spoke directly to her uncles, "My father... what happened to him?" Her expression indicated she would persist until she had an answer.

"Odel, tell her. What was his name?" The grandfather pleaded with his oldest son.

Conrad stepped closer to Odel, pointing a gun at his face in an attempt to persuade him to talk.

Odel spoke guardedly. "We went to Paris, but could not find him. We did not have a name or picture. He just vanished." His voice sounded heartless. "Then you infidels attacked our country. You Americans think you can come here and do whatever you want." His cold, cruel gaze shifted to Brianna.

"Oh, you don't have to worry about the Americans... you have to worry about me. Remember, I'm part Arab." Brianna looked directly into her grandfather's eyes. "I was born here, which gives me dual citizenship. It also gives me part of everything you own." She chuckled, a mocking laugh.

"You will never get anything I own," her grandfather insisted, jumping up, his voice intensifying.

"The truth is I don't want anything you have. Not one thing... you make me sick... all of you!" She spun around and slapped her grandfather again.

He raised his hand to hit her and noticed her eyes filled with pain and fury. He stopped.

Brianna turned to walk out the door.

Conrad quickly rendered Emir's two guards unconscious with a swift blow to the neck. Picking up their weapons, he took out the magazines, and stuffed them in his pocket.

The American bodyguard moved closer to Odel. If the size difference wasn't enough to frighten the older brother, the tone of voice, and the outrage in his eyes should have been. "I have only one thing to say... this ends now. If anything ever happens to Brianna, or if her life is threatened in any way, I will hold you three personally responsible. I will hunt you down, and I will kill you like a wild boar. Understand?" He stuck one of his pistols forcefully in Odel's nose. "I asked you a question. Do you understand?" There was no doubt at this point Conrad was in complete control of the situation.

"Yes," the brother mumbled reluctantly.

"That's not a threat. It's a promise. If anything ever happens to Brianna, I will come after you with the United States military. Believe me, there is not a rock anywhere on this planet you could hide under. Trust me on this."

Conrad pushed Odel with such force that he went flying over the couch, landing at the feet of his father.

As Brianna stepped into the foyer, she noticed her grandmother heading to the front door with only a small bag in her hand.

"Woman, where are you going? Get back in here," Emir shouted to his wife.

With boldness and determination, she turned to face her husband of many years, and spoke forcefully, in a way she had never done before. "You have bossed me around long enough, and I am tired of you calling me 'Woman.' My name is Miridia. I am the mother of Mira... and the proud grandmother of Brianna Bays. You can talk to my lawyer." She spun around in a huff.

Stepping closer to her granddaughter, she studied the features of her face. The resemblance was uncanny—she could see Mira in her. The scene was touching—a grandmother meeting her long-lost granddaughter for the first time. No one else mattered. Miridia stroked Brianna's face gently and began to weep quietly, tears of sorrow and regret.

She walked out the front door to a waiting car and her chauffer, never looking back at her husband.

Brianna watched her grief-stricken grandmother walk away. She realized something good had come from their encounter—she helped give freedom to one imprisoned soul, her grandmother.

Conrad interrupted her thoughts. "Brianna, we need to leave now."

The bodyguard backed his way to the door, still aiming his weapons at Odel and Adel.

Without warning, Conrad grabbed Adel and shoved him against the wall. "His name, what was his name?" He shouted to the younger, more timid brother, realizing he had hardly spoken the entire time.

"We never knew his name. We only heard Mira say it once, and it was not clear." Adel was trembling with fear.

"What was it?" Conrad asked, shoving the barrel of the gun into his nose.

"Barrett! We never knew if that was his first or last name. The only thing we know is that he is dead."

"How do you know that?" Conrad questioned the terrified man further.

A slow, evil grin came to his face. "He died in prison. We would have killed her, too..." he nodded toward Briana, "...but we just could not catch up to that devil child."

Conrad's temper flared. With full force, he stuck Adel in the head with the palm of his hand, knocking his head against the wall. Unconscious, the brother fell to the floor in a heap.

Without hesitation, Conrad stepped in front of Brianna protectively.

Together they walked through the foyer. When he opened the front door, two more of Emir's bodyguards were aware something was amiss and challenged them with guns drawn. They never had a chance. Conrad took both of them down, disarming them in one swift move.

Bruno noticed what was happening and quickly neutralized the one remaining guard who was standing close to the military vehicle.

Brianna sprinted to the Humvee and slipped into the backseat. Conrad and her bodyguards followed. They passed through the gates and sped away. The rest of the caravan followed.

Conrad stared at Brianna, unsure how to respond. Was the confrontation worth it? He gently reached for her hand and noticed it trembling. He was amazed by her strength and determination. He desperately wanted to take her in his arms and hold her, comfort her, but he knew she didn't think of him that way. He was her bodyguard, a good friend, nothing more, and he must stay focused on protecting her.

In the safety of the vehicle, Brianna replayed the events in her mind. Tears welled up. It was impossible to understand. How could a man kill his own daughter or sister because she loved someone of a different religion? No answer blew across her aching heart, and no words could comfort her.

Later, Emir Murat would protest to the Iraqi and American authorities, but his request was ignored.

SIXTEEN

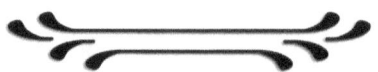

The Heart in Stone

For you created my inmost being;
You knit me together in my mother's womb.
Psalm 139:13

There was only one thing left for Brianna to do in Iraq—visit her mother's grave.

When the vehicle arrived at the secluded, run-down cemetery, a local caretaker greeted them. The old burial sites were hard to find due to the overgrowth of weeds and brush. Drifted sand obscured many of the tombstones.

"I'm looking for the grave of Mirada Mira Murat," Brianna announced in Arabic.

The aged caretaker nodded his head. "Ah, Mira. Yes, I know her well. I will show you," he replied in broken English.

Conrad walked next to Brianna, holding her hand, as she carried a bouquet of flowers to her mother's grave.

The old man spoke in short, choppy sentences. "Mira is buried next to her infant. Sadly, they were killed when bombs hit the hospital during war. There is no tombstone for the baby. I believe Mira's mother brought the flat rock. That is the only headstone. Her name was on it. Time has weathered it. She seldom has a visitor." The caretaker spoke about it like it was a hospital bed, not a grave.

It was necessary to step over rocks and debris that were littering the path. The man kept talking while they walked. "Six or seven months ago a woman... another American came to visit."

Brianna immediately knew he was referring to Sonya.

The old caretaker continued, "I believe her mother comes by every year. I think it's on Mira's birthday. She leaves a single red rose. She still grieves this many years later. She cries for long time on her knees, moving back and forth. She still is sad over her daughter's death."

Brianna fought back tears thinking of her grandmother.

Finally, they arrived at the site. It was out of the way, nothing special, and exactly as Sonya had said—the tombstone was a flat rock.

"Has anyone else ever come to visit?" Conrad asked the caretaker.

"No. No." The man answered readily.

Brianna stood solemnly. Chills ran through her, knowing she was this close to the remains of her mother. She could not shake the strange feeling... a feeling of hopelessness. She was overcome with sadness, realizing next to her mother's body was a baby, an infant, who never had a chance at life. Her only consolation was that the unknown baby was in the arms of Jesus.

Brianna turned to the caretaker. "Please. Try to remember. This means a lot to me. Have there been any other visitors?"

He looked into her bright eyes and suddenly recalled something. "Yes. I do remember one. Fifteen or twenty years ago a man came. He was young." The caretaker paused, trying to recollect the faded memories. "I remember him because he had blue eyes... like yours. He told me he knew Mira. I had to chase him away. He ruined the gravestone... carved images in it." He shook his head, obviously still distressed by the action of the visitor.

Brianna moved closer to the tombstone and knelt. She laid the flowers beside the rock sadly, and brushed the sand off the tombstone with her hand. When she pulled back her long hair and blew at the headstone to clean it further, the morning sun highlighted her birthmark.

When the dust cleared, she was shocked to realize that the stone had not been defaced—a heart had been scratched into it. Brianna gasped and looked up to see the expression on her bodyguard's face.

Conrad's eyes focused on the etched heart, and then he shifted his gaze to Brianna.

She jumped up excitedly and faced the kind caretaker. "Can you tell me anything else about this man?" Her voice demonstrated the urgency of what she was asking.

He shook his head. "No, no. It was a long time ago. I don't remember."

"Please. It is very important to me," she said, putting her hand gently on his shoulder.

His mind searched for anything that could help the anxious woman. He finally spoke. "I recall he was young, dressed very nice. I remember the blue eyes... they were bright blue. He spoke English and Arabic. I am sure he was American. As I recall..." he paused, "...I think he had light brown hair." He shook his head, almost as if he was in pain. "It has been too many years... too many years."

She faced Conrad. "It was my father. I know it was. He did come back." She looked down at the flat rock. "But why did he scratch the heart on the stone?"

Brianna looked back at the aged caretaker. "I know it's been a long time. How many years after Mira was buried did this man come?"

The old man pondered, trying to put all past recollections in place. "About five years. Yes, I believe that's right."

"Five years." Brianna looked down at her mother's grave. "He knows Mira is buried here, but does he think it's her baby buried next to her?"

Conrad's response was quick and certain. "Brianna, your father might have put that heart on the grave to let you know he was looking for you."

Brianna's eyes narrowed and then brightened with a hopeful glint.

She turned her attention back to the caretaker. "Do you know who I am?"

"Oh yes! My grandchildren love you. You are Brianna Bays," he said with a sincere smile.

She took his hand again. "Please, will you do something for me?"

"Yes."

"If that man ever comes back, will you tell him his daughter is looking for him? Tell him who I am. Tell him... tell him that I want to meet him."

"Yes. I can do that. I will gladly do that!" He nodded his head vigorously.

The entertainer reached in her pocket, pulled out a large amount of folded Iraqi money, and handed it to him. "Take this money, and take care of my mother's grave. If anyone tries to hurt it, or if anyone comes to visit, please let me know." She handed him a card with her personal cell phone number on it.

He waved his hand. "No, no, no... I can't take that. I will do it for you, not for money."

Insistent, Brianna placed the money in his hand. "Take it. You can buy your grandchildren some clothes or something. Please, do it for me."

He stared at the large sum of money, amazed at her generosity. "Will you do something for me?"

"Anything!"

He took his cell phone out of his pocket. "Can I get a picture of you with me? I would be proud to show it to my grandchildren."

"I would love to." Brianna put her arm around the Iraqi caretaker, and Conrad snapped the picture—the elderly man had a huge smile.

The entertainer thanked him again, and gave him a kiss on the cheek.

Conrad took her hand as they strolled back to the vehicle. Brianna looked back a number of times at her mother's grave. As they walked, she spoke, "Conrad, you know what that means? My father was alive at least five years after my mother died. He still could be alive." A sense of joy and peace spread over her. Maybe, just maybe, her father was still alive. Did she dare hope?

"I don't know," Conrad said. "Your uncles told us that he died in prison, but I don't believe they were telling us everything. Why didn't they give us more details? I think they killed him... or at least, they think they did." He sounded both hopeful and doubtful.

"I will still hold out hope," Brianna said, searching Conrad's eyes. She smiled, grabbing his arm tight as they walked down the path.

"At this point, that's all we have... hope. We will hold onto that!" Conrad said smiling.

After spending a week in Afghanistan entertaining the troops, Brianna and her bodyguards returned to Bagdad.

Conrad and Brianna went to the hospital to talk with the mysterious nurse, but she was nowhere to be found—another dead-end for the disheartened entertainer.

It was time to say goodbye to her newfound friends. Among them were more than a dozen army personnel, as well as several Marines who had escorted her safely around Iraq and Afghanistan. She thanked each of them personally, posing in photos with them, or giving them a kiss on the cheek. Brianna was proud of the brave men and women of valor serving in this faraway land defending freedom for her and all Americans.

It seemed strange for Brianna to be back in the Middle East, but it seemed stranger still to leave it. She wanted to stay, but knew what she needed to do next. Out there somewhere, her father might be alive. Perhaps he was still looking for his baby girl. At least now, she had a small glimmer of hope.

SEVENTEEN

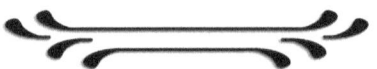

The Startling Encounter

So do not fear, for I am with you; do not be dismayed,
For I am your God. I will strengthen you and help you;
I will uphold you with my righteous right hand.
Isaiah 41:10

The flight back to America was tedious. Even though Brianna was in the comfort of her own plane, she was edgy. It was a rare occurrence when her music could not provide solace for her, but this was one of those times. The large number of concerts in the three weeks in Iraq and Afghanistan wore her out physically, but it was the confrontation with her family, which had taken a toll on her emotionally.

She kept replaying the scene in her mind. The coldness, the cruelty of her family still gave her chills.

Her thoughts drifted to the most poignant part of the trip—visiting her mother's grave, the mother she would never know. She couldn't shake the memories—the conversation with the caretaker, the heart etched in the rock. The one thing that kept her going was the spark of hope that her father could be alive. After twenty years, he could have forgotten about her, or considered her dead and moved on with his life. There was also the possibility that her father was deceased. She had to be prepared for the worst.

What she would face next would be what she dreaded and feared most—the meeting with her adoptive father. There was no other way to look it—she destroyed his life. How would he treat her? Would he even talk to her? She would not blame him if he slammed the door in her face... or worse. She knew she deserved it.

Bruno tried his best to get Brianna to smile at his silly jokes. Conrad and the others attempted to get her mind off the upcoming encounter. They tried to persuade her to sing and play the guitar, but nothing worked. Her stomach was in knots as she felt the weight of her guilt and responsibility. She stared silently out the window into the distance.

Their plane was scheduled to land in Casper, Wyoming, where Ethan Anderson now lived. Sonya would be waiting for the star upon her arrival.

Brianna missed her good friend during their tour to the Middle East, but Sonya knew it was vital to stay behind and prepare for the next step in the entertainer's life.

The meeting would be a surprise for Ethan, but Brianna and Sonya surmised that would be the only way he would talk to her. He certainly wouldn't agree to a planned visit... why should he?

The hum of the engines lulled Brianna deeper into her private thoughts. She couldn't get the meeting with her grandparents out of her mind. She pitied her grandmother; the poor woman had been lied to all those years. As for her grandfather and uncles, she despised them. Brianna knew that would be something she would have to deal with as a Christian. How can you forgive someone for killing your mother? It was unforgivable. Wasn't it?

Then it hit her. What she did was equally destructive. She was seeking forgiveness from Ethan. Her lies tore apart Ethan's family, destroyed him financially, and put him in prison where he was abandoned, beaten, and abused. She ruined his life. Yet, she was seeking his forgiveness. How ironic!

She realized that forgiveness needed to go both ways. She had to forgive what her grandfather did to her, and she had to ask for forgiveness for what she did to Ethan. She had a sick feeling in her gut, and didn't know if forgiveness was possible in either case.

When the plane landed, Sonya was waiting with a rental van, ready to take them to Ethan's home. The ride was silent, but much prayer took place. Sonya and Conrad prayed the meeting would be cordial and healing could begin. Brianna prayed for strength to do what she knew would be extremely difficult.

Upon entering the shoddy trailer park, Brianna immediately could see exactly how far Ethan had fallen. Abandoned, broken-down cars and trailers cluttered the area. They drove by a group of men sitting outside drinking beer with their music blaring; a couple of them were throwing rocks at empty bottles. Barking dogs and parents yelling at their children were some of the many unpleasant sounds in the noisy trailer park.

Brianna couldn't help but think of how different it was from her upbringing after Ethan adopted her.

Their large van seemed out of place. It came to a halt in front of a run-down, singlewide mobile home; the shutters and screens were torn, and the steps and front porch rotting away.

Silently, everyone stared at the dumpy trailer.

Brianna wiped away a single tear. "I must stay strong," she whispered.

Conrad spoke softly, "Should I come in with you?"

"No," Brianna answered with certainty. "This is one part of my life I must face alone."

"What if he gets violent?" Cathy asked.

"He has never hurt me; I don't think he ever would." Brianna answered with assurance.

"Time in the pen changes a man," Jonathan warned.

"Not Ethan... I hope." She took a deep breath, opened the car door, and stepped out. Jonathan handed her the guitar case from the back seat.

Concerned, Conrad dished out more instructions. "Brianna, keep your phone in your hand at all times. Don't be afraid to put him down if he gets physical with you. You know how to defend yourself. If you need us for any reason, push the star button and we'll be there in seconds."

She nodded her head and began the slow walk up the broken steps. She stood at the door mustering the courage to go further, and fighting the urge to run the other direction.

Standing nervously in front of the dilapidated door, she could hardly believe her ears. Music was playing a familiar melody—a song from her latest CD.

Could he possibly know who she was? Is there any way he could have discovered that Janna Anderson was actually Brianna Bays? All her life she had gone out of her way to hide her birthmark from the press and the authorities, making sure no one knew her true identity. No... it must be a coincidence.

She took a deep breath and lifted a silent prayer. *Lord, give me the strength to do this, and the wisdom to know what to say. I can't do it by myself. I desperately need You!*

With trembling hands, she knocked.

She heard footsteps. The door creaked open slowly.

Standing in front of the superstar was a thin man with a rough beard. He wore a stained shirt, torn jeans, and no shoes. His greasy hair had grown down to his shoulders. He looked old, and his face seemed cold, hard. He certainly did not look like the same man she remembered, yet there was something familiar about his eyes. She stared at the man, speechless. Yes, those eyes belonged to Ethan Anderson—the man who cared for her six years, taught her how to play the guitar, sing, write music, and ride a bike. He was the man who protected her and taught her how to pray.

Her mind was racing. She recalled when the boys came knocking on the door, Ethan would politely say, "Come back in ten years." She smiled lightly at the memory, and then shook her head to help her focus.

The man stared back, but there was no smile on his face, no upbeat voice, no sparkle in his eyes. Yet, she was certain his face registered surprise when he saw her.

After he paused for what seemed like an eternity, he greeted her. "Well, if it isn't the one and only Brianna Bays. To what do I owe this visit?"

Brianna straightened and cleared her throat, trying to sound composed. "May I come in?"

"By all means, come into my humble abode," he said sarcastically, swinging the door open, and pointing around his empty trailer.

Standing by the door, Ethan noticed the van. He saw Conrad by the hood watching intently, and Bruno by the car door. "I see you brought your own army," he chuckled nervously.

Brianna jumped at the sound of the door closing. Perhaps she was more than a little frightened, more than a little uneasy.

He turned to see Brianna looking around. "My, you sure have become a beautiful woman. I always knew you would be. I had to fight those young boys off with a stick," he said, swinging his arm pretending to be holding a stick.

He walked over to the small portable CD player and turned it off.

"You know who I am?" She forced herself to focus.

"Of course I do. I've been listening to your latest CD... I recognize your voice." He gave her a crooked grin. "I recall helping you write a few of those songs. Do you think I have a court case against you?" Again, he chuckled. "As you can see, I have been living a life of luxury with the royalties you've been sending me."

She faced him, not knowing how to respond because she knew he was right. Brianna clenched her hands and nodded. "I didn't come to attack you."

Ethan looked skeptical. "You know, I've been listening to your latest CD. That third song, *What I Really Want*, I still think you should have ended with a high C. You could have held the last measure longer, you know... for effect."

"You're right. I forgot you had suggested that to me." Brianna was having a difficult time reading him. She wondered where the conversation was heading.

Ethan rubbed behind his ears. "So you didn't come to attack me. I sure hope not; your bodyguards could make mincemeat out of me." He stared at her for a moment, his face blank.

"Have a seat." He pointed to a well-worn sofa. "The place isn't clean, but at least it's not cluttered. I wasn't expecting company. Can't afford much on $140 a week, but I get by. People tell me I could get food stamps, but you know that I never take a handout." Ethan, noticeably nervous, spoke hurriedly, and jumbled.

Responding to his request, Brianna sat down on the sofa anxiously clinging to her guitar case.

Ethan sat in a wobbly chair a few feet from her. He stared at her and an uncomfortable silence fell between them.

At a loss for words, she wondered where to start. She had replayed this scene many times in her mind through the years, but it wasn't going as she had envisioned. Words did not come easily.

Ethan walked over to her and stared silently at the cross necklace she wore.

It startled her when he pulled back her hair revealing her birthmark. "You still have the mark. That's good. I was afraid you would have had it removed by now. That's a gift from God, you know." He returned to his chair as if nothing happened.

A shiver ran down Brianna's back. Glancing around the room, Ethan picked up a glass. "Oh, look at me. What a rude host I am. Can I get you a drink?" He rushed toward the kitchen. "I don't have much, but what I have is yours."

"No, thank you. Please sit down. We need to talk." Brianna took a deep, steadying breath.

He glared at her, but reluctantly sat back down. "We need to talk. We need to talk." His voice grew louder. "What do you mean, we need to talk? It's been over ten years since I last heard from you."

He started to laugh, a laugh that made Brianna shiver.

Ethan continued, "Let me see. How did that go? It's been years... you don't write... you don't call." His voice, his tone, everything about him was frightening Brianna. Was this visit a mistake? She was becoming increasingly more uncomfortable.

The man who was her father at one time, stood and walked closer to her. He bent over and leaned forward, stopping inches from her face. "You have my undivided attention. What do we need to talk about?" He emphasized the word "we."

He stared at her for a long minute. Brianna noticed his eyes become moist. Then suddenly, his demeanor changed again, and he sat back down. "What do we have to talk about?" His voice was calm.

Silence settled over them as Brianna tried to gather her thoughts.

"I've come to apologize." Brianna's heart beat louder, faster.

"Apologize for what, Janna? Lying, destroying my marriage, my relationship with my children? Do you know I have never seen them? Ten years... and I have never even seen a picture of my three children." His gaze turned toward the ceiling as he tried to remember what they looked like. "Of course, I did hear what happened to them. Robert Cain kept me up to date."

Brianna couldn't move... couldn't speak... couldn't run. She sat motionless, barely even breathing.

Ethan's tone suggested the worst was yet to come. His eyes rested on her, but his thoughts seemed to be elsewhere. "It's hard to follow in the footsteps of a condemned man accused of abusing his children. I heard Eric ended up getting a fifteen-year-old girl pregnant, shirked his responsibilities, dropped out of school, and ran away. He joined a street gang in L.A. where he killed a rival gang member. Then he just disappeared. Rumor has it... he was killed in a street fight over drugs. Lonnie drank himself to death in a binge one night. What wasted lives! Did you know Lonnie was gifted? Robert told me his IQ had been tested when he was twelve, and it was almost off the chart. Two years later, he was dead. I would have gone to their funerals, but even dead, there is a fifty-foot barrier for me."

Unexpected tears pooled in Brianna's eyes, but she blinked them away. She must remain strong.

"Matter of fact, if the cops knew you were a few feet from me right now, I would be arrested. You aren't going to call them, are you?"

She didn't respond to his sarcasm.

"Now, where was I? Oh yes, Alana. That girl made something of herself. She got pregnant when she was fourteen, but ended the pregnancy with an abortion. You know, out of sight... out of mind. She dropped out of school at fifteen, and ran away with a drummer. That didn't end up too well; he left her broken on the streets of L.A. Last I heard she was in and out of drug clinics, and waiting on tables in northern California."

Brianna couldn't believe what she was hearing. She groaned and sank a little lower in the sofa.

"Of course, Susan didn't fare any better. I heard she was working at a convenience store in Oklahoma City. Yes, Robert has kept me informed." Ethan tapped his fingers on his knees.

Reacting physically to the heartbreaking news, she struggled for her next breath. Brianna felt lightheaded.

"And then there's Dad." Ethan's mind drifted into the past, a happy time in his life. "God rest his soul. How I miss him. He stood by me until the very end. He tried to get in touch with his grandchildren, but wasn't allowed. They treated him like he was a leper or something. He was killed by a hit-and-run driver, had his identity stolen, and lost almost everything. The little he had left, the government took. They said he owed back taxes. How a dead man who had everything stolen from him can owe taxes is beyond me." He shook his head, sadness overwhelmed him.

Brianna wanted to disappear. However, she couldn't move—she sat, paralyzed with fear and regret.

"Dad was always there to help America. In the end, they were there for him, too." His mocking laugh scared Brianna. "With my father dead and no home to go to, I was left to the wolves in the big house. Boy, did they have a heyday with me." He noticed his trembling hand, quickly clutched it, and brought it to his chest to help stop the shaking. Then his gaze drifted past her. "They even took our ocean home near Corpus Christi."

Brianna noticed his wandering mind and shaking hands, and realized he must be seriously ill. She didn't say anything, his expression told the story... the abuse, and beatings in prison obviously had a lasting effect on him.

"So apologize all you want. Ten years of torture, that's what it's been. The only job I can get is washing dishes. Every week the police come questioning where I was the night before because some kid in the area had been abused. I can't go to the playground or even the library without being forced to leave. God forbid if the local preacher would stop by and ask me to come to church. The deacons would nail his hide to the church door. So go on, apologize... I'm listening."

This wasn't the reunion Brianna had dreamed about... had hoped for. No, it was turning into a nightmare. Who could blame Ethan for his hatred and bitterness?

Ethan stood and folded his arms. "Go ahead and apologize. I'm all ears. But don't give me a hug because the police will break down the door and arrest me. That's happened twice—I was sleeping both times."

Startling Brianna, Ethan turned quickly and ran toward a back room. He pointed to his bedroom shouting, "I was just sleeping when the door was kicked in. They pulled me from my bed, took me in handcuffs in my underwear to the police station where I... I had to prove my whereabouts at a certain time."

Outside, Conrad and the others could hear Ethan's elevated voice, but would do nothing to help unless Brianna requested it.

An ache settled in Brianna's heart and tears erupted from her eyes. She fought to get the words out. "I didn't mean for all that to happen. I just wanted freedom. I needed to get away." Trying to gain control of her emotions, she hesitated.

Then she poured out her story. "There was a girl at school who told me when she wanted a new family she created a story of abuse. Just like that, she would get a new family. I never thought of the consequences to my lies. I didn't know anyone would get hurt... especially you."

Ethan's voice exploded. "Hurt? Of *course* people get hurt when you lie. Lies destroy lives. Wow, listen to me! I just made a title to a new song, Lies Destroy Lives. Let's see, how we can sing that?"

Brianna could take no more. She stood, looking directly at him. "Will you please listen to me? If you ever cared about me, please listen."

His demeanor changed again, his voice softened. "Cared about you? You're my little girl. I've always cared about you."

His sudden mood changes disturbed Brianna.

Through her tears, she noticed a big scrapbook on the kitchen table and was drawn to it. Intrigued, she opened it. She scanned each page filled with photographs, recollections of another time and place. Her hands began to shake. Pictures from the time she was a six-year-old in Kuwait, through her time living with Ethan covered the first pages. The following pages contained recent pictures from newspapers and magazines, tastefully organized. Brianna was shocked to see a photo of her receiving her first Motion Picture Award. Near the back of the album were covers of all of her CDs. By the last page, her tears had stopped.

She finally had the courage to look at Ethan. "You have kept track of me. Why?" She didn't blink.

"Like I said, you're my little girl. I needed to do that. I have every one of your CDs; I played them so much that I wore them out and had to buy new ones. That's all I listen to." A hint of a sparkle appeared in his eyes as he talked.

"Why?" Staring at Ethan, Brianna felt the extent of her selfish choices. Her heart was pounding loudly.

"Maybe it's a way I like to torture myself." His voice grew softer. "I watched you at the awards and heard what you said. Did you mean it?"

Slowly she closed the book. She turned it back to the first page, which was blank. Judging by the faded color a picture must have been removed.

She shifted her gaze back to Ethan. "Yes, I meant every word... from the bottom of my heart."

Her eyes focused past Ethan to a bookshelf where something caught her attention, something she had not seen since she was a child. On the crooked shelf sat an old stuffed animal. She walked over and gently picked it up as memories flooded her mind. "Deb Zghir," she cried out. "My teddy bear... you kept it all these years." She pulled it close to her chest and hugged it, recalling the time at the airport when Ethan bought it for her. "Why did you keep it?"

"It's the only thing I have left. Everything else is gone." He said the words calmly.

Brianna's eyes were clear and intense, her words deliberate. "I'm sorry about that. I only recently found out that Grandpa died. He was very special to me and treated me kindly."

She picked up the guitar case, walked over, and handed it to him. "I wanted to return this to you. It helped shape me into the person I am today."

He opened the case. His jaw dropped as he gazed at the guitar he had given her the day Susan shattered hers. It was in perfect condition, including the red heart he painted as a reminder of Janna.

Ethan's voice choked with emotion. "It's in great shape. You took good care of it." He touched it. More memories raced through his mind.

The scene was moving, but just as quickly was over! Ethan snapped back to reality slamming the case shut. "I don't play anymore!" He shoved it toward Brianna, hanging his head sadly.

Brianna blinked her eyes open and waited for Ethan to look up. As he moved his eyes upward, their eyes met. Neither of them could pull their gaze away from each other for some time.

"I've come to say I'm sorry." Her voice cracked.

Then it happened again. Ethan's mood changed, the sarcasm returned. "Wow! Listen to that. There's another song title... I Have Come to Say I'm Sorry. You need to come more often—we could put all the other artists out of business. Well, now wait a minute, wasn't there a song with that title released in the sixties? Yes... by that blind dude. What was his name?" Ethan looked around the room, putting his hand to his chin, trying to remember.

"Please, listen to me. Please!" Brianna pleaded desperately.

"I'm listening. What reason did you have to lie about me? Why did you have to destroy my life? Tell me. I'm dying of curiosity." Bitterness dripped from his words.

Brianna began crying uncontrollably, and soon her entire body was quivering. It took a while for her to calm down enough to speak. "You were too protective of me. I grew tired of it." As soon as the words came out, Brianna knew she shouldn't have said them... it was not the truth. It was time for honest answers... no more lies!

"Oh, I'm sorry. I thought good parents protected their children," he answered defensively.

"You don't understand. It wasn't you; it was Susan. She hated me. I couldn't do anything right in her eyes. I thought it would help you if I was out of the picture." By now, her words were not clear, due to her intense sobbing. "I know you did your best, but all I wanted was my real mother and father. I wanted my daddy."

Ethan stood shouting, "So you wanted your daddy. You wanted your daddy!"

"Yes. I needed to know who my father was."

"Well Janna, let me tell you who your father was. I was your father... I am your father."

"No! I mean my real father," she shot back.

Ethan placed his hands on her shoulders, staring into her big blue eyes, and shouted, "Janna, look at me. I am your father!"

"No, you don't understand. I mean, my real father... not just the name on the birth certificate. I mean my biological father." Why couldn't he understand what she was saying? She sounded frustrated.

Ethan shook her gently trying to snap her into reality. Inches from her face, he insisted, "Mandy Dawn, look at me, look at my eyes. I am your real father. Mira, your mother, was my wife!"

Brianna stilled, letting the truth settle. She stopped sobbing when she began to grasp what he was saying. How could he call her that name? Only she and Sonya knew the real name on her birth record. How could he know her mother's name?

Shocked, she gasped, putting her hands over her mouth. Dizziness overcame her, and she began to fall, but Ethan's hands caught her.

The entertainer tried to collect her thoughts. Then she breathed loud and long, staring at Ethan. "You know my real name... how is that possible? You... are... my real father, my birth father?"

"Sit down and let me explain. It's a long story." He released his grip on her. She slowly walked backwards until she collapsed in a chair. Ethan grabbed another chair and put it directly in front of her, so close their knees touched.

He closed his eyes and took a deep breath. When he opened his eyes, he looked directly at Brianna.

For a brief time, Brianna saw the former Ethan—kindness shone in his eyes, his voice displayed concern. He was calm, thinking clearly.

Ethan took her hand tenderly, and touched the bracelet she wore. "I met your mother, Mira, in Paris. I remember her wearing this beautiful bracelet. Obviously, you found out what happened to her." He paused. A tear began its descent down the side of his cheek.

After all this time, Brianna was getting answers. She waited twenty-three years for this. She felt like she couldn't breathe, couldn't move, or she might miss something. Her expression showed her anticipation, her eagerness to know the whole truth.

He explained. "I was attending college in Paris. I was studying to be a linguist, and she was in my class. Well, she was actually my teacher." He grinned. "I thought she was the most beautiful woman in the world, but never expected what would happen between us."

A half-smile came over Brianna. "Oh... of course, that's why Sonya couldn't find you. Who would have thought my mother was dating one of her students?"

Ethan stroked softly his daughter's hand. "One day after class I noticed she had a flat tire on her car and I helped change it. We hit it off from the start. We just began talking and never stopped." He smiled as he recalled the events. "We had known each other for only a short time when we realized we were madly in love."

He stood up and started to pace the floor. He was obviously agitated, but at the same time savoring each moment of his past. It was the first time he ever told anyone their love story.

"Every free moment we spent together. We had an amazing adventure in the City of Love. We would go up the Eiffel Tower at night, and I would hold her for hours as we watched the beauty of the city—the colors, the lights, the traffic below. We would make jokes about the little toy cars. You could see them, but not hear them. It was like we were in another world, just the two of us. No worries. No schedules."

He continued sharing. "Coming from a desert country, she would say that the one thing she wanted to do more than anything was visit the snow-capped Rocky Mountains. She had seen pictures of them, and found it hard to believe something that magnificent really existed."

Brianna could hardly believe she was finally hearing the truth about her mother and father—how they met, and fell in love. She sat breathless, reeling in every detail.

"She was a year older than me, and we kept our relationship quiet because of the student-teacher thing. Nobody knew we were involved. Paris is a big city and we got lost in it. We would walk the streets day and night, talking about everything—ourselves, our families, the future, and God. She was curious about Jesus since I often talked about my personal relationship with Him. One day I explained it to her. We had actually dated for about six weeks, when she turned to me and said, 'I want to know this Jesus for myself. How can I do that?'"

Relishing the moment, Brianna tried to capture the sights and sounds of that momentous occasion.

"Of course I was thrilled to pray with her. I was unaware at the time that I was signing her death warrant. One thousand feet above Paris, late at night, she became a Christian, rejecting the religion of her family. I was delighted, but I noticed a change in her a few days later. I found out she had told her parents about her conversion. She had hoped to invite them to meet Jesus." There was a long pause before he continued. "Her father ordered her home. In fact, her brothers were coming to get her."

Brianna sighed, afraid to hear the rest of the story.

"I asked your mother to marry me and she agreed readily. As my wife, she would be able to get into America easier. We wasted no time; we married immediately." Another smile came to his hardened face. "It was a small wedding in a chapel, the same place we spent our honeymoon. I gave her the cross necklace that you're wearing as a wedding gift. I didn't have time to get her a ring." Ethan's demeanor remained calm as Brianna tenderly touched the cross. "I remember our tiny cottage, just outside Paris, as though it was yesterday. It was the most wonderful weekend of my life. We were two young lovers without a care in the world. In fact, you were conceived there. We never even thought about her getting pregnant, nor the ramifications of it."

Overwhelmed with sadness, Brianna shook her head. "May I ask you a question?" She removed the cross and handed it to him. "What do the numbers and letters on this cross mean?"

He instantly recalled, "1C1347."

"Yes. You remember?"

"It's the love chapter in the Bible... 1 Corinthians 13:4-7. *Love is patient, love is kind. It does not envy, it does not boast, it is not proud. It does not dishonor others, it is not self-seeking, it is not easily angered, it keeps no record of wrongs. Love does not delight in evil but rejoices with the truth. It always protects, always trusts, always hopes, always perseveres.*"

Ethan looked heavenward and a tear slipped from his eye. "Always protects... I couldn't do that. I could not protect the love of my life. What kind of man was I?"

His shaking stopped. Ethan's mood became melancholy as he delved deeper into his past. "She went to work three days later, but when I arrived at class, the other students said she never showed up. I found out later that her brothers had abducted her from school. There was a scuffle and police were called, but they did nothing. By the time I found out, they were on the way back to Baghdad totally against her will. I could do nothing about it. I was heartbroken, helpless."

Brianna exhaled, her frustration was evident.

"I called my dad and told him the entire story. He was concerned because he knew about her family, and he thought my life might be in danger. The circumstances in Iraq made it impossible for anyone to help. It was two months before I heard a word from her. She called to tell how much she missed me. Her father restricted her from leaving the house. I wanted so badly to go to her, but Mira insisted I stay away. She told me they would kill me, and the police would look the other way. At that point, they had no idea who I was, and she wanted to keep it that way to protect me."

Ethan's words became more difficult to get out with each breath. "That's when my wife told me she was pregnant. She dared not tell her family, or she and the baby would be killed. I always thought she was exaggerating about her violent family. Surely grandparents would not harm a baby, not their own flesh and blood." He shook his head in disbelief.

The pain in his eyes was almost more than Brianna could bear.

"My father explained that most Muslims were not that way, but her family was extreme. They would kill both of us, no questions asked. Dad couldn't risk helping my wife escape their clutches, but he could help me stay in touch with my sweet Mira. He had many Muslim friends he could trust."

Brianna glanced at her necklace, then back to her father.

"There was one family in Baghdad he had known for years, good people—Dafi and Saahira. They would help protect Mira and the baby. Even as powerful as Mira's father was, they said they would do what they could. I felt bad putting their lives at risk, but I didn't know where else to turn. Come to find out, Saahira was a nurse at a hospital in Baghdad. In the dark of night, your mother finally escaped from her evil family and stayed with this couple. Eventually that nurse took your mother to the hospital where you were born."

Brianna said, "I think I met her, but I went back to the hospital to talk to her and she couldn't be found."

He continued with the painful details. "They kept in close contact with me during your birth. She and her husband had planned to get you and Mira out of Iraq through Kuwait. Unfortunately, Saddam had other plans—he attacked Kuwait, and Mira was stuck in Iraq."

Ethan reached into his pocket and pulled out his worn wallet. Removing a photo, which he had laminated for protection, he handed it to her.

Brianna assumed it was the missing picture from the front of the scrapbook. It was one in the series of pictures taken of Mira and her baby at the hospital. Staring at the photo of her mother, Brianna could not hold back her tears.

Ethan went on. "She had this picture and a few others taken, and sent them to me. Years later, Susan found the other photos and destroyed them in a jealous rage."

His voice weakened. "The nurse was bringing you back from being fed when she noticed Mira's brothers in the hall. Instead of returning you to your crib, she took you to another room. She hurried back to move Mira and the other baby who was in your crib. It was too late—they were both already dead. Of course, with your grandfather's money, the whole thing was covered up. Later at the funeral, the family saw a picture of Mira holding the baby and noticed the birthmark. The brothers knew there was no birthmark on the baby they killed, so they suspected you were still alive. They returned to the hospital with the photo, and questioned our nurse friend about the baby with the distinctive feature. She told you had died. The brothers obviously did not believe her. I don't think your grandmother, Mira's mother, ever knew the truth about her husband and sons."

By now, tears were flowing freely down Brianna's face as she thought of the heartbreaking story of love, which ended so tragically.

"The nurse took you home for the first three years of your life. She was your mother by all accounts and kept in touch with me."

"That's why she looked so familiar when I saw her," Brianna cried.

Ethan nodded his head in agreement. "Saahira knew your uncles had checked all the orphanages and had not found you. She heard that everyone in the hospital was being screened and their lives were at risk. You were in danger, so they took you to a small orphanage close to Kuwait. The people at the orphanage protected you until our friends could get you out of Iraq safely. They had strict instructions that you were not to be adopted; your father would return for you as soon as he could. I tried everything to get you out of the country, so I could hold you, and care for you, but every avenue closed."

He cleared his throat. "I learned that Mira's brothers were using the birthmark to try to locate you. My father told me there was a huge reward for both you and me—dead or alive. Evidently, Mira accidentally let my name slip once. She called me Barrett, which is my middle name. My dad said her family didn't know if it was my first or last name. Fortunately, all of my documents said Ethan B. Anderson, so their search for me came to a dead-end."

Everything was starting to make sense to Brianna. All the pieces of the puzzle, her life, were beginning to fit together. "They told Conrad they were looking for Barrett, but could never find you."

Ethan raised his brow. "Oh, so you have met your uncles and grandfather. What do you think of them? A lot of family love, huh?"

He continued to stare into her tear-filled eyes. "They were getting closer and closer to you. Money can buy a lot of information."

"Don't I know that!" Brianna stated emphatically, realizing that is how she received all her information—she bought it.

"I don't know what I would have done without Dafi and Saahira."

"So, it wasn't that nobody wanted me. All this time, I thought I was unadoptable because I was flawed. The truth was that I was never adopted because my real father was coming back for me." Brianna's voice was mixed with sorrow and relief.

Ethan began pacing the floor. "Yes, it was because of my orders that you were never adopted. Dafi and Saahira risked their lives more than once to protect you. Finally, the big break came. I managed to get into Iraq for business. At the same time, the orphanage was taken over by Saddam's regime; he would use the building to house his army. The people in charge were fired, and the children were dispersed to different parts of the country. Our friends were informed that you had been sold to a group of businessmen and taken to Kuwait. That long black hair and dark blue eyes of yours caught their attention. They knew you were worth a lot of money in the adult movie industry. I knew I had to act fast, or possibly lose you forever. My father was a good friend of one of the princes in Kuwait. With that man's help, we found your location and rescued you along with two dozen other girls. I almost lost you to those people in Asia."

Brianna cried, "You were the man at my mother's grave that the caretaker talked about, weren't you?"

"You know about that? My, you have been busy. Yes, I had to stop and say goodbye. I was six years late, but I carved a heart in the rock that served as her tombstone."

"What did the heart mean?"

"It meant two things—my love for Mira, and my love for you. I talked with your mother seven times before her murder. I remember each conversation like it happened yesterday. She loved you so much. She told me how beautiful you were, especially the heart-shaped birthmark, and that you were a gift from God. We both believed God marked you for a reason."

Relief was making its way through her because she was finally getting the answers she had longed to hear.

"I received the photos of you the same day that I was notified of your mother's death. The birthmark on your forehead became the only link to you. Surely, Gods plan. I put that heart on the tombstone with the hope that one day you would see it, and realize that I was alive. We deliberately circulated a rumor that I was dead. However, Mira's powerful family kept searching for you. They would have killed you if they had found you, even in America. "

They were both still for a long time. Neither could understand.

He continued. "When I got to the house in Kuwait, I spotted you immediately." He said with a father's love, "I didn't need the blue eyes, or the birthmark to recognize you. I just knew it was you." Ethan looked at Brianna through his tears. "My heart skipped when I saw you. I wanted to run up and hug you, but I needed to keep my cool. Nobody could know who you were."

"Did Susan know about me?" Brianna finally spoke.

"Yes. I told her all about you. She was all right with it at first, but when Eric and the twins came into the world, she changed. It was all about her— her needs, her desires. She was jealous of my relationship with your mother. It was sad."

"Why did you not tell me about this before?"

"Like I said, Mira's parents were influential people. I didn't think I could disclose this information without putting your life in danger. Her evil relatives found out later you were in the United States. My father showed me a flyer written in Arabic. They had sent it to all the mosques in America, searching for a girl with a heart-shaped birthmark on her forehead. I could not risk anybody else knowing you were here. The fewer people who knew about it, the safer you would be. It was extremely difficult since I worked with people of the Muslim faith at the school... that was all the more reason to be secretive."

His eyes met hers. Ethan questioned, "Let me ask you this, would you have done things differently if I had told you?"

"I don't know. I can't answer that. I was a mixed-up teenager searching for something. I was so confused, and Susan made things worse. Now I understand why you never took me to work with you, or never introduced me to any of your business associates. Things are finally starting to make sense. I thought I was an embarrassment to you, but you were protecting me all along. Did your lawyer know?"

Ethan nodded. "He knew everything from the beginning. Robert set up the adoption. He helped me as much as he could, even today. He informed me when you disappeared, and I feared they had killed you. When he called me on your seventeenth birthday with the news you were alive, I was overjoyed."

Brianna stood. With a nervous voice, she tried to keep her focus. "I destroyed your life, your family. You spent six years in prison for a lie I told. Your father died while you were in jail. Now you live in these horrible conditions. Why... why didn't you stand up for yourself? Why didn't you defend yourself in court?"

Without hesitation, Ethan confided. "It would have been nationwide news. Word would have leaked out about the birthmark. If your identity had been discovered, your life would have been in jeopardy. There was no way I could have kept you safe. Their hate would have caught up to you and killed you. I was not willing to risk that. For Mira's sake and yours, I had to protect you—that's what a father does. Whatever the cost, he should shield his children from harm. God is a Father like that. He promised to protect His children. He has done that for you, hasn't He?"

There was complete silence. Brianna could not find the words to speak. She thought about all the things she had done. Her selfish actions destroyed many lives. The damage was done, nothing could undo it.

More thoughts flooded her mind. It was Ethan who made her into the woman she was today. Much of her music, the tunes that launched her into stardom, in reality, belonged to him. They were a team. If only she had listened to him. She would not have had to endure the torment and abuse she experienced on her way to the top. So many regrets! So many consequences! If only she could turn back time.

Ethan had taught her that Jesus was the way. Yet, she had to find out for herself, the hard way, ten years later.

What about forgiveness? She certainly didn't deserve it. How do you ask forgiveness from someone whose life you destroyed?

Brianna suddenly felt a surge of strength—she knew where it came from. Without talking herself out of it any longer, the singer walked over to her broken father.

Unsure how to respond to her, Ethan turned his back.

She reached for him with trembling hands. "Can... can you ever forgive me?"

He exhaled. The frustration and anger were evident in his tone. "Forgive you for lying, cheating me out of my family, and stealing my life? Forgive you for having me locked up in prison where I was terribly mistreated? How can I forgive you?"

She touched his shoulder, and he pulled further away.

The daughter who needed her daddy, wanted to hug him, and weep in his arms, but couldn't tolerate more rejection.

Next, she did what she had done all her life when circumstances seemed overwhelming—she bolted, slamming the door behind her. She darted to the car, never giving her father a chance to reply, or to extend his forgiveness. What if he couldn't forgive her? The heartbreak would be too much. So she ran.

In the stillness of the room, a crushed Ethan Anderson fell to his knees and tearfully poured out his heart to God.

Prayer was the only thing that made sense... and it had been years since he had prayed.

EIGHTEEN

The Surprising Confession

A time to search and a time to give up,
a time to keep and a time to throw away.
Ecclesiastes 3:6

The ride to the airport in Casper was anything but quiet. Brianna told Sonya and her friends what had happened, and that she found her real father. They simply listened.

More secrets exposed... more lies uncovered... more questions answered.

Brianna needed to do one more thing. Even though fear and dread descended on her, the entertainer knew she would not, could not, be free of her burden until she returned to where it all started—Mesa, Arizona. Not certain what she would do when she got there, she asked Sonya to arrange the flight right away.

Sonya phoned the pilot, "We're going straight to Mesa, Arizona. Make the flight arrangements."

The flight to Arizona was quiet and uneventful.

By early evening they had arrived at their destination and were settled in a small, but comfortable, condo in Mesa.

After a quiet night, forsaking her usual morning run, Brianna met the others for an early breakfast.

After their meal, Brianna put her cell phone and a few things in her pocket, and stood by the front door. She spoke directly to Conrad and Sonya. "I have never asked this before, but I need some time by myself. I'm going to take a walk to clear my head. Please, let me have what I'm asking for. The next decision I must make on my own. I'll be okay... let me go. Alone."

Even though they were uneasy about it, they knew she was right.

Conrad didn't like it, but he understood. He gave her an Arizona Diamondback cap and sunglasses to wear on her way out the door.

They all watched Brianna walk down the sidewalk until she disappeared from sight. With certainty, they knew she was not alone... God was with her. The small group of friends gathered for a prayer of protection on her.

The entertainer wandered the streets of Mesa for hours as she tried to clear her head. The star stopped at a small outdoor café and bought a bottle of cold water. Several people took a second look at her. A few asked if she was Brianna Bays, but she smiled and answered politely, "My name is Mandy Dawn Anderson."

"You sure look like Brianna," they would reply.

"I get that a lot." She smiled.

She walked until she could walk no more, and then sat on a nearby bench for a short break. Glancing at her watch, she realized she had been traipsing around the city for several hours. No wonder she needed a breather! She took a sip of water, and uttered a simple, silent prayer. *God, what next? Why did You bring me here?*

Even though she believed God worked in mysterious ways, and that He would make His will known to her in the right time, it still astonished her when she looked up and directly across the street was the Maricopa County Court House. She nodded her head in agreement. *Okay, Lord. I know what You're asking of me. I will be obedient. Please, give me strength.*

She took a few moments to reflect on her complicated life—her birth, her time at the orphanage, the adoption and how everything fell into place. She could clearly see God's protecting hand had been on her all her life. When she tried to do it on her own, she made a mess of things. This past year she discovered how to have a personal relationship with Jesus, and it was the best decision of her life.

People noticed the change in her, especially the outpouring of love for those around her. She felt peace, and experienced complete, undeserved forgiveness. What indescribable joy she felt!

Without God, she surely could not pursue the unfinished business awaiting her. It was time. She was ready. He would be with her; He was in control.

She stood, took her cell phone out of her pocket, and made the call she knew would change her life. "Sonya, I'm going to turn myself in. Will you come with me?"

"Where are you?" Her friend's voice didn't show surprise, almost as if she was expecting the announcement.

She glanced across the street. "I'm at the Maricopa County Courthouse. I believe God wants me to end this charade where it all began."

Unsure how to respond, Sonya asked, "Are you prepared for this, my friend?"

Brianna spoke with certainty. "Yes. Yes, I am. I don't know what tomorrow holds, but I'm sure who holds tomorrow."

"I'm proud of you! I'll be there in a few minutes. Wait for me!"

Brianna sat back down on the block bench looking at the building where her destiny would be decided. What would the outcome be? Was prison in her future?

There was an unusual chill in the air—perhaps it was her nerves.

Oblivious to the sights and sounds around her, she bowed her head to pray. She felt God's presence as words to one of her songs replayed in her mind, helping soothe her emotions.

You were there all along,
Waiting to pick me up...
You came shining,
Just as I knew you would.

Before the prayer ended, she felt a light touch on her shoulder. When she saw Conrad, her heartbeat was anything but normal.

The entertainer should have realized her extraordinary bodyguard wouldn't let her go alone. He had been following her discreetly all morning, never once letting her out of his sight.

"Sonya called me," he confessed.

Surprising even herself, she jumped up, slipped her arms around his muscular shoulders, and squeezed him tight. For a moment, it was only the two of them; nothing or nobody else mattered. She felt comfort and safe in his arms and was relieved he was there.

Sonya's car interrupted the tender moment. Jumping out of the vehicle, she ran over to Brianna. The star broke her hold on Conrad and threw her arms around Sonya. "Are you sure you're ready for this?"

"Yes. It's something I need to do." Without any more explanation, she clutched Conrad's hand, then Sonya's. Brianna knew she could count on them. Hand-in-hand, the three of them crossed the street and entered the courthouse.

Brianna bravely stepped up to the receptionist, her friends standing on each side of her.

The middle-aged woman behind the desk asked, "May I help you?"

Sonya readily responded in an upbeat voice. "We would like to talk to the District Attorney, Carol Moore."

"May I ask the reason for your visit?"

"Yes, my client would like to confess to a crime," Sonya stated, nodding towards Brianna.

The receptionist took a closer look at the woman in front of her. "You're Brianna Bays, aren't you?"

Sonya observed Brianna, wondering how she would respond.

"My name is Mandy Dawn Anderson." Brianna smiled.

"I see. You sure look like Brianna Bays. My kids have all her CDs. She's a good role model for them."

Sadness engulfed the entertainer when she realized how much of her life had been lies. No more lies—it was time for the truth to set her free.

The receptionist picked up her phone. "Yes, Carol, we have a Mandy Dawn Anderson here. She wants to confess to a crime." She listened and then looked up at Brianna. "No, I don't think she's dangerous. Are you dangerous?" she smiled warmly.

"No." Sonya stated, "She's definitely not dangerous."

Nonetheless, seconds later, two police officers escorted them to the district attorney's office.

As they walked through the waiting area, the whispering began. One person said, "I'm sure that's Brianna Bays. I wonder what she's doing here."

The star wasn't troubled by the murmurings, she strode ahead focused on her mission.

Carol Moore stepped out of her office to greet Brianna and her friends. She motioned for the two police officers to leave, and they readily responded.

"Aren't you Brianna Bays?" Moore asked.

"My name is Mandy Dawn Anderson. Brianna Bays is really someone else... someone I once knew. As a child, I was Janna Anderson." Her piercing eyes showed the gravity of the situation.

Moore's expression displayed her surprise. "Janna Anderson... I remember that case. That was about ten or eleven years ago. I worked diligently putting that pervert away. Please, come on in."

Brianna's heart sank when she heard the negative accusation about her father.

The three stepped into Moore's office.

The prosecuting attorney walked behind her desk and sat down. "Have a seat." Moore pointed to some chairs in front of her desk. Dropping her friendly tone, her voice expressed urgency. "Okay, what is this all about?"

Sonya made the introductions. "I'm Sonya Ellis, Miss Anderson's attorney, and this is Conrad Thompson, a close friend."

Brianna squeezed her friend's hands, still not wanting to let go of them.

Sonya filled her lungs and kept her focus. "She has a confession to make."

Brianna intended to do this with her head held high, not that she was proud of any of it, but because it was the right thing to do. Boldly, Brianna said, "Eleven years ago I lied about a crime, which sent an innocent man to prison. I destroyed his life."

Moore's expression changed to confusion. It was evident in her body language that she tensed up. Since she began practicing law, her worst fear was that she would send an innocent person to prison. She took a deep breath. "I remember that trial clearly. It was my first real case as an assistant prosecuting attorney for the county." She paused, reflecting on the trial, the huge media event that jump-started her career. "You do realize the state represented you, and the only evidence was your written testimony?"

"I do." Brianna sat perfectly still, unaware of anything around her.

"If what you say is true... you are guilty of perjury... a very serious crime. Are you aware of that?"

Brianna nodded her head in agreement.

Conrad sat next to her, barely breathing.

Moore's expression softened. "Why are you coming forward eleven years later?"

"Do you want the real reason, or do you want the legal reason?" Brianna asked.

"Is there a difference?" Moore's confusion was noticeable.

"To some people there would be."

"Well, let's start with the real reason," the prosecuting attorney responded.

Brianna cleared her throat. "I was convicted of my sin when I met Jesus. He totally forgave me, but made it clear that in order to be at peace with myself, I needed to ask forgiveness of those I have wronged."

The attorney's eyes widened. "I understand. You see, I'm a Christian now also. I have to say, you have more courage than many Christians. They accept the gift of salvation from God, but often do not walk the walk, or talk the talk. I admire you for this."

Brianna forced a weak smile.

Sonya interrupted. "As Brianna's lawyer, I am requesting that all charges against her be dropped."

Surprised, Moore questioned, "And your reasoning?"

"First off, my client was just twelve... she was underage at the time of the accusation. Secondly, I have read all the transcripts related to the case. Much was hearsay. It seems words were put in the young girl's mouth. And thirdly, I believe there may be a statute of limitations for this even though the law is vague."

Moore thought about what Sonya said. She looked at Brianna without saying anything. Eventually her thoughts became words. "I understand what you are saying. Let me first address your confession. If what you say is true, many people need to apologize. I, for one. I mean... I... I put Ethan Anderson in prison. Yes, you were only twelve, and that does play a big part in the process." She sighed. "And as much as I hate to admit it, many of us who talked to you did put words in your mouth."

The remorseful prosecuting attorney continued. "When Judge Summers became a federal judge, and when Ethan Anderson's father died, I was determined to make sure Mr. Anderson served hard prison time. I did everything in my power to facilitate his incarceration. I heard he was mistreated in prison. The fact is... the system failed him miserably. I will have to come to terms with my part in all of this later... as an attorney, but more importantly as a Christian."

This isn't what Brianna expected. Her heart was beating fast, her hands sweaty.

Moore continued. "I'm sure your lawyer has told you what could happen. However, I must explain it myself." She shifted her position in the chair. "There is what we call a statute of limitations. That means a person cannot be tried for something that happened more than seven years ago. It's been over ten years. I'm not really certain if that would apply in this case, but as the prosecuting attorney, I am the one who submits the court cases."

Moore reflected on the trial that launched her career. "As far as criminal action, we will not press any charges. Putting it bluntly, if we did, we would open this entire office up to an internal investigation. That would not be good for any of us. We made mistakes. However, civil action is different."

"Meaning?" Brianna asked.

"Simply put, it means the man you put behind bars can sue you for everything you have. You said you are asking for forgiveness... have you contacted him?"

"Yes, I have." Brianna's eyes instantly began to fill.

"How did he take it?"

Brianna thought back to the day before, when she discovered Ethan was her real father. "It's complicated... very complicated. I think it would be better to ask, how did *I* take it?"

"I don't understand."

Not wanting to divulge more personal information, Brianna changed the subject. "What is my next step? I want to come clean for all my wrongs. No more secrets."

"Like I said, legally we won't do anything. Your case is closed."

Brianna walked over to a picture on the wall of George Washington kneeling in prayer. She stared at the famous art piece wondering what the first president would have done in her situation. She recalled the old legend about Washington as a young person. *I cannot tell a lie. I chopped down the cherry tree.* She smiled at the thought.

All eyes in the room were on Brianna; everyone was being respectful of the time she needed to pull her thoughts together.

On the wall directly beside Moore's desk was a picture of a young man dressed in army fatigues—a soldier standing in front of an American flag. The entertainer walked closer, staring intently at the picture. "Is this your son?" Brianna asked with an element of surprise.

Moore boasted, "Yes, he's an MP. He's currently serving in Iraq." Her eyes shone a little brighter.

"My, what a small world," Brianna whispered. She recalled the same soldier from her recent tour in Iraq. He had been one of the MPs who protected her, escorting her around the area. "You must be very proud of him."

"I am." The mother's face beamed.

During the conversation, Brianna suddenly realized what she had to do. "Sonya, call a press conference."

"When and where?" Sonya didn't hesitate.

"Here... where it all began... tomorrow morning at ten. Ms. Moore, will you come to it?"

"Yes, I will, but why? What's this all about?" Moore shot a questioning look at the star.

"I want to be honest with my fans."

"Sure, I'll be there. I wouldn't miss it."

Brianna looked directly into the prosecutor's eyes. "Thank you."

"No, Miss Bays." Moore hit a key on the computer keyboard, and turned the monitor for Brianna to see. It was a picture taken in Iraq. The star was posing with her arm around the prosecuting attorney's son. "I need to thank you." Carol wiped away some fresh tears.

Brianna studied the picture, smiling, and remembering the brave soldier.

"For what?" Brianna asked.

"For remembering our troops... especially my son. And for being truthful—your fans will respect you for it."

Moore stood. "Who knows? There may be people out there who are contemplating doing what you did. They may change their minds when they realize the grave consequences."

Brianna nodded.

"I am ashamed of my part in this. The evidence was not there. Ethan Anderson should never have been convicted. The problem is in such a case, emotions run high. It's almost impossible for a prosecutor to lose. And truthfully, I was trying to make a name for myself." Moore lowered her head shamefully.

Brianna thought about her words for a brief time, and then her voice perked up. "By the way, your son is a fine young man. I appreciated his protection, and enjoyed getting to know him. I pray he is well."

"Yes. He will be home in a couple weeks." The mother smiled.

"I'm glad to hear that. We pray for the troops during our prayer time every day."

"Thank you, again."

Brianna reached her hand to Conrad, who gladly held it. Words could not describe the admiration he had for his friend. Her actions demonstrated courage, and an eagerness to be in the will of God. She amazed him. Maybe that's why when he was close to her, he felt his pulse racing.

Moore smiled at Brianna. "Miss Bays?"

"It's Mandy... Mandy Dawn Anderson."

"Well, Mandy Dawn Anderson... welcome to the family of God!"

A heartfelt smile took over Brianna's face.

NINETEEN

The Public Disclosure

Love is patient, love is kind... it keeps no record of wrongs.
Love does not delight in evil but rejoices with the truth.
1 Corinthians 13:4-6

Immediately following the announcement of the press conference, the Internet was active. Facebook, Twitter, and all the social media were predicting what the entertainer's big announcement would be.

Gossip was running rampant among the media, many expecting a wedding announcement, or perhaps the release of a new CD or movie deal. The Arizona city was buzzing with excitement that perhaps Brianna's newest movie would be filmed in Mesa.

Still others feared a negative announcement, something like drugs. Even though Brianna preached against drugs at her concerts, she may have fallen—many stars do.

Soon enough, the mystery would be solved.

A giant crowd of reporters and fans gathered to hear the announcement from the world-renowned superstar.

On a typically warm morning in Mesa, Brianna walked out and stood in front of a bank of microphones. Sonya, Conrad, and the district attorney followed. The sight of Carol Moore confused many reporters—they couldn't imagine why she was there.

In a noticeably different mood than her usual chipper self, Brianna nervously stared straight ahead. "Good morning. Thanks for coming."

A hush fell over the crowd who was eagerly awaiting the news.

She paused. "What I am about to say is difficult. I wasn't sure where to begin, so I wrote a statement that I will read. After I'm finished, I will not take any questions."

With that, she began to read. "We all do things in our lives, which we later regret. Most of the time, they don't affect others to the extent of what

I have done. For years reporters have tried to dig up details about my life. Because of circumstances in my childhood, my past has been kept private... even to me. Recently the secrets of my past have been revealed. I used other names to hide my identity, but it has been in recent months that I discovered my real name is Mandy Dawn Anderson."

A reporter in the crowd yelled, "Why all the secrets, Mandy?"

Brianna ignored the remark, determined to stay with the script. "I'm ashamed to admit that when I was twelve, I falsely accused my adoptive father of a crime he didn't commit. I lied, committing perjury."

Some snide comments came from the media, but she ignored them. "My adoptive father, Ethan Anderson, was the kindest, most gentle father a child could ever have." She hesitated, fighting emotions that were close to the surface

Brianna glanced into the still gathering, then back at her notes. "This morning I want to tell the world my story."

Silence reigned over the anxious crowd.

"I was born in Baghdad, Iraq, on February 13, 1991, during the Gulf War. My mother, an Iraqi Muslim, met my father, a devout Christian, while she taught at a university in Paris. My mother converted to Christianity, and they married secretly. They were deeply in love." Brianna shuffled her notes.

The singer's voice cracked when she spoke about her mother's murder, and the killing of the helpless newborn. "They soon realized they had killed the wrong baby, and they began a hunt to kill me. The search continued until a few weeks ago."

The bizarre story kept the crowd interested as they waited for more, anything for a juicy headline.

Forging ahead, Brianna spoke about the nurse at the hospital, and the impact she had on her life. She even disclosed the fact that she was almost sold as a child harlot.

At times it seemed like the events she was relating happened to someone else, and she was an outsider looking in.

It was difficult to share her story, but when she began to talk about Ethan, it became even harder. She told what happened when Ethan first laid eyes on her at the orphanage. "His voice was kind, his eyes so caring. He told me that I was special, a gift from God. Only now do I realize the importance of his words."

This was not the information the press expected, but still newsworthy material, possibly even a bigger story than they imagined. It certainly would tug on the readers' heartstrings.

She was hesitant to detail her rebellious teen years. Nevertheless, she knew it was necessary. Maybe some young people were going through the same struggles. Perhaps her honesty could steer them in the right direction—one changed life would make it worthwhile. "Just before I turned fifteen, I ran away. For the next two years, I lived on the streets using my music to survive. I did things I deeply regret. Until one day, I was given the opportunity to perform at a small restaurant. I'll never forget the day Sonya came into my life." Brianna glanced at Sonya.

In response, Sonya smiled and winked at her.

Brianna returned a sad smile, not her usual radiant one. She was extremely grateful for Sonya's friendship and support. She never could have made it to this day without her and Conrad.

The singer took a deep breath and continued reading. "All along, certain questions kept hounding me. Who were my real parents? Whatever happened to Ethan Anderson, the man who had taken me in, loved me as a child, and protected me more than I ever knew? Just a few days ago, I finally learned the truth."

A fresh batch of tears stung her eyes, but she blinked them away. Would she be able to finish this?

She glanced at Conrad and he rewarded her with a smile, giving her the strength to continue.

"About a year ago, I hit rock bottom. That is a story I will share another time. I realized I could not keep living a life of lies, and I gave my heart to Jesus Christ. My life changed drastically after that."

She thought she heard a couple people in the crowd shout words of affirmation, others were murmuring. Good or bad, she wasn't sure, and at that point, it didn't matter.

She continued reading, "My ultimate goal was to find out who my real parents were. When you have plenty of money, you can buy a lot of information."

Brianna cast a look into the audience, then quickly back to her notes. "I was on a mission, and nothing could stop me. One of the things I needed to do was visit my mother's grave. I also wanted to confront those who murdered her, one of the most difficult things I've ever done."

The mood of the audience grew even more somber.

"However, the identity of my birth father continued to be a mystery... every lead turned out to be a dead-end. Unknown to me, my father had already been a part of my life. Recently, I discovered that my birth father was Ethan Anderson, the very man who rescued me from a life of horror. The same man I lied about... the same man who was sent to prison for six long years for a crime he didn't commit."

Fighting tears, she took a deep breath. "My life was in danger, and I didn't know it. My mother's family realized I was still alive, and Ethan knew they would kill me. My father had been protecting me all along."

She swallowed hard, trying to keep her composure. "I know many of you are thinking, in a world of six billion people how could my uncles find me? Why couldn't I hide? Why couldn't my money buy me safety?"

Brianna hesitated for a second, and then pulled back her hair exposing her birthmark. "Only my closest friends knew about this birthmark. No one has ever captured it on film. So... here is your chance. Take pictures if you want. No more secrets!"

Some reporters gasped, obviously stunned by the entertainer's disclosure. Six years, tens of thousands of photos, and it was never detected. Cameras were snapping everywhere. The media would not miss the opportunity to share photos of the mark on the mega star's forehead, or shoot close-up photos to add interest to the shocking story. What an account it would be!

Brianna would not be deterred. "Ethan had never seen me as a baby. His only clue came from a small photo of my mother holding me in the hospital. When he saw me at that orphanage in Kuwait, he picked me up, looked at my birthmark, and told me that it was a gift from God. Now I understand what he meant. It was the only evidence that I existed; it was the only way I could be identified. By going to prison, Ethan protected me. He sacrificed his career, his family, his life, and even his reputation. He could have exposed my lies, but he chose to protect me—his love for me was that strong. I pray that someday it will be again."

A few reporters interrupted, shouting questions. "How could you do it, Mandy?"

Brianna stayed with the script. "I know you are wondering why I lied. After all, I had a good home, certainly better than any of my foster homes. Even though I had serious problems with my stepmother, why would I resort to destroying the one person who really cared for me, my father? I keep asking myself the same question, but unfortunately, I still don't have an answer. I'm not trying to justify my actions, just trying to sort out my confusion at that rebellious time in my life. There is no excuse for what I did."

A reporter tried to push through the crowd to get closer, but security quickly removed him.

"You see, I didn't know who my mother and father were so there was a huge void in my life. Everyone at school had parents. I had a stepmother who resented me, and an adoptive father whose marriage was in trouble because of me. I allowed the influence of a peer to cloud my judgment. I chose a path of destruction. It was all about me... myself. No one else mattered. I thought everyone would be better off if I was out of the picture."

Brianna knew what she was about to say was touchy. She didn't want to hurt the Muslim community, yet knew she couldn't hold back. "Also, I was being pulled in two different directions—I was reared six years as a Muslim, the next six as a Christian. I had no idea what to believe."

Brianna's voice sounded dry. Grateful she brought a water bottle, she took a few sips. "As success came to my life, a few things hounded me. First, my intense desire to locate my birth parents. Second, was the guilt of destroying a good and decent man. Add to that, my spiritual condition... I had pushed God out of my life."

Brianna cleared her throat. "I could not see that emotionally I was spiraling out of control, but those around me could. One day I hit a brick wall. Fortunately when that day came, my friends were there to help me pick up the pieces." Brianna could not look at Conrad and Sonya—she would not be able to control the tears.

She continued reading. "It took a lot of soul-searching, but with the help of my close friends, I found the real answer to my problems. I realized that I was a sinner, saved by grace. Not perfect, but forgiven. That's when I entered a personal relationship with Jesus Christ."

The crowd was still quiet, most scribbling on their pads. Many reporters had microphones, hoping for a private word with the star—all wanting the juicy details.

"I sent my lawyer, Sonya Ellis, on a quest. Regardless of the cost, I wanted her to find out everything she could about my background. That search led me to where I am today."

Brianna looked into the sea of reporters. She had not intended to leave her notes, but somehow she did. Pulled from her script, she spoke straight from her heart. "I know what I did was wrong, and I deserve to be punished. Therefore, yesterday I turned myself in to the local authorities. I am ready to face justice. I know nothing can erase what I have done. It will always be embedded in my mind, and the consequences will linger forever."

The entertainer noticed a star-struck teen standing in the front row with the reporters. She was wearing a Brianna Bays t-shirt. The entertainer could see the confusion in the girl's eyes.

She hated to disappoint her fans, but knew she had to finish. "Yesterday at the courthouse, a mother commented that Brianna Bays was a good role model for her children. That statement hurt deeply. Although I tried to be a good role model, I had dark secrets from my past. I have not been the example I should have been because I have not been totally honest."

Brianna looked eye-to-eye with the young fan in front. "I am asking for forgiveness from my fans who I have disappointed. Please forgive me. I thank God because He already has. I know there is nothing that can change or repair the damage I have done. But maybe, just maybe, what I am doing today will affect one life, even just one." By now tears were running freely down her face. She stepped back. There was nothing more she could say; she had done her part.

Sonya came close to Brianna, wrapped her arms around her, and embraced her.

A woman approached the microphone. "My name is Carol Moore, and I am the District Attorney of Maricopa County." She cleared her throat. "I was greatly disturbed when Brianna Bays came into my office yesterday and told me this entire story. She is not the only one who needs to ask for forgiveness."

Brianna listened from the background.

Moore continued. "I did everything in my power to destroy Ethan Anderson. I went out of my way to convict him and send him to jail. When his case came up for review, I did everything in my power to have him sent to state prison. My actions were appalling, and I deeply regret them. I owe Mr. Anderson an apology. I also apologize to you, the public. I am sorry."

The attorney's face registered sorrow, disgrace. "I have talked with the judge and my staff lawyers, and we all commend Brianna Bays for coming forward. We have concluded that because of her age at the time of the trial, and the amount of community service she has rendered, including supporting the troops overseas, there will be no further action from my office. However, that does not rule out civil action in the future from others. That's all I have to say. Thank you."

It started with murmurings, but within seconds grew into a loud rumbling. One voice boomed over the noise, "Does that mean Ms. Bays gets off scot-free?"

The district attorney glared at the man who asked the question. "I would say that would be up to Ms. Bays and the man she falsely accused."

Another voice yelled, "How can we contact him? Is he available?"

"I don't know the answer to that. Please direct those questions to Ms. Bays or her attorney."

The restless crowd was growing more agitated.

Sonya released her hold on the remorseful entertainer. Brianna lost herself in Conrad's open arms, where she felt protected, safe, even amidst such chaos.

Sonya came to the microphone. "My name is Sonya Ellis. I am Brianna Bays' personal attorney, manager, and close friend. Let me first say, it's tragic these events ever occurred. Unfortunately, things like this happen every day. Abuse is rampant in our society. Until we realize all life is to be valued, from the womb to the tomb, it will continue. There are thousands of children, and senior adults for that matter, whose abuse goes unreported. Other times innocent people are tried, judged, and sentenced. Our system is not perfect and mistakes will occur."

Looking sternly at the press, Sonya defended her friend. "As for Ms. Bays, she has paid for what she has done in more ways than you can imagine. The pain and regret never leave her. I can personally testify to the mental anguish that she has put herself through the last six years. She has been in her own private prison."

A reporter shouted, "Has Brianna been in touch with the victim?"

Sonya thought it ironic that the accused, Ethan Anderson, in reality, ended up the victim—how pitiful! She couldn't comment. "Additional questions may be directed to my office. Thank you."

Unwilling to let it drop, another reporter piped up, "Brianna, did you say you're asking for forgiveness from your father?"

The crowd was silent as everyone waited for a response.

With a tear-stained face, Brianna eyed the reporter.

The same reporter shouted, "Do you think he will forgive you, do you think he can ever forgive you?"

The press thought they deserved an answer, and many in the crowd shouted remarks inferring as much.

Having no answers, Brianna lowered her head, and turned to walk away.

Suddenly, from the back of the crowd, a voice bellowed above all others. "I believe I can answer that."

All heads turned to find the source of the comment.

Brianna immediately froze.

The man had been listening to the entire press conference, and now was weaving his way through the mass of reporters and photographers.

"And you are?" A reporter pushed a microphone in front of him when he walked by.

The mysterious man ignored the reporter and the question, pushing his way toward the front.

All eyes focused on him as he came face-to-face with Brianna Bays.

For a moment, he stared at her, and then turned his gaze to the crowd. He stepped to the microphone.

Brianna stood motionless in the protecting arms of her bodyguard.

"You asked this young woman if the man she falsely accused could ever forgive her."

The crowd grew louder, still demanding answers.

"Let me answer that. My name is Ethan Anderson. I am the father of Brianna Bays." Clean-shaven, with a haircut, and dressed in khakis and a navy blue polo shirt, he looked like a different man than the one she confronted a couple days before.

Brianna couldn't move or speak.

"Yes, my life has been a living hell for the last eleven years because of lies of a rebellious teenager. There's more to it than that. You asked if I could forgive her. The other day, my daughter asked me the same question. I was not certain how to respond. Her lies ruined my life, and I spent six years in prison for a crime I didn't commit. I lost my wife, my children, my family, my career, and my dignity."

Ethan's voice sounded nervous. "I don't blame all of what happened on my daughter. Society and the justice system let me down. The assistant prosecuting attorney did all she could to put me away, not because I was guilty, but because I was a man. The system was stacked against me from the beginning."

Carol Moore sadly nodded her head in agreement.

He blinked to clear his vision and mind and then continued. "I repeatedly mulled over the same questions—could I forgive her? Would I forgive her? Since my daughter's surprising visit, I have thought of nothing else. I never answered her when she asked for forgiveness. The words of my late father kept replaying in my mind. 'One of these days, she will come back and ask for forgiveness. We must be ready to give it to her.'"

Ethan took a deep, cleansing breath, and exhaled slowly. His eyes began to fill. "Finally, I realized that I must forgive her as Christ forgave me. Jesus gave His life to save ours. He didn't have to... He just did... because He loves us. He loves us, even though we don't deserve it. You asked me, can I forgive her? Forgiveness comes from the heart. If I didn't or couldn't, what sort of father would I be? You see, Mandy Dawn Anderson is my daughter. No matter what she has done, she always was, and always will be my little girl."

He turned to face Brianna, speaking to her as if no one else was listening. "Mandy, I loved your mother. There is no way I could have ever abandoned you. You are part of Mira, and part of me. I love you unconditionally. How can I not forgive you? How can I not continue to love you? You're my daughter... and that will never change. I love you." With that, Ethan held his arms open wide.

Within seconds, Brianna bounded into her father's arms sobbing. "Daddy, I'm sorry... I'm so sorry."

Both were weeping tears of remorse, but more than that—tears of joy. After all the years of heartbreak, the father and daughter were finally reunited!

Many in the audience were wiping away tears. All were moved by the human drama that had played out before their eyes.

Ethan's tone was kind, warm, and reassuring as he tenderly spoke only to his daughter. "It's all right. We're together... that's all that matters now."

The moment had come. There was complete, total forgiveness. They had come full circle, and their lives would never be the same.

Sonya stepped to the microphone. Barely able to speak, she ended the news conference. "Like I said, any more questions, contact my office. Thank you."

The press began to charge toward the steps, trying to get close-up shots of the superstar with her father.

Sonya, Brianna, and Ethan rushed into the courthouse to escape any more cameras and questions. Within seconds, Brianna's bodyguards protectively blocked the door of the courthouse allowing the father and daughter their needed privacy.

When they entered the building, Carol Moore greeted them. "You talked about forgiveness out there, Mr. Anderson. As I look back on your trial, I know I was just trying to make a name for myself. I made a case against you with no real evidence. You're right... I was biased because you're a man. Let me assure you, it will never happen again. I have learned a good lesson. In the future, all evidence will be weighed and evaluated fairly. I can guarantee that. I ask you... can you forgive me?" She extended her hand to Ethan.

He reciprocated with dignity, and shook the hand of the woman who attacked him so viscously in the courtroom over ten years earlier. "It's a fresh start. The past is over. Mandy and I have a lot of father-daughter time to make up. I certainly do not have the time, or the energy to hold a grudge. Yes, I forgive you."

Ethan turned, pulling his daughter close to his side.

Brianna held Ethan tight, not wanting to let go of the father she had long sought. With tears in her azure eyes, Brianna asked Ethan a question. "Daddy, can we go to the ocean?"

Ethan was too choked up to reply. He looked at his daughter remembering the times long ago when she asked him the same question. It was a moment of love and forgiveness. Neither wanted the special moment to end. It was freedom from a confinement that had imprisoned each of them for more than a decade.

TWENTY

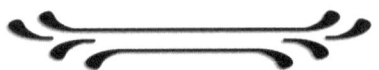

The Island Escape

A time to tear and a time to mend.
Ecclesiastes 3:7

Following the news conference, the media was even more relentless in pursuing her. To escape the constant hounding of the reporters, Brianna, Ethan, Sonya, and her four bodyguards retreated to the star's luxurious private island in the Caribbean. Two weeks of rest and relaxation would benefit all of them. Most of all, it would be a time of rebuilding the relationship between Ethan and his daughter.

Upon arrival at her lavish island getaway, the group relaxed, sipping lemonade, on the balcony overlooking the beautiful white-sand beach.

Ethan commented on her exquisite home-away-from-home. "How on earth did you ever purchase your own island?"

Brianna and Sonya looked at each other and broke out laughing.

"Do you want to tell him?" Sonya asked.

"No, you go ahead. I'm really kind of embarrassed about the whole thing,"

Sonya began. "Brianna was touring in Mexico about four years ago when a nicely groomed lawyer came to her dressing room. Of course, Conrad was suspicious of the man so he stayed while they talked. The man told her that he had an offer she couldn't refuse. His client was a big fan of hers, and had to quickly unload his Caribbean hideaway. Come to find out, his client was El Perno Rey."

Ethan's eyes widened, "The Mexican drug lord?"

"None other!" Sonya smiled. "He had been captured by the Mexican government, and was being held in an Arizona prison for security reasons. He had built this fortress over the span of twelve years, complete with guard towers, surveillance cameras, and a ten-foot cement fence around the entire place. He even had a surveillance area on the beach. Nobody could get on or off without him knowing it."

Sonya continued. "Anyway, Rey offered the place to superstar, Brianna Bays, for $430,000 with two stipulations."

Brianna rolled her eyes, laughing.

"She had to pay immediately in American cash... and in person."

"In person? Didn't that make you suspicious?" Ethan asked.

Brianna responded, "At first it did, but it was at an Arizona prison, so I figured it would be safe."

Sonya added, "He just wanted to meet his favorite entertainer, and at the same time unload his property so the government didn't seize it. To make a long story short, this place is worth over twenty million dollars. A good return on her money, don't you think?"

Ethan smiled at the story. He looked proudly at his successful daughter. "God protected you all along, didn't He?"

Brianna reached for his hand and squeezed it. "Yes, Daddy, God took care of me on my rough journey. He had a plan for me... for us. I can see it clearly now."

"This place is amazing," Ethan said.

Sonya agreed. "Brianna turned the twenty-two room guard house into a guest house where her island staff could live year round. The small house overlooking the ocean, which used to be the servant's quarters, was turned into her music sanctuary. She loves spending time there in solitude writing music."

Brianna interrupted. "Oh, Daddy! You've got to see that room! It's the most peaceful place on earth. I'll take you there later."

During their time in the tropics, Ethan and Brianna would walk the beach for hours, sharing tales of their past lives, and revealing honest feelings with each other—both good and bad.

Brianna soaked up the stories her dad told her about her mother.

Ethan loved to hear tales about her life as a superstar, her rise to the top of the entertainment world. He was proud of her, knowing she did not follow the path many superstars do with drugs, men, and wild parties.

The father-daughter duo played music together, just as they did many years before. The others would listen to their beautiful harmony and smile, amazed at what God had done in their lives—evidence that nothing was too big for Him!

Both of them realized it would take a lot of time and effort to completely restore their relationship, but they were committed to it, believing that one day their bond would be stronger than it ever was. The time in the Caribbean Islands was a perfect start!

The more Ethan and Brianna conversed, the more they realized two things still needed to be done. First, as painful as it would be, they needed to confront Susan. Second, they wanted to visit Mira's grave... but this time it would be together.

TWENTY-ONE

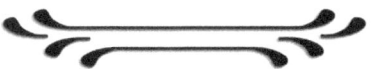

The Fatal Consequences

...a time to be silent and a time to speak.
Ecclesiastes 3:7b

Sonya managed to track Susan down. She was living with her parents in Phoenix.

However, she was unable to locate Alana, the only surviving sibling. Sadly, none of Ethan's children ever knew that their older sister became one of the most successful entertainers in the world. Brianna was a true Cinderella story—the siblings and stepmother ended up with nothing!

Ethan was hoping Susan could give them more information on Alana's whereabouts.

As they drove up the driveway to his former in-laws home, Ethan recalled the many times over the years he had visited. Some joyful times, others he would rather not remember.

Brianna wished she had fond memories of her time with her grandparents. She dreaded their visits because Susan's parents treated her like a stranger, not a granddaughter. Her stomach churned at the unpleasant memories. She would rather run from them, yet, she couldn't—there was no more running! She had to face them head on.

The house was not as nice as they recalled; it was showing its years of neglect.

Conrad pulled up to the door. He smiled at Brianna, trying to lift her spirits. Then he prayed a silent prayer for strength, courage, and wisdom as they faced another ugly part of their past.

Ethan and Brianna held hands as they walked to the door. Neither knew what surprises were in store for them. The only assurance they had was that no matter what happened, this time they would face it together.

Ethan rang the doorbell.

While they waited, Brianna glanced around at the broken shutters, which at one time made the house charming. The once-striking landscape was now overgrown with weeds and crabgrass.

Finally, the door squeaked open. In front of them stood an older woman they assumed must be Susan's mother. Obviously, the years had not been good to her; she appeared gaunt and haggard.

She stared at Ethan first, and then shifted her gaze to Brianna. For a time, no one said anything. Finally recognizing them, the woman screamed. She stepped back from the door with her hands covering her mouth, acting as if she had seen a ghost.

Quickly a man joined her to check out the commotion. He eyed the two visitors. "Ethan, is that you?" Susan's father asked, unable to hide the look of astonishment.

"Yes, sir." Neither Ethan's voice, nor his face showed any reaction.

The elderly man returned his eyes to Brianna examining her closely. There was no denying it, the black hair and bright blue eyes gave evidence of who she was. "It's true... Janna really is Brianna Bays!"

Brianna's eyebrows lifted. She uttered a short, nervous chuckle, uncertain what to say.

Ethan spoke curtly. "We would like to talk with Susan."

"So would we," the man replied sadly.

"May we come in?" Ethan asked.

"I'm sorry, yes, please come in."

He glanced at his wife, who was still speechless. "Martha, get our guests some lemonade."

"No thanks. We won't be long. Just long enough to tell Susan how we feel and say goodbye. Then we will be on our way." Ethan's answer seemed rehearsed.

"Ethan, you need to know that she is just a shell of a human being. Please don't be hard on her. She has been through a lot," the heartbroken father responded.

"And we haven't?" Ethan retorted, his tone sounding harsher than he wanted.

"I'm sorry. I didn't mean it like that. As you can see by the condition of our house, we're not doing very well. We've spent our entire life savings on Susan and her problems. She made one bad choice after another... in life... and with men." The father quickly added, "You not being one of them. You were a good man for her, and I'm sorry things didn't work out for the two of you."

Ethan was trying to keep his cool. "I seem to recall our last conversation was quite different. You weren't exactly civil to me."

The former father-in-law, regretful, hung his head. "Yes, you're right. I'm sorry. I didn't know the whole story."

"Please, just get her. We want to get this over with, so we can get on with our lives." Ethan's voice grew impatient.

"I'll be back in a few minutes. Please be seated in the study." He pointed to a worn sofa in a quaint room off the foyer.

Ethan and Brianna looked around the memory-filled room while they waited. One wall was dedicated to pictures of Susan during her beauty queen days. Trophies of their only daughter adorned the shelves. Another wall displayed a few family pictures of Susan and her children in their younger days. There were no photos of the siblings when they were older and not even one picture of Ethan or Brianna. They had been cropped out of the family pictures. Obviously, Susan's parents wanted nothing to remind them of those painful years.

Ethan sadly shook his head. "It was like we never existed."

They heard the doorknob turn, and they turned to see the elderly couple helping a frail woman into the room.

Brianna gasped aloud when she saw the woman, hoping no one else heard her sound of surprise.

Ethan closed his eyes and turned away. He could hardly face her; his stomach was upset.

Could it be Susan? Her hair was gray and thin with noticeable bald patches. Nothing but skin covered her feeble bones. Her face was no longer beautiful with her jaw protruding. Her nose was crooked; it had been broken in a beating by her last husband. Her teeth had yellowed and decayed. However, her eyes were the worst part—they no longer sparkled, and were sunken and dull. Her feet barely lifted; no longer was the sound of her heals clicking the floor, only the shuffle of dragging feet.

The woman looked at the visitors. A small flicker came to her eyes when she appeared to recognize Ethan.

The frail woman slowly walked over to Brianna. With shaking hands, she brushed the younger woman's hair to the side exposing her forehead. She pulled back when she noticed the birthmark, and immediately began sobbing uncontrollably.

Ethan put his arm around his daughter's shoulder and pulled her closer—neither knew what to say or do. The scene in front of them was dismal, tragic.

"She's anorexic." Susan's dad broke the silence. "Her mind is slow. Sometimes she's incoherent."

The father cleared his throat, and in a shaky voice told his daughter's heartbreaking story. "After your divorce, she returned to the cosmetic firm.

She ended up having a sordid affair with one of the top executives, a married man. When the board found out about it, they were both fired. They began their own cosmetic company with my financial backing, and eventually married. The marriage only lasted two years. Next thing we knew, he left the country with one of the models, and all the money the firm had in the bank. When the police finally caught up to them in Jamaica, the money was gone. Susan was left with nothing but the bills, which ultimately became my responsibility."

Brianna's eyes unexpectedly began to fill.

Susan's heartbroken father continued. "She started drinking and going out with men who were big partiers. She realized that if she was going to be successful she needed to get her figure back. The competition was strong, and the older she got the more difficult it was to compete with the younger girls. She became even more obsessed with beauty. She began losing weight any way she could. At first she became a vegetarian, and then started forcing herself to throw up. She took pills, which made all her food pass through her quickly—anything to lose a pound. She got to the point where she just stopped eating. Before we knew it, she was anorexic, bulimic, and an alcoholic."

Ethan wanted to run... as far away as he could. However he stayed, listening to the painful testimony of a woman he once loved, a woman who at one time seemed to have the world at her fingertips.

Susan's father continued, at times his voice broke. "She could not get a job let alone keep one. All the men she was involved with just used her. She married two more times, both to men who enjoyed beating her. Finally one day, we received the dreaded call from the police saying Susan was in the hospital in critical condition. Her husband had spent an hour in a drunken rage, tearing the house apart, beating her up, and then tossing her out the door in her nightgown. The neighbors found her and called 911. After a long recovery in the hospital, she moved in with us. Her husband was hauled to jail."

Brianna was weeping quietly. She realized her life could have ended just as tragically. The comparisons with her own life were great; she was grateful for God's hand of protection through it all, but sad for her former stepmother.

The father pressed on, but each word took an effort. "She has been like this ever since. It is so heartbreaking because she has done this to herself. She's locked in a world of her own. I accept responsibility because I enabled her, never allowing her to face consequences for her behavior. Something I deeply regret."

The man moved his gaze to Ethan, and drew in a deep breath. "Do you know what happened to your children?"

Ethan nodded his head, barely able to speak. "All except Alana—what happened to her?"

The grandfather sadly shook his head. "We lost track of her, but her life has been a mess. We tried to help the best we could. Your children were too far gone when we realized they were headed down the wrong path. After your divorce, they never went back to church. They just seemed to drift on their own."

Ethan walked over to Susan, but she turned away. He put his hand softly on her bony shoulder and gently turned her around.

His ex-wife stared at the floor, and then finally transferred her eyes to Ethan. Without warning, Susan wrapped her arms around her former husband's neck and cried. "I'm sorry. I'm sorry. I did love you. I always will. Forgive me."

Reluctantly, Ethan put his arms around her, pulling her head close to his chest.

Brianna watched through teary eyes. Any love for Susan had been destroyed when she was a child. Yet, her heart broke for the woman, knowing what she needed more than anything was a relationship with God.

With the former beauty queen still in his arms, Ethan faced her father. "I have often wondered why Susan did not tell the court that Janna was my birth daughter."

The father gave a grim smile. "I never understood that myself. She never told me anything about it until I read about your reunion in the paper a few weeks ago. Then she finally opened up."

Tim took Susan by the hand, and sat her down on the sofa next to her mother; he sat on her other side. Softly he said, "Honey, tell Ethan what you told me."

Susan looked at the floor, then around the room, afraid to make eye contact, obviously suffering from paranoia. Finally she spoke slowly, choosing her words cautiously.

"I... didn't... I... went into the courtroom to destroy you and that girl. I intended to tell the world who she really was." Susan stammered, "I hated her so much, and I hated you. Not you as much as the love you had for your precious Mira. I felt I could never measure up. Our love could never be as strong as the love you shared with her."

Every word took an effort. "But when I saw you..." She faced Ethan, sobbing. "When I saw you in that courtroom, a broken man who had done nothing wrong, I realized that it was I who was wrong. I decided I could not hurt you by telling the truth about Janna and her identity. I realized you were doing what you had to as a father—protecting your child. At that moment, I understood. When I walked out of the courtroom and stopped next to you, I wanted to hug you, ask for forgiveness, and tell you I loved you. Then I saw the reporters, the lights, the cameras, and I knew the public awaited me. I lifted my head and walked toward my destiny. I was so jealous of the love you once had for Mira, I failed to see the love you had for me."

Ethan allowed himself to feel the pain in her voice.

Susan looked down. "My life was okay for a couple years... I was traveling a lot and keeping busy. I married my boss, and we lived a lavish lifestyle for about a year, until I found out he had been cheating on me."

She babbled on. "Then there were our children... there was never any time for them. Dad would call and say that he and Mom couldn't handle them, but I never responded. Look at how they turned out. I don't blame you, Dad." She looked at her dad, attempting to smile, but it wouldn't come.

Tim nodded his head in agreement. It was too late and unproductive to play the blame game.

Briefly, Susan made eye contact with her former husband, and then quickly turned away. "Then I did something I knew I should never have done. Ethan, if you hate me now, you'll hate me even more when you hear what else I have to say."

Her father interrupted her. "Honey, you don't need to tell him. Your therapist said you don't need to, if you don't want to."

"She also said if I didn't, the guilt would consume me. He must know... they must know." Susan turned and faced Ethan. At the same time, Brianna grabbed her father's arm, holding him tight. The daughter was terrified of what Susan was about to disclose.

Tim put his arm around his daughter, and softly rubbed her thin, frail shoulders—a reminder that he supported her, no matter what.

"A little more than a year after the trial, I was doing a photo shoot in Egypt to promote a new line of cosmetics." Susan rose slowly and walked over to the window, staring out. Her voice was monotone, and her face blank. "I never go outside anymore... it scares me." She paused briefly, and then continued with her story, still staring outdoors. "I could use the excuse I was tired, but the fact is, I just said it. It was during an interview with an Arab newspaper. Somehow the question of you came up, and then the question of Janna. When it was over, I had told them about the adoption of a little Iraqi girl with the heart-shaped birthmark."

Ethan's eyes opened wide, still unsure what was coming.

She continued to gaze out the window. "Back home a few months later, there was a knock at the door. They said they were reporters, but all the questions were about you and the girl with the birthmark. When I finally figured out they were not really reporters, it was too late. They threatened me, and said that my parents would have an unfortunate accident if I didn't tell them where the girl was." She slowly walked over and sat down, almost collapsing onto the couch.

Ethan was waiting... fearful of what was to come.

"During their threats, I... I... told them you had every right to her because you were her actual birth father."

Ethan shook his head, a mixture of pain and sorrow evident in his eyes.

Not deterred, she went on. "They were ecstatic. They were ranting in Arabic and English. Then they blurted out that they were Mira's brothers. They said they had the responsibility to kill both of you. It was then I realized that everything you told me was true. All the Muslims I had ever known were kind and respectful. I never believed people like those evil men existed. You warned me many times, but I never listened. They said they would hunt you and Janna down and kill you."

Brianna blinked, unable to move or speak. Was this really happening?

"I had no idea where Janna was. The police and family services had questioned me many times after she ran away from the foster home. I knew you were locked away somewhere, so I assumed you'd be safe. Regretfully, I gave them your dad's address just to get them to leave. They said if I told anybody about them, they would kill my parents and our children. They claimed Allah gave them that right."

Ethan felt like the air was knocked out of him. He tried to catch his breath, but couldn't.

"They left, and I immediately ran to the phone to call your father to warn him. As I started to make the call, I stopped, and thought about the consequences. I hung up the phone."

Looking directly into Ethan's confused eyes, Susan forced herself to proceed. "I never thought they would hurt your dad. Days later, I heard the news of your father being killed while he walked to his car. The report said it was an accident, a hit-and-run driver. The newspaper reported that a black truck with two men hit him and fled the scene. I knew it was the same men because I saw them leave my house in a black truck."

Tears began to well up in Ethan's eyes at the revelation. Everything was starting to add up. "They killed my dad!" The knots in his stomach grew tighter.

Brianna cried out. "I'm sorry, Daddy... it's my fault."

What if he blamed her for Grandpa's death? She had come so far to find her father. She couldn't risk losing him again.

"No, it's not," Ethan instantly replied.

"No, it's my fault," Susan snapped. "If I had the courage, I would have called the police and reported the threat."

Ethan's voice grew forceful. "It's nobody's fault. It's this crazy, mad world. People can't get along; religions can't get along. To kill innocent people in the name of god is a dreadful atrocity."

As he said the words, he thought about the man of Arab descent who stabbed him in prison. Everything began to make sense. "They came after me too, didn't they?"

Susan nodded her head. Regret and sorrow clouded her worn face.

"They tried to have me killed in prison," Ethan said to Brianna.

"Your lives are in danger again. They know who you are now. They will find and kill you," Susan warned them, clearly concerned.

"No, Susan... it's over. They will never try to harm us again." Ethan attempted to put her mind at ease.

Susan's dad interrupted, "What makes you think that? How can you be sure?"

Brianna finally spoke. "A few months ago, I confronted them. Conrad told them in no uncertain terms that if they ever tried to harm me, or anyone I love, they would have to face his wrath, and that of the United States military."

Susan asked, "Who is Conrad?"

"He's my bodyguard—a special man in my life." Brianna smiled as it occurred to her that she had never referred to Conrad that way before.

"It's really over?" Relief showed on Susan's face.

"Yes, it's over." Ethan shifted his eyes to Susan, who was nestled between her parents on the sofa. Right or wrong, her parents sacrificed much for their daughter. Ethan knew Susan would be safe with them. He realized there was nothing more he could do for her. If he ever felt revenge or malice toward his ex-wife, it was gone. She had suffered enough for her bad choices. The main difference between them was that Ethan had found a way out—his faith. Susan, on the other hand, never would. She was locked in her own little world... where she would remain.

He knew it was time to say goodbye to Susan forever.

Helping her to her feet, Ethan held her hand one last time. As he looked into her eyes, he said softly, "Susan, I want you to know that I forgive you." He kissed her on the forehead, then slowly turned and walked away.

Ethan glanced back at Susan one final time. For a split-second, he envisioned the beauty she once wore, and felt the love he once had for her. Both were destroyed by years of neglect, selfish choices, and sin.

He opened the door for his daughter, and looked back at Susan's parents. "I trust you'll continue to take care of her," Ethan said with a caring heart.

Tim put his arm around Susan's emaciated shoulders, "We can do no less. After all, she's our daughter... and we love her."

Ethan understood what he was saying. He nodded in agreement and said goodbye.

One last time, Brianna looked back at the woman who should have been her mother. She should have loved and protected her at all costs. If she had, perhaps none of this would ever have happened... to any of them. So many consequences. So many regrets.

Brianna's heart was heavy.

Just before Brianna stepped outside, she smiled, and waved to her former stepmother. It was her way of saying, "I forgive you."

Susan raised her hand slowly, and smiled back. It was the first time Brianna had ever seen her stepmother smile at her, and it ended up being the last time.

Susan could never forgive herself for the pain and embarrassment she caused her family. She knew if she had defended Ethan in court, she could have protected him from years of anguish. If she had loved Janna as a daughter, everything would have been different. If she had been the mother she should have, the tragedies in her children's lives might have been avoided. Her days were filled with regrets; her nights were consumed with nightmares. She couldn't take anymore.

It was another scorching night in Mesa, only seven months after the meeting with Ethan and Brianna. Susan lay on the sofa in the den with just the table lamp dimly lit, and swallowed a full bottle of pills. She stared at the many trophies of her beauty pageant days, and then focused on the largest picture on the wall—a photo, which only showed her and the three children. Ethan and Janna had been cropped out, just as in real life.

She began to weep at her life of failure. She wept until she fell asleep... and never woke up.

Brianna and Ethan came to pay their final respects at the small graveside service.

Susan's suicide came days after Alana died in a motel room from an accidental drug overdose. Sadly, it was on her eighteenth birthday.

Ethan and Brianna had tried to contact Alana, but never found her. The entertainer wanted to reconnect with her sister and tell her about the saving grace of Jesus.

Alana was like many of the young people in her generation, she thought she had time... but her time ran out.

TWENTY-TWO

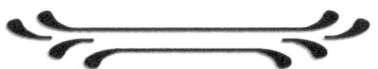

The Tearful Goodbyes

...a time to mourn
Ecclesiastes 3:4

The original plan was for Ethan and Brianna to visit Mira's grave together. After hashing it over, they decided to take an additional step, and bring Mira's body back to America. She deserved a decent burial, and they both wanted her nearby, even if it was only her remains.

After using their political pull, and at the request of the President of the United States, Iraq agreed to release the body of Brianna's mother.

Ethan, Brianna, and her bodyguards flew to Iraq on the star's private jet.

Aahil, Sonya's late husband's friend, greeted them at the airport. He would chauffeur them around Iraq during their stay.

Their first stop was Mira's grave.

The caretaker at the cemetery recognized them, and welcomed them with a huge smile. He shouted excitedly, "You found him!"

Brianna returned the smile, nodding her head enthusiastically.

Respecting their privacy, the caretaker left them alone as they knelt by the grave of their loved one.

Later he would help remove the casket, and say his own goodbye to Mira. After all, he felt like he knew her.

After the cemetery visit, Brianna and Ethan returned to the hospital where Brianna was born. As they drove up to the birth wing, the words in English caught their attention. It read, "Brianna Bays Birth Place." It was somewhat ironic, and a fitting tribute, which even the hospital officials did not realize. It was named after her because she had donated the money to have it built. In reality, it was Brianna Bays' birthplace... an interesting play on words!

The hospital administration permitted them to spend some quiet time in the room where Brianna was born, and her mother died. Neither of them spoke, each with private thoughts and prayers.

As they turned to leave, the nurse Brianna had talked with on her earlier visit was standing in the doorway.

"Saahira!" Ethan blurted out as he greeted the nurse. It had been sixteen years since Brianna's father had seen her.

The nurse threw her arms around Ethan in a warm embrace.

With a glimmer of a smile, Ethan said, "How can I thank you for all you did to protect my daughter?"

The nurse backed up. "You don't have to thank me. It was my job to protect my patients, and I didn't do my job well that night."

Saahira faced Brianna. "Your eyes... I remember them so well. You were only three the last time I saw you. Oh, how you cried when I left you at the orphanage. It broke my heart to leave you, but I was afraid your uncles were getting close to finding you. It was the only way I could protect you." She gently brushed Brianna's cheek. "Do you remember me?"

Brianna's only recollection was a face of a woman in white saying goodbye in Arabic. "Yes, I have a faint memory."

The nurse continued, "For a couple years you were safe. I thought your father would return quickly. I couldn't chance coming to see you—I was afraid I was being watched. To keep you safe from your uncles, you were moved from one orphanage to another. One day the people at the orphanage notified us that the authorities had shut them down. It was not a good time in my people's history; the government was corrupt. You and the other girls were sold to a group of child traffickers in Asia, and were going to be shipped out through Kuwait. I felt helpless. I didn't know what to do. It was then your father showed up unexpectedly at my door. It must have been a total God-thing. Ethan knew he had to act fast, so he enlisted the help of his father. His dad called a friend, a prince in Kuwait, and they devised a plan to rescue the girls."

Brianna studied the nurse thoughtfully, listening intently.

Saahira took Brianna's hand and held it as she told the story. "I was afraid the plan would fail, and we would lose you forever. A couple days later, a group of Kuwaiti military personnel stormed the orphanage. Your father was with them!"

Ethan took a deep breath, and took over the details of the conversation. "It was a twofold plan—rescue you and the other girls, and shut down the child traffickers. It had to be perfect timing. Praise God it was. Saahira and her family risked their lives for us. The Iraqi military murdered her husband, not because of you, but because of his stand against the corrupt government. They came into their house one night, dragged him into the street, and beat him to death." His expression froze, and for a few seconds he stared at his nurse friend.

Brianna hugged Saahira. "I'm so sorry. You and your husband suffered greatly."

Saahira shook her head sadly. "It's not your fault. It was just the way our country was."

"How can I ever repay you?" Brianna asked.

"You already have! The new birth addition was a godsend. It would never have happened without you. Right now, that is my life... the children... the precious children." The nurse mustered a small, but heartfelt smile of gratitude.

Brianna looked directly into her eyes. "If there is ever anything, anything at all, I can do for you and this hospital, please let me know. Promise me that."

"I promise." The nurse smiled. "Thank you."

Brianna hugged her one last time.

Just before Brianna left the room, she stood quietly, staring at the place where she had been born. She envisioned her mother lying in bed, holding her as an infant to her breast. Angelically, her mother looked up at her, smiling serenely.

A tear came to Brianna's eyes as the scene faded.

She looked heavenward, knowing that her mother was looking down at her, proud of the woman she had become. She felt peace.

It was time to leave Iraq. Goodbyes were more difficult than anyone expected.

Brianna's grandmother, Miridia, came to the airport to bid farewell to her granddaughter... and to Mira.

The day Brianna confronted Emir and his sons was the last time Miridia would ever set foot in her home. She would never return to that miserable existence.

Later that year, a car bomb killed her two sons, Odel and Adel. Rumors spread that it was one of their own bombs, but their mother never knew for sure.

Miridia inherited the family fortune after a fellow businessman killed her husband during an argument—he was shot in the back of the head.

Their evil empire had fallen. Perhaps it was justice.

Ethan and Brianna never had to fear them again.

Miridia was thrilled to finally meet the man who stole her precious Mira's heart. They felt a special bond, something that only the two of them understood. Their embrace was heartwarming.

Although it was nearing departure time, Brianna's grandmother took her aside. "You look like your mama, but you sure have your daddy's eyes," she said repeatedly.

She had noticed Brianna wearing the charm bracelet, which Sonya had received in the old cigar box with Mira's belongings.

Making sure no one else was within earshot, she pointed to the bracelet. "Honey, that was a gift from my mother who, received it from her mother." She smiled. "It is believed that it goes back almost twenty-five hundred years."

She whispered as she explained the history of the valuable heirloom. "I took this to an old Jewish jeweler and asked him what it was worth. He asked if he could have it for a couple days to examine it. I had no idea of its value. I had only heard stories passed down through generations. When I returned later, he locked the door, and pulled the shades. It scared me. He explained that most jewelers would only recognize the diamond and gold, and estimate the value at about two-thousand dollars."

Brianna raised one eyebrow, intrigued by what her grandmother was saying.

"The jeweler asked where it came from, so I told him the story." She put her lips closer to Brianna's ears and held her hand. "The fact is this bracelet came from the greatest king of all times, King Cyrus. He was known as the great conqueror. He had this bracelet made for his beloved wife, Cassandra. It is said that she had black hair, and blue eyes, like you. As the queen, she was loved by all of her subjects. The king adored her, and sent scouting parties to all corners of the world looking for the rarest gems. It took five years for them to return. Nobody ever knew where the jewels were found."

The grandmother continued telling the incredible story. "The jeweler explained his discovery. Come to find out, embedded in each charm is an extremely rare gemstone. Some of these gems have only recently been rediscovered. In some cases, less than ten are in existence." The old woman pointed to each rare gem and called it by name.

Brianna could hardly believe what she was hearing. She swallowed hard.

"When I asked him what the bracelet was worth, he laughed. Mandy, my child, this bracelet is one of the most valuable pieces of jewelry on the face of this earth. The jeweler told me that no monetary value could be placed on it."

Brianna leaned in closer.

The grandmother whispered, "My husband never knew its value. If he did, he would have taken it from me, and I never would have been able to pass it on to my children. I gave this to your mother when she left for France. I remember that day clearly."

She pulled her granddaughter's head close, giving her a kiss on the forehead. "So... let's just keep it our secret. Okay?"

Brianna smiled, nodding her head. "It's our secret, Grandma."

The entertainer was never certain if the story was true or not. Nonetheless, she kept it a secret because that was her grandmother's wish. It was a tale she would pass down to her own children when the time was right.

She embraced her grandmother, grateful for the opportunity to get to know her.

They waved to each other as Brianna boarded her plane.

The entertainer glanced back at her grandmother, then down at the charm bracelet, and smiled.

Hours later, they flew into a private airport near Denver, Colorado. It was a dreary, misty afternoon.

Sonya was there to meet them; she had spent the last couple of weeks preparing for this special tribute.

Fortunately, they were far from the media as the white hearse backed close to the plane.

The bodyguards and Ethan carried the casket, and Brianna walked behind them. Her heart was touched as she watched her father help carry the casket bearing the remains of his wife, Mira Anderson—the woman he dearly loved, for much too short of a span.

After the casket was loaded into the hearse, Ethan took Brianna's hand, helping her into the car. There were only two vehicles accompanying the hearse as it drove to a small cemetery in the foothills of Colorado.

Mira had dreamed of visiting the Rocky Mountains, but this was the best Ethan and Brianna could do. She was buried under a tall pine tree, which was surrounded by golden Aspens. It was a spectacular place to be laid to rest.

Pastor Jeremiah, from Buffalo, New York, was honored to perform the small graveside service.

Brianna and Ethan sang an A cappella arrangement of Amazing Grace. The harmony was indescribable.

The flat rock, which served as a headstone in Iraq was embedded into a large granite tombstone honoring her memory. Ethan's hand-carved heart stood out for all to see.

The tombstone bore the inscription:

Mira M. Anderson
wife of Ethan, and mother of Mandy
You will always be loved and remembered.

"The faithful love of the Lord never ends!
His mercies never cease."
Lamentations 3:22

TWENTY-THREE

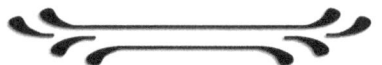

The City of Love

*Now then, stand still and see this greet thing the
LORD is about to do before your eyes!*
1 Samuel 12:16

Before Brianna's past became known to the world, she had been
working diligently on her latest CD project. Interestingly, every song on
the CD had to do with her search for her parents, and her life's
transformation by God. After the reconciliation with her father, Brianna
released the new CD, which quickly raced to the top of the charts.

A couple weeks after Brianna's mother's body was buried, the world-
renowned star set off on a twelve-month world tour.

She would be traveling without her long-time mentor, and trusted
friend, Sonya. It was time for the attorney to begin a new life of her own.
The past seven years Sonya Ellis had immersed herself into the career of
Brianna Bays, leaving no time for her own life. She had no regrets—she
was thankful to be involved in the rise of one of America's most
successful entertainers. She was even more thrilled to witness the life-
changing experience, the personal encounter, Brianna had with God. He
answered the prayers of Sonya and Conrad in a miraculous way. She
would be eternally grateful for her part in Brianna's conversion.

Sonya had heard it said, "All good things must come to an end." That
was certainly true for her at this stage of her life. The decision came after
much soul searching, prayers, and tears.

Through the years, a strong bond tied the group together. The transition
would be an adjustment for all of them. No doubt, Sonya's departure
would create a huge void. However, they sent her off with well wishes.
After all, with modern technology she would only be a phone call away.

Since Ethan's restored relationship with God... and with Brianna, he
had become more like the man he once was. With Conrad's help, her

father took over as manager. His people skills and knowledge of the world made him a perfect fit for the job. In addition, it would give him more time with his daughter... perhaps it was a way to make up for the lost years.

Ethan and the bodyguards accompanied Brianna on the tour that broke world records for attendance. Performances in Rome, Moscow, Tokyo, Beijing, Berlin, and many other cities sold out within minutes.

The entertainer boldly shared her faith at each show. Many of her fans rejoiced, realizing how dramatically the star's life had changed. Some came to think of Brianna as a member of the family, or a close friend, perhaps because she had openly shared her personal experiences and failures with them.

All members of the group had special times on the tour that they would remember forever.

Beyond any doubt, the most memorable for Brianna came in Paris, France.

The father-daughter duo spent three days in Paris visiting Ethan's favorite spots—places that he and her mother had frequented as young lovers. They walked for hours around the great city, retracing the steps of her parents nearly twenty-five years before.

At the Eiffel Tower, Ethan showed his daughter where he proposed to Mira. It was an emotional moment for each of them.

Later they drove out of the city to the little getaway Ethan remembered vividly. It was there the couple was married and spent that extraordinary weekend. Brianna and Ethan sat on a bench, silently staring at the memorable place.

The father eventually broke the silence, telling his daughter information he had never shared before. "After I heard the news that your mother died, I needed to be close to her. We had only been together in Paris, so I came here. I spent a few weeks alone. I felt empty. I walked where we had walked together, even ate at the same restaurants. I spent hours every day at the Eiffel Tower. Much of the time, I stood in the exact spot where I proposed to her, remembering that day. Somehow, I sensed her presence."

Brianna never grew tired of hearing Ethan talk about her mother. Enthralled she held on to every word.

Ethan watched a young couple walk into the secluded getaway, wondering if they were getting married as he and Mira did many years before.

He continued. "I drove by this place repeatedly. Sometimes I stopped and walked around the grounds. Occasionally, I sat on a bench, like this one, remembering our special times. Many times, all I could do was weep—I could not believe she was gone forever. At the same time, I wanted to hold you in my arms, but I couldn't get to you. I felt totally helpless, dead inside."

"Oh, Daddy, I can't imagine the pain you suffered. I wish I could have known her." She didn't know what else she could say, the pain still evident in her father's eyes every time he discussed Mira. She hugged him, as they stared at the little cottage.

So many memories... so little time!

Too soon, the moment was gone.

It was back to business. Tens of thousands of fans showed up for the two concerts in Paris. Brianna told each audience how important the City of Love was to her.

After the final concert in Paris, Ethan said he was tired and going to bed early. Brianna thought it strange, and was afraid her father was ill. He had looked slightly pale. "I'm fine. I'm just very tired."

"Have you been taking your medicine?" Brianna asked, sounding more like a nurse than his daughter.

Her doting tickled Ethan. "Yes. As I said, I'm tired. It has been a busy few months. I just want to relax tonight. Before I retire for the evening, maybe I will challenge Bruno to a game of chess. He beat me last time, and I can't allow that. I have a reputation you know." He laughed.

Brianna was concerned, but realized that maybe her father could benefit from the extra rest.

"You and Conrad go enjoy the sights. Make sure you go to the top of the Eiffel Tower. It's spectacular. Romantic things can happen there this time of night." Ethan winked.

Brianna blushed, looking up at her good-looking bodyguard. Readily, she accepted her father's advice, and grabbed Conrad's hand. "Let's do this. I need some fun."

She gave her father a quick peck on the cheek. "I love you, Daddy."

He replied, "I love you to, Hon. Now run along and enjoy this beautiful night."

Ethan watched as the two left, but not before Brianna looked back and smiled at him.

The mega-star and her bodyguard took the long walk to the Eiffel Tower, holding hands, and chatting about little things that happened during the tour. When they reached the base of the tower, they looked up at the lofty structure, one of the most magnificent landmarks in the world. It was still amazing to them.

They stepped aboard the elevator. When they got out on the first level, they silently viewed the sparkling lights of the city. Then without warning, the entertainer mischievously pushed Conrad. "Can't catch me!" Brianna said, as she sprinted up the stairs to the next level.

Conrad was up for her teasing and began chasing her up the stairs—two kids caught up in a game of tag. He was always amazed at her physical fitness. He caught her on the second floor. When he reached her, she fell back into his arms. They studied each other, and there was a comfortable silence between them. A minute passed, then two. They gazed into each other's eyes as time stood still.

Brianna reminded herself to breathe. After a pause, she sighed, and shifted her position. Still in the warmth and strength of his arms, they both unconsciously turned to view the city lights. The entertainer's heart was pounding! Drawing in a sharp breath, she pointed to the tiny cars on the street below in an effort to lighten the moment. She was amazed at the splendor of the Arc de Triomphe in its brilliance.

Conrad fought the impulse, the burning desire to kiss Brianna. He rambled rather nervously, hoping she didn't notice the tenseness in his voice. "The Arc was Napoleon's idea, but it was never finished while he was in power. The emperor and his new bride marched through a wooden replica of the arc. After the French leader died, his body was paraded through the city and under the completed structure."

"You know a lot about French history... I'm impressed." She smiled, still feeling the heat between them.

"I had some free time while on leave and came here with Bruno. I have always been interested in Napoleon's life. It was a fascinating time in history." Suddenly he stopped talking, realizing he was babbling.

He searched Brianna's eyes. "I have never heard you talk about politics or history. Do you have any opinions?"

Brianna responded with a lighthearted laugh. "Only if I can put it in a song! It has been that way my whole life. My music drives me every day—the next song, the next tune, the next lyrics."

"Is it haunting? I mean, do the melodies haunt you? Are they constantly going through your head day and night?"

"I don't think haunt is the right word. However, they do seem to control me. I hear them repeatedly. When I put one down on paper, the next one begins. They just never seem to end." She rolled her eyes, aware of what an oddity it was.

"Why do you think that happens?"

"I blame my father. When I first met him, he was always singing about everything and anything. He told me that my mother was an accomplished pianist. So maybe it just runs in my genes." Brianna smiled. "I could play the piano extremely well when I was eight, a little bit of everything—Beethoven, Bach, and the Beatles."

Conrad laughed at the contrast in her musical taste.

"I'm also a perfectionist, but you probably have that figured out by now. I put my all into everything I do."

As they chatted, Conrad was happy to have the perfect opening for what he wanted to say. He cleared his throat. "How about in a relationship?" He said the words calmly, but inside he was shaking.

"What do you mean?" Her response was quick; her heartbeat felt like it doubled in speed.

Why were they both nervous? They had spent endless hours together through the years. They laughed, played, and cried, yet, this was different. There was an unusual awkwardness between them.

Conrad persisted. "I mean if you found the right man, would you give the relationship your all?"

"Why, Conrad... I think you're blushing." She lightly ran her finger over the side of his face, giving herself a little more time to figure out how to reply.

Conrad raised an eyebrow, patiently waiting for an answer. The question was one he had thought and prayed about for a long time.

Brianna loved the twinkle in his eyes when he smiled. She leaned closer. "The answer is yes. When I find the right man, I will give the relationship my all." Her voice was breathy, beyond excited. "I would even slow down my entertaining schedule."

They both laughed, easing the tension.

They began walking at a relaxed pace, oblivious to the people around them. The tourists didn't notice the entertainer either—all appeared locked in their own private worlds.

Conrad bought ice cream cones at the small restaurant on that floor. As he handed a cone to her, his finger brushed her hand.

A giggle surfaced from between her lips... she felt like a school girl.

Nervously, they entered the elevator. Neither spoke as they rose to the top floor.

When they exited the elevator, they walked next to each other enjoying the cold treat, hand-in-hand, still silent.

Finishing the last bite of ice cream, Brianna came to a stop, and lightly touched the railing. "This is where my dad proposed to my mother. This very spot... June, 1990."

Conrad remained quiet as Brianna commanded the conversation. "This place somehow makes me feel closer to my mother."

They gazed at the twinkling lights, awed by the beauty of the city.

Conrad released her hand, and slipped out of sight.

Brianna turned to see where he had gone.

Conrad, the man who had protected her since the beginning of her career, was on one knee in front of her, holding a spectacular diamond ring.

She was grateful for the darkness—maybe he wouldn't notice the heat in her cheeks, or the tears that started streaming down her face.

"Brianna, as your bodyguard, I have been near you day and night, hardly ever leaving your side the past seven years. The moment I saw you, I fell madly in love with you. For years I dreamed of this day, and wondered how I could make it extra special for you." He took a deep breath. "This morning I asked your father for your hand in marriage, and he kindly gave me his blessing. It meant a lot to me when he said he would be proud to have me as his son. He even suggested this spot for me to propose. He was right; it's perfect."

Surprised, Brianna brought her hands to her face. For a moment, she held her breath. She noticed an older couple observing the scene, faces beaming.

Conrad stood. Holding her hands in his, he looked deeper into her blue eyes. "Brianna, I have taken care of you for many years, and I would like to take care of you forever. Will you give me the honor of being my wife? Think of it this way, you won't have to pay me a salary anymore." He laughed tensely.

She nodded her head, barely able to utter the word, "Yes." A smile of consent lit her face.

Conrad placed the engagement ring on her trembling finger.

She repeated herself a few more times, each time louder than the last, "Yes... yes... yes! I will happily marry you."

For that moment it was only the two of them.

He moved closer, getting a whiff of her perfume. A passionate kiss sealed the special moment. It left no doubt of his feelings. It was their first romantic kiss, and certainly, worth the waiting; it left them breathless. Then, they embraced, a time neither wanted to end.

Brianna drew in a deep breath. Finally able to speak, she shared her feelings. "I fell in love with you the first time I saw you, too." She batted her long eyelashes at him. "I could not take my eyes off you. I knew you were the right one, but I had to get my life in order first. I'm sorry it took this long."

Conrad tipped her face, looking deeper into her amazing blue eyes.

Looking serenely into his face, Brianna said, "There were many times I was afraid I was going to lose you before I could come to terms with my past. Thank you for waiting for me. I love you, Conrad Thompson."

He pulled her closer. "I could never abandon you. I believe you were the woman God prepared for me. It hurt me to see your pain as you searched for something that was right in front of you all along. However, I knew God would show you His plan in His time. Brianna, I love you. You have been worth the wait. I want to spend the rest of my life with you by my side."

Brianna could hardly believe how blessed she was. To have a godly man who wanted to honor, cherish, and protect her all the days of her life... could things be any better?

God's hand of protection had been on her; His angels surely surrounded her through every stage of her life. He did have a plan, and this very special man would play a big part in it.

As the dam of tears broke in Brianna's eyes, Conrad took out his handkerchief and tenderly wiped them away.

Neither could speak as they held each other tight, making their own memories, and savoring the moment.

The wedding plans began before they finished their tour.

The announcement that the number one bachelorette in the world was going to marry her bodyguard, an ex-Marine, left many soldiers' heartbroken. Some of her fans thought she would marry another entertainer or actor like many stars do. She always said she would never do that; she felt that most of the Hollywood-type were too wrapped up in themselves. She wanted to marry a man who would care for her through thick and thin—a man like her father.

She still could not comprehend the love her father had for her, the sacrifices he made to protect her. She knew Conrad had many of the same qualities as her dad. There was no doubt that her bodyguard was the man that God had chosen for her... her soul mate... for life.

TWENTY-FOUR

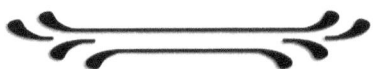

The Shocking Discovery

And we know that in all things God works for the good of those
who love him, who have been called according to his purpose.
Romans 8:28

The day after Brianna's concert in Berlin, her caravan arrived at the Landstuhl Regional Medical Center, located near the U.S. Air base at Ramstein, Germany. The facility is one of the major hospitals for the American soldiers wounded in Afghanistan and Iraq.

Brianna would spend much of the day in the intensive care unit visiting injured servicemen and women. Her schedule allowed stopping long enough to talk with each soldier, sign an autograph, or snap a picture. She felt that was her duty to those who have sacrificed for their country.

An army chaplain escorted Brianna around the ICU introducing her to the wounded GI's, while he handed out Gideon New Testaments. Her heart was heavy—some of the soldiers were teetering between life and death. Standing by the bedside, she whispered a prayer for each of them.

She followed the chaplain to a private room. Before they entered, he filled her in on the patient and his condition. "This is Specialist Andrews. He is only nineteen. Wounded in Afghanistan, this soldier is quite the hero. He killed four enemy combatants who had infiltrated a secure location, and in the process saved several lives. This brave soldier took bullets to the chest, arm, and head. His vest protected his chest, the arm injury is superficial, but the head wound is life-threatening. If he lives, he may lose vision in his right eye. With the bullet still lodged in his head, they're not sure the extent of brain damage he may have. His left side is paralyzed; the doctors hope it's not permanent. Surgery can't be performed until the swelling in the brain goes down. His outlook is bleak. He's extremely bitter and refuses to see his family. From what I gather, he's had a difficult life."

The chaplain opened the door and whispered, "He's probably asleep."

Brianna walked quietly to the GI's bed and looked down at the sleeping man. Various tubes in his body showed the serious extent of his injuries. The haunting beeps of the heart monitor interrupted the quietness of the room. The right side of his swollen face was heavily bandaged. One look and she immediately pitied him.

Despite the injuries, she could tell he was a good-looking man. The gold ring on his finger captured her attention. Hopefully, somewhere an anxious young wife was praying for her wounded husband.

The chaplain took a New Testament from his pocket and placed it on the stand next to a picture. "I'll be right outside if you need me," he said softly.

"Thank you," she said, picking up the photo and studying it. The uniformed soldier was holding a pre-school aged boy, standing in front of the American flag. Sitting in front of him, an attractive young woman held a smaller child. Brianna had to smile when she noticed the little girl and her big blue eyes. "She's cute!" Brianna whispered, returning the photo to the nightstand.

She gently touched the Bible, hoping the soldier could find solace from its pages. The entertainer looked around the small room, tastefully decorated with flowers and cards. Brianna glanced one more time at the resting soldier, closed her eyes, uttered a silent prayer, and turned to leave.

A hand grasped her arm, startling her. In a feeble voice, the patient said, "Nurse, please help me."

Brianna glanced at the young GI, and smiled in her usual way, a smile that brightened any room.

He murmured, "I have a wife and kids at home. Can you send them a message for me?"

She was not sure if he was delirious, but she would give this hurting soldier every bit of attention he needed. "I'd be honored to convey a message. Where does your family live?" Without waiting for his response, she continued. "I'll personally see that your family gets it."

Barely opening his good eye, he gazed toward the ceiling. "They live in a coastal city in Alabama called Gulf Shores."

"Oh, I've been there. When I was a young girl, I played in a softball tournament in Gulf Shores one summer. It's a nice place to raise a family."

Brianna moved a little closer to him. "I was noticing your photo. You have a good looking family. How old are your kids?"

"Weston will be three in September, and Rachel is almost two." He shifted his position to get more comfortable; his face grimaced with pain. "I became a daddy when I was too young, but my family means the world to me. I'm just afraid that now I won't be able to be the husband and father I should be. I don't know if Gabi will still love me."

Brianna pulled a chair next to the bed confirming her interest in the soldier. "What message do you want me to convey to your family?"

"Tell them I love them... and I think about them all the time."

"I'd be honored to do that. I'd like to hear more about your wife. You said her name was Gabi?"

"Yes, Gabriella. I've known her since I was fourteen. She was a year younger than me. We were childhood sweethearts. We did many things we shouldn't have done... I realize that now. I should have respected her more than I did. If I could only do it over..." The soldier's voice grew softer with each word until it stopped.

"I hear you." Empathy for the soldier filled Brianna's heart. She wondered if he had fallen asleep.

After a brief pause, he continued weaving his story. "Gabi was too good for me. I was trouble, and her parents knew it. I got her pregnant at fifteen. When her parents learned about it, they made me stay away. When my son was born, I was not even allowed to see him."

He looked through his blurry vision at the kind stranger, noticing her brilliant blue eyes and jet-black hair, apparently still thinking she was his nurse. "Let me ask you something. Why is it that good girls go for bad guys?" He waited for a response.

Brianna frowned, unsure how to answer the question because she too had fallen into that trap. She fumbled for words. "Um... um... that's a question for the ages. Maybe it's the chase. Kids search for acceptance; they want to be cool. I really don't know the answer, but it happens far too often."

His uninjured eye drifted back to her face. "You're not a nurse, are you? Who are you?"

"I'm Brianna Bays, and I'm visiting wounded soldiers today... heroes like you."

"Brianna Bays? How do I know that name?"

"I'm an entertainer, singer, and actress." Brianna studied the weakened patient's reaction.

He slowly turned his face away. "Oh, you're one of those." His demeanor changed, and his voice chilled. "What do you folks get out of doing this? I mean coming over here and showing us how important you are. Is it an ego thing or what?"

"No, believe me, it's not an ego thing. It's called supporting our troops. Helping lift their morale—it's the least we can do." Brianna replied candidly, baffled by his negative response.

"Why not join the army and help fight? Put your life on the line and see what it's really like." He paused, and there was an uncomfortable silence between them.

Brianna didn't move.

He finally continued in a subdued voice. "Brianna Bays... seems like I have heard about you. You're a singer... what did you sing?"

"Some of my biggest hits have been, Coming Home, In the Eyes of a Shattered Love, and Before There Was Rain."

"*Before There Was Rain*—I know that one! A haunting melody. I'm a hard rocker, but I know of you. After all, who doesn't know of the great Brianna Bays? Please forgive me, but I have a bullet lodged inside my brain that's playing havoc on my memory." His voice drifted off.

Again, there was a hesitation. Suddenly he perked up. "You sure can play a mean guitar... for a girl."

She smiled.

He winced in pain. "I played guitar in a rock band when I was sixteen, but when I wasn't permitted to see Gabi, I hit the road."

The GI reached for a cup of water from the stand slowly. Brianna noticed his struggle, grabbed the cup, and held it close so he could sip from the straw.

He continued his story. "The band spent a year in California, and then went to New York. Had a successful gig there. I managed to save enough money to fly back to get Gabi and Weston."

He tried to get more comfortable, but couldn't. "Gabi left early for school, but instead went to the airport where I was waiting. It was the first time I ever saw my little boy. We flew back to New York and eloped. When she called her parents they were furious." A small smile came to his puffy lips as he recalled the memorable day. "We changed our name, so her parents couldn't find us."

Brianna was hanging on to every word the soldier said.

He shifted his focus to her face again. "There is something special when a child calls you, 'Daddy.' I think it's the best feeling in the world."

Brianna saw a tear in the young man's eye. He obviously adored his family.

The soldier's mood seemed brighter. "I enjoy talking with you... you're a good listener. How much time do you have? I mean, you must have a crazy schedule, do you have to leave soon?"

"I have as much time as you want. My next concert is in Moscow three days from now." She chuckled.

He thought about that for a second. "Moscow. Wow! Did you sell many tickets?"

"I'm doing a concert on Red Square; over one-hundred thousand tickets were sold."

"Gee, that must put a lot of money in your purse."

"Not really. As a matter of fact, every dime goes to the starving children in that country." Brianna smiled sheepishly.

"That's nice. I guess I really misjudged you."

"I understand. There is a certain stereotype with entertainers, and unfortunately, many fit the bill!" She flashed a weak smile. "I'm interested in your life. Please finish your story."

"Right after we returned to New York, Gabi got pregnant again. Just before my baby girl was born, the entire band got busted for drugs. Kind of sad, we had a lot of potential. The other members of the band had prior arrests, so they had to do jail time. The judge saw my family, and since I had no past record, was lenient with me; he gave me the choice of jail or military time. I chose military—figured the benefits were better. I could get my college paid for, and my family would be taken care of." He looked at the medical equipment around him, and chuckled sarcastically. "Maybe I made the wrong choice."

Brianna fluffed his pillow, and then leaned closer to him, trying to make out his words.

The patient's tone was subdued. "We moved to Alabama and rented a small house close to the ocean. Gabi landed a job at a cell phone store making good money. My little Rachel was born, the cutest girl you ever saw with huge, saucer-like eyes." He raised his hand weakly and gestured toward the picture.

"I noticed her. She's adorable. I bet you can't wait to see them."

"That's not going to happen," he said, looking contrite.

"Why not?" Brianna questioned.

"I don't want them to see me like this. The bullet is still in my brain. Doctors say I have a fifty-fifty chance of making it through surgery. Even if surgery is successful, I may be blind in the right eye. They said I could have trouble walking, but I'm more worried about mental problems. What if I flip out and hurt Gabi or my children? I wouldn't be able to live with myself. As long as I'm thinking clearly, I'm not willing to risk it."

He reached for Brianna's hand, holding it like a concerned friend. "What will happen to my wife and kids?"

Brianna took her other hand and cupped his. "Let's look at the positive. You're still alive, and your family loves you. I'm sure they will accept you, no matter what. I'll pray for you every day. I'm going to pray that one day you will take moonlight walks along the sandy beaches with Gabi, and you'll be the father that you want to be."

"Pray? Are you serious? You're going to pray for me? Don't waste your time." His voice became cynical and apprehension coursed through him. He released her hand and turned away.

"Oh, believe me, it's not a waste of time—I consider it a privilege." Her voice was still kind, but direct.

He obviously didn't want to look at her. "Don't give me any of your self-righteous lingo. You have no idea what I've gone through. I came from a religious family... what hypocrites! I finally left home and lived on the streets. How could you possibly understand?" He shifted his gaze back to her. "I bet you own five houses around the world."

Brianna took a deep, steadying breath. "As a matter of fact, I own seven houses, but five of them are for sale. And yes, I do understand. When I was fifteen, I lived on the streets, and believe me; I had to give up a lot more than you did... just to survive." Her voice demonstrated the urgency of her message. The hurt showed in her eyes anytime she talked about her past mistakes.

The soldier looked at the entertainer, and realized she also had a history, possibly more complicated than his. "I'm sorry. It probably is a lot worse for a girl. I have a daughter, and I never would want her living on the street. Never!"

He was quiet for a second, and then added, "I have these nagging thoughts from my past. I lied, stole, and even almost killed a man. I have nightmares about those things." He looked straight into her eyes. "Do you have regrets about what you did? I mean, does your past ever eat you up?"

Brianna let loose a long sigh. "If only you knew! My past haunted me until I finally stopped running from God and made peace with Him. I thought what I did was unforgiveable. I lied about my father, and that lie sent him to prison and destroyed his life. One day, I had a total meltdown. I fell on my knees and gave my life to God. When I came to understand His love, I finally knew the power of forgiveness. Since I entered into a personal relationship with Jesus Christ, I have not been the same. The guilt rarely returns, but if it does, I spend extra time in the Bible. You see, all my regrets and sins are nothing compared to God's love and mercy. An old hymn says, *He took my sins and my sorrows and made them His very own.* Jesus did that because He knew we could not bear them alone."

The wounded GI was taking in every word the entertainer said.

In a soft voice, Brianna asked, "Do you know God... I mean personally?"

"I know of him. I went to church for a while until my father went to prison. And my mother, well, she's a drunk, and never gave a hoot about us kids."

Brianna's eyes grew misty. "I can relate to that." A sad smile played on her lips.

She touched his shoulder. "I sense forgiveness is needed between you and your parents. Without it, you'll become bitter and resentful. With God's love anything is possible... even forgiveness." Brianna stared at the soldier who was hurting physically, mentally, and spiritually. Her heart was touched by his honesty

He blew out a breath, and sadness flickered across his face.

"I'll go in person and talk with Gabi, Weston, and Rachel, but you must promise me three things." She paused briefly. "You won't give up, you'll read the New Testament, and you'll try to mend things with your parents. Deal?" She extended her hand to the wounded soldier.

He stared at her hand, and weakly grasped it. "I'll read the book, and I won't give up... but, mending things with my parents... that will be difficult. There's too much hurt there, but I will try. Brianna Bays, you have a deal!"

As they shook on their deal, he groaned. "Ouch! You have a strong handshake!"

"I was taught that many years ago." She giggled.

In the hospital room, Brianna prayed with the suffering GI. She prayed for his upcoming operation, his family, his future, and his salvation.

When it was finished, he looked up. "Thank you for taking the time to talk with me."

The soldier noticed the diamond ring on her hand. "Looks like you have someone special in your life."

She smiled. "Yes, I'm newly engaged."

"I bet he's some big actor."

Brianna countered, laughing. "Not really. As a matter of fact, he's my bodyguard—an ex-Marine."

"You mean... he is a Marine. Once a Marine..."

Brianna joined him, "...always a Marine."

They both laughed and it relieved any leftover tension.

"Conrad keeps telling me that," Brianna said.

"He's a lucky man."

"With the baggage from my past, I think I'm the lucky one—just like your Gabriella."

Brianna stood, looking down at the soldier. "By the way, I understand you're quite the hero."

"A hero? Me? Do you know who I saved?" His voice was thick with cynicism.

"No, I don't."

"I saved three politicians—two Afghans and some American senator. I was walking by, just off patrol, headed to the mess hall, when this truck crashed through the gates firing away. My training kicked in, and I turned my weapon on the vehicle as it approached, emptying my clip. Boom! Next thing I remember was waking up here. I was told I was the only thing between the truck and the dignitaries. But, I don't consider myself a hero... I was just doing my job."

"Don't sell yourself short. To me, and your family, you're a hero. To the politicians' families, you certainly are a hero."

"Well, you're right there. I got cards and flowers from each of the families. One of those cards mentioned God." He stopped talking, trying to figure the best way to phrase his question. "Ma'am, if there is a God, why do so many bad things happen? I mean, I saw some very religious men die."

Her eyes were clear and intense, and her voice unwavering. "Yes, a lot of bad things do happen, but not because of God. It's because of sin and man's disobedience. God never promised us a trouble-free life, but he did promise to help us through the difficult times."

Brianna picked up one of the cards and looked at it. Surprised, she said, "This card is signed by Harold Ashton."

"Right," he answered nonchalantly.

"He's the vice president of the United States, not a senator."

"Well, he used to be a senator." The soldier grinned.

"No wonder you have a room all by yourself." Brianna returned the card.

They both laughed. It felt good to lighten the mood, even briefly.

"I have to go. I sure have enjoyed our visit. Specialist Andrews, I predict you'll have a complete recovery, and one day you'll walk your daughter down the aisle at her wedding. I think it will be one of the hardest things you ever do in your life."

He questioned her further. "Why do you say that?"

"To give away your daughter, that's..." Brianna stopped talking. Her eyes looked heavenward as she realized her own father would be giving her away soon. "It must be one of the most difficult things a father ever does."

"Yes, but at the same time, it might be the proudest." He smiled.

"I believe that's true." Brianna blinked away a tear.

"I sense you love your father very much."

"You don't know the half of it... I spent most of my life searching for him. I could write a book about what I had to do to find him, and what my father went through to get to this point. In fact, someday I'm going to do just that... write a book. Right now, I just praise God my dad is back in my life."

He picked up the Bible and brought it to his chest. "I will keep my part of the bargain... will you keep yours?"

Brianna reflected on her promise. "You can count on that! Before the sun sets tonight, I'll make the call. When I get back to the States, I'll personally visit your wife and children."

The entertainer pulled her hair back and bent over to give the soldier a kiss on the cheek. Without realizing it, she exposed her birthmark.

The young man was startled when he spotted the heart-shaped mark on her forehead.

Brianna smiled and turned to leave.

He stared at the celebrity as she walked away.

After only a couple steps, the soldier desperately cried out, "Janna?"

She stopped dead in her tracks, uncertain if she had heard him correctly.

The soldier lifted his head as high as he could and once again cried out, "Janna, is that you?"

Shocked, she turned to face him; her eyes pierced the young soldier's eyes. How could he know her adopted name?

The GI's heart monitor sped up signaling an alarm at the nurses' station. "It is you, isn't it? Janna, it's really you." He began to thrash around, emotionally out of control, trying to reach her. He shouted, "It's me, Eric... your brother!"

Gasping for air, Brianna's head began to spin. She covered her face with her hands, her mind raced with childhood memories of playing with Eric on the beach.

With lightning speed, she rushed to his bed, collapsing at his side. Brianna tenderly laid her head on his chest, weeping uncontrollably. "Eric... Eric, is it really you?"

The chaplain, who had been watching from the hallway, noticed Brianna fall onto the soldier, and wasted no time bursting into the room to find out what was happening. "Ms. Bays, is everything all right?"

Clutching her long-lost brother, Brianna shouted to the chaplain, "Please, get my father, quickly!"

The baffled chaplain went to the corridor and called on his two-way radio, "Bring Brianna Bays' father up to room 314, stat!"

A nurse ran in to see why the patient's monitor was sounding. Peering at the entertainer, she spoke sternly, "What is going on here?"

The GI cried, "Just leave us. Please, leave us alone."

The puzzled nurse checked the monitor and the IV to make sure everything was functioning properly. "Well... I'll be right out here if you need me." Slowly turning, she glanced back a number of times, and reluctantly closed the door.

Minutes later, Ethan and Conrad sprinted down the hallway followed by a number of military personnel. "What's going on?" Ethan peered through the large window of the room demanding an answer from the bewildered chaplain.

"I'm not certain, sir. Everything seemed to be fine, and then suddenly your daughter collapsed onto the wounded soldier."

Ethan burst into the room with Conrad following closely.

The confused men saw Brianna clinging to the wounded soldier who had his arm clutched around her.

Ethan approached them cautiously, not knowing what to expect. In a calm, but concerned voice, he asked, "Mandy, is everything all right?"

His daughter turned her head, staring at her father. Through unbidden tears, she cried, "Daddy, its Eric. It's my brother, Eric!"

Ethan looked down at the injured man. As their eyes met, the dazed father cried out, "Eric! Son, is it really you?"

Choked with emotion, Eric spoke from his heart. "Dad, I'm sorry for all you had to go through. Janna told me the truth."

Ethan dropped to his knees next to his son's bedside. His hands were moving nervously, unsure what to do. He wanted to hug his son, but was afraid he might hurt him. He did the only thing he could think of... he slipped his left arm around his daughter's shoulders, and his other hand gently cupped his long-lost son's head. Through sobs, Ethan cried the only words he could, "Thank you, God!" Then, he laid his head on the pillow next to Eric. The prodigal son had returned!

Still uncertain of the unfolding developments, Conrad could tell that another piece in his fiancée's puzzle, another vital part of her past, was revealed. There was no doubt that the mighty hand of God had moved again, doing exceedingly above what they ever dreamed or asked.

That night Brianna's private jet left Ramstein to pick up Gabi and the kids in Alabama.

When the plane returned to Germany, Brianna excitedly greeted her new sister-in-law, Gabi. Eric's wife had difficulty grasping the news that her husband's sister was one of the most successful entertainers in the world, who happened to be her all-time favorite singer. Gabi had followed Brianna's music from the beginning of her career.

Brianna could hardly wait to meet her niece, Rachel. A huge smile crept across her face when she saw the girl's big, blue, saucer-like eyes.

Ethan was ecstatic to meet his grandchildren. While holding his grandson, Weston, in his arms, he whispered a prayer of thanks.

The father kept vigil at his son's bedside. Whatever the future held, Eric would not face it alone. His family would be there for him... every step of the way.

After her Moscow concert, Brianna rushed back to the hospital to be with the family as they awaited the results of Eric's lengthy surgery. They spent much of the time in the prayer room with Gabriella. They felt confident that Eric was in God's hands.

When the operation was over, the surgeon burst through the door with the news they were awaiting. "Everything went well during surgery. When the soldier awakens, we will know for sure if we saved his eye. Future plans call for extensive rehabilitation."

When the time came for the doctor to remove the bandages, the family was there. The room was hushed. Anxiety was replaced with exuberance as one-by-one Eric called everyone by name. His sight had been completely restored.

The hospital room buzzed with excitement as Gabi and Brianna embraced, weeping tears of joy. Ethan immediately thanked God for answered prayer. It was a moment none of them would ever forget.

Her newfound relationship with Eric changed Brianna's life significantly. The entertainer knew she couldn't cancel her concert tour, but was committed to spend as much time with her brother as possible. At least twice a week, she would fly to the hospital to visit him, closely keeping track of his recovery.

The doctors were amazed at his progress. There was no permanent brain damage and within days, Eric was walking. His stamina was remarkable—a full recovery was expected.

When the tour was completed, Brianna flew the entire family back to America.

Eric would continue his rehabilitation with the best therapists and doctors in the world... his sister would see to that!

TWENTY-FIVE

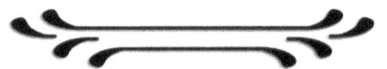

The Big Day

...and a time to dance
Ecclesiastes 3:4

The next step in Brianna's journey was an occasion she had looked forward to all her life. As a child, she always dreamed of having her wedding at the ocean home in Corpus Christi. Unfortunately, it had been sold to help pay mounting bills and pay off the remaining obligations after her grandfather died.

As a wedding gift, Brianna surprised her father with the deed to the property, which held such special memories.

Ecstatic, Ethan said, "I'm supposed to give you the wedding gift—not the other way around, silly."

"Daddy, you gave me the best wedding gift anyone could give... you! Being able to share this moment with my father is a dream-come-true."

It was a fairytale wedding. The beach overlooking the sea during sunset, with hues of crimson, tangerine, and pink, made the perfect backdrop. The scent of the ocean, coupled with the sound of the crashing waves, complimented the romantic scene.

The couple's treasured friends all took part in the special event. Bruno took his job as best man seriously, much to everyone's surprise.

Eric and Jonathan, the groomsmen, looked debonair in their tuxedos.

Long-time friend and confidant, Sonya Ellis, was thrilled to be the maid of honor.

Gabriella and Cathy were gorgeous bridesmaids in their sleeveless, navy-blue gowns.

Everyone smiled when they saw Weston, the ring bearer, in his tux. He looked like a miniature version of his father.

Rachel, the flower girl, was adorable as she skipped down the aisle. She stole the show when she spilled all the rose petals in one spot. Everyone laughed.

Pastor Jeremiah flew in from Buffalo to perform the ceremony. When they were at his church, he had a fleeting thought that perhaps one day the couple would wed. He was honored to be a part of the joyous occasion.

It was a perfect line-up... for a perfect day!

The proud father walked his daughter, Mandy Dawn Anderson, down the aisle to wed her true love, Conrad Mark Thompson. To Ethan, his sweet girl would always be Mandy, the name given when she was born. To the rest of the world, she would still be Brianna Bays.

The bride had never looked more exquisite. Her black hair, against her white chiffon dress was stunning. Her face radiated sheer joy.

Brianna took the groom's breath away, when she appeared. Conrad, the giant of a man, wiped away a tear at the first glimpse of his beautiful bride.

When Pastor Jeremiah asked the traditional question, "Who gives this woman to be married to this man?" Ethan boldly proclaimed, "Her mother and I."

A big smile came to Brianna. She fixed her eyes upon her father with a look only a daughter could give. Swinging her arms around his neck, she whispered, "I love you, Daddy."

The father placed his daughter's hand in Conrad's palm and stepped away.

Ethan watched Brianna join arms with her soon-to-be husband as they took their place in front of Pastor Jeremiah.

Ethan moved by Sonya. She slipped her arm through his, and tried to imagine how difficult this day must be for him. After all, he just gave his precious daughter away, a child he had waited so long to claim as his own. Their lives would be different now. Happiness mingled with sadness enveloped the proud father.

Weston's squirming at the front brought smiles to the entire wedding party and the guests. The youngster enjoyed the attention.

Little Rachel ran full force toward her grandpa. Ethan released his grip on Sonya, bent down, and lifted his granddaughter.

Brianna noticed her father holding Rachel and smiled. Perhaps it was God's way of easing her mind. She realized her Dad would be all right... he had another little girl to occupy his time, care for, and make music with.

As the waves crashed to the shore, the bride looked at her handsome groom. Then her eyes shifted heavenward, and she mouthed the words, "Thank you."

Among the guests was Mira's mother. Miridia was thrilled to share this day with her granddaughter and family.

It was indeed a time of rejoicing. God orchestrated it... ordained it... and now would bless this special union.

The couple spent their honeymoon on a remote island in the Philippines. Brianna's other bodyguards did not make the trip. It was time for the newlyweds to be alone.

TWENTY-SIX

The Journey Ends

The LORD is righteous in all his ways and faithful in all he does.
Psalm 145:17

Sonya Ellis

Within days after the honeymooners returned from their unforgettable trip, Brianna began preparing for another big event. She would be the matron of honor at Sonya's wedding.

The lawyer finally stopped running from Harry Stillman. She remembered what Cathy said years before, "If you want to get the right man, run from him... eventually you will catch him!"

That was true with Sonya. When she finally found time to search her heart, she realized she had fallen in love with Harry years ago, and couldn't imagine her life without him.

She and Harry would return to Los Angeles and open a small law firm, which dealt exclusively with adoptions. Fortunately, she never had to charge for her services since an anonymous donor had contributed a substantial amount of money for that purpose. Sonya always knew who the donor was, but never let on. She would continue to be Brianna's personal lawyer.

Nothing made Sonya more delighted than to see young children united with loving parents. She thanked Brianna Bays for that. From the beginning, Sonya noticed that everywhere Brianna went, she helped a child in need.

Sonya and Harry adopted five children, ages four to thirteen—siblings, orphaned when their parents were killed in a plane crash.

A couple times a year Sonya and her family would fly to the Caribbean, or the Texas retreat to visit their close friends, Brianna and Conrad Thompson.

Bruno Strauss

Bruno returned to Germany where he became the head of security for the chancellor of that country. Once a year he would return with his family to Brianna's Caribbean refuge and get together with the others to reconnect and reminisce. He continued making people laugh with his character imitations, which never improved.

Jonathan & Cathy Turner

Jonathan and Cathy remained with Brianna and Conrad as personal bodyguards and chefs. They started their own family, and lived in a spacious home on the Caribbean island. They took up sailing in their free time.

Eric & Gabriella Andrews

Eric and his family moved close to his father's ocean front home in Texas. He started his own Christian band, which became successful. His favorite things to do were moonlight walks on the beach with Gabi, and hunting shells with his children. He spent as much time as he could with his father.

Ethan Anderson

Ethan moved into his Corpus Christi beach home. He loved spending time with his grandchildren—especially when they created music.

He started a flourishing music publishing company. Much of the music came from Brianna Bays.

Eventually, Ethan found love again. He married a local music teacher on his forty-seventh birthday.

He and his wife visited his daughter and son-in-law frequently.

Brianna Bays

One year after her wedding, Brianna Bays faced the press again to make an announcement. She and her husband, Conrad, would be permanently moving to their home in the Caribbean.

Her professional career as an actress, singer, and entertainer was over. A new chapter of her life was about to begin. She announced that she and

Conrad were expecting twins. Her new role would be that of a mother—the most important job she could ever have.

Later that year, she bore twins, a boy, and a girl. They named their daughter after Brianna's mother, "Mira Grace." Their son they called, "Ethan Jeremiah."

Brianna Bays was gone forever. She was Mandy Dawn Thompson now.

She would never act or perform again, but she would continue doing what she loved best—singing. While she no longer sang for thousands of fans in concert halls around the world, she would perform a limited number of concerts for charities and churches.

Most of all, she enjoyed singing her children to sleep every night, just as her father had done with her so many years ago.

As Mandy rocked her babies, memories of her childhood flooded her mind. It seemed like yesterday she was running down the sandy beach with her brother chasing her. She would look up to see her daddy standing tall against the blue sky with arms wide open. As she jumped into her father's strong arms, he would envelop her with a giant hug, and she'd giggle. Then he would pick up Eric and do the same thing.

A loving father—that describes Ethan. Even though she walked away from it all as a young girl, her forgiving father was ready to receive her back. Much like the Heavenly Father. No matter who you are, or what you have done, He waits with open arms for your return.

As for Brianna Bays, her *Quest for Forgiveness* was fulfilled.

www.ingramcontent.com/pod-product-compliance
Lightning Source LLC
Chambersburg PA
CBHW030029180626
46810CB00001B/275